THE SCHOLAR THE SEER AND THE OUTLAW FAE

E. M. RENSING

THE SCHOLAR THE SEER & THE OUTLAW FAE

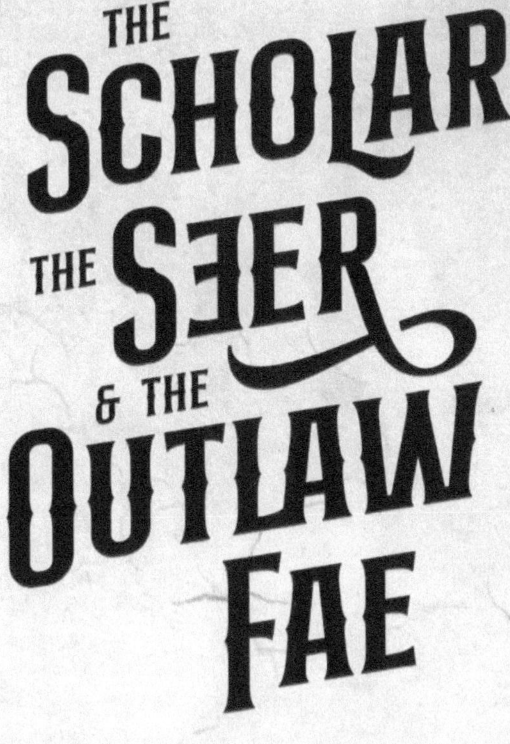

E. M. RENSING

ALSO BY E. M. RENSING

The Heliosphere Trilogy
The Lighthouse of Kuiper
The Ariums of Earth
The Cathedrals of Mars

The Abiota Series
Source Code
Unity Code
Numina Code
Domain Code
Virch Code
Anyon Code

Sci-Fi Fantasy Retellings
Engines of Winter

CENTRAL COLORADO MINING TERRITORY
N
NW
NE
W
E
SW
SE
S
SAWATCH RANGE
ELK RANGE
BLACK CANYON
GUNNISON
UNCOMPAHGRE PLATEAU
POWDERHORN WILDERNESS
OURAY
LOST BARTON MINE
SAN JUAN RANGE

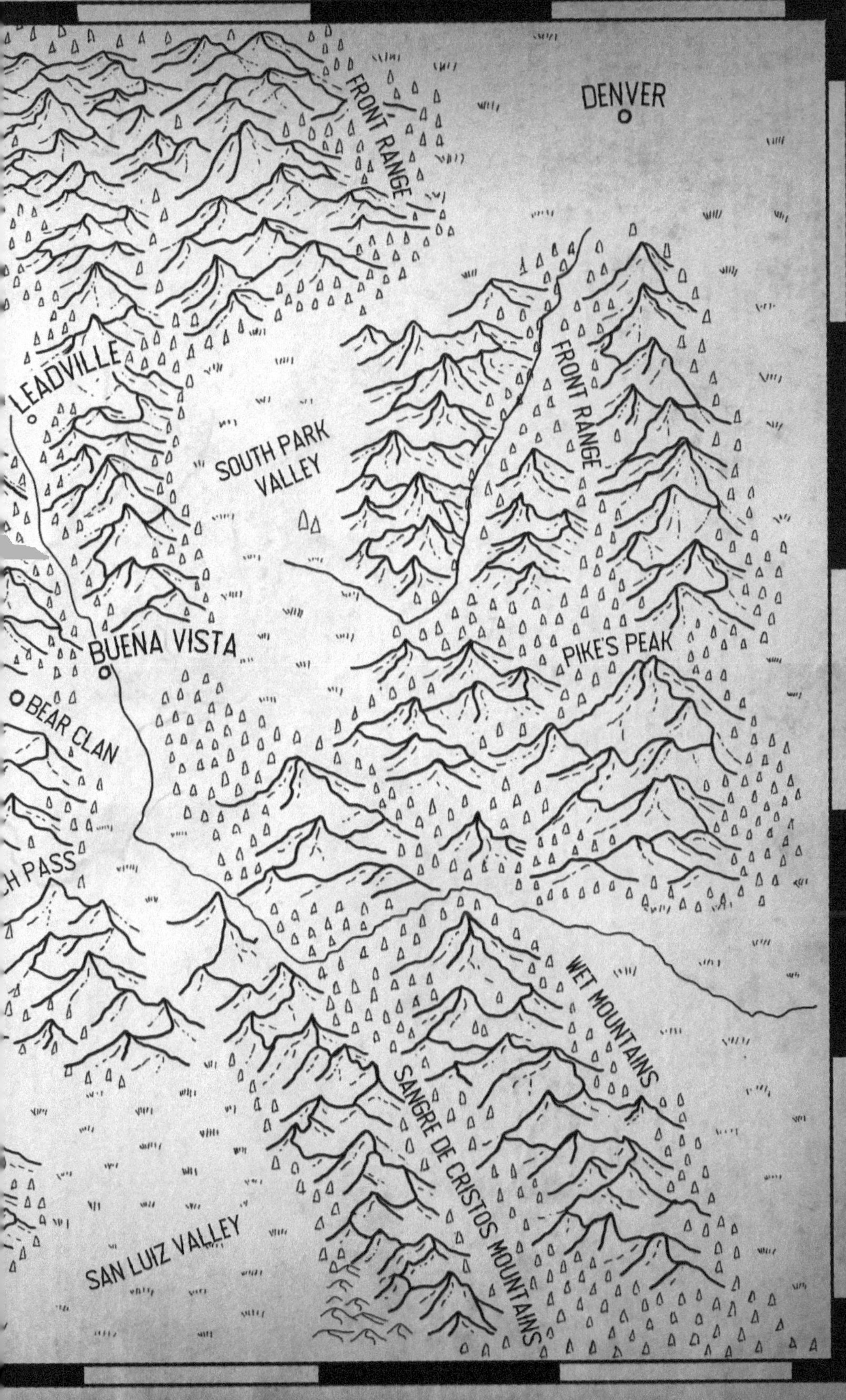

DENVER
FRONT RANGE
FRONT RANGE
LEADVILLE
SOUTH PARK VALLEY
BUENA VISTA
BEAR CLAN
PIKE'S PEAK
H PASS
WET MOUNTAINS
SANGRE DE CRISTOS MOUNTAINS
SAN LUIZ VALLEY

BOOK ONE
STONE

CHAPTER ONE

Dust ran through his fingers. Fine, dark. It blew away on the predawn wind, every trace of the moisture it once carried already gone. Blood. It was blood. Deer blood.

A grand stag, the creature had been. Its size prodigious, its antler rack impressive. Now very little of it was left—even the bones were collapsing, the body in a highly advanced state of decay.

Across the small clearing where he was crouched, he heard the caw of a crow. Nowhere could he escape those damned birds. Ireland, Virginia, Georgia, Colorado, they were everywhere.

"You disapprove?" he sneered and dusted the desiccated vitae from his hands. "Then perhaps you should not have banished me to this hell."

The bird cocked its head, its beady eyes baleful and blank at the same time. He laughed at himself for reading anything into this, letting his mind wander back to other times, better times.

"You are not they," he said, chuckling. "No longer can the Morrigan can take flight in this world. The humans banished you in turn, did they not?" He looked back down at the carcass in front of him. It should not have fallen apart so quickly. This curse of his was getting worse. It took all his willpower to contain it now, and even then, it leaked. Blood from a wound. Light from a star. He had barely had time to read the signs before the stag's organs had failed, the augury fading, the prophecy they carried almost lost.

Divination, interpreting the death throes of the animal to discern what the future might hold.

He should never have been reduced to this.

Well, he had trusted others to handle his problems, and look where that had landed him. What was it the Americans said around here? "If you want a job done right, you have to do it yourself." No more mistakes. No more misplaced trust.

Beyond the edge of the clearing, footsteps.

Only one man would dare approach him here.

"What is it, Lukas?" he asked softly.

"I'm thinkin' it was a fine animal. Would have made a grand meal."

He snorted, turning away from his divinations for a moment to consider his number two man. Always subservient, this one, hunched in on himself, wary. But then, that wasn't a terrible thing, considering what Lukas was. Subduing his kind was a challenge, but a necessary one. These Laignech Fáelad were tough, mean, and most importantly, partially immune to his... problematic nature. "You and the lads have supplies enough. This animal served a higher purpose than base digestion."

"Did the stag tell you what you wanted to know?"

The impertinence of it. "Yes. All my preparations are complete. Every stone set in motion has rolled to its proper position. At last."

"You sure?"

"The signs are unwavering. But what about you, Lukas? What does your nose tell you?"

"Whole world smells like dying leaves and fading days, boss. Can't smell destiny through that."

"Of course we can. Autumn. An auspicious time. The right time. The veil thins. It must be now."

"It won't be so easy gettin' there, boss. Storms've been comin' early this year. The mountains ain't our friends."

"Nothing in this damned land is, my friend. Ancient and wild this place was once, and it shall be so again. You will see. There are other forces at work here." And he reached out, almost gentle, for the stag's skull. Its rack was still attached. Five points. What a lovely beast. It had been almost a shame to kill it. But then, all died in the end. All came to its end. "You take the lads on, as agreed. I shall meet up with you later."

"But the mountains—"

"Do not worry about the mountains. I shall bring them to heel," he said, and watched the skull crack apart, crumbling in his palm. "All that is will be brought low. Of that, you can be sure."

"The boys'll be mighty glad of something to do," Lukas said carefully. "We'll go, just like you said."

"Do that," he said, and regarded his man. Not quite human, and not quite not. Caught between two worlds. But then, weren't they all? "Grab the one with power. I know you and Diego can smell it. Make no mistakes, Lukas. We cannot afford it."

"Yes, boss."

"I was not always like this, Lukas, and once we reach our goal, I shall be whole again. Then, nothing the humans build will save them. Then, we shall remind them of the old ways."

Lukas nodded his head and replaced his hat, slipping off back into the forest, back to the camp, back to the men.

The man who was not a man at all watched his lieutenant go.

This was not as it had been. Once, he had commanded legions. Possessed the powers of the storm and the flood, the ending of all things. Now, he had only a ragtag gang of outlaws at his disposal and his connection to his powers was broken, uncertain and unreliable. But he had waited centuries for this opportunity, prodding events, shaping choices, pulling on the threads of fate. All for this. If he did not take advantage of it here, now, right now, there was no telling when he would have another chance.

Too much was changing in this grubby human world. This time was an inflection point, a moment of history where the old ways were dying, but not yet dead. The way home might be lost forever, if he did not take the path now.

He could wait no longer.

The crow, still clinging to its branch, cawed at him again, and then hopped lightly into the air, winging away into the twilight. He watched it go, transfixed, his mind remembering that final battlefield.

He snapped off one of the antlers, chewing on it thoughtfully even as it crumbled to nothing in his mouth, and looked east. From this vantage point, perched on the crest of a foothill, he could see the lights of civilization far below.

Destiny beckoned.

CHAPTER TWO

Smoke billowed out across the platform, enveloping Charlotte Roseingrave. Thick and gritty, dark and unpleasant, it stirred old, unwelcome fears.

It was just a locomotive, she told herself as unease gripped her. Nothing to worry about at all. She was anxious about the deadline she was under back at the workshop. Concerned about the shipment she was here to retrieve. Nothing unnatural about it. Nothing.

Except there was.

There always was.

On the edge of the platform. On the edge of her vision.

Somebody watching her.

A man. Pale hair, pale face. Dressed in the latest fashion, sack coat the color of a winter storm, silk waistcoat underneath as bright as spring leaves. But it was the eyes, his eyes, that chilled her. Brilliant, piercing skin and bones, gazing into her very—

"Miss Roseingrave?"

Charlotte almost jumped out of her skin. It was a man who had spoken, but not the one who had emerged from the smoke. No, this man was dressed in the simple, rough uniform of the porters who worked here at Union Station, loading and unloading cargo.

"Yes?" she asked, pulling herself together.

"We're ready to open the boxcar now." The porter pointed. "Although as I said before, you and your sister don't need bother your pretty selves with this dirty business."

Charlotte looked back at where she had seen the figure. The smoke was clearing now, the train's boiler finally spooling down. The people were now beginning to disembark from the passenger cars, up the way. The man, or whatever he was, was gone.

A figment of your imagination, she told herself, *a trick of the light.*

She didn't believe it.

She never did.

Charlotte smoothed down her black wool skirt, making the tools on her chatelaine tinkle like wind chimes. "This is the West, sir," she told the porter. "Everything out here is a dirty business."

"Then let's get this over with," he sighed, and waved her on to follow him.

They'd already had a long argument with the head of Union Station's cargo supervisor, Charlotte and her sister had. That man had made it quite clear he didn't appreciate a pair of women mucking about in his business. But as Charlotte had told him, she didn't appreciate her shipments going missing. It had already happened twice this month and Mr. Dunn down at the opera house was getting twitchy about it.

"Who would you rather deal with," Charlotte had finally asked the supervisor after a half hour or arguing, "me, a seamstress, or Mr. Tabor himself?"

Mr. Tabor was the richest man in the state, behind Mr. Barton. And as fond as he was of his opera house, he was as likely to come down to Union Station to argue over a crate of dry goods as he was to fly. But dropping his name had had the desired effect. It had gotten her what she wanted—access to the boxcar—but certainly no warmth. Charlotte didn't need any of Mama's old tricks to tell that the porters did not want her here.

Celeste was already down there, laughing and joking with a few more of the porters as they waited for approval to open the boxcar doors. She had the goods manifest in hand. Charlotte envied her sister and the ease she had with people; of the two of them, only Celeste had inherited their mother's outgoing personality.

Or maybe, Charlotte thought in her more uncharitable moments, it was just that Celeste had not inherited the family curse. As the eldest daughter, it was Charlotte's burden to bear alone.

"Sister!" Celeste called as Charlotte walked up. "Did you satisfy your curiosity about the rest of the train?"

Instead of answering her little sister, Charlotte held out her hand for the manifest. Celeste gave her a smile, not entirely false, and handed it over. Charlotte made a little show of looking it over. She had memorized the shipment's contents prior to coming down here, but sometimes, one had to put on a performance. Mama had taught them that.

"It looks like we have eleven crates altogether," Charlotte said, and held up the manifest for the porters to see, tapping the correct spot with a gloved finger. "Do you not agree?"

Most of them nodded. The youngest, barely fourteen, looked abashed. "I can't read, ma'am," he mumbled.

"We're teachin' him," the most senior porter said quickly, jumping in front of any disapproval either woman could voice. "He's my nephew. But he never did have much patience for school."

"You should learn," Celeste said encouragingly. "Mrs. Hardesty over on 11th Street runs a free night school for boys your age. She could teach you."

The boy smiled. Charlotte looked back down at the manifest. Eleven crates, two of which were replacements for goods already gone missing. "I do hope everything is here," she told the head porter.

"So do I, ma'am," he replied, and pulled out a fresh plug of tobacco to chew on.

The crates came out, one by one. Charlotte had specified that the lids be opened. Again, Mr. Tabor's name proved effective; she doubted her request alone would have gotten it done. Grunting and straining, the porters did as she asked, allowing her to review the contents before carrying the things over to the waiting wagon.

Celeste grew bored with the whole process after the third crate and retreated to the side again, chatting with the head porter. Charlotte tried to ignore it.

In truth, she worried about her sister's behavior incessantly. Twenty-one to Charlotte's twenty-four years, Celeste had always been the baby of the family, coddled by their mother. At least, that was how it had felt to Charlotte.

Celeste seemed to have no sense of danger at all, as if through willpower alone, she could prevent harm from ever coming to her. It had been annoying when they were children, but it had become a little more serious when Celeste had discovered that men found her attractive.

Back east, men behaved themselves, but out here in the West, everyone was quite forward. And why wouldn't they be?

Celeste and Charlotte had both inherited their mother's red hair, her delicate facial structure, her height and her slender build. But where Charlotte's hair was dark and smooth, Celeste's was an almost flaming orange with a curl that could not be brushed out. Where Charlotte attempted to downplay her appearance, Celeste accentuated it.

Back east, they would have been pretty girls, nothing exceptional. Out west, they were rare beauties, and Celeste exploited that to the fullest.

Out of habit and boredom, Charlotte believed, more than any real need or interest. It bothered her. They had honest, straightforward work now. There was no need to stoop to using any of Mama's old tricks to—

Something heavy hit the wagon.

"Last crate, ma'am," the head porter announced.

Charlotte double-checked her list, then glanced back over the wagon. "That is crate number ten."

"I understand that, ma'am."

"There are supposed to be eleven."

He smiled at her, patronizing. "To be fair, Miss Roseingrave, the shipping manifest only lists items, not the exact shipping arrangements."

"Our New York City supplier uses a standard-size crate," Charlotte said, "that fits exactly twelve of these fifteen-yard bolts. Therefore, the math dictates that for a shipment of one hundred and twenty-five bolts, we have eleven crates, not ten."

"Maybe the thicknesses are different."

"And maybe you have neglected to pull my final crate out of the boxcar," Charlotte said, irritated now, and stepped forward. "I want to see inside."

The head porter got between her and the boxcar. "I wouldn't want you to snag your pretty dress in such a rough place, ma'am."

"Let me through."

"That ain't the arrangement."

"The arrangement was for me to observe the off-loading of all crates. We are missing one."

"Ma'am, if you were a man and calling me a liar—"

But before anything truly stupid could happen, the tension was broken by a cry from Celeste. All eyes snapped to her.

She was bent over now, supporting herself with one hand, leaning hard on another pile of boxes being unloaded from the next car over. One of the porters made to help her, but she waved him away.

"A terrible thing has happened here," Celeste said, voice wavering.

Several of the porters exchanged uncomfortable looks.

"What's she talking about?" the head porter asked Charlotte.

Blast it, Charlotte thought, and didn't even need to fake her sigh. Of course her sister would resort to this.

"What's going on?" the head porter asked.

Affecting a shake in her limbs, Celeste pulled herself back up straight, one hand stretching dramatically out in front of her. "They speak to me, the unsettled spirits of this city. There is one, very new to all of this, who says he met his end recently in... Oh, it's horrible!" And she sobbed again, almost collapsing to the ground.

Charlotte rushed over to her, catching her before she fell. "Celeste, this is not necessary. It's—"

"No, I know, sister. But every soul had a story, and this one met such a bad end." Celeste was actually crying now. She pretended to make a valiant effort to pull back the tears. "He wants his story... no, he wants his murderer to be known." She looked around. The men around them were transfixed, rooted to the spot. It was quite a crowd now. Their entire team, along with a dozen others who had been unloading nearby cars, were gathering around. Out of fear or morbid interest, Charlotte didn't know. Usually, it was a combination of both. "I see...cards. Yes, cards, and poker chips. And a smell, strong and nasty. It burns the nose. Like raw chemicals, like—"

"Like liquor?" one of the men asked.

"Yes, I suppose. I don't know," Celeste said, and closed her eyes again, giving another little cry. "Last Friday! A man, tumbled after a game gone wrong. He says...he says his killer was... Ah, it's too terrible."

The head porter looked around at his men, nervous and angry and very much on edge. "There are no murderers here!"

Celeste shook her head, one delicately gloved hand against her temple.

She was the very picture of some swooning heroine from a *Harper's Weekly* story.

"It is not you, Mr. Henry," she said. "They say you are a fine husband, a good provider for your wife and three children. But your men, perhaps... It is never clear when the spirits speak... Ahh, but they show me... I see a marquee, a huge painted sign with a horse..."

"The White Mustang Tavern?" one of the men blurted out.

"Ahh, you know it!" Celeste said and looked at the one who had spoken. She had blue eyes, huge beneath long eyelashes, and she fixed those on him now. He started quaking. "Perhaps it is you they speak of."

"There are no criminals here," the head porter insisted again, less sure now.

"There are," Celeste insisted, voice trembling now. She was shaking. "They watch us, you know. They know all our secrets. If only I could understand them now, we might know who killed poor Michael Roderick down on Fourteenth Street last Friday."

A crate hit the platform.

Charlotte looked at the two men who had just brought it out of the train.

"We ain't criminals," one of them said.

Celeste nodded and took a deep, shuddering breath. Then she made quite the show of collapsing down onto a box. "I lost the connection," she said, and tried to smile. Her face was wet. "I suppose we will never know who killed that poor man." And then she started sobbing in earnest.

"Put that on the wagon, would you?" Charlotte asked the head porter, pulling Celeste to her feet. The sooner this farce stopped, the better.

The head porter, looking quite irate now, barked a few orders. The crowd that had gathered around them dispersed. The men who had brought out the final crate carried it off to the wagon, crossing themselves and muttering about ghosts. All retreated down to other, safer cars. The two sisters were left alone at the end of the platform.

Celeste grinned at Charlotte, tears still hot on her cheeks.

"Dirty thieving bastards," she commented.

"I should slap you for talking like that," Charlotte snapped back, and offered her sister a handkerchief. "And now look at this. You've gotten my dress all wet."

"You wanted the goods, we got the goods," Celeste replied smugly, wiping her eyes. She was quite good at forcing tears; her pale freckled face was flushed red from the effort. "Or was your plan to simply argue them into submission?"

"My plan was to stick to the facts, not charlatanism."

"And look how well that was working out for us," Celeste said as they headed to the wagon. "Emotion, Charlotte, not logic. That's how one gets through to people who do not wish to listen."

Charlotte sighed. "How did you know about the dead man?"

"Men die here all the time."

"This particular dead man?"

"You need to keep up with the city gossip," Celeste said, and circled around to the front of the wagon. The oxen team was waiting patiently. She clambered up into the driver's seat, offering Charlotte a hand up. "Denver is awash in such stories."

"You don't help our reputations," Charlotte said, and climbed up next to her sister, retrieving the driving reins. "Behaving like this."

"Our reputations are already set," Celeste said, cross now. "Everyone knows who we are. The daughters of the great Madame Aine, trance medium extraordinaire, world-famous Spiritualist. Why shouldn't I use that to get what we need?"

"Mr. Dunn won't be happy when he hears about this," Charlotte said.

"Mr. Dunn isn't happy with anything," Celeste retorted. "I'm sure he'll be displeased that we've finally solved the theft problem, because now he can't complain about it."

Charlotte actually smiled at that. "We still shouldn't do things like that."

"You know it only works because people want to believe in it," Celeste replied, somewhat smug. "Isn't that what Mama always said? Give the people what they want?"

I've never wanted it, Charlotte almost said, thinking about the figure watching her on the platform. To her little sister, the whole thing was a grand, hilarious game.

But Charlotte knew. There was nothing hilarious about this at all.

"People are fools," Charlotte told her sister and flicked the reins. The obliging ox team trundled off, into the dusty Denver streets.

CHAPTER THREE

"I say, young man, might you help a poor traveler out?"

"You talk funny, mister. Where you from?"

"I'm from England," Thomas Leighton told the boy he had just stopped, smiling. "London, if you can believe that. And I must confess, I am having a hard time understanding this board."

Thomas indicated the schedule board in front of him. It graced the wall between the inside hall and the outside platforms here at Denver's Union Station. It was of the latest style, the moveable letters spelling out line names and timetables still a brilliant, fresh white. The building had only been completed a year or two before, judging by the dedication plaque he'd seen in the entrance hall. A simple collection of plain stonework and curved brick, it wouldn't have held a candle to even Grand Central Station back in New York City.

Below it, the wall was plastered with less official things; flyers for public lectures, announcements, offers of horses or goods for sale, wanted posters, featuring criminals. One of them stood out quite prominently. Eli Horn, wanted for horse thievery and murder. A five-hundred-dollar reward. Substantial, he'd thought.

The boy nodded at him. "Sure, mister. What do you need to know?"

"What any of these train lines are. I've looked all around the station, but I cannot seem to find anything to help me decipher which of these comes from the town of Leadville. Do you know it?"

"Leadville? Ain't ever been there myself," the boy said, but pointed. "That's the one you're lookin' for, mister. The Denver, South Park, and Pacific Railroad."

Thomas found the correct entry on the board. His glasses were horribly smudged, he realized, and pulled them off, cleaning them with his handkerchief. "Did I see the time right? The train gets in at half past six tonight?"

"Yessir. It's normally quite prompt."

"Are you sure of that?"

The boy nodded. "Of course. I work here," he said proudly. "With my uncle."

Thomas looked up at the board again, considering. The last telegraph from his patron, four days ago in Chicago, had said they would meet at Union Station when Thomas's train got in on the sixteenth of October.

But it was only three o'clock now.

The boy looked at him expectantly, and Thomas sighed. "I was to meet somebody here. A Mr. Lane Barton. He said he was concluding some business in Leadville first. I don't suppose you—"

"Mr. Barton!" the boy exclaimed. "He's famous, what with his mines and silver and all. He lives up on Capitol Hill in a fine ol' mansion. You ever been to Capitol Hill?"

Thomas smiled despite himself. "No, I haven't."

"Well, you should see it! It's a grand place!"

Thomas considered his options. Waiting around Denver's Union Station, or even exploring the town a little, was not an unwelcome prospect. Perhaps he could even find a place to sit down, get a bite to eat, and get back to work on his current translation project. But he had luggage to consider, important luggage, that Mr. Barton would no doubt want secure and safe, and who knew if this place could supply that? "I do have a few crates of goods for Mr. Barton that I should like to see delivered as soon as possible. You said his house is known?"

"Well known, sir. We move a lot of goods for him. Oysters and coffee and whatnot."

"Is there a way I can send my luggage on to his house while I wait for him here?"

The boy nodded. "My uncle can help you with that, sir." And he gestured. "C'mon, he's working out on the platform now."

The boy's uncle, it turned out, was the head porter, in charge of unloading the very train Thomas had come in on. The man was big with rough hands and a sunburned face but shook Thomas's hand warmly enough.

"Anything for Mr. Barton," he said.

The cargo area of the train depot was organized, it seemed, crates and boxes moving about with that industrious efficiency that Thomas had come to associate with Americans. There was a great deal of chatter amongst the porters, swapping jokes with each other or good-natured insults with drivers working on loading up their wagons. Horses stomped their feet and ox teams lowed. It was, Thomas thought, a well-run place.

"And this is mine?" Thomas asked as they walked up to a small group of crates clustered all together. They were four feet by four feet to a side and came up to his waist. By this point in their journey, they were covered in shipping stamps. It had taken him several months and not a small amount of effort to pull these tomes together.

"It's all here," the head porter said defensively.

"I wasn't questioning your integrity, but things do get lost in transit."

"What, you want to accuse me of theft, too? This is an honest outfit."

"I never said it wasn't," Thomas said, a little surprised at the man's defensiveness. "And it would be a foolish thing to steal anyway."

"What do you mean?" the porter asked.

Thomas rapped on the top of one of the crates. "Books, my good man. Books. Old books, at that. Not much use out here on the frontier, I suspect."

"What kind of books?" the boy asked.

"All kinds," he said. "Mr. Barton had a rather eclectic list he wanted filled. Some of these are quite rare."

"Rare books gettin' shipped to our town," the head porter said, shaking his head. "Times are a-changin'."

"Indeed," Thomas said, and his eye settled on one of the crates. "There's a spot of water here. Might I open it and check for damage?"

The head porter crossed his arms. "I prefer not to open cargo out here."

"If something has happened in transit…"

"You're as bad as that Roseingrave woman," he grumbled.

And at that name, Thomas's ears perked up. "Roseingrave? As in, the medium?"

"Yes, that's the one! She can see spirits!" the boy said.

"Hush," the head porter told his nephew. "It's bad enough she was talkin' to you 'bout school when there's work to be done, but that little show she put on here—"

"But Uncle, somebody really did die last Friday!"

"Somebody dies here every Friday. There ain't nuthin' remarkable 'bout that at all."

Thomas looked at his crates again, considering.

"Your nephew mentioned that I might be able to have this delivered to Mr. Barton's address without trouble?" he asked.

"We'll put it on Mr. Barton's tab," the porter said. "We have an arrangement with him."

"I certainly hope so," he said. "Mr. Barton would be quite cross if he did not receive this shipment."

"Anything for Mr. Barton," the head porter said seriously.

They were obliged to wait a few more minutes while Thomas's luggage was loaded and secured to his exacting expectations. He tried to offer the head porter a little something for his trouble, but the man waved it away.

The boy, on the other hand, was waiting by Thomas's side, gaze both expectant and hopeful.

Thomas smiled and handed a quarter to the boy, who wrapped a grubby hand around it with a look of surprised reverence. It was probably too much to have paid the boy, but Mr. Barton had provided Thomas a substantial stipend for the journey, and here at its end, it only seemed fair.

"Thank you for your assistance, young man. Now, if you can do me another favor, there'll be another of those for you."

"What's that?"

"Show me where I can find Mrs. Roseingrave."

It had been a long week's journey from New York City, but even that was something of a marvel. Once, in the not-too-distant past, it would have taken a man months to hack his way across the North American continent. Now, thanks to an ever-expanding rail system, the trip took mere days.

Traveling across America had been quite the experience. The fine cities of the East Coast, while not comparable to London, held a sort of modern charm, stuffed to the gills with every new innovation and idea the Americans could come up with.

As Thomas had moved west, however, the cities grew smaller, less cultured. He had spent a few days in St. Louis; the gateway to the frontier, some people called it. He had found the place utterly lacking in charm and had passed the time reviewing his reference material and sending a few final letters from the hotel.

Denver, on the other hand, was a city with dreams of grandeur, he thought as they passed back through Union Station. He hadn't expected anything like this. Open prairie and raw wilderness, he'd thought, judging off some of the travelogues he'd read. To see something this urbane out here in the middle of the American West was jarring.

The edges of the map were being drawn in. "And we shall all be the poorer for it," he muttered to himself as they passed out into the streets.

"Beggin' your pardon, sir?" the boy asked.

"Nothing," Thomas replied. "Just thinking out loud."

The boy nodded. "What brings you out to Denver, sir?"

"Research," Thomas told him.

"Whaddaya research?"

"Psychical phenomena," Thomas replied, and at the boy's questioning look, he clarified. "Ghosts, spirits, supernatural happenings."

"There's a job for that?"

"I don't suppose you've ever heard of the Academy for Psychical Inquiry?"

"You work for an academy? You must be awful smart, mister."

Thomas sighed. Anything more about all that and he was going to start lying to this boy, and that didn't seem fair. Curiosity deserved to be rewarded, not manipulated. That was the Holzworths' position, the position of the Academy itself, and despite Thomas's recent disagreements with the Academy's illustrious founders, he still wholeheartedly agreed with the philosophy.

"It's a group in England seeking to bring a little scientific rigor to the world of Spiritualism," he told the boy. "They look at mediums, performances, things like that."

The boy smiled, finally catching on. "That's why you want to see the Roseingraves!" he exclaimed and launched into a story about one of Mrs. Roseingrave's daughters, just today, meeting a dead man on the train platform.

Thomas listened with half an ear, distracted by his own thoughts but still trying to pick out the details from the boy's account. There was truth everywhere—as Mrs. Holzworth always said—but personal reports usually told you more about the observer's biases than anything else.

Denver proper turned out to be as surprising as its station. Stone and brick edifices rose tall and proud along its downtown streets, with more buildings under construction. Women in fine silk dresses promenaded down the sidewalks, carrying bags and baskets and towing small children along behind. The dusty streets were clogged with traffic, wagons and horses and cattle. Men in rough plains shirts and leather chaps rose past brightly painted buggies. Signage hung everywhere the Americans could shove it, and many of these were advertisements. It was chaotic, messy, lacking in any greater design. Nevertheless, the place had a kind of earnestness to it, big and bold and shameless. Thomas took it all in, a little amazed. Not what he had expected at all.

But soon enough, they were nearing what appeared to be a grand opera house, worthy of any city in Europe and flanked by a small cluster of outbuildings. One of these appeared to be a stable, the others workshops.

What was Madame Aine Roseingrave doing in a place like this? Perhaps working on some kind of case or collaborating on a performance—she gave few public demonstrations, and Thomas had never heard of a séance delivered in an opera house, but this was America. Who knew what they might get up to here?

There was sawing and hammering going on here, horses whinnying and oxen lowing and all the sounds of industry one might expect.

"Are you sure Mrs. Roseingrave is here?"

The boy nodded. "They came to pick up fabric for Mr. Dunn. He's the manager here, you know."

"Fabric?"

"Fabric, all shiny-like."

Seamstress work, then. Very strange. But if that was the answer, that was the answer, so Thomas offered the boy another quarter to wait for him and headed to the building with the SEWING ROOMS sign hanging above the main double door.

Inside, he could hear two women quarreling.

Thomas took stock of himself before knocking. He was a bit of a mess. He had brought his secretary bag with him, sending his own steamer trunk on with the rest of the luggage to Mr. Barton's house. The thing was stuffed to bursting. His suit was badly wrinkled from the train ride, and he was certain he needed to wash his face from the smoke.

Still, this was possibly the only chance he would have to speak to Mrs. Roseingrave prior to Mr. Barton inserting himself into the situation, and as Mrs. Holzworth always said, it was best practice to question people separately.

Gathering himself, he knocked.

The arguing inside stopped.

The door jerked open.

Standing there was a slim woman with flaming red hair and fine features, her pale skin heavily freckled and her eyes a glittering blue. Her black wool dress was trimmed with purple. Half mourning? He wondered who might have died.

"May I help you?" she asked cautiously.

"I am told that I can find the Roseingrave family here," Thomas replied, considering her. She bore a strong resemblance to the descriptions he had heard of Mrs. Roseingrave's daughters. They were mentioned on occasion in articles about Madame Aine. *Borderlands* especially was interested in the family. Thomas supposed this daughter was Celeste, the younger sister who was said to assist her mother in séances these days.

"And who told you that, Mister..."

"Oh, Leighton. Thomas Leighton," he said, and took off his hat, tucking it under his arm. A shock of dark hair flopped down over his forehead, loosed from its pomade. "I was looking for Madame Aine."

"Her name was Anna Roseingrave," another woman said, so like the first that they could have only been sisters. Unlike her sister, though, her dress was pure black. The only color on her at all was a silver chatelaine of fine Celtic design at her waist. Her hair was darker and her blue eyes more burdened. Charlotte, he guessed, the elder sister who served as her mother's publicist and performance manager. "Madame Aine was her stage name."

"Yes, of course. I meant no disrespect. I have been corresponding with her, and our mutual benefactor Mr. Barton, these last months, and I have been very eager to meet with her."

The sisters exchanged a look. "I don't remember her mentioning a Mr. Leighton," the second one said.

"Well, here, I have her last letter," he said, fumbling for his bag. Despite the overstuffed nature of the thing, he located the paper easily enough and handed it over. The first sister, the one in purple, grabbed for it.

"This is Mama's handwriting," she mused, reviewing it. "You're an investigator? With the British Academy for Psychical Inquiry?"

Thomas shifted his bag around, feeling a little guilty now. "I prefer the term 'researcher,' actually. Some of, er, my overzealous colleagues have made 'investigator' synonymous with 'debunker.'"

"No wonder there," the sister in all black said. "I can't imagine they'd ever find anything real."

She was elbowed by the one in purple trim. "Charlotte!"

"What, should I lie to him, Celeste?" The elder sister shook her head. "I am sorry for your trouble, coming all this way from England, but whatever our mother promised you, she cannot provide it."

"And why is that?" he asked.

"Our mother's dead, Mr. Leighton."

Chapter Four

The pronouncement hit Thomas hard. An ocean crossed, thousands of miles traveled, and this was the result? He frowned, looking back and forth between the two women. "I don't understand."

"Her health had been declining for some time," the younger Miss Roseingrave said sadly. "Her heart finally gave out a few weeks after we arrived here."

"She was looking forward to a stay out in Glenwood Springs," the elder sister added. "We never got there."

"I cannot believe this," Thomas said. "I got her last correspondence only a few days before I departed England, and I have been in contact with Mr. Barton since then, via telegraph. He said nothing of this either."

"Mama didn't say anything to us about taking on a commission with Mr. Barton," the elder sister said. "And I would know. I handled all her bookings."

"So I've been told," Thomas replied. He glanced at the flame-haired younger sister. She was reading the letter again with obvious care.

"It's most likely related to his son," the younger sister told the elder. "Remember when he went missing? Even you couldn't have missed that local gossip."

The older sister just looked irritated now. "Is there anything we can do for you, Mr. Leighton? Perhaps directions to her grave, or something equally morbid? Lord knows we've had plenty of strange requests from the local Spiritualist community."

"There's a Spiritualist community out here?"

"Spiritualists are everywhere. Mama wouldn't have come this way if there wasn't money in it." The elder Miss Roseingrave sighed. "Mr. Leighton, I do apologize for all your trouble, but since our mother is no longer with us, I do not see what—"

"Perhaps the two of you could help," Thomas interrupted. The younger Miss Roseingrave seemed to perk up. The elder frowned. "Your mother has, er, had, the best accuracy rate of any medium in North America, surpassing even the famed Mrs. Piper from Boston, whom the Academy has—"

"Why would the Academy be interested in Mama?" the younger sister asked, interrupting. "I've heard that they refuse to study any medium who charges for his or her work."

Thomas hesitated. "I do not believe that a medium charging for her services is an indication of fraud."

"All working mediums are frauds, Mr. Leighton," the elder sister said. "Including our mother."

"Charlotte!" the younger snapped.

The elder looked exasperated. "What, am I to protect Mama's reputation even now?"

"Even that would be fine information to capture," Thomas said quickly, sensing the argument that was coming. "I do not believe there is a single account of a medium, or a medium's assistant, revealing the tricks employed by the profession. I know Madame Aine's methods were—"

"Her name was Anna Roseingrave," the elder sister said firmly.

Thomas had assisted in many investigations over the past few years, as a fellow with the Academy, but never had he encountered anything like this. It was strange. "We had an arrangement, your mother and me. She had agreed upon a fee for—"

The elder sister bristled. "We are not for sale, sir."

"I'm not implying that you are, nor your mother. Mr. Barton had something he wished her to examine for him."

"His dead son," the younger sister mused.

"I am glad Mama never had the chance to exploit his grief," the elder sister said, and went over to the door, opening it. "Now, if you please Mr. Leighton, we are quite busy here today."

He looked around the workroom, the shelves stuffed with bolts of fabric of all colors and description, along with a great deal of other things. Seamstress work did not pay very well and was quite grueling to boot. Still, he sensed a great deal of pride in these two and had no wish to offend them further. He took the elder Miss Roseingrave's not-so-subtle hint and replaced his hat, stepping outside.

"I am to stay here in Denver for the foreseeable future," he said, unwilling to leave without a fight. "I have other business here in the Colorado area, so—"

"Like what?" the younger sister asked.

"A survey of the local folklore," he said. "Such things are my primary interest, you see."

"I have no doubt you'll hear many interesting stories," the younger sister said. "Miners are a superstitious lot."

"Good day to you," the elder sister added.

The door slammed shut behind him.

What a strange encounter.

Outside, the boy from the train station was waiting for him. Thomas was glad to see him; in truth, he wasn't quite sure what to do with himself next.

"Did you get the answers you needed, sir?" the boy asked.

"Not quite yet, my boy," Thomas said, making a decision, and pulled out two quarters. One he handed over, the other he held up in reserve. "Now, can you show me where I might find a bite to eat while I wait for the mountain line to get in? Nothing too expensive or boisterous, if you please, and close to the station if possible."

Eyes wide at the sight of the coin, the boy nodded.

That place turned out to be a hotel facing onto the main square in front of Union Station that served what the boy insisted was fine food. Thomas ordered a steak and an ale—there seemed to be plenty of both out here in this part of the country, and while the beer was poor, the beef was excellent.

In between bites, Thomas looked back over the translation he was currently working on. Ogham script, a meticulous copy of a rubbing he had taken on his last sojourn through Ireland. It had no bearing on the present situation, but it gave him something to focus on. Thomas had come too far, risked too much, to find Anna Roseingrave dead and have her daughter slam the door in his face. What would Mr. Barton say when he—

"Beggin' your pardon, sir, but she was inquiring about you over at the station."

Thomas looked up from his notebooks, still chewing, to see a steel-haired woman of perhaps fifty standing there. She was the sort of woman he'd seen all over in America: proud, forthright, with the thick wrists and simple dress of one used to working with her hands. She was also frowning, as if she already disapproved of him.

"Mr. Leighton, I presume?" she asked. "I'm Mrs. Coulton. Mr. Barton is my employer."

"Yes, yes, of course," he said, wiping his mouth and standing up. "How good to meet you."

"I got your package up at the house and realized that something must have been mixed up. Mr. Barton believed you were coming in tomorrow, not today."

"Ah," Thomas said. So that was why Mr. Barton, or some proxy, had not been at the station. "I apologize for the inconvenience."

Mrs. Coulton sighed a little and looked at the boy. "You can run along now."

Thomas held out another quarter. The boy grabbed it, eyes wide, and bobbing his head, ran out of the hotel.

Mrs. Coulton stared after him, lip curled. "You shouldn't do that," she said. "His family's as likely to spend that money on drink as they are on anything else. If he doesn't get robbed for it, or get you robbed later."

Thomas thought about London, where yes, such things were extremely common. Perhaps they were common here, too, but there was a different feel to things here. "Why shouldn't I tip a young man who's doing an honest day's work?"

She sniffed. "Well, I suppose being generous is no vice. But I do have the buggy here, if you would accompany me up to the house."

Thomas nodded and gathered up his notebooks, almost knocking his beer over in his haste. "Of course, Mrs. Coulton, lead away, please."

"You can finish your food, if you'd like," she told him, slightly bemused.

"Nonsense," he said, and swept the books back into his satchel. "I wouldn't dream of keeping a lady waiting."

The buggy waiting for him out front was as fine a model as he had ever seen. Its team of chestnuts was perfectly matched, every surface of the buggy polished, the leather seats well-padded and soft. He was about to inquire where the driver was when Mrs. Coulton began unhitching the team from the post.

"Something wrong?" she asked.

Thomas shook himself. "Back home, women typically don't drive carriages."

"Needs must," she told him, and pulled herself up into the seat.

Only hesitating a moment more, he followed.

Mrs. Coulton must have needed to drive the buggy often, because she handled it expertly. The streets of Denver were broad, dusty, and very busy, but she guided them through it with a light touch and easy commands.

"What did you send to my house?" Mrs. Coulton asked as she drove.

"Books," Thomas replied. "Your employer put in quite a large order from London. I agreed to chaperone them."

"More books," Mrs. Coulton sighed. Her face had disappeared under a broad quilted bonnet, practical, not fashionable. The sun, Thomas could feel, was quite harsh here. "Why must there be more books? More books, more nonsense. Some of it is borderline heretical, if you ask me."

She was terribly free with her opinions for a servant, Thomas thought, but didn't say it. "Some might say that one man's heresy is another man's truth," he said. "Just ask the Catholics."

Mrs. Coulton shook her head and flicked the reins, but he thought he saw a smile in the shadow of her bonnet. "You and Mr. Barton are going to get along famously," she told him.

Denver was a young city, only a decade or two old, but it was flush with wealth rolling down out of the mountains to the west. The silver boom had created an entire generation of new-money millionaires here, and Thomas was fascinated by the streets around them.

Passing through the small downtown, they were obliged to navigate around the foundations of what, Mrs. Coulton assured him, would someday be the grandest statehouse west of the Mississippi. The Americans seemed to take a great deal of pride in their public buildings, emulating the classical styles of Greece and Rome in some deliberate invocation of that fabled democratic past.

But there was still aristocracy here, of a kind, and Thomas soon found himself in it.

The neighborhood south of the half-finished capitol building was fine indeed. Stone and wood mansions in the latest style stood proudly above the road. Finally, they stopped at a grand place of red stone and intricately carved wood.

Mrs. Coulton walked him briskly through the house. It was of the latest design, with well-appointed rooms flowing into each other. Thomas commented on the craftsmanship several times, to which she just shrugged.

There was a set of rooms near the back of the house with the doors closed. Mrs. Coulton made no attempt to show him what was in those. The kitchen, perhaps, he thought, and then she was leading him up the stairs.

"And these will be your rooms, while you're staying with us," Mrs. Coulton said finally, gesturing at a door about halfway down the main hall. "You're welcome to wash up or change or whatever you'd like. Mr. Barton will be in around seven o'clock."

"Of course," Thomas said, looking around. His nose was stinging now, dry and uncomfortable. "I'm looking forward to meeting him." He brought up a handkerchief to his upper lip and saw blood come away.

"Nosebleeds are common here, especially if you come by train and don't take the long way across the prairie by wagon," Mrs. Coulton said, but offered no other comment on it.

Thomas balled up the handkerchief. "I should like to unload the books I brought him."

"The library's on the main floor, all the way to the back of the house," she replied.

So that was what was behind those closed doors. "You don't hold with your employer's interests, do you?"

"My employer can do whatever he likes," she replied. "It's his money."

This was certainly not the kind of servant Thomas was used to dealing with. "Well, I shall get everything ready for him, if that is alright with you."

She shook her head. "Supper will be ready at half past eight. I trust that will give you both enough time to review the new...reading material."

"Quite," he agreed.

But then the woman was gone again.

Strange creature, Thomas thought, and looked to his steamer trunk, brought up here earlier by some unseen staff. It would be a good thing to change his suit; after days on the train, he could practically feel the soot in his coat. It would need a thorough brushing later.

Books first. Then he could figure out what to do about this mess with the Roseingrave sisters.

CHAPTER FIVE

"Do you have any idea how much Mr. Barton was offering Mama to do that séance?" Celeste was seated on the room's only chair, her current sewing project spread out in front of her on top of the barrel that they used as a table. "Any idea at all?"

Charlotte rubbed her forehead. This was the last thing she wanted to talk to her sister about. "Eight hundred dollars. What difference does it make?"

"What difference would that not make?"

Charlotte ignored the question, instead turning another page in her old storybook. The pages were brittle with age, yellowed and stained, and yet somehow, the images were still as bright as they had ever been.

The book had been a gift from her grandmother, some family heirloom brought to America from the west of Ireland, written in the old language. "Wise stories from the old country," Grandmother used to say when she'd read them to the girls, stories about the Fir Bolg and Fomorians and Tuatha Dé Danann, who had fled to the hills and dwindled, becoming all manner of faery folk. Gods and monsters and heroes.

Some of the stories, like those of Cú Chulainn, used to make Charlotte laugh. Others, like the Children of Lir, made her weep. But whoever had written them down here had written them down all wrong, because these were different than the versions Charlotte had read about in newer translations.

Still, she often found herself reading it after a brush with the things she didn't want to see. There was comfort here; she could still hear Grandmother's voice reading the words to her, never translating the Gaelic to English, and there was one specific story she sought out often, the one she sought now.

"You're counting money we don't have, Celeste," Charlotte said. "We're not doing it."

"You don't have to do anything," Celeste said. "But I could—"

"What?" Charlotte asked, interrupting. She turned another page. Why didn't the thing have a proper chapter listing? "Lie to him? About his missing son?"

"Missing but presumed dead," Celeste countered. "And Mr. Barton must think him dead if he was reaching out to Mama."

Charlotte held her tongue. She knew exactly why Mr. Barton had reached out to their mother. Or, at least, she knew enough of it to know she wanted nothing to do with it. "You're wasting oil, Celeste. Put out that lamp. We should go to bed."

"You're reading," her sister threw back. "Why don't you stop?"

It was a fair point. Not that Charlotte was going to concede that to her sister. She looked up from her book, glancing around at their cramped little apartment.

It wasn't much, just a small room on the upper floor of the opera's workhouse with a bed, an old woodburning stove, and their little barrel table, scrounged from the streets. Perhaps these spaces had been meant as something else originally, but they made fine little apartments.

A few other women lived up here on the same floor in other rooms, like Miss Rachel Westinghouse at the end of the hall, a native New Yorker who had come west for her fiancé only to find out after she arrived that he had run off with another woman, or Mrs. Sarah Dresden, who had two small children and never spoke about her past.

They had a small communal kitchen on the main floor and took turns with baths, and Mr. Dunn, the manager here, didn't charge them rent as long as they kept working. It was as pleasant a place as an unmarried woman could find on the frontier.

But it was tight.

In the weeks after Mama had died, Charlotte and Celeste had sold as much as they could bear to. Some things, like Mama's clothes, had been difficult to part with. Other things, like her steamer trunk full of tricks, should have been easy to discard. And yet, the sisters had fought over that thing bitterly. Celeste had eventually won the argument. Mostly because she had started weeping when Charlotte had pressed her on it. There wasn't much in there that had value to anyone else out here anyway, Charlotte had figured, but it did make the space in their already cramped room even more cramped.

"Does Mr. Dunn know you took materials from the workroom for your own personal project?" Charlotte asked.

Celeste huffed and shook out the skirt she was working on. "I took a wool remnant from last year's performance of *The Doctor of Alcantara*. Nobody cares about it."

"Do you think he won't fire us if he finds out?"

"He'd likely just fire me," Celeste said, "but then, what would it matter? I'd have a patented new riding skirt to profit from. Imagine that, Charlotte, my pattern in *The Delineator*! 'We offer today the new Roseingrave skirt, a simple yet elegant style for any woman finding herself employed on horseback in the West.' Wouldn't that be grand?"

"What do you know about horses?" Charlotte sighed, still leafing through the book. The thing had opened to the book's account of Cath Maighe Tuireadh, a bloody and violent tale she had no stomach for today.

"I know that riding sidesaddle is a fool's mission out here, and current styles don't permit anything astride," Celeste shot back.

"Any woman who needs to ride astride wears trousers," Charlotte replied absently, pausing. The illustration on this page looked familiar, but the story wasn't.

Her younger sister set her work aside, clearly frustrated. "Eight hundred dollars, Charlotte! With another four hundred upon successfully contacting the spirits!"

"Nobody pays a medium twelve hundred dollars for their services."

"Mr. Barton is rich, and he wants to know what happened to his son," Celeste said. "And that is simple enough to guess. He is dead. He died of natural causes, was killed by some wild animal, or truly was murdered by another prospector. That's why they've never found the body. Men would roll it off a cliff or bury it and a bear would eat him."

"That's positively morbid, Celeste."

"What I mean is that whatever happened, the body won't likely be found, so who could prove me wrong?" Celeste stood up, hands animated, pacing. "Twelve hundred dollars, Charlotte. Imagine what we could do with twelve hundred dollars. We could establish ourselves in San Francisco. I could find myself a nice respectable gentleman to marry, and you could open a dress shop or mope about or whatever it is that would make you happy."

"We can't, Celeste. Not like this."

"Why not?"

Charlotte hesitated, fingers pausing. Celeste had always been so flippant, never taking their mother's work as anything more than a game. Celeste had never had to deal with the fallout, the consequences, the reality of it all.

"Charlotte?" Celeste was right next to her now, sitting on Mama's old steamer trunk. "Why can't we take this job on?"

Charlotte sighed and tried to lay the book aside, but Celeste laid a hand on it before she could.

"Maybe I should ask him," she said, and tapped the illustration on the left-hand page. "Surely he wouldn't like to see us starving."

Charlotte looked down and closed her eyes. Blast it. She'd found the page she was looking for. "Celeste..."

Celeste cupped a hand around her mouth. "Mr. Faery, do you suppose you might help us with a séance?"

Jerking the book away, Charlotte glanced down at the story. It was a simple tale, near the end of the book, consisting of no more than a single page with the illustration opposite. A simple, fanciful thing, as all the stories of the fair folk were, about a lord who abducted a chieftain's wife and in recompense, sent one of his warriors to watch over her baby daughter, the warrior bound by oath to watch over her and all of her kin, until the stars burned out.

One of Grandmother's favorite stories, that one.

"Our family's story," Grandmother had always told her. "Your story."

The wife in the story had seen the faery lord first; she'd had the Sight, the ability to see into Tir na nAill, Sight that was granted to the daughter left behind and all firstborn daughters to follow. At least, that was the story.

Charlotte had never believed it. Birthright? More like a curse.

"Stop that," Charlotte snapped.

"Why? Do you think he might show up?" Celeste smiled at her, something hard and angry in her eyes. "Maybe he could tell me how you knew about the twelve hundred dollars."

Cold washed through Charlotte as she realized her mistake. She had been so distracted, she hadn't even thought about what she was saying.

Celeste had been leading her on. "I saw the letter Mr. Leighton handed you," she offered quickly.

"No, you didn't," Celeste snapped back. "You're lying. I can tell, because you were never any good at it." There was fury in her little sister's eyes now. "Mr. Barton came to you, didn't he? You, who handled all of Mama's bookings. He came to you first! And don't lie to me about this!"

Blast it. "Fine. Yes, we spoke."

"And you didn't think to mention this to me?"

"Mama was dead, Celeste!"

"I can do this!" Celeste yelled. "Why are we grubbing for pennies, working for that horrid Mr. Dunn in this horrid place, when we could be using what Mama taught us instead? Why didn't you tell me?!"

There were a dozen things Charlotte could have said to that, but giving voice to any of them would have been even more of a disaster.

Instead, she grabbed her shawl and stormed out of the room.

The night was cold outside. Winter was on its way, and here on the high plains, the air seldom held on to daytime warmth. The shawl Charlotte had grabbed was not quite enough to block out the chill.

She wrapped herself up tighter, hugging the shawl to herself, and breathed out. Little clouds formed in front of her mouth. Charlotte wandered a little way away from the workshop's back door, away from where her sister might look for her first. Anger warred with guilt in her breast.

Mr. Leighton had not been wrong. Mama had had an excellent accuracy rate, but Mama's séance performances were just that. Performances. Both Charlotte and Celeste knew every one of her tricks.

Fake hands, ghostly silk shawls, sticks hidden under one's skirt that allowed a medium to make a table dance or create ominous thumps from beneath the floorboards. Leading questions. Vague statements. A carefully cultivated aura of mystery, a fine stage presence. One did not need to speak to spirits to discern what a séance's attendees wanted to see, and then, it was just a matter of giving it to them. The tricks of the trade were legion, and effective, and the worst part was that nobody seemed to mind. Even the most ardent Spiritualists would admit that the pageantry of the séance, the uncertainty, was part of the appeal.

That was Mama's business.

And yet, Charlotte knew that it was not parlor tricks or insightful comments that people wanted.

No, it was the times—the very rare few times—when things weren't faked that had earned Mama the reputation she enjoyed.

But for every object that appeared without explanation, every automatic drawing that accurately showed some hidden family secret, there were horrors. That séance in Cincinnati where the shades of the dead, lost when a paddle wheeler sank, showed up at the house, dripping and burbling water as they pawed at the guests, causing several women to faint from shock. The time in St. Louis when their client, Mr. Trent, suffered a heart attack after that...that thing summoned up from the basement shoved a hand through the man's chest. The famous incident back in 1875, the one that had earned Mama her reputation, where every object in the drawing room had levitated three feet in the air before crashing down again, injuring the client's twelve-year-old son and destroying several priceless family antiques.

Mama had the Sight. Charlotte knew this was true. Mama had been Grandmother's eldest daughter, only daughter. And there were too many things that had happened in their lives that could not be explained any other way. And yet, Charlotte had never spoken to her mother about it. Not since that one time, that only time, the week after Grandmother died. When Charlotte had learned just how dangerous the spirits could be.

Back then, Mama had promised Charlotte that no harm would ever come to her again, that nothing would touch her, that Mama's work wouldn't be a problem for her.

How could it not be, Charlotte thought again, now, bitter. The only way to truly keep out all the horror was to never engage with it in the first place. To even play at séance was to risk sanity and safety and soul.

"It's a cold night for such cold thoughts. You'd best go back inside, lass."

She froze.

It was a man's voice, soft but laced with warning.

"Who speaks?" she demanded, jerking around, trying to find the source of the voice. The chatelaine still on her waist jingled its soft, silvery notes. "Who are you?"

"It's not safe."

Nobody. There was nobody there. The alley was empty. Charlotte pulled her shawl tightly around her shoulders, ice in her veins. The worst thing she could do was answer, she knew, and she touched the little crucifix she wore under the collar of her dress. Yes, ignoring that voice was—

But then she saw the door.

The workshop door, closed and latched carefully behind her, was yawning open wide.

Heart suddenly hammering in her chest, she hurried inside. The door resisted hard as she tried to close it, the hinges protesting, rust flaking to the ground. Charlotte ran the toe of her boot through the small pile, kneeling down to get a better look at it. Glancing up again, she could see that the bottom hinge was half gone, the remaining fragments pitted with decay.

"What in the world?" she muttered to herself.

And then, behind her, came a creaking, groaning sound from above, like breaking wood.

And then a potbellied stove, bright with fire, crashed to the workshop floor not five feet from where she was standing and exploded.

For a single moment, time seemed to stop. Charlotte saw the cast iron of the stove shatter apart like glass, flying out in all directions. The logs within, already turned half to charcoal, burst, sending burning chunks of wood across the workshop, including one massive one, headed right for her face.

But the wood didn't hit her. No, it was deflected in mid-air, embers spraying out in all directions. It was as if it had collided with the curved edge of some invisible shield. The sheer shock of that was enough to stop her dead, staring at the strange phenomenon, even as old memories threatened to overwhelm her. Another night, another fire, a—

"Fire!" a woman's voice screamed from upstairs, and the spell was broken. The shield was gone, the air around her now full of burning ash.

"Celeste!" Charlotte didn't even stop to think. She raced to the back of the workshop, dodging the burning wood that was scattered everywhere, taking the stairs as fast as she could.

Upstairs, doors were being flung open, smoke billowing into the hall, as women in all manner of dress piled out, many of them clutching bags or children. The only light was from the burning walls inside every room, and even that was starting to be obscured by smoke.

"Where's my sister?!" she yelled at one of their neighbors, grabbing her by the elbow, but the woman just shook her head and kept running.

Charlotte reached the door to their tiny room, eyes and throat stinging.

She coughed and tried to open the door. The rough wood was warm, and the knob was hot and it wouldn't give.

"Celeste!" she screamed, banging on it.

"Charlotte!" came a cry from inside. "It won't open!"

Charlotte closed her eyes for a moment, thinking about the explosion downstairs, thinking about Grandmother's old stories. Nothing was natural about this fire. She could feel that in her bones. Something had started it. Something...otherworldly. "If that was you out there, we could use some help right about now," she muttered.

But perhaps his help wasn't needed after all, because just then Celeste fell out into the hall, the door jerking open in a blast of heat.

Inside their room, Charlotte could see, fire was everywhere. Licking up the walls, engulfing the simple pallet where they slept. The stove seemed to have crumbled apart; the only sign it was there at all was a rusted pipe leading to the roof. The contents of the trunk, all their clothes, were scattered about the floor and burning now, as if Celeste had been desperately searching for something inside.

Celeste's eyes were wild, and Charlotte had to grab her to keep her from going back in the room. "Mama's trunk!" she wailed. "Grandmother's book!"

Charlotte glanced back at the room. There it was, sitting on the barrel that was itself now on fire. "We can't!" she yelled, heart twisting inside her chest, and dragged her younger sister away.

Getting out of the workhouse was bedlam.

Sarah had her smaller child in her arms, the older one screaming furiously, biting at her. Celeste, recovering now, snatched the little boy up and they all rushed for the stairs. Old Mrs. Williams tripped going down, and only Celeste's intervention saved her from falling.

Skirts ripped, children screamed. They tumbled out onto the main floor. More fire was licking its way up the walls and through the stacks of fabric. Wool and silk were not normally so flammable, but in the presence of so much heat, combustion seemed inevitable. The air was growing black, even as the fire burned and burned and burned.

The small group of women halted, Mrs. Williams doubled over with hacking, the children's screams stuttering now.

"Which way's the door?" Celeste coughed.

Charlotte looked around desperately, fighting down old memories that were trying to surface again. *Please,* she thought, eyes watering, feeling the breath being choked from her lungs, *please not like this.*

And then, noise. Wood breaking. Some of their group screamed, but then the air currents shifted. A tunnel of clear air formed in the smoke, guiding them out.

"That way," she said, lungs screaming at her, and grabbed for her sister's hand. The little boy was fighting Celeste hard, twisting out of her arms. Charlotte grabbed him before he could get away. "Everyone! This way!"

It wasn't far to the door. Clutching hands or holding on to clothing, the group of women made their way out of the burning structure, into the clean air of the high plains night. Dazed, Charlotte realized there was a growing crowd out there in the courtyard, lookers-on, neighbors, even a fire brigade already getting to work.

Charlotte passed the little boy in her arms back to his mother and looked at the small, huddled group. Smoke-streaked faces looked back at her. "Is everyone here?" she asked, mentally counting as she spoke.

Seven, there were seven of them, along with four children. Something in her gut settled. That was everybody.

They'd all made it out alive.

"That was everything we had," Celeste muttered beside her, facing the building.

Charlotte turned. Despite the best attempts of the local fire brigade, it looked as if the building would be entirely consumed.

Despair filled her. All she had were the clothes she was wearing and her grandmother's chatelaine, still hooked onto her belt. They'd never had much, not with the itinerant life that Mama had lived, but back in their room were Grandmother's splendid old book and their only photograph of their father, and of course, there was the money to think of. Neither of them had grabbed their purse.

"What are we going to do?" Celeste asked.

Charlotte stood there, watching their entire world burn. "I don't know."

So distracted was she by the sight, she failed to notice the dark figure behind her, slipping away into the shadows once again.

CHAPTER SIX

Lane Barton swept into the mansion with all the energy of a stampeding rhinoceros. Loud, dangerous, and utterly in charge.

Thomas barely noticed him.

After changing his suit and unpacking a few small items, Thomas had come back downstairs. The mansion had seemed abandoned, with only the clink of dishes from some distant and unseen kitchen to inform him that anybody was here at all. Thomas had headed through the doors he had seen earlier, hoping to ask Mrs. Coulton a few questions about his patron, but instead found himself in an extensive cabinet of curiosities.

It was a grand space, at least twice as large as the room Thomas had been granted and stuffed full of wonders. Preserved animal specimens fought for space with metal models and huge chunks of exotic minerals on the room's many shelves. Pottery from Persia sat next to old brass sextants and the fossils of long-dead sea creatures. A fine Egyptian bust was displayed with a trio of shrunken heads from New Guinea and urns from the old Hellenic period. Rows and rows of drawers promised everything from Indian arrowheads to rare art. A seal skeleton hung on silver wire from the ceiling. Nothing was cataloged, nothing organized, but it was impressive in scale and scope.

"Ahh, Thomas!" a booming voice called out, a hand slapping down on Thomas's shoulder. "May I call you Thomas? I hate standing on formalities. Gets in the way of getting things done!"

Thomas pulled himself away from his contemplation of a particularly nice example of late-dynasty Moghul statuary. He could hardly do otherwise. Lane Barton was not a man to be denied. A big man, broad and tall, possessed of an exuberance that threatened to burst out of him at any moment. He was dressed quite simply, as if wearing anything more than work clothes was an obligation he found irritating. His features were broad and open, and it seemed he smiled quite easily, for he wore a huge grin now.

"Thomas is fine, Mr. Barton," he said a little stiffly, and readjusted his sack coat around his shoulders.

"Lane, Lane, call me Lane! What did I just say about formalities?" He chuckled, rubbing his hands together as he came up alongside Thomas. "Ahh yes, this one. Took me quite a bit of finagling to get it over here, let me assure you. Had to bring it across the Pacific on a trader out of Hong Kong."

"It seems it was worth the effort, Mr. Barton. This is quite the collection."

Barton started walking again, heading for the doors at the end of the room. "Eh, it's adequate. I know a few men who have better, but they're all back east, and who wants to live there? Out here is where everything is happening right now. Out here is where a man can make his fortune."

Lane Barton's fortune was, from what Thomas had heard, significant. As the founder and owner of a series of highly successful mines, he extracted everything from quartz to gold from the mountains here. This room only confirmed how lucrative that work was.

"I see quite a few pieces from the Mediterranean," Thomas commented as he followed, not wishing to get dragged into a discussion about money. "Did you collect these personally?"

"Me? A few, yes, but not as many as I'd like. I have a few agents who work on my behalf, and a few friends as well, such as you now, I assume. It is good to have such contacts in the Academy for Psychical Inquiry." The American rubbed his hands together, pausing at the door. "Were you able to acquire the books I requested?"

"Yes, of course," Thomas said, feeling a small stab of guilt at the mention of the Academy. He squashed it. Yes, Thomas had not parted well with Mr. Holzworth, but surely that didn't have any bearing on this case. He was here to solve this mystery that Mr. Barton had presented to the Academy, and that was exactly what he was going to do.

"Excellent! Now, show me what you brought."

The silver baron's library was adjacent to the cabinet, a set of simple doors leading into a round room set into the mansion's front round turret. The library was designed like a gallery: two stories, with a small catwalk ringing the upper floor. The bookcases ran the full width and height of both the bottom and top floor, shaped to fit perfectly against the curved wall. Ladders with brass fittings allowed access to the shelves, while a small spiral staircase led from the ground floor to the first. A pair of comfortable leather chairs, along with a small table, dominated the ground floor. Here, the invisible staff had brought Thomas's crates.

Seeing the shipment, Mr. Barton breezed right past Thomas, as happy as a child receiving a new toy.

"As you can see," Thomas said as Barton began pulling titles from their straw packing, "I was able to locate most of the titles you requested, and for the ones I could not, I attempted to source suitable replacements. The subject of classical Celtic folklore is experiencing something of a revival right now, and—"

"The original text for *The Book of Invasions*!" Barton said, gleefully paging through a massive tome. "This is excellent."

"I am still working on the verse translation you requested," Thomas said. "I'm afraid our institutional knowledge of old Gaelic is quite poor. Reference material is hard to come by. It's been slow going." Barton looked at him. Thomas shook his head. "There is no love lost between the English and the Irish. I'm afraid that much of Ireland's cultural heritage has been destroyed by various lords and bureaucrats over the centuries. Old prejudices die hard."

"Spend a few months out here and you'll realize how ridiculous that all is," Barton said dismissively. "Out here, all that matters is what a man can do, not what he is or where he came from."

"I'm afraid the same cannot be said for Europe," Thomas said drily.

Barton laughed and closed the book. He set it aside and reached for another. "I hope you're enjoying your visit to our country."

"I haven't had much time for touring, but the land I've seen from train windows has been..." And Thomas trailed off. Mr. Barton had just placed the book—a very expensive and difficult find, at that—on a shelf next to a tome about archaeologic discoveries in Rome. There were piles of books everywhere, stacked ten high on the floor and across the shelves. "Excuse me, Mr. Barton, but—"

"Lane."

"Sir?"

"Lane."

Thomas didn't like the way Mr. Barton was looking at him, but there was nothing to do but to press on. "Sir, forgive my impudence, but do you not have a catalog system for all of this? Or do Americans use a different system than what I am familiar with?"

Mr. Barton looked around, like he wasn't quite sure what Thomas meant, then laughed. "Oh, of course. I'm going through a bit of an expansion right now. My goal for this collection, for this house, in fact, is to turn it into a destination for Spiritualists. A place to read and grow in one's understanding of esoteric matters."

"A kind of psychical research society or club?" Thomas guessed.

"An institute. I am still working on it, of course. My new primary residence in Leadville is almost complete, and this place will need a director. Somebody who can code and organize all of this for me. But it is damned hard to lure a trained professional out here to Denver. It's hard enough getting Mrs. Coulton to dust the place!" He laughed again and gestured at the chairs. "Now please, let's talk. I want your impressions of my case."

"I do not know if we will be able to meet your original intent for this investigation," Thomas said. "I have found out, just today, that Mrs. Anna Roseingrave is dead."

"Yes, yes, she did pass away a few months ago."

Irritation flared in Thomas. "Might you have notified me in some way?"

The silver baron seemed to sober a little at that. "I apologize I was not here when you arrived. I most certainly would have told you then. And I'll be square with you, I wanted my books."

"I would have ensured your books arrived," Thomas assured him. "Although perhaps with a different courier."

Mr. Barton nodded and picked up a small handbell from the table. Ringing it, he laughed. "A dry sense of humor. I like that in a man."

Thomas did not bother mentioning he was not attempting to be funny. "Er, quite. But sir, the entire idea was to have Mrs. Roseingrave use her abilities to pull some answers from that artifact you have up in Leadville. Without her—"

"The show must go on, Thomas!" Mr. Barton looked at the bell, then back through the open doors to the front foyer of the house. He rang again. "Damned annoying business, these bells, but Mrs. Coulton does not like it when I holler at her. Now where is she?"

"How do you propose holding a séance if the medium has died, Mr.

Barton?" Thomas pressed. "While there have been stories of deceased mediums reappearing at séances to help the younger generation, it's hardly an exact science."

"There you are, Thomas, joking again. Damn it all. Mrs. Coulton!"

That last bit was yelled, and the housekeeper finally appeared in the doorway.

"Yes, Mr. Barton?" she asked. The words were pleasant, but her expression sour. She was looking around at the books as if they might eat her.

"Bring up a bottle of wine for my guest and I, would you? One of the 60s Bordeauxs, perhaps."

"Of course, Mr. Barton."

"And supper?"

"Ready at half past eight. As always."

"Good, that gives us plenty of time to talk!"

She retreated quickly, and Mr. Barton shook his head. "It is hard to find good help these days. She doesn't approve of my collection, you see. Does not care for Spiritualism in any of its forms," Mr. Barton said. "But she keeps a good house, so I keep her on." He smiled again. "Now, what were we talking about?"

"The Roseingrave sisters and their deceased mother," Thomas said.

"Ah yes, a sad business. Did they agree to do the séance?"

Thomas blinked. "Excuse me?"

"You went to see the daughters, did you not?"

"Yes, but—"

"Mrs. Roseingrave was a rare talent. One in a million. One in a billion, perhaps." Mr. Barton got up, began pacing around. "Full-blooded Irish, you know, by way of Savannah, Georgia. Have you ever been to Savannah?"

"No, I did not get the chance to—"

"I was there during the war. Now, I'm not going to make excuses for General Sherman, nor apologize for him. The war was what it was, and it was very unpleasant for all involved. But thanks to him, I did spend a few months in Savannah. It is... Have you ever seen a ghost yourself, Thomas?"

"As someone who considers himself a student of science," he said cautiously, "I must say that we have no evidence for such things, and it's not been for lack of trying. And yet, also as a student of science, I cannot logically rule it out."

Mr. Barton laughed and waggled a finger. "You believe. All of you working at the Academy believe. And you should. There is much we don't understand about the world. Knowledge that's been forgotten, I say." And he waved a hand around at his books. "Knowledge I wish to draw back together and share as broadly as I may."

"Sir, about the sisters—"

"Yes, well, according to my research, such talents as what Mrs. Roseingrave had are often passed from mother to daughter, and both Miss Charlotte and Miss Celeste, especially, are said to have helped with her work."

And then Thomas realized why he'd been allowed to come all this way without being informed about Mrs. Roseingrave's death. "You hoped I could persuade them to undertake the séance."

Just then, Mrs. Coulton was back with a tray, an open bottle of wine and two glasses carried on its gleaming surface. Pewter and cut crystal.

"Thank you, Mrs. Coulton," Mr. Barton said as she poured them both a glass. "Is it steak for supper?"

"Rib eye with carrots. As you requested."

"Excellent!" he enthused but waited until she was gone again before resuming their discussion. "Yes, Thomas, I hoped you could convince them, or at least the older sister, Charlotte. She was quite unresponsive when last I spoke to her. I even offered her a generous bonus, and she turned me down." Mr. Barton said this as if it had been an extreme offense. If Thomas had to guess, he'd say that the silver baron wasn't used to being told no.

"They may not be so keen to speak to me." *Again,* he added silently. "I am an investigator."

"But a sympathetic one," Mr. Barton said. "Isn't that correct?"

"I..." Thomas said and faltered. He took a sip of the wine—an excellent vintage, this—and looked around the library. He chose his next words very carefully. A true Spiritualist would not have been pleased with what Miss Charlotte Roseingrave had told him. "I think the demand for true psychical phenomena far exceeds the supply. But are there yet things in this world that we do not understand? Assuredly so. And the photographs you sent of the object indicate to me that this is something worth looking into further." Thomas shook his head. "At the very least, it is not the type of hoax we normally see."

"It is not a hoax," Mr. Barton said, a dangerous note creeping into his voice.

"I did not mean to imply that I believed—"

"My son vanished six months ago, Thomas, along with a dozen other men, trusted men, and the nephew of my business partner. All I have as evidence of their fates is that object in the back garden of my Leadville home." Angry. He was definitely growing angry now. "I will have my answers as to how they met their fate and what that fate was. Conventional investigative techniques are no good out here in the mountains, and I have exhausted all the answers a laboratory may provide. Only a medium can provide me with the truth."

"Sir," Thomas said honestly, "I do not think the Roseingrave sisters are the ones who can furnish you with that information."

He smiled. "These sisters... I understand that there was a great deal of stagecraft in Madame Aine's regular performances. That is only understandable. Séances are entertainment first, and she had children to feed. Believe me, I know how that goes. But Mrs. Roseingrave assured me she would be able to ascertain the truth for me. She was so confident that she agreed to have an investigator present, to guarantee her findings."

"Yes, I understand that, but—"

"But nothing," Mr. Barton said, and all the previous geniality was gone now. He paced over to the window. "Those girls are going to uphold their mother's promise to me. I will accept no other outcome."

Thomas didn't quite know what to say to that. What had the elder sister told him? *Our mother was a fraud.* Suddenly, he regretted his trip out here. When he had seen the photographs, he'd known that it had to be investigated, no matter what Mr. Holzworth had thought. But the whole situation seemed so simple, so easy, back in England. The reality of it, now that he was here, was quite clearly much more complicated.

"Oh, would you look at that?" Mr. Barton mused, hand to the window. "Looks like something is on fire downtown."

CHAPTER SEVEN

"It's a fine piece, to be sure, but silver? All the fine ladies are wearing gold."

Charlotte folded her hands on the countertop, despair in her heart. "Who has ever heard of a gold chatelaine?"

"Like it or don't, miss. I can't sell this." And the jeweler put away his loupe. He was short with broad shoulders and a hard, disapproving face. He had the faintest hint of an accent that Charlotte couldn't place. German, maybe. He also had a reputation for being thorny, angry, perpetually irritated. She hadn't wanted to come here. But she'd already tried everywhere else. Dvalinsson Fine Jewelry and Novelties was her last option.

"You are the fourth dealer in town to tell me that this is worthless. But I do not believe this is so."

The jeweler handed her back her chatelaine. In his huge rough hand, it looked like a child's trinket. He handled it gingerly, as if it might burn him. "I am not saying it is worthless, miss. I am saying I cannot sell it. Now, if there's nothing else, I have work to do."

"This is the rarest sort of antique," Charlotte said, hurrying after him as he tried to walk away. "My grandmother had it converted from a brooch she brought over from Ireland itself."

He snorted. "If it's Irish, then I might know a few people who'd buy it just for the pleasure of melting it down."

"Even if you did melt it down, would it not have value?"

At that, the jeweler paused. He looked at her, considering. "You are Mrs. Anna Roseingrave's daughter, aren't you?"

Her mother, her mother. Always her mother. Was there no way to escape that blighted legacy? "Yes, sir, I am."

"Then you should know, Miss Roseingrave, that the tools of a witch often bear the echo of her emotion for a long time after they're parted. And weapons are worse," he said. He placed the chatelaine back into her hand, then laid his hand on top of hers, gently closing her fingers around the little object. "Don't inflict your grief on anyone else by selling this on."

She blinked, as surprised by the touch as she was by the words. There was an immense strength in his fingers, and the quiet admonishment was unbearable. As if a mountain peak had taken form and descended to the city to admonish her for some unknown slight. "I'm afraid I don't understand your meaning, Mr. Dvalinsson."

"Then understand this, Miss Roseingrave. I want you out. Now." And he pointed. "Good luck to you, but I won't do business with your kind."

Heading out the door of the shop, Charlotte found herself once again on the broad, busy byway of 16th Street. Here, tall brick and stone buildings rose on both sides of the street, of fine construction, none older than a few years. Nearby, a group of wealthy bachelors was going about their morning, boisterous and loud as they talked amongst themselves. The sun was bright but the air cool, and the trees that poked around the edges of the buildings were thick with leaves, still turning red for autumn.

It was a day when nothing should have been wrong at all.

Instead, Charlotte's entire world had fallen apart. She had thought losing Mama was bad. This was worse.

All the women who had lived at the workshop, suddenly finding themselves homeless, had been offered shelter at the local Methodist church. It had been a kind offer, and one that had surprised Charlotte. She and Reverend Hinkle were not on the best of terms, and she knew that as soon as he realized the Roseingraves were in his rectory, they would be thrown out. So this morning, she'd washed her face, brushed down her dress as best she could, and, stomach grumbling in hunger, gone out.

The opera house would no doubt soon reconstitute its costume and prop departments; the new season was already underway, and the next production was slated to premiere in only a month or so. But that effort would take some time. That left both her and her sister without a means of supporting themselves for the foreseeable future. This chatelaine was all she had to sell, and nobody would buy it. The thought of it made her angry.

"I see you were unsuccessful!"

Charlotte pulled her attention away from the autumn day. There was Celeste, waiting for her.

"What are you doing here?" Charlotte called back and clipped her chatelaine back to her waistband as she walked over.

Her younger sister shook her head. "No luck selling Grandmother's chatelaine?"

Charlotte tried not to let her irritation show. "I would never sell the brooch itself. I was wondering about a few of the small implements, like my scissors. They are silver-plated, after all."

"You're a bad liar," Celeste replied.

I'm an excellent liar, Charlotte thought, but just sighed and started walking. There was a dry goods shop over on 14th Street that had a small selection of sewing accoutrements. Perhaps she'd try there. "What are you doing here, Celeste?"

"I reckoned you'd talk to the smaller shops first. Wouldn't start here. Mr. Dvalinsson's reputation precedes him, after all. So everyone else has told you no as well?"

Celeste may have phrased it like a question, but Charlotte knew her sister well enough to know that she wasn't really asking. It was one of those questions designed to continue a conversation, to lead somebody somewhere they might not otherwise go, and Charlotte refused to take the bait.

"What do you want, Celeste?"

"Other than to stop my dear older sister from selling the last of our family heirlooms without so much as asking my opinion?"

"It's not your decision. Grandmother left the chatelaine to me."

Celeste pulled a face. "Grandmother left everything to you. Her chatelaine, her book..."

"A book we no longer have," Charlotte snapped, the grief of that reminder making her angry. "What is your point?"

"Reverend Hinkle sought me out this morning. He wants us out by tonight." Celeste sniffed. "Some man of God he is."

Charlotte chewed the inside of her cheek. Her sister was more right than she knew. The head pastor of the biggest church in town was one of the biggest hypocrites she had ever met, but talking to Celeste about how she knew that was...inadvisable.

"Do you suppose he hates us because we're Catholic or because we're Spiritualists?" Charlotte asked, trying to lighten her tone, trying to make small talk.

"Are you really either?" Celeste countered. "You're too cynical to be a Spiritualist, Charlotte, and you're too guilt-ridden to be Catholic."

"What does that say about you?" Charlotte shot back, exasperated now.

Celeste ignored the question. "Did Mr. Dvalinsson tell you there's no market for Irish goods?" She grinned at Charlotte's reaction. "He did, didn't he?"

Charlotte sighed. They turned the corner down Wyncoop Street. "I understand it back east, but out here..."

Celeste tapped a finger against her cheek. "You know who would buy a rare ethnic object?"

"Don't, Celeste."

"Mr. Barton. He has quite the collection."

"What use would a man have for a chatelaine?"

"The cabinet of curiosities at his mansion is very well curated."

And that hurt Charlotte's heart, the idea of her grandmother's precious chatelaine pinned up and framed like some rare species of jungle insect on the wall of some millionaire's home. At least selling it would mean it would be used, worn, loved. But regardless, that couldn't be why Celeste wanted to talk to the silver baron. "We are not talking to Mr. Barton."

"Why not?"

"We are not mediums!"

"Oh, I know what you told that investigator yesterday, but what difference does it make?" Celeste said. "If everyone gets what they want—"

Charlotte stopped, clenching a fist. "What people want, Celeste, is the truth. Not lies, not comfort, not illusion. They want the truth! We can't give it to them. You can't tell that man what happened to his son!"

"Like I said last night, I know what happened to his son. He's dead, and no body will ever be found." Celeste spread her hands. "Not even you, my dear inflexible sister, can possibly turn down twelve hundred dollars at a time like this."

Charlotte stopped walking, a realization hitting her.

The cabinet.

While there were many stories in the pages of Spiritualist publications like *Borderlands* attesting to the reality of psychic powers, Charlotte had never seen such things. Her own gifts, unwanted as they were, didn't extend into mind reading. But Mama always said that observation and a sound understanding of human nature could look like magic under the right circumstances.

And with Celeste mentioning that blasted cabinet...

"Celeste," she groaned.

Her sister smiled her most winsome smile. "You left without a word to me this morning, Charlotte, in order to seek out some way of dealing with our financial situation. Why shouldn't I return the favor?"

Charlotte stared at her younger sister. "Please tell me you're joking."

"Not at all," Celeste said, and reached into a pocket, producing a narrow pocketbook that she certainly had not had before. She proudly held it open, revealing a small stack of bills inside. Twenty-dollar bills. Five of them. "Our advance."

A hundred dollars. Charlotte could barely wrap her head around that. A hundred dollars? "What did you promise him?"

"Nothing, other than agreeing to do the séance. Did I tell you the best part?" Celeste asked, clearly enjoying this. "We have an invitation to join him on his private railcar tomorrow morning."

Charlotte frowned. "He wants to do a séance on a train?"

"He wants to do the séance in Leadville. He's invited us to stay at his house there, for as long as it takes for us to get him in contact with his son. First class, Charlotte, all the way."

Leadville. That was right. He had mentioned Leadville. But he had been incredibly cagey about why he wanted to do the séance in Leadville, and Charlotte hadn't pushed him on it. Perhaps Mama had known.

But Celeste seemed to take Charlotte's hesitation for agreement. She laughed and folded the new pocketbook up under her elbow, starting to stroll again. "I say we go get ourselves a bath and a good lunch, and a room at the hotel, and have a fine day. And tomorrow—"

"Celeste!"

"—tomorrow, we set out for the mountains nice and early, enjoy Mr. Barton's generous hospitality, give him what he wants, get paid, and then be on our way to California again. Finally. And leave all of this behind."

Charlotte wavered.

"Come, sister," Celeste said urgently, clutching Charlotte's hand. "What is the problem? It's a grand plan!"

In the bright Colorado day, it would be easy for Charlotte to pretend that what she had seen last night had just been a figment of her imagination.

That the fire, the exploding stove, the tunnel in the smoke, all of it was just some child's fancy.

But she could not pretend.

She could not ignore the truth of that fire. This world of spirits that was once again, always, forced on her against her will.

But her stomach was grumbling painfully now, and practicality had to win out.

"I suppose we're already committed," Charlotte grumbled.

Celeste smiled and gave her an enthusiastic hug. "Then you'll help?"

"You'll do it on your own," Charlotte replied, but grudgingly returned the embrace. "But I shall come. Maybe I can keep you from getting us thrown in prison for fraud."

"Fraud? Hardly. We're the daughters of Madame Aine, the greatest trance medium the world has ever seen," Celeste said, laughing. "There's nothing we can't do."

"We should share at least a little bit of this with the others from the workshop," Charlotte said as an afterthought. Whatever had been lurking in the dark, whatever had started the fire, it had been there for her. She could feel it in her bones. The others didn't deserve to suffer for it. "I won't leave them all destitute."

Celeste rolled her eyes but slipped her arm into Charlotte's and started pulling her along. "Mr. Barton gave me two hundred. I already gave the other women ten dollars each," she said.

"Very kind of you," Charlotte said grudgingly, but shook her head. "And now, of course, I can't give the money back."

"You are predictable, sister."

"I don't appreciate being boxed in."

"I know," Celeste said. "But you're also too proud to go back and ask for something you've already rejected. You know this is our only option right now. You couldn't take it, but I could. So I did."

There was a hard note in her sister's words. Disappointment, maybe. Charlotte felt bad, hearing it. Celeste had ever been the baby of the family. It had always fallen to Charlotte to take care of her, and here, today, she had failed.

Charlotte squeezed her sister's elbow and shook her head, setting off again. "Do you think the hotel will take single women?"

"They'll take our money," Celeste said, clearly excited now. "I'll make sure of it. Now, after Leadville, we'll have to check routes, but I don't think it will take more than a few days to reach California. I was thinking that somewhere a little more out of the way would be nice. San Diego, for example, is supposed to be…"

And then Celeste was chatting, the earlier anger seemingly forgotten.

Charlotte let her sister ramble on, walking through the streets of Denver, allowing herself to contemplate that future. The odds were good, she thought, that Mr. Barton would see them both arrested, but surely there was no harm in dreaming.

She didn't notice the figure behind her, slipping from shadow to shadow, following them all the while.

Chapter Eight

Aspens.

They were aspens.

Golden-yellow with autumn's touch, spade-shaped leaves rustled around her. The last wind of evening, the final touch of the sun's warmth. White-barked trees stretched their branches overhead. Ferns grew in the shadows. She could hear the sound of rushing water and the singing of owls. It was all more real than real.

Then.

Gunshots. Screaming. Smoke.

A battle was being fought. A wolf was howling.

A figure was coming toward her through the grove. Roughly man-shaped, but she instinctively knew there was nothing human about it at all. Where it stepped, birds fell silent. Trees died. The gunfire grew closer.

You can't be here.

The figure was coming closer, dragging darkness with it. Not the darkness of night, but an altogether more horrible darkness where the moon and the stars no longer had any purchase on reality.

She wanted to scream. She wanted to run.

She couldn't move.

A bullet whizzed by, so sudden and so real and so slow that she could see the ripples it left in the air. She watched it pass right by her face, almost leisurely, to impact into the desiccated bole of a young aspen. Its leaves, once so golden-yellow, now a death-dry brown, burst into flames.

You can't come here.

Something grabbed her arm. Dragging, pulling, trying to move her.

The figure was coming closer. She could almost make it out now, its features cast all in shadow, nearly invisible beneath the wide brim of its hat, a blood-red kerchief pulled up over its mouth, hair the color of ash, trench coat swirling as it—

Charlotte woke up.

She shot straight up in bed, fighting off the blanket, gulping for air. She almost fell out, barely catching herself, and closed her eyes, trying to breathe. Heart hammering. Palms weak. A dream-panic, following her out into the waking world.

Dreams.

How she hated the dreams.

As a little girl, Charlotte had never had them, not even in the darkest days after General Sherman had finally pulled out of Savannah, when the shades of the dead walked the streets in their legions. After Mama had taken up her Spiritualism work, such dreams had come to Charlotte often.

They had been pleasant, once. Magical, showing Charlotte things she never could have imagined. But after Grandmother had died, the dreams had become unbearable.

Dreams of soldiers, dying on the battlefield, heads blown open or chests a mess of blood. Dreams of creatures, watching her with never-human eyes that never closed and never looked away from her. Dreams of fire, like the fire in the hearth that one morning, after Grandmother died, when Charlotte had...

Winding a finger through the chain of the little crucifix she always wore, Charlotte mentally recited the Lord's Prayer, focusing all her attention on the words, using them as a shield to block out everything else. It usually helped.

Today, it took three iterations for the panic to subside to a dull ache.

Charlotte glanced over at her sister, sleeping soundly in the room's other bed. She looked perfectly at peace, one arm cast over the blanket, breath even and expression slack. For a moment, Charlotte hated her. Why didn't Celeste share this burden? Why was it Charlotte's alone to bear?

But that was a cruel question. Charlotte would never have chosen to inflict this on her sister. The Sight was hers alone, and it was her problem to deal with.

And yet...

The hotel they had chosen for tonight was the nicest in town, a sturdy, new red-brick building near Union Station and as well appointed as any you'd find back east. But despite the finery, the room was cold, had grown chill from the night, and Charlotte found herself shivering in her new nightgown. She'd sweated profusely, she realized. Even the sheets felt cold.

Swinging her bare feet out onto the fine knotted rug covering most of the floor, Charlotte tiptoed over to the little stove that heated the room. The fire they'd had last night had fallen to almost nothing. She picked up the tongs to drop in more coal.

Sparks flared as the first coal hit the embers, setting off memories. A bonfire in the deep woods. The yawning mouth of a huge fireplace hearth in an antebellum Savannah mansion, flames licking at her as she—

Celeste stirred. "It's cold," she muttered, turning over in bed.

Charlotte dropped another coal into the stove. They'd paid for the extra hopper. No point in letting it go to waste. No point in paying any heed to dreams and memories and all those things that weren't real.

"I'm taking care of it," she told her sister.

And yet, as she watched the fire roar back to life, Charlotte knew it in her bones...

They were walking into a disaster.

Mr. Barton had said the train would be ready to depart around nine o'clock that morning, so when Thomas woke at a quarter 'til six, he figured he had plenty of time.

He wanted a second look at that library.

Thomas, in his time at Oxford and later as part of the Academy, had been in many a library, public and private, and Mr. Barton yesterday, as they had unpacked the crates of books Thomas had brought from Europe, had described an ambitious plan for his psychical institute, the first and only of its kind west of Mississippi.

But none of it was going to come to pass while this collection was in such a shambles.

Thomas picked through the library now alone. Free of Mr. Barton's ceaseless energy, he was able to look at it a bit more critically.

The collection had certainly overgrown the space allotted for it. There were heaps of books piled on the floor or on tables, no place for them on the shelves. Including what was up on the upper floor, there were probably half as many books again here that had no home, and that wouldn't do.

Some other rooms in the mansion would have to be converted with shelving to house them. And then, of course, the place would need a proper catalog system, a reading room, a small lecture hall, a dedicated space for séances—always had to consider the séance, the backbone of all Spiritualist experiments—and a dozen other things. There were also quite a few antiquities in storage back east, or so Mr. Barton claimed, that would also need to find homes here.

How Mr. Barton had pulled so many books together in only a few years, Thomas had no idea. The breadth of the collection was impressive. Books on ancient Greece and Assyria—a most fascinating emerging field in the new archaeological studies—sat next to modern, handwritten notes on Apache folklore and ancient hand-lettered illuminated manuscripts. There were many newer works, but also a great number of antiques. Thomas wondered if Mr. Barton was aware that the two types of books had to be treated very differently in the archiving process, so as to ensure both were adequately taken care of.

Thomas suspected that nobody had said anything to Mr. Barton about this, or if they had, it had not factored into Mr. Barton's treatment of his collection. Over the past day or so, Thomas had arrived at the conclusion that Mr. Barton was the sort of man who would listen keenly to advice and then proceed in whatever direction he pleased, regardless.

It was one reason why Thomas had not told his new patron of the conversation he and Charlotte Roseingrave had had.

Thomas had not been in the room when the younger sister, Celeste, had arrived yesterday morning. More was the pity. He would have intercepted her at the door and tried to at least modulate Mr. Barton's expectations. Instead, he had come downstairs at the allowed time for breakfast and found the two of them deep in conversation in the front parlor.

"Ah, Thomas!" Mr. Barton said, waving in him. "Look at our good fortune this morning! The illustrious Miss Roseingrave has agreed to take on my commission."

The younger Miss Roseingrave smiled sweetly at Thomas. A warm, broad, somewhat secretive smile. "Good to see you again, Mr. Leighton," she said sweetly. Her voice, he noticed, had a much more distinct Southern drawl than it had had the day before at the workshop. "Won't you come join us? Mr. Barton, this is the best coffee I have had in a very long time."

There was a fine porcelain coffee carafe on an antique walnut table near her chair. Miss Roseingrave got up, skirt rustling, to pour Thomas a cup.

"You don't have to do that," Mr. Barton told her gently.

"Why not? I'm here," she replied, still sticky-sweet, and handed Thomas the cup where he stood, somewhat dumb, in the doorway. "I will let you add your own sugar and cream as you please."

Thomas still hadn't quite developed the palate for American-style coffee, but sugar did seem to help. He added a generous spoonful, stirring with a silver spoon from the serving platter. "I thought, after the conversation with your sister, that we wouldn't have the, er, pleasure of getting to see you in action."

"My sister is still in mourning for our mother. Her death impacted both of us, but..." And Miss Celeste Roseingrave affected a little sob, a sigh, then seemingly collected herself. "Well, my sister thinks we should not disrespect my mother by taking up in her profession so soon after her passing."

"And you?" Thomas asked, somewhat bemused.

"I think the best way of honoring our mother is continuing on with her work, the talents and skills she taught us so well."

"I quite agree," Mr. Barton said.

Thomas sipped his coffee, trying to hide his discomfort. He hated lying. He was not good at it, although he had had somewhat more experience with it of late. "Have you seen the pictures of the object your mother had agreed to read for us?" he asked pointedly.

Miss Roseingrave laughed and waved that off. "It's better if I don't. No preconceived notions, no influences on my judgement, less chance of doubt on your part. If I go in blind, then it makes your data better. Isn't that correct, Mr. Leighton?"

The younger Roseingrave sister was smooth. Thomas had to give her that. He couldn't see the elder sister, Charlotte, being able to pull off that sort of thing. She seemed the sort to charge straight through a situation with blunt, uncompromising honesty. Perhaps that was why she was so obviously reluctant to work as a medium herself.

It was a profession that required at least a degree of theatricality. Even some of the best mediums from the past few decades had had a strong sense of showmanship. There was talking to spirits and then there was making those conversations interesting to the audience, who could only hear one side of the exchange. Alleged exchange, Mrs. Holzworth would have said.

Thomas had to admit to himself, he had been quite convinced Madame Aine had the talent. Not for trickery, but for true spirit communication. He would not have come out here, risked what he had, if he had not believed in her. Finding her dead and her daughters in her place, so different from what he'd expected, was more than a little disappointing.

Still, depending on how these séances went, there was still a chance Thomas could save his career, even considering his last conversation with the director of the Academy for Psychical Inquiry, where they had fought about—

Then, there. Something caught his eye. A book, sitting on the room's small table, well-worn and clearly loved.

A children's book, it seemed.

Frowning, Thomas picked it up. An illustrated set of tales, Irish folklore, with fine old art. He didn't recognize it, and he had read many such books over the past few years. Something new, then. Interesting.

"Mr. Leighton."

He snapped the book shut, turning around. It was Mrs. Coulton, wearing her usual sour expression. "Yes?" Thomas asked.

"Breakfast will be served in a few minutes in the dining room. Mr. Barton has requested your presence."

"Of course," he said. He hefted the book. "Do you suppose he would mind if I borrowed a little reading material for our excursion to the mountains?"

"I doubt it," she said.

"Then I shall take this up to my room, and be down shortly," he told her.

She nodded and headed out again.

Thomas breathed in deep, feeling the thin air sting his sinuses again, but he smiled to himself. Whatever happened in Leadville, it was sure to be illuminating.

"It's not too late to pull back from this," Charlotte said as she followed her sister through Denver's Union Station.

"Pull back from what?" Celeste replied, smug. "Our payday? I already took his deposit, Charlotte. Remember?"

"I know, but Celeste, this is a bad idea."

"You were fine with this yesterday!"

"You forced this on me yesterday," Charlotte hissed at her. "Mr. Barton is one of the wealthiest men in this state. If he finds out..."

"Mr. Barton wants what everybody wants," Celeste replied in a low voice. "Closure. I don't have to speak to the dead to give him that."

"That is not the point," Charlotte replied, struggling to keep her tone quiet and even. "We have an investigator with us. From the Academy, no less. They've staked their entire organizational reputation on exposing fraudulent mediums."

"In order to find the real ones."

"Which you aren't!"

"Then maybe you shouldn't have told him Mama was a fraud."

"Maybe you shouldn't continue Mama's legacy of lying!"

They were nearly to the big doors that led out onto the platform, and Celeste finally turned around. She held up a hand, open in supplication. "I know you always hated Mama doing this," she said quietly, "but in the last twenty years, can you think of anything, one single solitary moment with any of her friends or competitors that proved that this so-called 'spirit world' actually exists?"

Charlotte didn't trust herself to speak.

Celeste, as usual, took her silence for agreement.

"Me neither. I don't know what happens after we die, but we certainly aren't staying here on Earth to provide parlor entertainment for bored silver barons," Celeste said, and there was a plea in her words now. "I slept in a real bed last night, in a room with a fireplace and carpet on the floor. Carpet, Charlotte! I am tired of working twelve-hour days with nothing to show for it. I want—"

"Celeste, please listen to me—"

"I shall finish what I am saying! I want to make it to California and make my own way in the world. I don't agree with everything Mama did over the years, but at least it was honest work."

"There was nothing honest about what Mama did," Charlotte countered. Celeste was clearly on the edge of tears, but whether those were real or false, Charlotte wasn't sure. It bothered her that she couldn't tell.

"It could have been worse," Celeste snapped back. "She could have sold herself like the women down at the Golden Dove."

Charlotte glared at her. "How dare you say something like that?"

"Tell me I'm wrong," Celeste replied. For a moment, the two sisters stared at each other. Then Celeste reached for Charlotte's hand, softening again. "All Mr. Barton likely wants is a few nice words about his son, a little bit of evidence that it's real, and a good show. I can provide all of that, especially if you help."

"I already told you, I am not going to help with this!"

Celeste looked at her, and Charlotte regretted her words immediately. She was fairly certain that the pain on her sister's face was genuine, because it passed quickly, hidden instead behind a mask of anger.

"Tell me why, at least," Celeste asked. "Why are you so against this? I've never understood this hatred you have of Mama's work."

Charlotte wavered then. Considered telling her sister everything. About what she saw. About the hidden things that had plagued her every day of her life.

But doing so right now likely would have angered Celeste even more or led to begging and pleading to use it to aid them now, neither of which Charlotte wanted to deal with.

Grandmother's stories were all just faery tales. Including the one about the family protector.

There was no help to be found in that other world.

Only pain and fear and death.

"It's dishonest," Charlotte said instead.

Celeste leaned in. "You're lying, like you always lie," she replied, and turned on her heel, heading out into the sunlight. "Come, sister! We'll miss our train!"

Charlotte caught a glimpse of something. That same man from before; brilliant silk waistcoat, piercing blue eyes. Watching her. From the shadows of trees, golden leaves rustling in the breeze.

Foreboding rolled through Charlotte. She hurried out onto the platform after her little sister. This business needed to end, and if telling Celeste the truth was the only way to do that...

"Celeste, wait!"

But it was too late. Celeste was already at the first-class car, talking happily with two men. Mr. Barton and that investigator, Mr. Leighton. She waved cheerfully as Charlotte caught up. "Charlotte! Ah, good you are here! Is all well with our luggage?"

Charlotte's earlier, more charitable mood died immediately. Celeste's voice was light and happy, as if nothing at all were wrong.

Lying again.

Forcing Charlotte to lie.

This alone would have made Charlotte hate their mother's work. Lies bred like rabbits. Once the first was told, an entire litter of others soon followed.

"You know we haven't anything to take with us," Charlotte replied. "I was distracted by something I saw in a shadow, that's all."

Celeste smiled. Smug. She knew she'd won this.

Mr. Barton tilted his hat. "Wonderful to see you again, Miss Roseingrave," he said, and it sounded genuine. "I'm so pleased we could work something out. You were so adamantly against this when I first brought you the proposal."

"Our mother's death was quite the tragedy, as you can imagine," Charlotte said. "Even the thought of speaking to the dead causes me unparalleled pain." At least that, she thought, wasn't a lie.

"You'll forgive us for the delay, won't you?" Celeste said, reaching out to squeeze Mr. Barton's hand gently. "Emotions are one of the weaknesses of the female sex."

If Charlotte could have rolled her eyes, she would have.

But Mr. Barton just patted her hand. "Of course, my dear, of course. I am just glad you have agreed to do it before the last artifact I have of my son has completely rusted away."

"What do you mean?" Charlotte asked sharply.

But Celeste laughed. "Shh, remember, Mr. Barton, no details," she said.

Mr. Barton smiled. Charlotte cared nothing for the expression on his face. "It will be wonderful to host two such lovely ladies as you at my new house. But I think the train is about to leave, so shall we?"

Charlotte caught sight of the station clock, a great thing of wrought iron and glass, suspended from the fretwork rafters. The train was actually three minutes late in departing. No doubt it was waiting for Mr. Barton to board.

About to answer, Charlotte felt something behind her. She glanced back once more. That strange man had come outside, leaning against a pillar, half-lost in shadow.

And Charlotte all but fled for the safety of the train.

Chapter Nine

Thomas had been on many trains here in America since arriving in New York City, but this one was something of a surprise. He had not expected to find anything so fine in so rough a place.

The car was sumptuous: dark-stained cherrywood paneling, full carpet, crystal fixtures. Leather chairs had been arranged artfully around the huge windows, so one could dine or play cards or enjoy the scenery on a whim. A few were even turned away, as if deliberately for privacy. The elder Roseingrave sister had taken one of those chairs immediately, speaking to nobody but the attendant serving drinks. The younger sister had, by comparison, positioned herself at one of the tables. She made small talk with Mr. Barton, and her manner indicated a kind of detached, aristocratic boredom, as if she rode on such cars every day.

Thomas was fairly certain that she did not.

As the train headed west, the city soon fell away, replaced by low rolling hills dotted here and there with outcroppings of trees. The grade grew steep, and they began to climb up through the Front Range of the American Rockies. Thomas had been to the Alps once, as a boy, but the landscape unfolding around him now was different by far.

It was drier here, thanks to the altitude and distance from the ocean. Junipers and pines predominated, low, scrubby trees in sage green scattered among the bright golds and reds of a more traditional autumn. Tall, scraggly prairie grass clung to the slopes, but the bones of the mountains peeked out in many places, great granite outcroppings falling away to a small river course that wound through the center of a shallow canyon. Snow glinted on high, distant peaks but the sky was a clear blue, the day bright outside the comfortable car.

The train stopped at a few stations here and there. Thomas could see the passengers climbing on and off the train from their window. Ranch hands and prospectors they seemed to him, rough men used to hard work. Nobody else entered their car.

A late lunch was served as the train started down from what appeared to be some kind of pass, curving down through highland plains toward its main stop at Buena Vista, where they would apparently be obliged to change trains for a local line. The meal was delicious. Roasted local trout with potatoes and cream sauce. Mr. Barton ate well, as did Thomas and the younger Miss Roseingrave, but the elder sister only took yet another glass of wine, still sitting off by herself. She had spoken to nobody since coming aboard.

"I funded this car myself, of course, and thank god that I did. This is a most uncomfortable journey in the benches in the standard cars," Mr. Barton said as he settled back down into one of the plush gallery chairs. "Mr. Leighton, I'm sure you're familiar with the new luxury cars running on European trains. I was so impressed during my visit to Italy last year that I simply had to bring the same thing here."

The staff was in the process of refreshing everyone's wine. It was a crisp, clear chardonnay, chilled with ice harvested last winter. Thomas had been surprised to learn the wine had come from California, and even more surprised to learn that the ice had come from the Great Lakes, far to the north; apparently there were not enough bodies of water in the Rockies to meet even the modest local demand.

Thomas accepted his own fresh glass, then almost dropped it as the train swayed dangerously. Wine sloshed out everywhere. He dabbed at his waistcoat with a handkerchief. "I have heard, yes, about such things," he said, distracted. "Not something one books on the Academy's dime, of course."

"Of course." Mr. Barton laughed. "There are many things that America does better than Europe, but the appreciation of culture is more developed there. The salons of Paris, the societies of your own country, Mr. Leighton. This is one of the things I wish to accomplish with my institute! Bringing some culture to these wild lands." He chuckled. "A new land for a new philosophy, wouldn't you agree?"

"You're starting a Spiritualist institute?" Miss Celeste Roseingrave asked. That smile had not budged from her lips since coming aboard. Thomas thought the elder sister's stony silence was preferable. "What a lovely idea."

"Perhaps you can come and give a lecture for me," Mr. Barton told her seriously. "I had very much hoped to make your mother part of our board of directors."

"My mother had her heart set on California," Miss Celeste Roseingrave said. "My father, god rest his soul, was a sailor after all. Colorado is beautiful, but she missed the ocean."

"Pfft, the ocean. Who needs it? Storms and humidity, that's what the water brings. But if you miss it so, California is not so far," Mr. Barton scoffed. "Why, we can make the journey coast to coast now in a few days by rail, whereas it used to take months on foot or by covered wagon. And that, Thomas"—and the silver baron turned the full weight of his attention back to Thomas—"is what I am getting at. The world is losing its mystery. Even I have trouble finding new claims in the mountains here. Everything seems to have been explored already! But Spiritualism, Spiritualism represents a new frontier."

Thomas nodded. "I have had such thoughts myself."

"Then you know how critical it is that we conquer this!"

"These things are not there to be conquered," a new voice said. It was the older Roseingrave sister. "They are...beyond us."

"I must politely disagree," Mr. Barton replied. "Is this not the glory of our age? Discovering the unknowable? Learning about that which was hidden? We now know the depth of our oceans and the distance to our moon. We can coax electricity from coal and the flow of water. We can describe our species' long and glorious past. All the secrets of nature are being uncovered. Why should the nature of the soul be any different?"

"Because this is not about nature as we experience it," the elder Miss Roseingrave replied. "The world of spirits is something that we can only touch but briefly. It defies rationalization. It laughs at our attempts to quantify it. We are tourists in that other world, Mr. Barton. Interlopers." She was standing now, a little unsteady on her feet, face flushed red. She waved her wine glass as the train hit a curve, and half her drink splashed out on the velvet-upholstered back of her chair. Nobody gave it any heed. "It is...it is as if we are on a train car, like this, moving through a darkened landscape in which wild things lurk. And it is only by the grace of God that those things do not crawl in here with us. You want to conquer the Otherworld, Mr.

Barton? You cannot. All you can do is survive when it decides to come for you."

The younger Roseingrave sister's smile had faltered; she was openly staring at the elder in what could only be deemed disbelief. Thomas found his fingers inching toward the notebook he always carried in the breast pocket of his jacket, wanting to write down what she was saying.

But Mr. Barton laughed, breaking the spell.

"Perhaps so," he chuckled, "and I would not gainsay the daughter of the great Madame Aine. I am sure you have forgotten more about these matters than I could ever hope to learn! But observing that world has great value, wouldn't you say?"

"Of course it does, Mr. Barton," the younger sister said, clearly making an effort to gain control of the discussion. "Both to science and the individual."

Mr. Barton nodded, as if he expected nothing less than his own ideas being confirmed. "And so, learning to observe that world more precisely and clearly would surely be one of the most important discoveries in human history. Who knows, we might even prove the existence of God."

"God has nothing to do with what's out there," the elder Miss Roseingrave said, and finished off what was left of her wine in one gulp. From seemingly nowhere, the attendant stepped forward to bring her another glass.

The younger one spoke up then. "Sister, don't you think you've had enough?"

"I don't think I have," the elder sister replied, and accepted the fresh glass. "It is not every day a man like Mr. Barton invites us to enjoy the fruits of his personal cellar."

"Perhaps you should eat something."

"Perhaps I don't feel like it."

Sensing the tension, Thomas stepped in. "It's a very Celtic viewpoint, isn't it?" he asked. "If we are to give credence to the idea of life after death and the presence of human spirits, then we must logically acknowledge those other spirits that so many other cultures throughout human history have claimed to witness. The Irish have a particularly strong connection to the entities of the Otherworld, in my experience, and do not view our respective worlds as so separate. But my own studies would indicate that not everything is friendly in the Land of Faery."

"Faery?" Mr. Barton laughed. "Are we talking about faeries now?"

"That would be what we call it in England, although I have seen some of the newer scholarship referring to such creatures collectively as fae. The term faery is indeed taking on some rather juvenile connotations of late," Thomas said. "But then, perhaps Miss Roseingrave's 'Otherworld' is a better term."

The elder Roseingrave sipped her new glass of wine and said nothing.

"Have you ever encountered such an entity, Miss Roseingrave?" Thomas asked, intrigued now.

"Oh please, gentlemen, let's avoid such wild conjectures!" the younger sister said. "The nature of séances limits contact with any such thing, if any such thing does exist. I have never heard of anyone encountering a...a nonhuman spirit or a fae or whatever you'd like to call them. The séance is about welcoming in those of our own kind who have passed on and wish to speak. It's not about painting your naked body blue and howling at the moon, as the ancient Celts are said to have done." She glared at her sister. "There is nothing pagan in what we do."

"Still, Miss Roseingrave, it's an intriguing notion, and one I have not considered before," Mr. Barton nodded. "Truly, your mother, your whole family, has great insight into these matters."

The elder sister ignored him and looked straight at Thomas instead. Her eyes looked a little glassy. "I have not met many Spiritualists who care about folklore, Mr. Leighton."

"As our esteemed patron says, it is a science of the soul and should be treated with appropriate rigor," Thomas replied. "But there are sciences of the past as well, archaeology and paleontology and the like. If the ancient Greeks and Romans teach us anything, it's that insight into human nature is not confined to the present day. There are likely many things about Spiritualism that we can learn from our ancestors, if we have the wit to see it." Without really meaning to, he pulled his notebook from an interior pocket of his coat. "Now, Miss Roseingrave, what did you mean exactly, about things out there in the darkness?"

The elder sister blinked, then rubbed a hand across her face. "Forgive me, Mr. Barton, I have made a fool of myself." The younger sister nodded a little. The elder sister leaned hard against the back of her chair. "Perhaps I should have a little something to eat."

"Of course, my dear, of course," Mr. Barton said, and picked up a handbell from the table.

Thomas extended a hand to help her to the railcar's table, but she shook her head and made her way over alone. The attendant came back in to give her the menu. Her sister stared daggers at her from across the table.

Mr. Barton, for his part, fished a cigar out of a small humidor beside his chair and snipped off the end. "This, I think, will be a most fascinating séance indeed."

They weren't even off the platform yet, Thomas stopping to help the ladies step down, when the already strange day got just a little stranger.

"Barton!" a deep, guttural voice boomed. "Barton, you miserable old bastard! We need to talk!"

Thomas looked at his patron, who just shook his head and pasted on a broad smile as he turned around. "Mikael! Good to see you, old friend!"

After switching trains in Buena Vista to a smaller local spur, they'd turned north up a narrow valley, climbing steeply again into deeper forest, finally arriving at Leadville. It was midafternoon, but the town was nestled against a series of peaks, and they were in the latter days of October now. The shadows were already long in Leadville.

And through those shadows, battering his way through the small crowd disembarking from the train, a sour-faced individual was stalking toward them. He was nearly as broad at the shoulder as he was tall, a squat, stocky man with a long beard and fury in his expression.

"Shove that horseshit, Barton," the man snapped in a faded Germanic accent. "I got your telegraph this morning. I want no part of this scheme."

"But Mikael," Mr. Barton said, laying a friendly hand on the other man's shoulder, clearly trying to calm him down, "it was your nephew who was out with my son. Aren't you the least bit curious what has—"

"No," the man said, and glared at the elder Roseingrave. "Whatever happened to my nephew happened. Having this pet witch of yours attempt to contact him after what was sent home after him is inviting disaster."

Thomas felt a squeeze at his hand; the elder Roseingrave sister was tightening her grip.

"I am merely the medium who shall be attempting contact with Mr. Barton's late son tonight," the younger sister said, forceful but with a

70

graceful smile on her lips. She extended a hand. "I would love for you to attend, Mister…"

"Dvalinsson," he said, spitting the word out.

"I would love for you to attend, Mr. Dvalinsson. Skeptics are always welcome. In fact, skeptics are my favorite guests at a séance." Her smile grew softer, more sly. "How can we progress in our understanding of psychical matters if everyone present believes that every dropped fork or furtive cough is the spirits speaking to us? It's unbearable sometimes!"

The younger Miss Roseingrave clearly thought this comment would be met with laughter from Mikael Dvalinsson, but if anything, his face grew darker. He turned back to Mr. Barton. "Whatever you do tonight, you leave my name the hell out of it."

"Please, old friend," Mr. Barton said. "There are ladies present."

The man snorted. "Believe me, Lane, if the ladies present here truly have the witchsight, a few bad words is the least of what they've experienced in their lives."

Again, the elder Miss Roseingrave's hand squeezed down on Thomas's.

Undeterred, the younger sister pressed on. "If your nephew was along on the expedition, perhaps we could—"

"My sister would skin me alive. You too, Barton, and you know it. There's no bringing those boys back, but at least they died in the mountains with rock under their feet and dirt under their fingernails. No good will come of disturbin' them now. As I said, especially after what followed them home." His eyes darted to Thomas. "And you, what are you supposed to be?"

There was weight in that gaze, an anger that felt older than the mountains around them. Very strange. But Thomas held himself up. "I am here to observe and record the séance. A… data point, if you will, in the annals of the Academy of Psychical Inquiry."

"Research. Bah. Data." And Mikael Dvalinsson spat on the ground. "This obsession with science will be the death of us all."

"Mikael, please…"

"Do anything in my name tonight and I'll sue you to high heaven, Barton." He looked at the Roseingraves. "My nephew stays out of this."

The younger sister seemed genuinely flummoxed, and it was the elder who spoke up. "If you do not wish for your nephew to be asked to speak, Mr. Dvalinsson, then we shall respect that."

Mikael Dvalinsson wasn't impressed. He narrowed his eyes. "This isn't back east, where the land's been paved over and beaten down. This is the West, missy, and things are different out here. Be careful where you tread."

"I—" the younger began.

"We understand completely," the elder Miss Roseingrave said, interrupting again. "And Mr. Dvalinsson, I hope it's alright to say that I am so sorry for your loss. I understand that—"

"What do any of you understand?" he grumbled, and strode away, back into the crowd.

For a moment, none of them spoke.

Then Mr. Barton laughed and adjusted his hat. "Mikael's a good prospector, the best, but he does have his quirks. Who doesn't, though, out here, eh? Don't worry about him. Come on. My buggy will be waiting, and after that, my new house."

The younger sister recovered herself from the shock and smiled. "It would be good to wash up and meditate before the séance."

"Of course, of course. Anything you need, my dear." And he offered her his arm.

Watching them walk off for a moment, Thomas turned back to the elder sister. She was still gripping his hand tightly. "Are you alright?" he asked. He felt bad for her; frontier or not, there was no excuse for a man cursing and carrying on like that in front of a woman.

She took a deep breath and looked down at her hand, like she'd forgotten about it completely. She let go. "That was unexpected is all."

"It was quite rude," Thomas said carefully. She was very pale. "Are you certain you're alright?"

"My sister is intent on defrauding one of the richest men west of the Mississippi," the elder Roseingrave sister told him, and headed off, toward where the buggy waited. "Why should I be alright?"

Thomas wasn't sure if the accusation in her words was intentional or not. He felt it all the same. "I was not able to stop her from offering," he said, and started walking with her. "And as you pointed out, it is not so easy to convince a Spiritualist that spirit communication isn't real."

"Oh, so it's not real now?" she asked, arching an eyebrow.

"You said it was not," he retorted.

She just sniffed and picked up her pace.

CHAPTER TEN

The buggy ride back to Mr. Barton's house did nothing to improve Charlotte's mood, nor the sick feeling in her stomach; she had not done it on purpose, but she realized now that she had indeed drunk too much wine on the train. Between the alcohol and the altitude, her head was aching.

Served her right, she thought glumly.

Charlotte didn't talk on the buggy ride, letting her sister continue to take the lead on that. A pleasant but constant stream of conversation had been one of Mama's favorite interrogation techniques. Little details about the client's life, or the life of their deceased loved one, could easily be teased out and then smoothed over again, lost under a sea of inconsequential words. Most people never noticed it was happening.

It was one of those little tricks of the medium trade that Charlotte had never liked. Always felt dishonest to her. But she didn't stop it. Celeste was going to need whatever information she could pull out of Mr. Barton for the séance tonight, and Charlotte truly had no desire to see her sister humiliate herself. That wasn't why she didn't interrupt it, though.

She was still mortified at her behavior on the train. She'd made an utter fool of herself. The Otherworld. Why had she mentioned the Otherworld?

Still, she had to admit, her sister had been right about one thing. It was good to get out of Denver. Leadville was nestled right in the heart of the

Rockies, surrounded by fine snowy peaks and filled with the sweet mountain air. The streets were well-maintained and the buildings pleasant, a testament to the wealth extracted from the silver mines. Passing by fine edifice after edifice, Charlotte almost found herself enjoying the sights.

But then the buggy stopped in front of a grand mansion, larger and more opulent than any other they had passed, stone dressed and wood gaily painted in the latest fashion, and that enjoyment evaporated.

"This is going to be my primary residence," Mr. Barton said as they disembarked. "As soon as we complete construction, of course. Cooler up here in the summers, you know, and closer to the mines."

Charlotte looked up at the beautiful facade, skirt gathered in one gloved hand as she stepped down from the buggy. There was something here. Not fear or anger or dread, all things she had felt before. No, nothing so prosaic. This was an absence, a lack of life, the end of light. A great, yawning abyss, ready to swallow them all.

"It's lovely," she lied, the words thick in her throat, hardly able to get them out.

"It's superlative," Celeste said, smiling at Mr. Barton. "You must be very proud."

"Yes, it's quite lovely. Incomplete, of course, and I must apologize for that. We are still missing some woodwork on the second floor, and most of the final furnishings, except for your rooms, ladies. But please, Miss Roseingrave, if you would..."

"Of course."

As the rest of their small party headed up the front stairs to the door, Charlotte stayed rooted in place. She couldn't move. Every fiber of her being was telling her to run. She just stared at the house, wondering what was in there, praying she wouldn't find out.

A loud clatter behind her caused her to jump. But it was just their luggage hitting the ground, the driver talking to the pair of men who had emerged from around the side of the house to help unload the buggy.

"Are you alright?" Mr. Leighton asked for the second time in the past half hour, coming back down the steps.

Charlotte admonished herself. She really needed to stop making such a fool of herself.

"I'm fine." She stared back up at the house, fearing it, but forced herself to start walking anyway. "What does Mr. Barton want us to see here?"

"I believe it has to do with the photographs he sent the Academy of that object in his garden," Mr. Leighton replied as they headed into the house. "Photographs! By special courier, no less. Imagine the expense!"

"An object? Photographs?" She wracked her memory. "Mr. Barton said nothing of any object, and certainly did not provide me with photographs."

"On our advice, I'm afraid. Mrs. Holzworth was quite insistent that Mr. Barton not provide the photographs to any medium he might employ."

Charlotte was flummoxed. Why would a séance require photographs? Why would Mr. Barton go to the trouble and expense of sending such things to as renowned an organization as the Academy? Spirit photography was highly suspect, so what else would there be? What kind of importance would such things carry? "Surely the Academy would not be taken in by photographs of ghosts."

"No, of course not. The photographs were of an object in his garden. Proof, he said, of his great need for our assistance into his investigation."

This was much worse than she had thought. "I thought he just wanted to speak to his dead son."

Mr. Leighton gave her an apologetic look. "It is a bit more involved than that. Didn't your mother speak to you about this?"

Mama had apparently been conversing with both Mr. Barton and the Academy for a few months before her death, and Charlotte suspected this was the reason they had come to Colorado at all. But Mama had collapsed the day after they arrived in Denver, and her health had been Charlotte's most pressing concern.

"No. We barely spoke about this séance at all, my mother and I," Charlotte said honestly. "And neither did you, I might add. You might have mentioned something about this."

Stopping on the porch, Mr. Leighton gave her a wry smile. "I am sorry about that, Miss Roseingrave. Mrs. Holzworth's investigative technique favors blinds, you see. I am sure you've heard of her?"

"Of course I have. Her famous blind experiments, yes, I know. But I've already told you, my mother was a fraud," Charlotte said. "How could you let my sister walk into this unawares?"

"The experiment still must be allowed to run its course," Mr. Leighton said apologetically. "Complex and detailed conversations with the dead are one thing, but there seems to be a slight thread of psychical talent that runs through us all. It may be that your sister is able to identify the object in question or even pull some usable information from it."

Was he really that naive? Irritation warred with uncertainty in Charlotte's breast. "I assure you, she cannot."

Mr. Leighton put a finger to his lips and pointed inside, where Mr. Barton and Celeste were clearly talking about something. "Let us see what happens."

Irritation won out, and she dropped his elbow. "This is not science," she insisted. But with nothing else to do, she followed her sister into the house.

But immediately upon entering, Charlotte wished she had not.

The foyer was beautiful. Grand, even without all the woodwork being installed or carpets on the floor. But she couldn't focus on any of it.

All she could see was blackness.

Charlotte had never felt anything like this before. Dark things, she had encountered. Evil, she had brushed against more than she cared to. But this was beyond all that. This was standing naked in the dark after the sun went out, with nothing in the universe at all, not even God. It was terrifying.

And there was Mr. Barton smiling at her, like nothing at all was wrong.

"Ah, Miss Roseingrave, Mr. Leighton, good of you to join us," the silver baron said. "Celeste and I were just discussing Mrs. Piper's latest article in *Borderlands*. Such a fascinating woman."

"She is a wonder," Mr. Leighton agreed.

"I haven't read it," Charlotte said, feeling as if the air was being crushed from her lungs. "I've been rather busy at the workshop."

Mr. Barton shook his head. "A pair of women as talented and beautiful as you and your sister should not be grubbing about for pennies, working for that odious Mr. Dunn." He nodded at Celeste. "You solve this mystery for me, and you shall be the most feted medium in America. Shall I show them now, Thomas?"

Mr. Leighton, off inspecting a large, vulgar Hellenic vase, started a little. He pulled back, blinking behind his spectacles. "Yes, yes, best let them see it now."

And that was when Charlotte realized what she was feeling.

The back garden of Mr. Barton's mansion was as unfinished as the inside. The bones of a fine English garden had been laid out behind the house, marked with string, some of the larger plants already settled in their beds, but none of the work had been accomplished.

For in the middle of it all was the source of all that darkness Charlotte had felt. A blight on the good green earth.

"Dear lord," Celeste breathed. "What is that?"

It was a mass of corroded metal, barely recognizable as anything man-made. It was lying in the center of a dead spot on the ground; for almost ten feet around the object, there was nothing but bare rock, surrounded by what looked like a low metal fence. The fence itself was rusted around the base. Charlotte had seen a great many things in her life, but this left her completely flummoxed.

Mr. Leighton, on the other hand, stepped carefully over the fence and knelt down by the strange object, a handkerchief in his hand. Carefully, he turned over some little bolt that had fallen off the main machine. It crumbled to red dust in his hand.

"This is far more corroded than in the photographs you sent us."

"It is," Mr. Barton replied. "I've been making regular observations on it, just as your organization asked. The effect may be accelerating, but I'm not sure. It's impossible to tell without a proper metallurgy laboratory, and mine is not fully established yet."

"Photographs?" Thomas asked.

"Taken weekly. I have to send the negatives to Denver for development. I have a set for your review."

Charlotte stared at the object. There was something in there. Something that was eating the light. Eating time itself, somehow. She could feel it in her bones, and she thought about the stove falling through the ceiling, the metal worn and rusted away as if it was a thousand years old.

Fire. Always fire. Taking her life away. Driving Celeste into Mr. Barton's employ.

Had they been pushed into this by some unseen force? The same force that had created this object? And if that was true...

"I've had the dirt sampled," Mr. Barton said, almost conversationally. "And cultured, using the absolute latest techniques. Nothing."

"Nothing?" Mr. Leighton asked and turned on his heel. "Nothing at all?"

"I've sent the samples to several different university labs. All tell me the same thing. Nothing grows in the petri dishes. They tell me that means this dirt is completely abiotic."

"I shall need those reports as well."

"Of course."

"Abiotic?" Celeste asked. Outwardly, her expression was measured, but Charlotte knew her sister well enough to know that she was scared. If ever there was a time for them to get out of this, it was now. "Culturing?"

"Yes, it's a relatively new technology," Mr. Leighton said absently, still examining the fence, "where a sample of, well, dirt in this instance, is scattered on a growth medium and incubated like a chicken egg, in order that we might see if there is bacteria or some other living thing within it. Mr. Barton, am I to understand that this means nothing can grow in any of this dirt?"

"Inside this circle," Mr. Barton corrected. "I've had potted plants placed inside of it and they don't last. Even the pots crumble. Indeed, anything will start to break down if left in here. Fascinating, really."

Celeste rubbed a hand over her mouth, clearly trying to hold herself together. "Mr. Barton, I am no scientist. I am not sure what help I can be to you here."

"I would like you to perform a reading on this object. That was one of your mother's specialities, wasn't it?"

Celeste visibly hesitated. Her sister was rattled, rattled badly. Served her right for lying to this man, Charlotte thought, and then dismissed the thought as cruel. They could fight about this later. Right now, they just had to get through it.

"It was," Charlotte said, stepping in, "but it is a hard talent to develop, and neither of us are as experienced as our mother. My sister may not be able to give you a full accounting of this mystery."

Her sister shot her a grateful look.

"Try," Mr. Barton said gently. "Please. As interesting as this phenomenon is, it is also only a hundred feet or so from my back door. And then, think of the town!"

"You're afraid of it spreading?" Charlotte asked.

"It has spread," he told her. "The effect was limited to just the ground under the object at first. Miss Roseingrave, if there is anything you may tell me..."

"Let me try," Celeste said. She took a deep breath and closed her eyes. "This is a drifter drill, used in mining operations," she said quietly, after pretending to be in deep concentration for a few moments, "one that was with your son's expedition, if I am not mistaken."

Mr. Barton's expression didn't change, but Charlotte noticed a slight twitch in his cheek. A hit. She communicated this to her sister by patting the apron of her own dress; the rustle of the fabric was a quiet but clear signal for yes. A no would have been indicated by a tap of her heel. One of Mama's many little ciphers.

"And...?" Mr. Barton asked.

"It came from far away, from... Ah! So much pain," Celeste continued. She swayed a little on her feet, and Charlotte automatically moved in to catch her. Celeste's eyelashes were wet when she raised her face. "I'm sorry," she said demurely. "Sometimes it can be overwhelming."

Mr. Leighton was busy taking notes, Charlotte saw. She sighed internally.

She had told the man what she had told him in the hopes that it would discourage him—or Celeste, for that matter—from pursuing this any further. But all she had done, it seemed, was guarantee their public disgrace. This scene of decay in the garden was quite beyond either of them. Charlotte had never heard of such a thing, not even in Grandmother's wildest stories. She had little hope that Celeste could spin a satisfying explanation, much less one that would hold up to scientific scrutiny.

Hopefully they could get out of the state before they were exposed.

Mr. Barton, however, grasped Celeste by the hand earnestly. Celeste reached for him with the other hand, and Charlotte let her go. It was working. Mr. Barton was hooked.

"It is quite alright, my dear," the silver baron was saying. "It did come from far away. My son was—"

Celeste shook her head, smiling weakly at him, as if exhausted. Her flaming orange hair was falling out of its coiffure now, an effect achieved by loosening up one's hairpins just a little bit and shaking the head just a bit too much. It spoke to extreme effort and was one of those subtle but effective subconscious parts of the overall performance.

"No, no, please, Mr. Barton. No details. Tell me nothing before the séance tonight. We have our esteemed investigator here, after all!" And Celeste gestured at Mr. Leighton. "That way, when we reach your son and he speaks with you, we shall all know it is genuine."

Mr. Barton patted her hand. "Of course, of course. Now, may I offer you some refreshments?"

"Yes, it would be good to stop moving," Celeste said. "Some quiet space to gather myself for tonight would be welcome."

"Why the fence, if I may ask?" Mr. Leighton asked, not looking up from his notebook.

"Ah, yes, that. It—"

"Please, gentlemen," Celeste said, pausing halfway up the back steps of the house, "let me take my leave first."

"Of course, of course," Mr. Barton said, and patiently waited until Celeste was back inside. He looked at Charlotte then. "She reminds me of your mother. Or at least, the stories I have heard about your mother."

"Yes, she really does take after our mother quite closely," Charlotte replied drily.

"And you? What do you see?" he asked.

Considering the seriousness of the thing in front of her, Charlotte took a risk. "I cannot tell you what supernatural force brought such an abomination as this into being. But whatever caused it"—and she gestured at the bare rock inside the fence—"it is not something to be trifled with."

"Have you ever seen something like this before?"

"I've never heard of something like this before," she said, "not even in my grandmother's stories."

"Stories?" Mr. Leighton asked, still inspecting the fence.

Charlotte swallowed. She shouldn't have said that. "My grandmother was the daughter of Irish immigrants, Mr. Barton, and grew up surrounded by her father's stories of the old country, where faeries lurk in every hill and ghosts hide behind every tree."

"Fascinating," Mr. Barton said, slightly less enthusiastic now, and turned back to Mr. Leighton. "The effect, as I was saying, was confined at first to the area immediately around the drill but spread quickly. My partner offered the fence as a means of restricting it, but it had already spread this far by the time we installed the thing."

"Your partner?" Mr. Leighton asked. "Was that Mikael Dvalisson?"

"Yes, it was on his suggestion. Iron, he said, iron was the thing we needed."

"Iron," Mr. Leighton mused. "How interesting. I should like to speak to your former partner, as opposed to this situation as he seemed to be."

"I can give you his address for you to make inquiries in person."

"That would be helpful, thank you," Mr. Leighton said, and finally put his pencil and notebook away. "Miss Roseingrave? Any thoughts?"

She shook herself. Staring at the drill was like staring at the Rapture. The end of all things. "Where is the séance to be held tonight, Mr. Barton?"

"Why, out here!" he declared, spreading his hands wide. "Just as your mother specified."

A chill went through her.

"Of course," was all she said. "Of course."

CHAPTER ELEVEN

That night at Mr. Barton's house brought nothing that Thomas had expected.

Despite the strong presence of Spiritualism in England, the social cachet of the séance had faded somewhat in recent years, ruined, Thomas suspected, by overbold fraudsters and an increasingly cynical audience. Still, even with that, Thomas had attended many, and in England, the séance had a certain rhythm to it.

A gathering of friends at a private home. Refreshments: food, drinks, maybe even a full formal dinner. Gathering in the drawing room or around the dining table. Some light talking as the medium settled into her trance. A few revelations, a few little demonstrations of spiritual influence, and then a lively debate that could stretch for days as to what, if anything, the group had witnessed that night.

This was not that. This was more akin to a carnival.

Mr. Barton's unfinished Leadville mansion was stuffed to the gills with the bored and the curious, drawn in by the promise of a fine show. Mrs. Coulton, brought along special for this it seemed, was directing a small army of servers, providing the throng with everything from champagne to French-style appetizers to fine fresh oysters, brought all the way from the Chesapeake by special chilled train car. Warm gas-fired sconces cast gentle light across the party, while an electrified chandelier in the grand entry provided another novelty for the crowd.

The younger Miss Roseingrave was playing her part expertly, circulating amongst the guests, making small talk, offering startling insights punctuated by dramatic pauses and closed eyes.

Thomas sipped at the rather excellent lager that Mr. Barton had offered him from his seat in the small front study, observing it all. He had withdrawn here to get out of the noise, yes, but also to write out a few notes.

Writing helped him think, and this was something that deserved careful thought. The elder sister had been quite insistent—strident, even—that there was no psychical gift in the family, nothing to any of this. And yet, the younger sister persisted in this display.

Was it all a game the two of them played? The elder sister seemed sincere, but so did the younger. PT Barnum, it was said, had taken to seeding false information about his shows in the American papers in order to generate interest. Perhaps this was a similar phenomenon.

A great deal of money was changing hands, too. This, Thomas had not expected.

Mr. Barton had offered a very generous fee to the Rosengraves, of course, but many of the guests insisted on contributing as well. This was not something Thomas was familiar with; he figured it was some kind of local custom. Americans seemed to be far more forward with their money, and less concerned about spending it, than the upper classes in Britain.

Then the sound of the crowd grew louder, only to fall silent a moment later, closed out again by the soft thud of heavy oak doors.

"Oh," he heard a female voice say. "I am sorry. I did not realize anyone was here. I shall go."

Thomas looked up from his journal, smiling automatically at the sight of the elder Miss Roseingrave standing there. In her black mourning dress, she seemed almost to be part of the shadows in the small room.

"No, please," he said quickly, and set his beer aside. While the drink was surprisingly good, he was mostly holding it for show, the pretense of being part of the party. "Please stay. I take it you're looking for some solitude?"

"I do not care for such large crowds," she said. Her face was strained, her words labored. "It is...exhausting."

"May I offer you a chair?" he asked, gesturing at one of the leather-backed armchairs by the room's carved stone fireplace, where a small fire was licking at well-dried local pine.

Miss Roseingrave just folded her arms, looking around. "What is this place?"

"Mr. Barton's private study. He said I could avail myself of it tonight." Thomas brandished his notebook. "I needed to jot down a few of my thoughts. Accurate recordkeeping is vital."

The study was well-appointed, fitted with dark wood bookshelves and a small, but thoroughly modern, safe. Windows looked out on the forest beyond. The shelves were only about half full here, as if Mr. Barton had not yet decided which books to bring from Denver.

"This is quite the collection," the elder Roseingrave sister commented, hand trailing along one shelf. Her gloved fingers brushed the spines of the books. "I have heard about Mr. Barton's library, but I thought it was all back in Denver, and..." She stopped. "Jules Verne?"

Thomas looked at the book she had stopped at. "Yes, I've noticed several tomes by that author here. Scattered, you know. Everything is jumbled together. Confused."

"Confused, yes. That is a good word for it."

Thomas set aside his notebook. "I must apologize, Miss Roseingrave. I was not trying to put you or your sister in a bad spot," he told her, drawing her attention. "I've had the pleasure of working with the Holzworths on a few cases, and—"

"That's the problem," she said, shaking her head.

He choked down the stab of annoyance at having his words cut off. "What do you mean?"

She pulled out a book, looking at the cover carefully before replacing it again. "You know people who investigate psychical phenomenon. Not those who believe in it to the exclusion of all else, like Mr. Barton. I would guess you do not fully grasp the danger this commission puts me and my sister in."

Thomas smiled. "You make him sound like a zealot."

"Everyone wants their ideas reinforced and their opinions made true," Miss Roseingrave replied. "This is what my mother offered our clients, and that's why they loved her."

"I would counter that curiosity, not faith, fuels most of the interest in séances."

"Mr. Barton is not merely curious. I don't know what he truly wants, but I hope he values the entertainment aspect of my sister's performance tonight, because that is the only substance he will receive."

"You're so certain of that?"

"Mr. Leighton, if there is life after death, as Rome tells us there is, then those who have passed are far beyond the concerns of the mortal world."

Thomas took a chance. "You are Catholic?"

She took another book off another shelf. "Mediums are not welcome at Mass."

"But you believe in it, don't you?" he asked. When she didn't answer, he pressed on. "You believe in the concept of saints? Of them listening to prayers and offering intercession? How is that different from asking for a loved one to speak to us?"

"Saints do not grab at the penitent's clothing. Saint Michael does not sit down at your dining room table and offer financial investment advice, nor does Napoleon seek to reunite you with an estranged family member," she replied. "Or any of the other foolish things I've seen over the years."

"But the very notion of miracles surely indicates some kind of common—"

She shut the book again, a little too forcefully, and moved on, her heels clicking on the parquet flooring.

Thomas sensed he had offended her, which had not been his intent, and changed the subject. "Your mother had an excellent accuracy rate. With mundane things. Place and type of death, family secrets, hidden bank accounts, that sort of thing."

"I remember the bank account case," Miss Roseingrave said, hesitating.

"How did your mother do it, if she didn't talk to the dead business partner?"

"Local gossip can tell you much, but the best information comes from direct conversations."

Thomas thought about that for a moment. The two sisters were much alike; similar height, similar build, well suited to the fashionable shape of the day. With that hair of theirs, and the fine elfin features that were so common with redheads, neither seemed suited for subterfuge. Surely any man speaking to the Roseingrave sisters would remember them.

"Did your mother employ a network of informants?" he asked.

"Too risky. Anyone you add into your confidence is one that can betray you later."

"Then how?"

Miss Roseingrave frowned for a moment and then laughed. It was a lovely sound. "Are you imagining one of us hooded and cloaked, going out into the night to meet somewhere in a dark alley?"

He smiled, rueful. "It is the image that sprang to mind, yes."

"It's nothing so exciting as that. My mother taught us the tricks for getting information out of our clients directly. Liquor, for example, is an excellent tongue-loosener. And like you must have seen on the train, long periods of chatter can be quite good for extracting information without the subject noticing. But Mama always told us that she had a guide who..." And she trailed off again, halting at the massive desk, positioned next to a broad bay window. Outside, the sun was beginning to set, and another carriage was pulling up in front of the mansion. But that wasn't what Miss Roseingrave was looking at. "What is this?"

Thomas went over to look. She had pulled a book out of his satchel, sitting there on the edge of the desk.

"I don't know. I brought it from Denver," he said. "Mr. Barton has many works, as you can see, and it is all so badly organized that—"

"*Tales of the Otherworld*," Miss Roseingrave read, heated now, and she opened the book, beginning to leaf through the first few pages. "Where did this come from?"

Thomas brightened. "You speak Gaelic?"

"Don't change the subject!" She stopped at a page and held it up. "How is this here?"

He looked at the page. There was indeed a dedication there, written in a confident hand. The only word he recognized was *Charlotte*. He blinked; he had not seen that before. "What do you mean?"

"This was my grandmother's! I've carried it with me all these years. I thought it lost in the fire last night!" She slammed the book shut with one hand, a flush stealing up her neck over the high collar of her dress. "You took it!"

"What?" Thomas asked, shocked now. "I would never."

"When you came to see us at the workshop, you must have sneaked up to our room and took it!"

"Miss Roseingrave, I do not appreciate being called a thief."

"How else would these be here?" she demanded, and he was shocked to see tears in her eyes, even as she shook with fury. "These were in my trunk! We took nothing with us! These cannot be here!"

"Perhaps it was some helpful spirit," a new voice broke in. Both of them turned. It was Mr. Barton, a glass of wine in each hand. He held one out to Miss Roseingrave, who refused it. Thomas took his own without comment.

"Perhaps it was apported here, brought back to you by a denizen of that Otherworld you spoke of. Your mother, perhaps."

Miss Roseingrave's face flushed bright red. "That seems unlikely to me," she said through clenched teeth.

"Unless you truly believe this fine English gentleman came all this way just to sneak into a young woman's bedroom and steal her grandmother's book of faery tales, there is no other explanation."

Something about that seemed to pierce the bubble of her anger, and she sagged, sinking back into that considered misery she wore about herself like a shroud.

Mr. Barton laughed. "We are just about ready to begin, if I can find Miss Celeste. Please allow me to escort you to the garden with us, Miss Roseingrave. Mr. Leighton, if you will..."

"Of course," Thomas said, and pocketed his notebook again.

"I'm afraid my sister's...gifts, and mine, don't always play nicely together," Miss Roseingrave said stiffly, and glanced meaningfully at Thomas. "I think it best I remain here."

"I shall have Mrs. Coulton bring you something. Chardonnay?"

"Thank you," she said, and turned her back on them both.

"Curious creatures, mediums," Mr. Barton commented as he led Thomas away, out of the study and back through the still-crowded house. "I've met many of them over the years, and they're all different."

"Do you believe the elder Miss Roseingrave is a medium as well?"

"Of course she is," Mr. Barton said seriously. "As I told you, my study of regional traditions indicates that the gift is passed along on the female side of a family line. There is no doubt in my mind they are both potent mediums. A shame we cannot have both sisters working together. Then I would be assured of answers."

Thomas nodded, digesting that, and looked around at the mass of people milling about in the grand spaces of the mansion. "This seems like too large a group for the séance," he observed.

"Yes, yes." The silver baron chuckled. "I've already selected the group for the séance itself. The rest of them here are welcome to continue drinking my booze and eating my food, but they shall stay inside."

"Why come at all then?" Thomas asked. "Is there a lack of entertainment here in Leadville?"

"There's plenty. But none like this." Mr. Barton took a sip of his own whiskey, smiling a little. It was a catlike expression, self-satisfied and anticipatory, the smile of a man used to getting exactly what he wanted. "Look at everyone we have here. My damned partner Dvalinsson isn't, of course, and you witnessed that disgraceful scene at the station today. There's no accounting for some people. At least we still have his beer."

"A prospector who's also a brewmaster?"

"One of his little side businesses. Excellent, isn't it?" Mr. Barton said, and then waved it away, pointing around the room again. "But ah, over there, that's Colonel Ramage, a senior cavalry officer we see here from time to time, when he's not chasing the Utes or some abominable horse thief through the mountains. And there, that elegant woman is Mrs. Valencia. She runs one of the better saloons in town. Mrs. Molly Brown is here, the woman by that Grecian bust. Always lovely to see her. And look at that." And he pointed, waving. A hard-faced man with a heavily tanned complexion nodded back and downed his wine in one go. "Dvalinsson isn't here but that damned Gregory Peck decided to show up. That old rival I told you about. Probably here to rub my face in the new mine he has down in the San Juans. The two of us have been fighting over claims all over this state for decades."

"You invited your business competitor?"

"Thomas, they all invited themselves!" Mr. Barton laughed and then waved. "Ahh, there is Miss Celeste Roseingrave now."

In her black dress, pale skin, and flaming orange hair, the younger Roseingrave sister looked positively ethereal in the flickering light, chatting happily with one of the guests. She glanced their way, holding up a hand in acknowledgment, and then turned back to the man she was talking to. He passed her an envelope, and she protested lightly as he pressed it into her hands. Then she nodded, kissed the man's cheek, and came over.

"Everyone wants answers," Mr. Barton observed. "But Giovanni over there is going to have to wait his turn. He is not among the guests outside tonight."

Thomas frowned. "Then why is he paying her?"

Mr. Barton shrugged. "What are you worried about? I've seen more ostentatious displays of wealth in Europe, by far."

"It was not a criticism of you," Thomas said evenly. "I just don't often see this, I suppose. The Academy for Psychical Inquiry does have a rule that they do not attend any séance with any medium who charges money for her services."

"Yes, yes, yes. That is what the reply to my first letter said. 'To ensure the purity of their research,' or some such nonsense. I am grateful they decided to relent and send you out."

On this, Thomas held his tongue.

"It's foolishness," Mr. Barton continued, and waved a hand around the room. "Scientific progress is fundamental, essential, to creating the world of tomorrow, I agree, but do you suppose anything in this house would exist without money? What development in engineering, what new medical treatment, what method of food preservation was undertaken merely for the sake of discovery? Money, my dear Thomas, money is what makes a thing worthwhile. Money is what makes a thing possible. The sciences that are pursued are the sciences that add value to human existence, and we recognize that value by paying for it. Mediums not charging money is the antithesis of progress."

Thomas was about to ask what he meant by that, but suddenly the younger Miss Roseingrave put up a hand, crying out.

"My friends!" she called as silence rippled through the house. "My friends, it is time for the spirits to approach! Mr. Barton, please, if you will."

"Of course," Mr. Barton said, rushing over to her. She grasped Mr. Barton's proffered hands tightly. "What do you need?"

"The table," she said, her voice taking on a singsong tone. "Let us go to the table."

That started a fresh round of chatter, and as if anticipating pushback to the choice of table guests, the servers were back out, puff pastry and fresh champagne carried on silver trays. But a few people began moving toward the back of the house.

Thomas let himself be led away, glancing back at the redheaded woman in the library. She had sunk down into a chair, her face in her hands. In her mourning dress, she was the very picture of grief. Something in him wanted to go back and comfort her.

But the mysterious appearance of the book thought lost to a fire spoke to...something, didn't it? Something that, just maybe, he would see explained here tonight.

CHAPTER TWELVE

Thomas was familiar with all the standard séance practices. While a dimly lit drawing room was a perennial favorite, some enterprising mediums held séances in public halls, lecture venues, even accommodating churches—although that was far less common these days. Madame Aine's performances out in the West, reports said, were marked by a peculiar choice of venue.

The reports, it seemed, were true.

The table in question was perfectly normal. Long, rectangular, it had seats enough for twelve, sixteen if all the sitters squeezed in a little tighter. Judging from the quality of the workmanship, it was likely intended to be the primary dining table for this residence.

Tonight, however, instead of being ensconced in some velvet-draped room, the séance table had been set up outside. Right on the edge of the strange iron fence. Lit with nothing more than a pair of candles in storm glass, the polished mahogany surface reflected the waxing moon. The garden itself backed onto the raw, wild forest of the mountains.

It was an eerie sight, and Thomas could not deny the feeling of foreboding that stirred now in his gut. Still, he was here to investigate, not get drawn into the theatricality of it all, and he forced himself to be analytical about the affair.

The table had clearly not been custom-built for séances, and thus, would not have any of the trapdoors or mechanics that allowed for tricks like spirit-hand manifestations or mysterious tapping. It was also far too big for something like levitation, most often achieved via a stick or lever concealed under a medium's skirt. There was no cabinet out here from which the younger Miss Roseingrave might venture forth draped in white silks, pretending to be a ghost. The elder sister had remained in the house, though, and Thomas could not rule out the possibility of her acting like a spirit.

But the two young women had lost everything in the fire a few nights back and had brought no luggage with them. Whatever props or other accoutrements they might have possessed were most surely gone.

How Miss Celeste Roseingrave planned to make this interesting, Thomas had no idea.

Despite the strange nature of the location, the séance began as many usually did, with Miss Roseingrave settling into a chair and allowing herself to drift into a trance. Thomas had seen this process take an hour or more at times. Under different conditions, of course. Far more pleasant conditions. Tonight, the air was chill, a breeze coming down from the mountains.

So it was only about ten minutes before anything happened. There was a sense of anticipation in the air, quiet murmuring all around. Thomas hung back, wishing for better light to write, and then—

"Someone is here with us," Miss Celeste Roseingrave announced, lifting her head again. "He wishes to speak."

Utter silence fell.

"He is young, sandy brown hair, a fine smile on his face." She closed her eyes, twisting her head. "He is covered in blood. Bullet wounds in his chest. He smiles. He has much to say."

"Is it my son?" Mr. Barton asked, sitting across from Miss Roseingrave.

She nodded slowly, as if her head had suddenly grown quite heavy. "Him and... others. Several others. All wounded unto death. They have come straight here, they say, to speak with us."

"They died months ago," somebody else said. The colonel, Thomas remembered. In the candlelight, the man's eyes were almost glowing gold.

"There is no time where they are," Miss Roseingrave said, and twisted her head, grimacing. "Ahh, what they suffered! An ambush, a betrayal...so much pain..."

Thomas wondered about the graphic details. Usually, in séances he'd been to, spirits were envisioned as clean and perfect, all wounds healed in death. Perhaps different imagery was required out here on the frontier.

"Where did he die?" Mr. Barton asked.

Miss Roseingrave was silent for a moment, twisting her head a few more times. "Among the aspens, he says," she told their patron, still using that singsong voice of hers. "Aspens and rock and I—paper! I need paper!"

A sketch pad had been set up on the table for precisely this reason; Madame Aine had drawn some breathtaking images while in trances, it was said, and it seemed that Celeste intended to take after her mother in this as well. She fumbled the pencil for a moment, before grasping it firmly and beginning to sketch with big, bold strokes.

"Among the aspens," she repeated. "The aspens."

"What are we supposed to be gettin' out of this, Barton?" That was Mr. Gregory Peck, down at the end of the table. "You've been tellin' everyone for months that your son found the best gold mine anywhere in the San Juan Mountains, nuggets the size of peanuts just layin' on the ground, but there ain't one shred of proof."

"It would seem he was killed for it," Mr. Barton snapped, and looked back to Miss Roseingrave. "Where did my son die?"

"In the aspens," she muttered, and flipped a page in the book. Something seemed to have changed. She was sketching faster now on this new page. Not trees, but the mouth of a cave. "There's the way, in there. That's the way to where he needs to go. That's where he has to be."

"Who?" Mr. Barton asked, voice starting to strain.

Miss Roseingrave's hand was flying now. She flipped another page, sketching faster and faster. Sweat stood out on her brow. Her teeth were clenched. Her entire body was shaking.

It wasn't just her. Everyone seemed uneasy. A nervous, unsettled mood had settled over the table. Even Thomas could feel it; a racing of the heart, the sensation of being watched.

"The darkness," she said, and she sounded scared now. "The darkness is there."

"Where did my son die?" Mr. Barton demanded. "Who killed him?"

"Can't see, can't see, can't see, the darkness..."

"This is bullshit," Mr. Peck snapped.

Mr. Barton ignored him completely, pounding the table in front of Celeste. "Where is my mine?!"

Celeste finally looked up, eyes wide and face pale. "They're here."

And the first gunshot rent the night.

Charlotte swirled her Chardonnay around in its fine cut crystal glass, watching the pale golden drink coat the sidese. It was an exceptional vintage. She wished she could have enjoyed it.

Mr. Barton was ostentatious with his wealth, as so many of Mama's clientele had been. Most of the time, Mama had said, they were just looking for novelty, some pleasant distraction from the monotony of life. Charlotte had always believed it was just her mother making excuses for herself, a justification for defrauding the ultrarich.

She sipped her wine. It really was exquisite.

With a sigh, she set the drink aside, reaching for her grandmother's book. Since arriving here, she had not been able to shake that feeling of...of nothingness. Charlotte had encountered such strong sensations before, where the feel of a thing or a place was so overwhelming she could not block it out. It had never been to her benefit.

It scared her to her core.

But if she had looked, then maybe she could have found Mr. Barton his answer. Perhaps her sister wouldn't be out there right now stirring up god only knew what from inside that iron ring.

The fire crackled as a log slipped, sending a flurry of sparks up into the air. It reminded Charlotte of another fire, another feeling, another moment of encounter with those places, those things, that lurked on the edge of sight.

They should never have come here. Charlotte knew that with the same certainty she knew that the sun would rise in the east tomorrow. But what she didn't know was what that...that thing was outside. The detail about the fence had immediately made Charlotte think about faeries; they were said to be repulsed by cold iron. But faeries, if such things were real, were supposed to be aligned with nature, with growing things, living things. All that death—

She tore her thoughts away.

She fingered the worn leather cover of the old book. It had been unfair to accuse Mr. Leighton of taking it. He couldn't have. This was the same book that she'd been reading right before the fight with Celeste. Before storming out. Before the fire. Long after Mr. Leighton had taken his leave of them.

It was possible that Celeste had saved it... but how? Had she smuggled the book out of the burning building under her petticoats? Kept it secret? Why? Would she have thought Charlotte would sell it? Or would Celeste have been planning some kind of grand practical joke?

It bothered Charlotte that she couldn't answer that question. She regretted the distance growing now between herself and her sister. Celeste was all the family she had left. If Charlotte lost her sister, too, she didn't know what she would do with herself.

A creak. The sound of boots, stepping very carefully. Barely audible above the quiet crackle of the fire in the study's hearth.

Charlotte sighed. "Mr. Leighton, if you are back for a second round of discussion—"

"From what the boss said, I thought you'd be outside right now."

It wasn't Mr. Leighton's accent.

It wasn't Mr. Leighton at all.

Her blood went cold. "Who are you?" she asked, voice hitching in her throat.

"Get up there, miss. There's a good girl," this newcomer said, waggling a huge rust-stained revolver at her. His face was concealed behind a red hand-kerchief, the paisley pattern of the fabric obscured by dark stains and shad-owed heavily by the brim of his hat. "Nobody needs to get hurt tonight."

"I don't have any money," she said, holding her hands out, open.

"We ain't here for your money, miss."

There was another one now. Circling her. This one's gun was still holstered, but he had a wicked-looking hunting knife in hand. "Stop chat-ting her up, Amos. Boss wants her brought in."

"We don't even know if she's the right one, Diego," the first one, Amos, said.

"Then ask her why don't ya?" This Diego smiled at her, his teeth like fangs. His eyes glinted yellow. "You the medium the boss wants?"

"I'm no medium," she said, heart pounding.

"You see? That's why we ask," Diego said to Amos, tone almost bored. "Kill her."

"Pity. She's a looker," Amos said, and raised the gun.

But no gunshot came.

A twang. A cough. Then blood trickled out of Amos's mouth.

The tip of a black stone arrowhead was protruding from his throat.

Charlotte stared at the man in horror as his body thumped to the floor, still twitching, the long shaft of the arrow planted in his neck like a flagpole. Then an arm grabbed her around the waist, hauling her back, crushing her. Diego. She gagged; the scent of him was rank, like that of a diseased animal.

"Well, well, look what we have here," Diego growled, his own gun drawn now, pointed straight out. He had Charlotte lifted half off the floor; her feet scrambled for purchase, kicking his shins, but he seemed not to notice. "Haven't seen one of your kind in a long time."

Charlotte was dimly aware of somebody standing in front of her. There. In the door. He was hazy, indistinct, like a mirage in the desert, but the arrowhead, glinting like glass, and the green silk of his waistcoat were clear to her.

A man holding a drawn bow, another stone-tipped arrow nocked to its string. But this was no Indian; his features, though indistinct, were quite pale, and when he spoke his voice had a distinct Irish lilt.

"You've never met one of my kind, animal."

The arm tightened around Charlotte's throat; her vision swam with gray spots. She couldn't speak, could barely breathe. She clawed at his hand, but her strength was ebbing fast. "Animal, is it?"

"Let her go."

"What, don't trust your aim?" the outlaw snarled, and drew Charlotte back. His strength was frightening.

Gunshots now. One, then many. Coming from outside.

"My aim's just fine," the Irishman said. "Doin' you a courtesy is all."

The man holding Charlotte started to speak but then yelped like a coyote, letting Charlotte go.

She fell forward, stumbling, off-balance.

An arrow was lodged in the outlaw's eye. He pawed at the shaft. "Ain't silver!" he yelled, blood pouring down his face, and lunged.

Something grabbed her arm. The Irishman. He swung her around, using her momentum to throw her behind him. A knife flashed out of some hidden place beneath his coat, whipping up to slash Diego across the arm.

The outlaw chuckled, tossing his own wicked-looking knife from hand to hand. "So we got ourselves a hero," he said.

The Irishman snorted.

And that was the end of any verbal exchange.

Charlotte had seen people killed before. Not in person, as it happened, but echoes of it, memories that seemed to soak into a bit of land or a building and imposed themselves on her through the Sight, no matter how much she tried to not to look. She'd seen them after they died, necks twisted by a bad fall or shot to death or, one terrible time, mauled by bears.

She had never seen anything like this.

Diego came on, almost too fast to follow. He threw himself at the Irishman, knocking him almost off his feet. The Irishman lost his grip on his bow. Raising his knife with both hands, he plunged his strange knife into the outlaw's back again and again, even as he was pushed back.

The shadows murmured, the fire guttering low in its hearth. Diego raised a hand, and it seemed to Charlotte then that it had grown, his fingers longer, capped with wicked claws. These he plunged down at the Irishman, going for his throat. Those claws raked the Irishman's exposed neck, cutting shallow furrows that shone with some fey light. Then the Irishman shifted and used the outlaw's own momentum to throw him into the study wall.

The impact rattled the entire room. Diego roared out in a voice that was far from human and pounced again.

He was on top of the Irishman now, ripping and clawing, like he was trying to tear him apart with his bare hands. He was twisting now, growing bigger, distinctly bigger, almost like...

"Charlotte! The desk!" the Irishman yelled. "The letter opener!"

Shaking herself out of the reverie she had fallen into, Charlotte realized she had backed up directly into that piece of furniture. The Irishman, from his back on the floor, kicked out with his legs and sent Diego flying across the room, straight into the fireplace. The outlaw roared and scrambled out, clothes burning as he knocked the Irishman once again to the ground.

Those memories suddenly threatened again. That fire, that fire in that other place, when she—

"Letter opener!"

She tore her eyes away, pulled her thoughts from the past, desperately looking—there, on a stand. A little silver letter opener the length of her hand.

"Throw it!"

She did. Her aim was terrible. He was forced to dive to reach it across the floor, Diego roaring at his heels. The outlaw threw himself down, jaws snapping, horribly distended now. Charlotte could have sworn she saw Diego's claws rip through the meat of her rescuer's arm. But then he was rolling, onto his back. The letter opener flashed above him in a glittering arc.

Diego fell to the ground, hands clutching at his neck. Through the blood gushing across his fingers, Charlotte could see that the damage was mortal. His throat was open to the vertebrae. He was still glaring at the Irishman, though, murderous hate in his one good eye. And, very intentionally, the Irishman, coming up to his knees, plunged the silver letter opener so deeply into the outlaw's eye socket that only the top inch was visible, right next to the snapped remnant of the arrow shaft.

The gunshots, so loud and vicious, dwindled. Out the window, from down the street, she could hear the pounding hooves of horses. Whooping and yelling was heard. A few more shots.

Then all fell silent.

Shock finally caught up with her, and Charlotte collapsed to her knees on the floor, dry heaving.

Something metallic and heavy scraped across the floor toward her. A big brass pot, reeking of tobacco.

"Best do that in the spittoon," her rescuer said. "I don't believe Lane Barton is the kind of man who'd take kindly to vomit on the floor."

She wanted to retort—the entire room was splattered with blood—but the smell of the thing sent her over the edge. Quite unprompted, her stomach emptied. As she finished, coughing, grimacing at the taste in her mouth, a clean, green paisley-print handkerchief was dropped on her lap.

She looked up, staring at the man who had saved her life. He was carefully wiping down the blade of his knife—black, and of an unfamiliar design —with a red-stained scrap of fabric. It took her a moment to realize he had taken the handkerchief from the dead man on the floor.

"Thank you," she said.

"No thanks are necessary," he replied. His voice was smooth, almost inhuman. It spoke to her of deep forests, of sunlit groves and hidden hills. It was— "My services are, quite unfortunately, guaranteed."

For a moment, Charlotte had no idea what he meant. And then she caught sight of Grandmother's book, tossed down on the floor.

"You," she said, realizing. "You are not real."

"Real as anything else in this mess of a world," he said, sheathing the knife again, tucking it away under his coat. He tossed the bloody rag back into the fire, contemptuous, and knelt down to offer her a hand up. "Unless you want to name your grandmother a liar."

"I don't believe in you."

"Doesn't matter what you believe in, Charlotte. You don't get a say in the matter. Neither do I, if you must know."

She stared at him for a few more moments before Mr. Leighton burst in through the doors of the library. "Miss Roseingrave!"

Charlotte half expected her savior to disappear. That was, indeed, what Grandmother's stories had always claimed about the man—if he was that man. But perhaps he was not, because there he still was, considering the two dead men on the study floor.

"I am quite alright," Charlotte replied to the very human researcher in front of her and gestured at the Irishman. "Thanks to him."

"One of Mr. Barton's guests?" Mr. Leighton asked.

The man turned. "An Englishman? Is there no escaping the plague of your kind?"

"And who are you, my good man?"

"I am the man who just saved Charlotte here from a brace of brigands," the man—who, according to Grandmother's stories, was not a man at all— said, gesturing at the dead bodies. "You'd think somebody would be grateful for that."

The researcher barely seemed to notice the jab. "Miss Roseingrave, I don't know how to tell you this, but your sister, she's..."

"Been killed?" the strange Irishman asked, voice utterly indifferent.

"No," Mr. Leighton replied, and took off his glasses, nervously polishing them with the linen handkerchief he kept in his jacket pocket. "Taken. Kidnapped, I'm afraid."

CHAPTER THIRTEEN

"And you are here on the invitation of Mr. Barton?"

Thomas looked past the deputy sheriff. The entire house was in a frightful state of disarray—furniture overturned, artifacts smashed, woodwork pockmarked with bullet holes.

But at the moment, all of Thomas's attention was focused on Miss Roseingrave. He could see her there, off in a small side drawing room, Mrs. Coulton by her side and her face buried in a handkerchief. The man who had saved her life was nowhere to be seen.

All the séance guests—all the ones who hadn't fled the gunshots or attempted to pursue the bandits themselves—were gathered right now in the main entrance hall. Clustered together, they were finishing drinks or starting new ones, talking quietly amongst themselves, all telling the same story to the authorities. The Leadville sheriff, along with several deputies and a group of concerned citizens, all armed to the teeth, had shown up a few minutes ago. Not soon enough to stop what had happened here.

Thomas's own impression of events was scattershot, fractured. After Miss Roseingrave's declaration at the table, gunshots had rent the night. The effect had been undeniable: people ran, dodged for cover, or sought to return fire. No bullets had fallen directly on the group, noise only, it seemed, meant to distract them. But outlaws had been everywhere, big, rough men with pistols and knives, knocking over chairs, scattering drinks, battering aside anybody who got in their way. Hell-bent on reaching their objective.

Which had turned out to be Miss Celeste Roseingrave.

The would-be medium hadn't moved from her spot during the commotion, caught up in some kind of trance. Thomas had attempted to reach her, only to be thrown into the iron fence by an immensely powerful man. It was only by the barest margin that Thomas avoided being impaled on the fence's top finials. Before he recovered, that outlaw had grabbed Miss Roseingrave a second later, dragging her out of her chair. She'd screamed then, but it had been too late. The outlaws, whooping and laughing, retreated fast, covering themselves with a rain of gunfire.

Some of the other men, Colonel Ramage among them, were embroiled in their own little battles and couldn't break free to pursue. Mr. Barton had run after them and had been beaten half to death for his trouble.

He was upstairs right now, unconscious.

Thomas burned with fury over the entire affair.

"Mr. Leighton?" the sheriff's deputy asked again.

"I'm sorry, but shouldn't you question us one at a time?" Thomas replied, a sudden thought coming to him out of his violence-addled brain.

The deputy sheriff, younger than Thomas by a few years, but with eyes that spoke to hard experience in his chosen field, raised an eyebrow. "Are you questioning me?"

"I'm an investigator, too, my good man, and separating witnesses is a much-admired practice amongst—"

"Yes, a psychical investigator, wasn't it? What is that? Looking for ghosts?"

"Not exactly," Thomas said.

"Deputy Miller, nobody here can question your dedication or your valor," Colonel Ramage declared broadly, coming over now. He had acquitted himself well during the attack in the garden, killing one of the outlaws and sheltering several of the female guests, all without ruining his dress uniform. He was a tall man, lean and lanky, with a powerful presence. At his rank and age—early fifties, Thomas judged—he was clearly used to being listened to and obeyed. "But clearly, they have a different way of doing things in England. Isn't that right, Mr. Leighton?"

"Err, quite," Thomas replied, not sure where this was going.

The deputy nodded. "Colonel. It's good to see you here tonight."

"I'd prefer it if we'd managed to kill more of the bastards and save poor Miss Roseingrave," he said, and clapped a heavy hand down on Thomas's shoulder, pushing him away. "If you don't mind, I'd like to speak with this one myself."

"Of course, sir."

The colonel didn't speak again until they were well out of earshot. "Psychical investigator, are you? I think we could use one of those right now." He led Thomas through the back door to the garden.

"I don't think this was done by spirits."

"Spirits." The colonel snorted. They both stepped out onto the back patio. Colonel Ramage closed the door carefully and looked around. "Tell anybody about this and I'll gut you myself, you understand?"

"Tell what?" Thomas asked, utterly confused now.

"This is pointless, wolf," somebody said from the séance table. A single lantern glowed there, a proper kerosene thing. Thomas realized it was the man who had saved the elder Miss Roseingrave. He was leafing through the sketchbook that the younger sister had drawn in. "What is this boy going to tell you?"

"He's with the Academy of Psychical Inquiry."

"And what are they? A pack of fat old scholars chasing their own tails."

"I want his opinion."

"Opinion on what?"

The colonel's eyes flashed gold as he glanced at Thomas. "You're an academic, yes? Somebody who studies the...supernatural?" And he walked over to the Irishman, holding out a hand. "Give me the book."

"Why should I?"

Colonel Ramage patted the sword at his side. Thomas had thought the weapon ceremonial, but the cavalry officer had used it to kill one of the attackers. "Iron is a component of steel, is it not?"

Miss Roseingrave's mysterious benefactor cocked his head, and then passed the sketchbook over to Colonel Ramage, who handed it in turn to Thomas.

Thomas had to step fully into the lantern light to see the drawing. He had not gotten a good look at it during the séance. On the pad, in a confident hand clearly trained for the task, was an artful sketch. It was of a narrow canyon, barely more than a cleft in the rock. A waterfall poured down a sheer cliff, and a cave mouth yawned beside it.

On the back of the opposite page were lines. Scratched, erratic lines.

And yet, when Thomas looked at it for a moment, he recognized a pattern within it. He frowned. How could that be?

"I recognized the men you killed back there, hill-dweller. Amos Newton," Colonel Ramage said, taking a seat himself. He pulled a pipe from a pocket, tamping a bit of tobacco down into it. "One of Eli Horn's boys."

"Eli Horn?" Thomas asked absently. Why did that name sound familiar?

The colonel struck a match, lighting his pipe. The scent of burning tobacco filled the night air. "Regional outlaw, as bad as they come. He's cut a path of terror from North Dakota to Mexico for the past fifteen years."

The stranger snorted. "Fifteen years and you haven't caught him? The American army has a wolf pack at their disposal and they can't catch one outlaw?"

"The bodies show the usual signs. Rapid aging, rusting weapons, and Diego, of course." Colonel Ramage gave a low growl, deep from his chest. "I know him, too. Almost the last of the damned Abbitt brood. But this"—and he indicated the notebook—"this is my true concern. This is Irish, is it not?"

"The most ancient of Irish writing," Thomas said, and laid the pad down. "I would need better light and my reference material to give you a proper translation of this all, as it does not seem to follow form."

"Form?"

"Most ogham script describes family relationships, as a means of identifying the individual. The Celts were highly tribal and—"

"You don't recognize any of it?"

Thomas pointed at the least warped line of script on the right side of the page. "This says 'father of B.'"

"B?" Colonel Ramage asked, eyebrow raised.

"I can't read the rest of it. It's not rendered properly."

"Pity," Ramage said, and took the sketchbook back.

"And what exactly are you planning on doing?" the Irishman asked.

"I shall do what I've been doing for the past fifteen years. Hunt Eli Horn down," the colonel replied.

"And not kill him," the Irishman replied sarcastically.

The colonel bristled. "You—"

"Clearly this hunt is beyond your abilities. The US military can't even get the Comanche under control. And this"—and the stranger waved a hand at the pad—"is far worse than anything you've faced before."

Thomas looked between them. "Forgive my ignorance, gentlemen, but what is going on here exactly?"

"Nothing you or I need concern ourselves with," the Irishman said, and stood. He took up his weapon, the strange native bow and its quiver Thomas had seen him with in the library. "Now, with your leave—"

"I have not given you permission to go anywhere."

And that was the elder Miss Roseingrave, standing on the back patio, arms crossed.

The stranger smiled at her. "You're alive. That's all that's required."

"Not tonight."

"My oath is fulfilled."

"It is not."

"It is," he said, and bowed his head a little. "As long as you are safe, your sister is of no concern to me."

"You'd let her die?"

The man shook his head and shoved back from the table, taking the sketch pad with him. "Good night to you all."

"You aren't going anywhere," Charlotte said, voice quavering a little. "I forbid it. You are going to help me find my sister."

Thomas was now thoroughly, thoroughly confused. He felt as if he had walked into some theater drama in the second act. He looked between them. "What am I missing here?"

Miss Roseingrave sighed. "This fine gentleman you see in front of you is bound to my family, sworn to the protection of our bloodline. Isn't that true?"

"You told me you don't believe in any of that," the Irishman said pointedly.

"And you said it doesn't matter what I believe. You are real, so I assume the rest of it's true, too," she said. The stranger said nothing. "I am going after my sister, and if you're to honor your oath, you'll have to accompany me."

The stranger looked to the colonel. "Would you mind, Colonel, letting me discuss this matter in private? This is family business."

The colonel gave him a hard look but stood. "This isn't the old world. Your kind don't hold power here. Mine do."

The Irishman gave a dramatic sigh. "No wonder this country's such a shambles."

"I'll keep the sheriff off of you, but I want you out of this town by tomorrow, hill-dweller."

"At the lady's pleasure, I'm sure."

And then, they were alone.

Charlotte settled down at the séance table, emotions warring within her.

Her grandmother had always told her stories of the family protector, an unfathomable creature who was bound to them. She had never believed it, though. How could she, when so much tragedy had befallen them? Why hadn't he saved Papa when Papa's ship went down with all hands in the Gulf? Why hadn't he saved Mama when her heart began to fail?

Why hadn't he saved Charlotte from the fire, all those years ago, the flames that still haunted her dreams?

And yet, here he was.

In the flesh. Smiling a mocking little smile at her. As if he was enjoying this.

"Charlotte," he acknowledged with a tip of his head, and held out Celeste's sketch pad to her.

She regarded him frostily.

He was a tall thing, lithe and lean, dressed in the finest and latest fashion. His clothing was impeccable, spotless and clean without a trace of the bloody fight from the study. His features were strong, and handsome, Charlotte supposed, if not for the uncomfortable otherworldliness that sat there. His fair hair was rather longer than most would keep it, pulled back again in a bunch at the back of his neck. His ears were ever so slightly pointed. But it was his eyes, his eyes, that gave him away as something other than a human man. Deep wells of emerald green, as ancient as the land around them.

He scared her.

"You know my name," she said, unable to keep the nervousness out of her voice. "What should we call you?"

"What are you?" Mr. Leighton added. "Colonel Ramage called you a hill-dweller. What does that mean?"

"He's one of the fair folk. The people of the hills," Charlotte said, miserable. "A faery. From Ireland, my family's country."

"Of a kind," the stranger replied. "It has been a long time since I was with my clan."

"Then perhaps the term 'fae' would be more accurate," Mr. Leighton said. "There are some now who are favoring that term as a means of properly encompassing the surprising breadth of—"

"Does this one ever shut up?" the stranger asked Charlotte and turned his attention to Mr. Leighton. "I am not some insect specimen for you to pin to a card and classify. But if you must call me something, Mr. Hallorman will suffice."

"A faery who calls himself Mister?" Mr. Leighton shook his head. "I do not mean this as an insult, Mr. Hallorman, but you do not strike me as a faery or fae or any other such thing. Not as I know them."

"Know us?" he snorted. "How would you know us? From books written by monks? Or perhaps from Tennyson poems? Your people behave like loggers in a forest, stripping bare things that they do not understand and can never replace, to be carted off and carved up for decoration in your homes."

"You've read Tennyson?" Mr. Leighton asked, pulling a small notebook from the inside of his jacket pocket. "That is fascinating. Can you tell me—"

Charlotte sighed and took the sketch pad. "Please do not antagonize him, Mr. Leighton," she said as she began to examine her sister's work. "He might choose to leave us entirely."

"Unfortunately, our current arrangement doesn't allow me to do so," Mr. Hallorman said. "You have ordered my involvement. I am now bound to see it through."

Charlotte bit her lip. "Invoking some kind of power—"

"Was not your intent, yes, I understand." He waved it away. "You have forsworn all utilization of your natural talents. And yet, how easy it is to forget your convictions when it is convenient."

"I find nothing convenient about my sister's kidnapping!" Charlotte snapped. The sketch on the paper in her hands was rendered in the usual fine detail—Celeste had always had an artistic hand—but it told Charlotte nothing on its own. "Who took her?"

"The gang that attacked this house tonight was an odd mixture," he said. "Mostly humans, but a few creatures among them. Men whose souls come in the shape of wolves."

Charlotte glanced over at Mr. Leighton. He was writing as fast as he could. Irritation spiked through her. She tried to set it aside. "That was the man you fought in the study, the one who looked so monstrous."

"Yes."

"Why did you need the letter opener?" she asked.

"The silver one that Mr. Barton had on his desk?" Mr. Leighton asked, still writing. "Werewolves are said to be repulsed by silver. So may we take that to be true?"

Mr. Hallorman looked at Charlotte. "Must I tolerate this Englishman?"

"Yes," she said, irritated now. "Now please, why was my sister kidnapped?"

"I have no idea. I assume that the posse that attacked tonight was acting on the orders of this Eli Horn that the colonel spoke of, but their reasons are not clear to me." Mr. Hallorman looked at the circle again. "I wonder, what power was being invoked here?"

"Aren't we taking a few liberties with the facts?" Charlotte asked. "Why should we assume that this circle and the séance and my sister's kidnapping are related?"

"Your sister was speaking of darkness," Mr. Hallorman said. "Darkness and somebody coming. She saw something. The ogham script provides it."

"Automatic writing is a farce," Charlotte protested.

Mr. Leighton shook his head. "On the contrary, the Academy has documented evidence that this may be one of the few true things to come out of séances."

Charlotte just stared at him.

"I am not here to debate the dubious value of the modern séance," Mr. Hallorman said, as the silence stretched out to an uncomfortable length, "but I can tell you that the fire in Denver that consumed what meagre resources you and your sister had, setting you on this course, was no accident."

"What?"

He waved that away. "I arrived too late to determine its cause. But it does seem clear to me that this séance was desired, perhaps even provoked."

"Provoked?" Mr. Leighton asked. "Are you saying this entire thing was a set-up merely to facilitate Miss Celeste Roseingrave's kidnapping?"

The faery didn't answer him, looking back to Charlotte instead. "What difference does it make now? If you are determined to retrieve your sister—"

"I am."

"Then we shall solve this mystery on the trail," the faery said, and pushed back from the table. "Get some rest. The next few days will be long and miserable, if we catch up to them at all."

"Ought we leave tonight?" Mr. Leighton asked.

Mr. Hallorman looked at him with an expression bordering on disgust.

"Of course not. We leave with the light. There is nothing we can do in the darkness. Besides, there is a chance, thin though it may be, that either the local sheriff or that damn wolf might catch them before they can get too far and save us all the trouble."

"But—" Charlotte began.

"That gang was mostly human. They won't get so far in the darkness, and you two will get nowhere. I assume you're going to insist on this soft-handed Londoner accompanying us?"

Charlotte realized Mr. Leighton was looking at her. She hadn't meant to drag him into this, but he was involved now, wasn't he? And in truth, she did not relish the idea of being alone in the wilderness, even for a day or two, with nothing but this...faery by her side. "Yes," she said. "But only if he'll come."

"Of course I will," he said. "Whatever I can do to make this right."

"Pity. I should have enjoyed the chance to glamour him," Mr. Hallorman said.

"And what's that?" Mr. Leighton asked, pencil back in hand.

Mr. Hallorman sighed dramatically. "Danu save me from the English."

BOOK TWO
SKY

CHAPTER FOURTEEN

Celeste woke the next morning with something poking her in the back. Something hard. No, everything was hard; she was on the ground, dirt below her fingers. She scraped at it, confused for a moment—had Reverend Hinkle really kicked them out so soon?—when it all came back to her.

The séance. The abduction. The wild ride through the night, thrown over some outlaw's saddle horn. Gunshots. Horses screaming. Then speed, the night air tearing loose her hair but unable to reach her lungs through the gag.

Eventually, all had gone black.

She was lying on the hard, bare ground, in a little hollow between a few large standing boulders, clustered so tight as to almost be a cave. Weak dawn light leaked around the edges and through the single open area, just in front of her. There was dead grass stuck in her hair now. What was this place, and more importantly, could she escape?

"Charlotte would love this," she muttered to herself as her fingers worked, picking out the grass. "Would probably tell me what a fool I was."

Charlotte. *Charlotte*. If Charlotte would have relented on her stance on séances months ago, then they could have easily earned enough for their tickets to San Francisco by now and Celeste could have been far away from all this damn frontier.

"Good. You're awake. 'Bout damn time."

It was a man, barely more than a silhouette in the weak light, eyes glowing gold, a bundle of clothes tucked under one elbow.

"Who are you?" she demanded, scared but determined not to show it.

"Lukas Abbitt, beggin' your pardon, ma'am." The man chuckled. Other voices, other laughter, joined in. More men outside the rocks, Celeste realized. Her heart sank. One man she could maybe talk her way past. Multiple would be much more difficult. "Ain't you gonna say 'thank you' for the hospitality, Miss Roseingrave?"

Heart hammering in her chest, she kept on a brave face. "Some hospitality, chaining up a woman like this."

More laughter came from behind him, and he threw that bundle at her. Clothes. A man's work shirt and trousers. "You're scared," he told her. "I can smell it on you. Now get dressed and be quick about it. We gots a lotta ground to cover today."

"I'm not going anywhere with you," Celeste said with the last bit of courage she had to summon.

Mr. Abbitt considered her refusal for a moment, then pulled out his revolver. Cocking the hammer back, he closed the distance between them and put the barrel to her forehead. "You've still got a sister, Miss Roseingrave," he growled. "If you don't behave all nice like, I can always go back and get her instead. The boss may not like it, but I figure you've both got the same blood, eh? That's all he usually cares 'bout."

The men around her were laughing uproariously now.

Celeste could feel herself starting to shake now, clutching the bundle.

He took a step back and waggled the gun at her. "Go on, missy."

"I shall not do anything with all these...onlookers."

Mr. Abbitt grinned at her, a lopsided, terrible grin. "You gonna deprive us of a little show? I thought you mediums were all about that sort of thing."

"I am not—"

But the protest died on her lips. He was pointing the gun at her again. "I was willin' ta risk it while you were still asleep, but I ain't turning my back on you awake. Get dressed."

"Fine," she said with as much dignity as she could muster. Then, laying the bundle aside, she started unbuttoning her bodice. It wasn't difficult; half the buttons were missing anyway, but her hands were shaking from shame and anger.

There were a few jeers at first, but the man who'd threatened her did push the posse back. Celeste ignored them as best she could, stripping down quickly. The clothes were too big for her. She left her boots on; there seemed to be no replacement for those. Then, tidying up her hair with as much dignity as was possible under the circumstances, she glared back at the man with gold eyes.

"That's better," he said, and indicated that she should follow him.

With no better option, she went.

Emerging from the rocks, Celeste saw men breaking up a rough, simple camp set among the pines. They were hidden in the wilderness, nowhere near anything that looked like a road. Her heart sank. There was no help here.

"Now, I'm to get you to the boss without a scratch on you, and that's what I aim to do," Mr. Abbitt said, and one of the men brought him a horse.

"Where are we going?" she asked.

"Don't make a damn bit o' difference to you, now does it? You ain't helpin' anyone. 'Cept maybe your sister by cooperating all nice like."

"Cooperate is all I do with her," Celeste grumbled to herself, but regretted it when he started laughing.

"You've got fire in your belly. The boss'll be pleased."

"Somebody ordered you to kidnap me?" she asked, incredulous.

"You think I waltzed on into civilization and took you all for myself, pretty as you please, thank you, ma'am?" Mr. Abbitt snorted, as if the very idea of it was unthinkable. "The boss wanted you snatched, so I did the snatchin'. Don't you worry your pretty little head. He has a way of makin' everything make sense." The man swung up onto the back of the saddle, keeping his feet out of the stirrups for the moment, and extended a hand down for Celeste. "Now if you please, miss. I'm gettin' mighty tired of threatenin' ta shoot you."

Celeste looked around again. The posse was substantial. Twelve, no, thirteen of them, and they all had horses. There was no way she could outrun them and nowhere to hide. Even if she could get away, they would find her and take her anyway. Or shoot her and go back for Charlotte. And as scared as Celeste was right now, she couldn't imagine Charlotte being able to handle something like this.

Her older sister was infuriatingly weak sometimes.

She took the hand and Mr. Abbitt hauled her up. His strength was shocking. She automatically shied away as he looped an arm around her waist. "Don't worry, miss, you and me gonna get to know each other real well."

Thomas had been under the impression that the new day would see them off in some dramatic fashion, galloping out of town into the sunrise.

Instead, it was all quite a bit more mundane.

And slow.

He woke and dressed quickly that morning, the sky barely light and the sun not yet above the edge of the mountain peaks. Thomas considered what to take very carefully. He was not unfamiliar with long rides, but this was no research expedition through the Scottish Highlands with no enemy more terrible than the local food.

No doubt they would need to ride fast and light, so most of his things would have to be left behind. He would have to ask Mr. Barton if that was alright. His notebooks would have to come, of course, and with the mystery of the ogham script to consider, a few reference books would be helpful as well. He would need something waterproof to wrap them in, and they would certainly need provisions, and—

His stomach grumbled at him.

Breakfast first, he decided.

The mansion was quiet, almost eerily so after the events of the night before. The bullet holes in the woodwork were invisible, all still cast in shadow. But there was light spilling from the front parlor, and it was there he headed.

Perhaps Mr. Barton had recovered sufficiently to make it down here. The silver baron struck Thomas as a man who was in constant motion.

But it was not Mr. Barton he found in the study.

"May I ask what you're doing?"

The elder Miss Roseingrave startled a bit. She was seated on one of the room's big armchairs, needle and thread in hand. Her fingers, stilled now momentarily, had been practically flying through the fabric. Thomas instantly felt guilty for interrupting her. But she just readjusted her thimble and kept working.

"I did not expect that anyone would be up so early. The light is better in here than in my room, and I lacked buttons to finish my work. Mrs. Coulton was kind enough to lend me a few," she said, continuing to work on a big length of black wool. "My apologies for the state you find me in."

She was not in her usual mourning dress. Instead, she wore an old housedress of deep blue calico, sprigged with tiny white and pink flowers. The color complimented her well, although Thomas had the impression that being seen out of mourning black was only increasing her already significant discomfort. Her face was flushed bright red, as though she was deeply embarrassed by all of this.

"You look fine," he said, and at that, she did look up. Thomas blanched. "Now it is I who must apologize. I did not mean for that to sound so—"

"Forward?" she asked, continuing to sew, fingers moving fast.

"Precisely so."

"It would not be the worst thing a man has ever said to me."

"What do you mean?"

"Some female mediums cultivate a salacious reputation, and there are still a distinct lack of women out here on the frontier. Men have a tendency to be very...direct," she replied shortly, as if eager to be done with the subject entirely. She picked up a button from a fine porcelain dish set on a side table. "Can I help you with something, Mr. Leighton?"

"No, no, I was merely wishing to..." And he trailed off. "What are you doing, if I may ask?"

She held up the wool she was working. It was the underskirt to her dress, Thomas realized, but partially disassembled. The front gore had separated from the two side gores almost the entire way up, with plackets and loops added. She was working on buttons.

"The modern cut of skirts is quite inappropriate for a trip on horseback," she told him. "I am modifying it."

"Might you not ride sidesaddle?" he asked. "There are some excellent models out there, I'm told, appropriate for cross-country pursuits."

"This is no hunt through the featureless countryside of your home, Englishman. Did you not see the mountains from the train?"

And that was Mr. Hallorman, still dressed in his long sack coat and silk waistcoat, sauntering in as if they were about to depart for the theater or a private dinner or some other such entertainment. He didn't bother to look at Thomas at all, instead nodding to Miss Roseingrave.

"Charlotte," he said. "You could always just procure yourself a pair of trousers. Instead, you wasted hours of rest time on this."

Miss Roseingrave threaded on the last button and pulled little scissors out of the holster hanging from her chatelaine to snip the thread. She didn't answer.

"What did you do with your petticoats?" Mr. Hallorman asked.

She didn't answer that either, standing and shaking out the skirt as she did so. Thomas realized the purpose of the loops. With the front gore detached from the sides, she would be able to sit astride a horse with little difficulty. The loops and buttons would allow her to close the skirt up again. The stitches on the plackets were nearly invisible. With her overskirt on, nobody would know the skirt had been altered at all.

"Clever," Thomas said, meaning it.

"It was my sister's design." And Miss Roseingrave held the thing across her chest like a shield. "I trust we'll be leaving as soon as we're able?"

"If that's what the lady commands," Mr. Hallorman replied, a mocking note in his voice.

"Then I suppose I command it," Miss Roseingrave told him, and all but fled the room.

The faery—still something Thomas could not quite credit—yawned and sat down in one of the small parlor's chairs, propping his feet up on the low center table. He looked around. "Do you think that servant woman is awake? Coffee sounds quite nice on a morning such as this." Then he looked at Thomas. "What is it, Englishman?"

"Beg your pardon?"

"Your thoughts are loud." The faery tapped his temple, dropping his feet again and leaning forward. "So what is it?"

Thomas realized then that he had no idea what this creature's abilities were. Even now, the Irish claimed that the fair folk possessed long life, the ability to change shape and cloud the minds of mortal men. Other stories referred to them as fallen angels, barely better than demons, although Thomas had always discounted this idea. But that was little to go on. Could this Mr. Hallorman truly read his mind? Know his thoughts?

It didn't matter, Thomas decided. They were to go on a journey together, he and Mr. Hallorman, and beginning that journey with lies did not seem like a good idea.

"I was just wondering...the stories about the fae don't exactly mention coffee."

Mr. Hallorman snorted. "Now I think you are using that term deliberately to anger me."

"What name would you give to—"

"Do you think me a fool, Englishman? To know the true name of a thing is to know it fully and thus, have power over it. Why would I help you with your little notes?" And Mr. Hallorman gestured contemptuously at the little book in Thomas's hand. The researcher hadn't even realized that he'd pulled it out. Feeling awkward, he tucked it away again. "But to answer your question, I do like coffee. And my people would have liked it, had we had it. What do you think we were? Angels, elevated far above the plane of earthly experiences? Hardly. We ate, we drank, we made love, made war, when and where and how we pleased. We were creatures of the earth, Englishman, who enjoyed our pleasures as much as any human ever could. More, I'd say. And while my kin have all withdrawn into the hills, I am still as bound to the corporeal realities of this world as you are."

"You speak of pleasure in this world, but you sound as if you resent it."

"Of course I do. Do you think it is by my will I am here? Do you think I have any desire to go chasing this darkness through the mountains? I do not. All the more reason to enjoy what I can. Now," he said, and stood, "let us go find that servant woman. There is much that needs to be done today, and I do not fancy doing any of it on an empty stomach."

CHAPTER FIFTEEN

Mrs. Coulton was soon found and persuaded to cook up breakfast for them both. Americans seemed to have an unhealthy obsession with beef, Thomas noted, as that was what the offering was: a thinly beaten piece of meat, dredged in flour and fried, then smothered with something Mrs. Coulton called red-eye gravy.

Mr. Hallorman insisted on eating right there in the kitchen, plate perched on the edge of a wood worktable, cutting off neat bits of steak with his strange black glass knife. Thomas was not exactly comfortable with the arrangement—it seemed quite the imposition on Mrs. Coulton, who was busy with breakfast preparations—but the dour woman warmed quickly to the presence of the faery. She even offered to go pack a few saddlebags for them before moving on to her other duties that morning.

Still smiling, she departed for the larder.

Leaving Thomas alone with Mr. Hallorman.

As he ate, Thomas considered the situation. He could not quite bring himself to believe that the creature in front of him was some figure out of Irish folklore. He wondered if he had ever truly believed his own assertions that folklore carried truth, that if spirits were real, then other beings might also be found by science someday.

It seemed like utter foolishness now.

Mr. Hallorman shot Thomas a baleful look. "Are you going to make notes of my eating habits?" he asked, and speared himself another bite of his own steak, sweeping it through the remainder of the gravy that coated the fine china plate. "Will my every move be documented for science?"

"No," Thomas said, searching for something to say. His eyes fell on the knife. "Er, what is that?"

Mr. Hallorman held up the black blade. A drop of gravy fell from its tip. "This?" he asked.

"That."

"Obsidian," he replied, and shoved another bite of breakfast into his mouth, chewing and talking at the same time. "A material much beloved before the Spanish brought gunpowder and steel. The humans used to use it to cut people's hearts from their chests. Fascinating practice, wouldn't you say?"

"I notice you carry a bow as well," Thomas continued, refusing to be baited. "Is that a, ahh, personal preference? Or does the, er, faery's rumored aversion to iron extend to all ferrous metals?"

"Ferrous metals." Mr. Hallorman finished his steak and reached for a dish towel on which to wipe his knife. "I don't think I care much for you, Englishman."

"I have done nothing to you, my good man."

"Nothing?" the faery demanded, teeth bared like an angry fox. There was something in Mr. Hallorman's eyes, his face, his very presence, something ancient and wild and very, very dangerous. "Nothing at all, Englishman? You sure of that?"

But what Mr. Hallorman meant, Thomas did not find out, because the kitchen door banged open at that moment and interrupted them.

"Now where in tarnation is my breakfast? Mrs. Coulton!"

It was Mr. Barton, standing there in the doorway. He looked terrible, leaning hard on the doorjamb, livid bruising covering most of his face, left eye completely black. He had a splint on his right hand, holding his last three fingers stiffly straight.

"She's packing a few saddlebags for us," Mr. Hallorman said, nonchalant once again. "We are going after Miss Celeste Roseingrave this morning, you know."

Mr. Barton grunted, then yelled again. "Mrs. Coulton!"

"Right here, sir," the housekeeper replied, reemerging from the pantry with a pair of full saddlebags. Miss Roseingrave was at her side.

"So you mean to follow your sister yourself?" Mr. Barton asked her.

Miss Roseingrave nodded. "Yes."

"It will be a rough road, Miss Roseingrave," Mr. Barton said, and looked down at his ruined hand. "Damn the authorities. They've failed to catch this Eli Horn for far too many years already, and look what happened? My new house damaged, my guests shot at, blood all over the floor of my study!"

"My apologies," Mr. Hallorman said, without a trace of regret in his voice at all.

Mr. Barton waved it away. "I'd come with you, put a bullet in Horn myself, if I was able to hold a set of reins. Nothing happens out west here unless one does it for oneself."

"Indeed," Mr. Hallorman said drily.

Mr. Barton nodded. "So, what can I do to assist? Horses?"

"I'll see to that," Mr. Hallorman replied.

"I am afraid I don't have any sidesaddles, Miss Roseingrave," the silver baron said, glancing at Charlotte.

She smoothed down her skirt. It truly was good work, Thomas found himself thinking. He never would have known she'd done anything to it if he hadn't seen her working on it. "I can ride astride when the situation calls for it," she said.

That got another nod, more approving this time, from the silver baron. "How about guns?"

Mr. Barton led them to a smaller room on the second floor that had not been open the night before for the party, and it was no surprise why: the room was filled with lovingly crafted wooden cases, long guns held in vertical rows like soldiers on a parade ground. Another cabinet held pistols in drawers. Unlike one lord's firearms collection back home, though, these were not highly decorated and lightly employed. These guns were all clearly utilitarian, meant to be used, and used hard.

"You have all this in your house?" Thomas wondered, looking around.

"Safest place for them," Mr. Barton replied easily. "Standard issue for my supervisors and foremen. This way, I know what they're carrying has been cared for right and won't jam."

"You supply your employees with guns?" Thomas asked.

"You have ammunition in here?" Mr. Hallorman asked, pulling out drawers.

"Of course," Mr. Barton said, pointing. "Bottom case."

"Charlotte," Mr. Hallorman said, indicating a drawer filled with small revolvers to her. She took one, a little awkward. "And you, Englishman? What'll be your pleasure?"

Thomas looked around. There must have been forty rifles in the room, but most were the same model. "I recognize these," he said, reaching for one. "Winchesters, I presume?"

"1873 repeater models, yes," Mr. Barton said, sitting down in the room's only chair. "I use those for my boys. Don't take any skill to achieve a rapid-fire response. Takes the same ammunition as those revolvers in there. Best gun to have on you out in the mountains."

"Are you worried about wild animals?"

"Shoot a bear with that, all you shall do is make it angry," Mr. Hallorman said. "You know how to use any of this, Englishman?"

"Of course," Thomas said, bristling. He reached for one of the rifles, lifting it, sighting it, barrel away from his companions. It was lighter than his father's old hunting rifle, and the pump-action features were unfamiliar. But it looked like a good-quality gun, and he said so.

"It's yours," Mr. Barton said. "Outlaws, in my house, killing my guests." He shook his head. "It's a bad business."

"You have no idea, Mr. Barton. Thomas, find a pistol you like." Mr. Hallorman tossed Thomas a hip holster and belt he'd pulled from a drawer. "Now, Barton, do you have any trail kit on hand? Bedrolls, pans, tinder and flint, that sort of thing?"

Mr. Barton sighed. "You'll want to see Mikael over at Black Mountain Mercantile for that."

"Mikael?" Thomas asked sharply. "The same Mikael Dvalinsson we encountered yesterday?"

"Indeed so. He owns the best dry goods store in town, along with the brewery, a water lease, and a few other odd and sundry businesses. You could go see Atkins, of course, but he charges more for lesser quality, and besides," Mr. Barton said, his tone dropping, "Dvalinsson owes me."

"Dvalinsson," Mr. Hallorman mused, still looking over the gun cases. "Now why does that name sound familiar?"

"Probably because that family of industrious miniature Germans is all over this state. Now, I can show you the way if..." And he trailed off, trying but failing to rise from his seat. He rubbed a hand across his brow, clearly frustrated. "I'll write you out a list of what all you'll need, if somebody will be kind enough to bring me some paper. Tell Mikael to put it all on my account. He's usually open early. But you'll have to go there yourself, I'm afraid."

"Just provide the directions," Mr. Hallorman said as Thomas tore a page from his notebook and held it out.

"Send Mrs. Coulton up when you leave," Mr. Barton said, taking both paper and pencil from Thomas. "And tell her I want my breakfast ready. I'm so damn hungry I could eat an elephant."

It was still quiet when they headed across town. The sun had not yet crested over the high mountains and much of Leadville was cast in shadow. It was cold; Mrs. Coulton had pressed a trail coat on Thomas before they had left the mansion. It was used, worn and patched in places, and slightly too large, but it kept the chill away.

If the elder Roseingrave sister was cold, wrapped in another borrowed overcoat, she gave no sign. She had spoken little this morning, and Thomas wondered if she felt the same as he did, like she was baggage being carted along by somebody far more experienced in these matters.

Projection, perhaps. And pragmatic; Thomas was a stranger in this rugged land, and suspected that his experience megalith hunting would be of little use. But meager experience was still experience, and he hoped he could bring it to bear for Miss Roseingrave. He did not like the idea of leaving her to the tender mercies of that faery who claimed to be bound to her.

The dry goods store sat on the south end of town. Mr. Hallorman had promised to meet them there with the horses; four or five, he deemed, would be necessary for this. He had not said where he intended to get them, nor how he would pay for them. Thomas wasn't sure he wanted the details.

"Are you alright with this?" he asked, pausing before he rapped on the door. "He was quite rude to you yesterday."

Miss Roseingrave looked at him, as if startled from some deep contemplation, and pulled her borrowed jacket tighter around her. The door faced west, and they were fully in shadow. "I have been called worse than 'witch' over the years."

Thomas nodded. But his knuckles never landed on the rough wood door. Before he had the chance to do anything, the door jerked open, and Mr. Dvalinsson was standing there in a leather apron, glaring at them.

"Well?" he demanded.

"My good man," Mr. Leighton began, "we are—"

"About to do something insanely stupid," the man snapped, but stepped away from the door anyway, leading them inside. "Well, don't stand out there like the fools that you are. Come in, and let's see what I can do for you."

Black Mountain Mercantile was a well-provisioned and exceptionally neat shop, two things that Thomas would have expected from one of German extraction. A pair of boys were waiting behind the counter; not Dvalinsson's sons, Thomas thought, as they had different coloring and were of standard height.

Mr. Dvalinsson took the list that Mr. Barton had written with surprising care; his hands looked as if they could have crushed bare rock, but he handled the paper delicately. "He might be a fool, but he knows these mountains," the prospector grunted. "But provisions for three. I don't suppose Barton's coming with you?"

"It's another man," Miss Roseingrave supplied. "A friend of the family, somebody who is deeply concerned for me and my sister."

Mr. Dvalinsson grunted again and passed the list off to one of the boys. They immediately got to work, pulling goods, rolling blankets, filling bags.

Thomas asked for a few things himself: a set of charcoal pencils, a fresh notebook, and a waterproof oilcloth wrapper for his books. The only things Miss Roseingrave requested were a hairbrush and a hat. Mr. Dvalinsson had a wide-brimmed rabbit-wool model in her size and handed it over himself.

"Thank you," she said, trying it on for fit. "I'm surprised to see a ladies' model here."

"You'd be surprised how many womenfolk I see come through this shop," he said.

Miss Roseingrave set the hat carefully down on the counter again, looking across the shop to where the boys were weighing out hardtack. "If you'll excuse the question, Mr. Dvalinsson, are you by chance related to the Mr. Dvalinsson that runs a jewelry store in Denver?"

"He's my cousin." The stocky man gave her a curious look. "Why do you ask?"

"The proprietor there refused to buy my chatelaine," she said, and pulled the little thing from her pocket, handing it across the counter. "Do you know why?"

This Mr. Dvalinsson took it gingerly, turning it over. Then he shook his head and handed it back. "Do you have any idea what this is?"

"It's a brooch my great-grandmother brought from Ireland."

"There ain't one of my clan who would take that on."

"Your cousin said much the same thing. Why?"

He smiled at her. "It's got magic beaten into it, seeress. Old magic. Deep magic. Powerful."

"Magic?" Thomas asked, a little startled.

"That's the English word for it, isn't it?"

"But magic?" Thomas repeated. "What do you know about—"

A glare from Mr. Dvalinsson silenced him. One of the boys came over to grab a box off a shelf behind them, and the prospector waited for him to leave before speaking again. "I prayed that Barton's plan to get Madame Aine up here would come to naught, but the old gods don't hold much sway in this world anymore, and Barton's a stubborn ass of a man. I tried to warn him directly, but he didn't want to listen."

"Do you know what took Miss Celeste Roseingrave?" Thomas asked, intrigued now.

"Between the ogham and the iron, I'd say it's something that hails from the islands," the strange little man said. "And if it is one of them who's taken your sister, Miss Roseingrave, there's only one reason for them to do that."

"Which is...?" she asked hesitantly.

"To drag her back to their realm, their corner of the Otherworld," he said, matter-of-fact about it, as if they were discussing the weather. "That's what those types always do in the end."

"Why do you say that?" Thomas asked.

For a little while, the prospector didn't answer, leaning on the edge of the counter. Finally, he roused himself, but his voice was quiet now, thoughtful instead of bombastic. "A word of warning to you, seeress. Your power hangs uneasily on you, but hang it does. Like a lamp in the night. Anything there can see it. Anything might be drawn in. Including those things that live in the deep places, the forgotten places. Things you might not want to deal with."

"I know," she said quietly.

"Then you be careful, Miss Roseingrave. That mine my nephew found was bad news, the sort of place one doesn't find often in this world. You go through that, step wrong, and you'll find yourself in one of those places where monsters still dwell." Then he pulled back, frowning across the shop. "Now, let's see if those boys have your kit ready to go."

They did indeed, it seemed, and just as the boys took the first armloads of gear out to the front of the mercantile shop, Mr. Hallorman arrived riding on a fine buckskin mare, three other horses in tow, compact animals mottled with huge spots of brown and black. Paints, Miss Roseingrave told him. They appeared both hardy and restless, as eager to start their day's labors as any other American Thomas had met here.

Mr. Dvalinsson came out to the front of the store to supervise the loading of the animals, but when he caught sight of Mr. Hallorman, his demeanor grew even more stony.

The faery would not even deign to look at the man.

Interesting, Thomas thought, and made a note in the book he always kept in the left interior breast pocket of his jacket.

The mercantile shop door slammed shut.

Mr. Dvalinsson was nowhere to be seen.

Only now did Mr. Hallorman hop down off his horse. The beaded fringe on his Sioux quiver clacked together. He clearly meant to direct the loading of the animals, but the boys were clearly used to this kind of thing and moved well.

"Where are you off to?" one boy asked as he worked. "Ain't no prospectin' trip, I reckon, this late in the year and all."

"Hunting monsters," Mr. Hallorman replied as he buckled the saddle-bags on his own mare.

The boy smiled at him. "Sounds like fun," he said.

"You have no idea."

"Why say something like that to him?" Miss Roseingrave asked as they were on their way again, headed out of town.

"He wanted an answer, that was the answer," Mr. Hallorman replied.

"And what of our answers?" Thomas pressed. "What manner of monster are we hunting? What could cause the strange decaying effect we saw in Mr. Barton's garden? I know we have the ogham script to indicate there is some connection to Irish mythology, but I confess, I cannot figure it out."

Hallorman said nothing. Miss Roseingrave sighed. "Mr. Hallorman, if I must bid you answer every time our companion here asks you a direct question..."

"Yes, yes," he grumbled, and shook his head. "I have my suspicions, of course, but naming an evil can draw it in. I do not wish to invoke anything. We shall not speculate on this matter further."

"But surely we must determine what we are up against!" Thomas protested.

"Why, Englishman?" Mr. Hallorman asked derisively. "So you can kill it yourself? You're here at the lady's behest only. Beyond being some kind of interesting bauble for her purse, I deem you irrelevant to this pursuit. Now" —and he sniffed the air—"we are fortunate we are already on the south side of town. The trail leads this way."

"How can you tell?" Miss Roseingrave asked.

"The reek of the gang's leader lingers even now," Hallorman said, adjusting the strap of his quiver across his chest. The beaded fringe whispered as it moved. "I'll be able to find him, as long as he does not get too far ahead of us."

"Reek?" Thomas asked.

"Wolves always stink," he said flatly.

Thomas wanted to ask what Mr. Hallorman meant by that, but the strange creature spurred his horse into a canter without a shred of additional explanation.

The hunt was on.

CHAPTER SIXTEEN

Under different circumstances, the day might have been a pleasant one.

Celeste was not quite sure where they were headed, but it seemed to be south, down through the valley that the train had passed through on its way north to Leadville. The countryside rolled by more slowly than on the train, and they were far from those tracks, but the far distant mountain peaks were somewhat recognizable. Celeste could pick out no specific features, however. Perhaps a woman raised here or one ranching here would be able to read such things with little difficulty. But the wilds of the Rockies were not Celeste's area of expertise.

What was, however, was people.

The posse that had snatched her back in Leadville was an unpleasant group. They were all rough men, prone to outbursts of brutal laughter and the tellers of terrible jokes. A few had thick Spanish accents, but that was not rare in this part of the country. They all spoke English, and they all had the easy attitudes of men who had worked alongside each other for many years.

They were older, too, or at least, they seemed old. There wasn't one of them that didn't have a tremble in his hands or the telltale stiffness of arthritis. Gray streaked their temples and wrinkles creased their faces. Only Mr. Abbitt seemed relatively young, and even he must have been in his early forties.

Strange. Celeste would have thought that men in the banditry business would be younger. Prematurely aged, perhaps, by hard living and long rides under the brutal Colorado sun. This could not be a lifestyle that was good for one's health.

They rode long and hard that day, stopping only when the sun was high overhead and they were passing a small stream. Both men and horses drank at the same time, the water getting confused from so many hands and muzzles. When Celeste turned up her nose at it, Lukas rolled his eyes but handed her his canteen. He had filled it upstream. Crystal clear and cold it was.

"Thank you," she told him. It didn't hurt to be polite. Not if one wanted to gain trust enough to sleep without being confined or to perhaps even get her own horse. Celeste knew she could not fight her way out of this mess, nor would she last long in the harsh mountains on her own. But there were many little settlements up here, and surely they would pass by one of those eventually. If she could charm her way free, escape close to one of those...

Mr. Abbitt smiled at her. There was definitely something wrong with his teeth, like they didn't fit in his head quite right. "Yer welcome, missy."

The afternoon brought more of the same miserable riding, out of the plains and up the slope of the mountains, into the forests that stood there. Flat land gave way to rolling, folded hills, and soon, a house appeared in the distance, perched on the crest of a far ridge.

"Don't get yer hopes up," Mr. Abbitt told Celeste in a half-mocking voice. "That ain't anybody who's gon' help you."

Riding into the homestead, the place looked to be in excellent repair, snug and homey, but it was silent. No children. No livestock. The silence was discomforting. What did it mean?

They all dismounted in the main yard between the buildings, Celeste struggling to stand as she was pulled off the horse by rough hands. There was laughter, coarse and mean, from the assembled group of men, and one of them yanked her up to standing.

"Lucky you, Lukas, havin' this in your lap all day!" the man laughed.

"Don't think so, Will. She moves around so much it's gonna wreck my horse's back."

The outlaw leered at her. "Whaddaya think? You give me the same courtesy of...movin' around?"

"Get off me," Celeste snapped, trying to wrench her arm away.

"Will," Mr. Abbitt warned, still atop his horse. He tossed the reins down now, though, starting to dismount. "Will, leave her alone."

"Why, so you can have all the fun?" the man laughed. He squeezed down on her arm; Celeste yelped.

"What are you gonna do to her exactly?"

Celeste was yanked back again. "Just havin' a little fun, Lukas."

"You heard what the boss said 'bout her. Unspoiled."

"I ain't gonna spoil her."

"I'm in charge here. I say what goes, and I say, we don't touch her."

"You're in charge for now. But maybe that can change, eh?"

For a moment, the two men stared at each other.

Then another voice broke in.

"Lukas, Will, you're scaring our poor guest half to death. Lukas, calm down. Will, let go of her."

The outlaw turned. "Boss, I ain't..."

"Let her go, Will. And I'll forgive the affront."

That voice was quiet, calm, collected. But like the rumble of distant thunder across the plains, it carried with it a threat. A promise of violence. A barely concealed sense of malice.

The man holding her arm turned pale. Released her immediately.

She followed his gaze. Another man had just walked up.

Tall and pale, long hair the color of wet ash falling around his shoulders. A battered, wide-brimmed Stetson hat sat on his head, casting his features in shadow. He was dressed the way the rest of them were, in simple clothes that had seen better days, and a long, ragged duster hung from his broad shoulders. A pair of well-used and well-cared-for guns were slung about his waist on hip holsters. His books were caked with dust. He could have been any man out here on the frontier.

But somehow, Celeste knew that wasn't the case. There was something about this man. Something she couldn't quite put her finger on. Something...unfathomable. Something familiar.

"Lukas," the man said. "I count three men lost, including your cousin. What happened?"

Celeste glanced over at Mr. Abbitt, whose body language had become submissive, almost fearful. Everyone else, standing in a loose circle around the three of them, seemed likewise subdued. It was as if water had been thrown on a fire.

They were afraid of this man.

"Ramage was there, boss," Mr. Abbitt said, almost apologetic.

"Colonel Ramage killed Diego?" The man's eyes narrowed. "You saw this?"

"Beggin' pardon and all but no. Ramage killed Timms. Diego went inside, he and Amos. Neither one came out." He shrugged. "No time to check what got 'im, boss. We got the girl and got out, like you said. Musta been that whelp of his that did it."

"Ramage never does go anywhere without that pathetic puppy following him," the newcomer said. "Pity about your cousin, eh?"

Mr. Abbitt shrugged. "Never did much like him, boss. But I'm sore 'bout losin' the chance to even the score with his killer."

The boss barked out a laugh and waved it off. "Don't worry, you'll have your chance to pay Ramage back for Diego and Cody and all the rest all too soon. All grudges will soon be satisfied. I'm sure you lads all acquitted yourselves well," he said, speaking now to the larger assembly. "It ain't easy when the full weight of the US government is on your tail. Bastards never do give us a moment's peace, do they?" There were a few murmurs, a few nods. The attitude, Celeste noticed, was shifting. Away from fear and toward something more eager. "But with her now, that all changes." Then his gaze fell on Celeste. "You sure she's the right one, Lukas? I rely on your nose for this."

"She looks right. And she was doin' the séance, like you said, boss."

The boss nodded, and his full attention fell on her. It was like staring into a hurricane. Celeste fought hard to meet his eye.

Here was the man she'd have to charm in order to get herself out of this mess.

"Forgive Will," he told her, almost kindly now. "The lads, they sometimes get a little overenthusiastic. But I assure you, no harm will come to you in your time with us. I trust you had a pleasant journey?"

"Pleasant?" she demanded, unable to stop herself, despite the situation. "There is nothing pleasant about being kidnapped."

Gray eyes watched her for a moment more. "Come in," he finally said to her, and gestured at the house. "Let us talk in private."

Hesitating for a second more, she looked around again. One man, or a dozen? "Who are you?" she asked.

He smiled at her. "They call me Eli Horn, Miss Roseingrave. Pleasure to make your acquaintance."

Eli Horn. She knew that name. She knew that face.

It was on wanted posters in every town and city and train station she'd been in for the past ten years.

"I must apologize for my man out there," Mr. Horn told her as he led Celeste into the kitchen. He placed his hat down on the linen tablecloth that covered the small table. The room was warm and smelt strongly of coffee; there was a pot brewing on the cast-iron stove, she realized. "They've been on the road for a long time, and they don't have much experience with the fairer sex. Please..." And he gestured at the stove. "Have a drink. Or help yourself to anything else you might like. There is still fresh bread in the cupboard there, and apples, too, I believe."

Celeste looked at the stove, then back to him, confused now. "What does the outlaw Eli Horn need with a farmhouse?"

"I never said it was mine, did I? Now please, Miss Roseingrave, get yourself some refreshment and sit down."

The last two words were still quiet, but far more forceful now. She found herself almost compelled to obey, and coffee did sound quite good. Celeste moved the pot off the heat, wrapping a cloth around the handle to do so, and poured herself a cup. There were indeed apples in the cupboard, but that was far too messy a thing to eat right now. She poured a second cup for the outlaw and brought them both over to the table.

His mouth quirked up in a grin. "Awfully considerate of you, Miss Roseingrave."

"You said you wanted to make this civilized," she replied, sitting down. Moving in the trousers felt strange. No skirt to sweep away. No bustle to consider. She felt naked, and the weight of this man's gaze wasn't helping. "So let me be civilized. Give me my dress back."

He laughed. "I have heard of your talents, but not your wit. What a fine thing to discover."

"You know who I am?" she asked, confused.

"Charlotte Rosengrave, the eldest daughter of Aine Roseingrave," he said expansively, and sipped at his coffee. "One of very few women on this entire continent who is possessed of the true Sight."

It was only with a supreme effort that Celeste kept herself in check. It was a pronouncement that demanded a response, however, so she choked one out. "My mother's name was Anna, Mr. Horn."

He chuckled. "What is a name, Miss Roseingrave? Anna may have been written on her birth certificate, or whatever it is that humans in these times do to codify such matters, but Aine was the name under which she labored, and the name that she used when claiming her power. Aine was the truth of her."

Celeste's head swam, trying to pull together the disparate threads of this conversation into some kind of sense. This outlaw Eli Horn had taken her because he thought she was Charlotte. He believed her mother to have genuine talent. He thought she herself had genuine talent. So that meant he wanted her for that. But why?

"Sir, if you wished to hire me for a séance, you could have just asked."

He laughed. Despite his rough appearance, it was a beautiful sound. So strange, she found herself thinking. "I am not exactly welcome in the kind of company you keep," he replied, smiling. "But my goals are larger than a simple séance. All my work, all my plans, and here you are."

"What plans?"

He picked up his coffee, pacing away toward the glass-paneled window over the kitchen sink. The sun was already behind the mountains to the west, but the day was not nearly done yet. Threadbare curtains hung in front of it. "Back home, Miss Roseingrave, there are many ways, many paths, one might follow into the old places, the deep places. And yet, all are barred to me. So I came here, you see, to the New World. Such paths are far less common here. Long have I searched, and only this year have I found what I need."

"Sir, I'm not sure I understand your meaning," she said honestly.

He turned, giving her a curious, confused look. "Can you not see... Ah, but then, you wouldn't. You see a human man standing before you, do you not?"

"What else would I see?" she challenged, mind still racing. What was this? It was a risk, responding that way, provoking him.

But his manner only grew melancholy. "What else indeed?"

"Sir," she pressed, "whatever it is you need, whatever trouble you may be in with the law, it did not require that you steal me from Mr. Barton's home."

"But it does, Miss Roseingrave," he told her. "It does. We have a long journey ahead of us, and we shall have to move quickly if we are to arrive in time."

"Séances do not normally require journeys."

"Did you not hear what I said to you? I do not want you for a séance. I need you to help me part the mists. To help me cross back into Tir na nAill."

And then, Celeste realized what he was talking about. Even if it made no sense at all. "You wish... you wish to go to Faeryland?" she asked, and then risked another smile, another little bit of wit, to cover up her own growing fear. She was in the clutches of a madman, it seemed. "I do not think there are horses to steal or stagecoaches to rob there."

"No, Miss Roseingrave, I do not go there to raid, although it is a fine idea. I merely wish to go home."

Before she could say anything, the outlaw Eli Horn squeezed his hand shut around the tin coffee mug he was holding. There was a slight creak, a sigh. Then the mug was no more, and dust was running from his closed fist.

Something ancient burned in his eyes.

"And you, my little fáith, are going to help me."

The sun was already behind the mountains by the time Mr. Hallorman steered them into a protected little dell. They had been working their way down the long narrow valley for most of the day; it had been almost noon when they set out from Leadville, and according to the little pocket watch on Charlotte's chatelaine, it was only around five.

"Why have we stopped?" she asked, spurring her horse forward.

"It will get dark quickly now," the faery told her, and gave his horse a pat. "Best care for the animals and bed down while there's still a little light left."

"But my sister could still be miles away."

"They're riding hard, it's true, but even they will be at the mercy of their horses and the light," he told her. "This is not a hunt that shall be finished in a single day."

"But—"

"Whatever this Eli Horn may be," Mr. Hallorman told her, and swung out of his saddle, "I should not like to encounter him in the dark."

He laid his reins across the back of his horse's neck. Where he had acquired the animals, Charlotte didn't know. They weren't the proper matched team that had pulled Mr. Barton's buggy the day before. These were mustangs, the same horses that might have been ridden by the Ute. They all seemed fond of Mr. Hallorman, though, and Charlotte's horse ambled over to him now, pushing its head into his hand.

"How then are we planning on rescuing Miss Celeste Roseingrave from these men?" Mr. Leighton said, dismounting himself.

Mr. Hallorman shot him a nasty look as he rubbed the horse's forelock. "A question you should have asked before we departed Leadville, Englishman."

"We will make it happen," Charlotte said firmly. "We shall find some opportunity. We will get my sister back."

Mr. Hallorman just grunted and began working on his horse's saddle girth.

Charlotte's horse, perhaps excited by the sight of its companion having its tack pulled, would not settle down enough for her to dismount. Mr. Leighton was obliged to hold its bridle so she could slide, awkwardly, from the saddle. The faery watched with derision in his eyes but made no effort to either help or explain his thoughts.

Making camp was a simple task, but one Charlotte was grateful for. While on her horse, she had felt as though she could ride for miles more, even through the dark. On the ground now, she realized just how tired she actually was.

They untacked the horses, gathered wood, shook out bedrolls still smelling of the factory, and settled in. Mr. Leighton, to her surprise, was handy with the flint and tinder that Mr. Hallorman had brought. They soon had a pleasant fire going, sausages and beans heating in a little Dutch oven in its flames.

"You've done this before?" Charlotte asked Mr. Leighton. The faery had stepped away; just out of the ring of firelight, she could see him rubbing down one of the horses with a handful of dry grass. She was working on buttoning up the last of her skirt's new closures. The arrangement was not the most comfortable thing in the world, but it had functioned well enough today. She felt a pang of guilt; Celeste had been so excited at her own invention, and Charlotte had been so dismissive of it. And here she was, taking advantage of her sister's cleverness. Something Charlotte would have to apologize for when she found Celeste again.

"I've undertaken several long trips through Scotland and western Ireland over the past few years," he told her. His spectacles glinted in the firelight as he cleaned them with a soft cloth from a pocket. "Those have been solo affairs, however, and without the sense of urgency we have now. Even Scotland's tallest peaks there do not compare to these." And he waved a hand at the dark line of mountains all around them, nearly black against the last light of the fading day. Stars were beginning to peek out now, sharp and bright. "And we do not have fae outlaws there."

He was smiling, she realized. An attempt at a joke maybe. But Charlotte did not much feel like laughing. "What were you looking for?"

"Monuments," he told her. "While most modern archaeology focuses on unraveling the mysteries of the more impressive ruins that dot the empire and much of Europe, there is much to be learned in our own lands. The ancient peoples of Britain built circles and barrows and even houses out of vast slabs of stone. Some of these are well known today, but there are plenty left to be discovered and studied by science."

"Barrows?"

"Tombs," he told her, and pulled out a well-worn journal. "See? We believe that sometimes entire generations of families may be interred together."

Charlotte looked at the illustration. It had been drawn in a careful but confident hand and passed over with watercolors. It was a great stone doorway leading into the darkness under a hill. A man-made hill, she assumed; more stones lined the perimeter, as if forming a stockade wall around the green, grassy top. "You draw well," she said, and handed it back.

"Entirely self-taught, I assure you," he told her. "My father didn't hold with such things."

His words were carefully neutral, but Charlotte still heard the bitterness there. It was something he clearly did not wish to elaborate on, and so, Charlotte did not pursue it.

"My mother was quite enthusiastic for us to learn both sketching and painting. She hired tutors for us wherever we went," she told him instead.

"That must have been nice."

"She wanted us to be able to assist with automatic drawing sessions during séances," she told him, and stirred the beans in the pot. "How do we know when this is ready?"

"Oh," he said, and smiled ruefully. "Whenever it's hot."

She picked up a spoonful of beans and let them drop again, watching them steam. "I would say we are there."

"I'll find the bowls," Mr. Leighton said, and went for one of the packs. "Mr. Hallorman, I say! Supper is ready!"

"Stop shouting," the faery grumbled, coming back into the circle of firelight. He stepped right past Mr. Leighton and reached into another pack, coming out with a set of tin plates and spoons. "You'll wake every creature between here and Denver, carrying on like that."

"I barely raised my voice."

Mr. Hallorman ignored him and took the ladle from Charlotte, dishing up a portion of beans and passing them to her. She took it, somewhat surprised by the gesture, but he didn't give her the space to comment on it. He served himself next and lounged back, legs folded and plate balanced on a knee.

Going for the last plate that Mr. Hallorman had left by the fire, Mr. Leighton was frowning. "It's not my intent nor my desire for things to be unpleasant between us," he said, grabbing the ladle. "If there is something I can do, Mr. Hallorman—"

"Oh, you were speaking to me?" the faery replied, contempt in his words.

"Gentlemen! We cannot be at odds," Charlotte said, glancing between them both. "If we are to get my sister back, we must be of one purpose."

The faery waved a hand at Mr. Leighton. "Charlotte, the oath that was made, seconding me in perpetuity to the protection of your family's bloodline, was made only to you. It was not made to whatever else you decided to drag along. We do not need him."

"I think we do," she said. "What of the ogham script?"

"I can read ogham just fine, lass."

"Then why didn't you tell us what it said back at the séance table?" Mr. Leighton challenged.

Mr. Hallorman didn't react, but Charlotte noticed his long fingers gripping the tin plate a little more tightly. "As you said, the only bit of it that was legible was 'father of B.' Hardly much to go on. It is more important right now to trust the trail and the land. That is what will let us find your sister, Charlotte." He scooped up a big spoonful of beans. "But whether we can get her back or not, I cannot say."

The reminder of potential failure cast a pall on the rest of the evening. Charlotte ate quickly and mechanically, then took her leave to get some sleep. Mr. Hallorman had protested this, but she was not about to undress in front of a man, any man, nor was she going to sleep in a laced corset.

"Protect me with your back turned," she had told him.

The infuriating creature had just chuckled.

So Charlotte lay some way away from the fire, half-naked with only her arm for a pillow, watching the stars hang silently overhead. The ground was hard. She was wrapped in a wool blanket that itched against the places not covered by her chemise. She thought it would take her forever to fall asleep, that the discomfort of it would keep her awake all night, that her fear and worry for her sister would consume her.

She was out in seconds.

Chapter Seventeen

Celeste woke before the sun was over the horizon. It wasn't that gradual wakefulness that normally came in the early morning. It was sharp like a shove. Like being pushed off a moving train, or into deep water.

They'd ridden on from the homestead yesterday, pressing on until the sun was down and the posse was grumbling, and now the sky overhead was gray, the eastern mountains rimmed with pink, a harsh breeze sweeping down toward them. There was a kind of rugged beauty in it.

Or there would have been, had her legs not been chained.

Smoke. Not fire, but tobacco, harsh and strong. Curling up from a pipe nearby, clutched in Mr. Horn's hand. He was in his shirtsleeves, vest open, no hat, boots cast off, staring at the dawn. His ashen hair wasn't gathered at the nape of his neck, like it had been yesterday, but fell loose around his shoulder. It seemed much longer than it had been before.

Celeste considered the situation. If she could find a crack, a flaw, maybe she could exploit it. Get them to let her go. So she started with the most logical question, the question anyone would ask.

"Why are you doing this to me? Really?"

"I told you yesterday. I need you to help me open a doorway." He breathed out smoke into the gray dawn air. "I need you to bring me home."

"Sir, I do not know how I can help you reach Tir na nAill."

Another puff of smoke. "Humanity has forgotten so much," he said.

"The old wisdom. The old ways. You threw it away. Burned it, on the pyres of your new gods."

"We only have one god, Mr. Horn."

"I do not speak of that which crowds you into churches," he said, a sudden and heated contempt in his words, "but the things your people truly worship. Your own knowledge, your own understanding. Your quest to subjugate the natural world beneath the boot of that thing you call science."

"I'm afraid I don't understand," Celeste said, utterly confused now.

He sighed, exhaling a mouthful of smoke, expression thoughtful now. "Do you know the stories of the Tuatha Dé Danann, lass? Your ancestors would. The ones who walked the earth long before humans, the ones humans drove under the hills."

"Sir, those are children's stories, and..."

She trailed off as he moved, as sudden and unexpected as a thunderstorm in the peaks. He did nothing threatening, instead sitting down beside her, close enough to touch. Involuntarily, she shrank back. He didn't acknowledge her discomfort at all, leaning into her instead.

"Surely," he said, his voice dropping, "if you talk to the dead, you talk to the others as well."

"Others?"

"Yes, the others." His manner was intense; she could detect no hint of dishonesty in him. Which meant he was either quite mad, believing all of this, or... "The ones in hiding or the ones who have surrendered themselves to stay here. Remnants of collapsed, forgotten realms, or the new ones just emerging to this existence. The ones who were never human, or have left humanity behind, like my friend Lukas over there. The others. We are rare, fáith, but I have to believe that you've seen them."

Celeste swallowed, trying to think of something to say. Over the past fifteen years, following Mama from city to city, crisscrossing America in the search for the next paying audience, the next generous client, Celeste had met many Spiritualists. Some were desperate, some were eager, some were disillusioned, but all were searching. All had certainty, but it was a false certainty. The kind of belief that demanded evidence, ritual, to sustain.

The only person Celeste had ever met who had talked about faeries as if they were real was her grandmother.

And yet...

Was this what Charlotte had been hiding from her, all this time?

Was that possible?

Was any of this possible?

But even as Celeste struggled against the emotion of such a realization, that analytical part of her mind whispered to her that she had to stay in control of this situation. Of this man. Of this...client. He wanted a performance. He wanted certainty. Even if he was delusional.

"I..." she began, struggling for the words, struggling to recall whatever scraps of Grandmother's stories that she could. She had never been all that attentive to them. "I've seen quite a few things in my life, sir, but I believe you are the first faery I have ever met."

He grunted. "The world has become loud now, a place full of iron and smoke. None of us are what we were. Now, see to yourself before my lads get up. We have a long day ahead of us."

Camp broke swiftly that morning. The outlaws, despite their ragged and worn appearance, appeared to be quite skilled at this sort of thing. Celeste did not care for the men's clothes she had been given to wear, but the trousers were at least warmer for riding horseback than a skirt would have been.

She was surprised when the outlaw leader handed her the reins of a horse.

"We'll go faster with you on your own animal," he told her, and held up a long rope. "And don't worry, I'll still be holding on."

Looking around at the laughing, leering faces of his gang, she was grateful it was him holding the rope, at least. "I didn't see a spare horse yesterday," she said.

"Will doesn't need it anymore," Eli Horn said.

She glanced over at Mr. Abbitt, who just nodded at her once. Knowing.

A chill went through her. "Did you—"

"Up you go, miss," Mr. Abbitt said with a leer, and patted the horse's side.

Five minutes later, they were out of camp, riding hard for the south, Celeste still trying to make sense of it all.

Celeste's mind was still racing, but whatever else was happening, she was alone in the wilderness with a dozen men, one of whom had pointed a gun at her already and another who had threatened even more unpleasant things. She had to endure until she could make her escape, and enduring, it seemed, meant giving this Eli Horn what he wanted.

But part of her, a very small part, was curious. And angry. And eager. What if these revelations about her family, about the world they lived in, were real and not the mere ravings of a madman?

What if it was real?

Over the past five years or so, since taking up this new life that his family so thoroughly disapproved of, Thomas had slept outside regularly, and was happy to discover he was not as sore as he had expected to be. But he was greeted by a pounding headache and a nosebleed. The altitude and dryness again, he supposed.

Despite the discomfort, the sunrise over the eastern peaks was a sight he had never seen before, and he sat there for a few moments, transfixed. Nowhere, anywhere in Britain, were there sunrises like this.

His bladder protested, however, and Thomas was obliged to drag himself from the warmth of his bedroll to relieve it. Considering that Miss Roseingrave was still sleeping, he went a bit further afield than he otherwise would have.

Coming back to camp again, he saw Mr. Hallorman working on tacking up the horses. The saddles used here in the American West were different than what Thomas was used to dealing with back home, heavy and broad, but the faery handled them as if they weighed nothing at all. He hefted one up and into place over the thick saddle blanket, then patted the buckskin's neck, coming around to speak to him softly. It sounded like Gaelic, a language Thomas was more familiar with in its written form. Even in the west of Ireland, it was hardly spoken anymore.

"I notice you did not tether them last night," Thomas commented.

Mr. Hallorman looked at him, then said something else to the horse and moved back to the saddle. "Why should I?"

"That is usually the done thing when on the trail. To ensure one's animals do not wander off during the night, I mean."

"Why should they wander? This mare and I have an understanding," he said, and tightened her girth, checking the fit. "She has agreed to help us. She is the matriarch of this little herd, and they will do as she says."

"Would they listen to a mare?"

"Your damned royal family is headed by a queen right now. Do you not listen to her?"

Thomas shook his head. He could not quite bring himself to think of Mr. Hallorman as a faery; it was a description that did not seem to fit him at all. He was an impertinent, difficult creature, with a sharp tongue and a great deal of disdain for everything. Or perhaps he was exactly what a faery was supposed to be, and it was only more recent ideas that had shifted, a misuse of a more ancient word.

"I thought herds were normally headed by stallions."

"Mares run their own herds. Stallions are more trouble than they're worth," Mr. Hallorman replied, and smiled as he gave his mare another pat. He left the bridle off for the moment and moved on to one of the paints. "Unless one needs that aggression in battle. Even horses know this."

"From what you insinuated yesterday, we might be facing such a thing."

Mr. Hallorman paused, another saddle blanket in hand. "I sincerely hope not."

"Then why pursue this course of action if you do not believe you can succeed?"

The faery threw a saddle blanket onto the withers of Thomas's paint. "I know you have only just made Charlotte's acquaintance, but if you knew her as I do, you would realize that doing anything else is futile. She would be out here alone without me if she had to be."

"You call her by her given name."

"I do."

"If I may ask, why?"

Mr. Hallorman pointed. "If you insist on pestering me, Englishman, at least be helpful." The faery was indicating a saddle. Thomas took the hint and picked it up for him, passing it over.

"It seems quite rude," Thomas said, "especially if you serve the family."

"Serve? Ha!" The faery laughed. "Have you ever been to Ireland?"

"Many times," Thomas said, and realized then how much the faery did remind him of some of the people he had encountered in that fair land's distant villages. "Are you saying that you are akin to those people?"

"The same land made us both. We might be very different, but in that, we are the same."

Thomas thought about that for a moment. "Even the Irish I have met would call a young woman by her family name."

"I have known Charlotte since she was born. I was there when she was born. I was there when she took her first steps, when her grandmother died, when her mother decided to start traveling." Mr. Hallorman finished with Thomas's horse and moved on to the next, talking as he worked. "I have walked beside the women of her family for a very long time. I have earned the familiarity."

"I do not think any woman would welcome a strange man to watch her give birth."

"You think of things too literally, Englishman. I was then as I am now, present and visible. My people have many ways of moving through the world unseen."

"I thought those ways involved the paths under the hills."

And that, finally, stopped Mr. Hallorman. He turned, brushing his hands off, and considered Thomas carefully. "Tir na nAill, the Otherworld, is not a singular place, cohesive and total, as your realm is. It is more akin to a... a castle, perhaps. There are the wider fields, beyond the walls and yet still under its protection, the barbican, the outlying defenses, that must be penetrated before proceeding into the inner courtyards and keep and dungeons."

"The Otherworld has dungeons?"

"Even our kind needs its prisons. My bond, my oath, to Charlotte's bloodline keeps me tethered to the human realm. But some of the shallower regions are still accessible to me, offering shelter and concealment like an overhanging lip of rock on a cliff face."

Thomas's fingers itched for his notebook. Here was not just information, but revelation. "That sounds as if it could be unpleasant."

Mr. Hallorman grinned at him then. "You have no idea, Englishman," he said, and then turned. By the remains of the campfire, Miss Roseingrave was stirring. "Help me with the packhorse. We shall leave as soon as Charlotte is ready. We have much ground to make up, if we wish to intercept this posse before they enter the mountains."

"What makes you think they will head into the mountains?"

But Mr. Hallorman just grunted and picked up the final saddle blanket.

The lesson for the morning, it seemed, was over.

The faery was true to his word: as soon as Miss Roseingrave was on her feet, they were on their way. At her suggestion, Thomas drank as much water as he could and filled his canteen again before heading off. The cold, crisp mountain water helped with his headache, although his sinuses still burned something fierce. They ate in the saddle, strips of beaten jerky flavored with juniper berries. Pemmican, Mr. Hallorman called it, and Thomas made a note to find the recipe before he left. The taste beat the canned meat he often took on expeditions back home by a mile.

For a few hours, they headed south, well off the main and well-traveled road. They had traveled this country already while on the train, and here and there, Thomas could see those tracks off in the distance. Mr. Hallorman said the trail of their quarry was so obvious even a blind man could see it, but all Thomas noticed were a few bent grasses.

The road under any other circumstances would have been lovely, golden prairie grasses flowing across rolling hills, sweeping up high slopes into the darker green of the pine forests that clung to the mountains. But beyond that were higher peaks, crowned with snow, stretching out forever. How were they going to find Miss Celeste Roseingrave in all this?

Mr. Hallorman, however, seemed reasonably sure of himself. "There won't be many paths they can take on horseback through here," he told Thomas when he pulled up his horse alongside his to ask. "The mountains narrow their options significantly, as well as slow their pace. We are fortunate they chose this route."

"This does not seem so fortunate to me," Miss Roseingrave said, trotting up beside them, her fair face shaded by the deep brim of her new hat.

"Changed your mind?" Mr. Hallorman asked, amusement in his voice. "Nothing would give me greater pleasure than to turn around."

She steered her horse around a particularly inconvenient rock. "I said we would find my sister, and we shall."

"Suit yourself," the strange creature said. "But this will become more difficult once they head into the mountains proper."

"What makes you think they will?" Thomas asked.

"I thought you were supposed to be the scholar here," Mr. Hallorman said derisively. "Do you not recall Celeste's drawing?"

Thomas did not think it would do much good to point out that he had brought the drawing with him. "Yes, of course. A waterfall set against a granite rock face. But that does not mean they are destined for the mountains."

"There was the rusting drill," Miss Roseingrave offered, "and the connection to Mr. Barton's son, who was on a mining survey."

Thomas shook his head. "We have no evidence that all these things are connected. Without more definitive data, we should not make definitive assumptions. I admit it is compelling, but what does it mean?"

"Mr. Dvalinsson said it was some kind of portal," Charlotte replied. "One that Eli Horn would take my sister through."

Mr. Leighton nodded then. "The stories do tell of humans being abducted by fae."

"It is not so simple as—" Mr. Hallorman began, and then abruptly fell silent, pulling his horse to a halt.

Looking ahead, Thomas saw what had stopped him.

On the top of the next rise was a dark figure seated on a dark horse. Watching them.

Mr. Hallorman stood up a little in his stirrups. "I should have known that damned wolf wasn't going to back off so easily," he grumbled, and muttering a command to his buckskin mare, set off for the interloper.

Thomas looked over at Miss Roseingrave. Her mouth was pinched, her eyes narrowed. "What is it?" he asked her.

She shook herself. "Nothing," she said, and spurred her own mount.

Thomas followed.

From a distance, he could tell that this newcomer was wearing some kind of uniform, and as they drew nearer, the details came into view: broad hat, blue shirt with yellow devices, blue trousers tucked into knee-high boots. Thomas half expected it to be Colonel Ramage, but it was clearly not that man. This one was younger, broader through the shoulders. He had light bronze skin, as if he'd spent his life in the harsh sun, and am impressively bushy mustache. He had a saber and rifle tied to the front of his saddle and full bags slung across the back of his horse.

"You must be the lady my alpha spoke of," he said as they drew near, leaning forward over his pommel. He tilted his hat to Miss Roseingrave, revealing dark hair cropped rather shorter than was fashionable. There was a slight drawl to his words, a regional accent Thomas couldn't place. "Ma'am."

She nodded back. "And you are?"

"Apologies, ma'am," he said, replacing his hat. "Allow me to introduce myself. Captain Peter Sirok, First Cavalry. Colonel Ramage asked me to accompany you. I'm here as a tracker, and for whatever else you might need."

"I don't need a tracker," Mr. Hallorman said. "My senses are as keen as yours."

"With respect, there's nobody better in all the West than one of Colonel Ramage's pack to get you through the country you're about to enter. Or does Ireland have such wild mountains?"

"It did once."

"Mountains this high?" Captain Sirok asked. Mr. Hallorman said nothing, and the cavalry officer laughed. "The weather alone'll kill a man, if you don't know what you're doing. And that might not be a problem for you, but I'm betting those two don't have any kind of...special protection."

"They have me."

The captain's smile didn't waver. "Truth is, somethin' like what happened the other night merits attention. Official attention, if you catch my drift. Can't have men gettin' killed in the home of such an important citizen as Mr. Barton. Women gettin' snatched. Bad business. The colonel had several requests to saddle up and pursue this gang in force. Official requests, from big important official men."

"So it's either you or the entire army, is it?" Mr. Hallorman asked.

"Me or the army."

The faery made a displeased sound in his throat, and Thomas was fairly certain he was about to tell this Captain Sirok to go to hell. But then, Miss Roseingrave stepped in.

"I am sure we shall find you indispensable, Captain Sirok," she said, and, looking meaningfully at Mr. Hallorman, added, "I don't see anything wrong with more help."

"As if the Englishman wasn't trouble enough, we must be burdened with this Laignech Fáelad," Mr. Hallorman muttered, but shook his head. "You follow me, you understand?"

"Colonel Ramage said you're the man in charge."

"Then I accept your expertise on these mountains and thank you for it."

The captain nodded. "First order of business, then, is showin' you fine people something I found up ahead."

CHAPTER EIGHTEEN

Captain Sirok joining the party was unexpected.

And yet...

Charlotte had dreamed the night before of a wolf running through the long grass, dark and sleek, leading her on into a storm rolling down off distant peaks. Strange dreams were nothing new in Charlotte's life and often held no particular meaning. But sometimes they seemed almost prophetic.

It's merely coincidence, she told herself now.

As she always told herself.

The cavalry officer was a strange man. There was something about him, something she could not quite place, that whispered of the wind and the moon, hunger and struggle. If she wanted to, if she looked...

But whatever else this Captain Sirok was, he was clearly an Army officer first, and that was a comforting thought.

"I am sorry to have to show a lady a sight like this," he told her as they crested a hill, "but we are on a hunt here."

"She can handle it," Mr. Hallorman replied before Charlotte even had a chance to answer.

She wanted to correct the faery, tell him it wasn't his place to speak for her, except they were approaching a cluster of buildings now, and the air was punched from her lungs.

Her whole life, Charlotte had been plagued by visions of death. Or rather, visions of what was left behind, lingering here, soaked into earth and brick like so much blood. Always, such things stirred some kind of feeling in her breast, letting her know they were coming before they materialized. Sometimes those feelings were light. Sometimes they were dark.

A shadow hung over this place.

Nothing is wrong, she tried to tell herself, and pulled her mind from that other place. How could anything be wrong? The sun was shining. The birds were singing in the trees. But there was no denying that the homestead itself was eerily quiet. There were no domestic animals, no pigs nor cattle nor horses, although the barn and its attached pens had clearly been built to accommodate them all.

"What is it you wanted us to see, Captain?" she asked, forcing the words out.

Captain Sirok nodded and headed toward the barn. "This."

There was a body there, laid out in the shadow of the wall. From her horse, it almost looked like a man who was merely asleep.

Almost.

The knot in Charlotte's chest tightened.

They halted. Sirok jumped lightly down from his horse. "Smelled this one from a mile or so away," he said, nudging the corpse with his boot. "Came to investigate. My apologies, ma'am. If not for this, I would have met up with you sooner."

"One of Eli Horn's men?" Mr. Leighton asked. Charlotte looked at him, and he shrugged. "It must have some kind of connection to our current quest for the good captain to bring us here."

"You are correct. This is Will Cooper, one of his newer boys," Captain Sirok said. "This one was arrested up near Cheyenne this past spring with half the rest of the crew for his involvement in a horse theft scheme."

"Arrested for horse theft and not hanged?" Mr. Hallorman asked.

"Horn staged a breakout."

"How?"

"Demolished part of the jail. Damnedest, er"—and Captain Sirok cast a glance back up at Charlotte, nodding apologetically—"strangest thing I've seen. This year, at least. Nobody reported any noise of explosives, but the whole back of a double-layer brick wall came a'tumblin' down, and the only bodies were the two sheriff's deputies we dug outta the rubble later."

"You saw this yourself?"

"I saw the aftermath. Weren't no dynamite that did it, either. No smell to it."

Charlotte was barely listening. Something was pulling at her, tugging at her, demanding her attention. Under any other circumstances, she would have said it was the dead man on the ground himself, but right now, she didn't think that was so. It felt... it felt like the void she had seen at Mr. Barton's house.

Her skin crawled with the wrongness of it.

"You said this man was young," Mr. Leighton was saying, still looking over the body.

"Nineteen, last report I saw," the cavalry officer replied.

"This man looks at least forty. Are you certain it's the same one?"

"Same facial scar, same height, same build, same smell," Captain Sirok replied, and at Mr. Leighton's questioning look, smiled. "My unit was the one that brought 'em in."

"There is a way to find out," Mr. Hallorman said. "Charlotte?"

"No," she said, feeling somewhat faint. That sensation was still tugging at her, threatening to drag her out of the saddle. Underneath her, her horse nickered nervously.

"What is it?" Mr. Leighton asked.

Charlotte looked toward the farmhouse, a solidly built two-story affair of fresh paint and milled boards. "I'm not sure," she said quietly.

Mr. Hallorman snorted, but offered no comment.

"Something's wrong with that place," Captain Sirok said, and gave Charlotte a curious look. "What are ya scared of?"

She fidgeted in the saddle, trying to regain her composure. "I'm fine."

He smiled at her. "You stink of fear."

"The house looks abandoned, if that's what you mean," Mr. Leighton commented, looking up, seemingly oblivious to Charlotte's increasing discomfort. "But this seems like a place where somebody invested a good deal of money."

"It does look like a nice place, too nice to abandon," Captain Sirok agreed. "But things like this ain't uncommon out here. People come out and hit a bad year and decide to move on, or realize the open country don't agree with them, or all kinds of fool things."

"Quiet," Mr. Hallorman ordered. "Lass, tell me, what do you see?"

"Nothing," she lied.

Dismounting, he gave his horse one last pat and came over to hers. "Come with me."

"What is it?" she replied.

"Come," he said, and loosed his obsidian knife in its leather sheath, "and I shall show you."

Charlotte was able to slide out of the saddle with a little more dignity this time and followed him with her chin high, determined not to lose her composure. But then Mr. Hallorman pushed open the door and all she wanted to do was run.

Inside, where there should have been a floor and walls and chairs and other such things, all she could see was darkness. The same yawning emptiness that she had felt in Mr. Barton's garden.

"Unsettling, I know," Mr. Hallorman said. "But ultimately harmless."

"Perhaps to you," Charlotte said, and grabbed for a porch column to steady herself. Her entire body had gone weak. "I can barely breathe."

"You feel like this because you won't acknowledge what's right in front of you," he told her. "It's not the Otherworld acting on you right now. It's your own body."

"What do you mean?"

"You anticipate horror, so that's what you experience. Now come." And he pointed inside.

Charlotte took another deep breath and was about to tell him off when Mr. Leighton was there at her elbow, holding out a hand.

"Are you alright, Miss Roseingrave?"

She took his proffered hand, feeling better for the contact. Bracing herself against him, Charlotte straightened up. She still felt as if she might pass out at any moment. Her heart was hammering in her chest. That anxious, hot energy still flooded her limbs. But she smoothed down her wrinkled dress, trying to regain some of her dignity.

"Thank you, Mr. Leighton," she said, and nodded. "If Mr. Hallorman believes we should see this, then let us go see it."

As a little child, Charlotte had often been asked by Grandmother about the things she saw. Grandmother had always been eager to hear about whatever

Charlotte had seen or felt or heard, encouraging her to share, proud of her when she did. Back then, Charlotte had thought it all a grand game. But after her grandmother died, something changed. The whispers from the shadows were no longer fun, the things she saw no longer whimsical and beautiful. And then, of course, had come the night with the fire. The night when they had told her to—

That night was the first and last time she and her mother had ever spoken of the Sight. Charlotte could no longer recall the conversation in any detail; no words came to mind. But what she did remember was the way it made her feel.

Mama knew about the whispers. Mama had the power, just like Gran, to hold the shadows back. Charlotte had pleaded with her then to step back from the séances, the readings, all of it.

Mama had not.

After that betrayal by her mother, Charlotte had quickly learned not to say anything to anybody. Most people thought it was ridiculous and would laugh at her. But Mama's Spiritualist friends would have treated her even worse. They would have hailed her as a saint, had they known she could see the spirits, and then stoned her as a heretic for telling them the truth.

Mr. Leighton, holding her hand, said nothing of any kind. His silence was welcome, as was his presence. She held on, like a drowning woman to a rope from a ship.

As they stepped over the threshold, Mr. Leighton going first, the darkness obscuring Charlotte's normal vision seemed to fade. The rooms were still cast in a strange twilight, but even that was light enough for her to pick out details.

The house was a quaint little two-story thing, the downstairs divided into parlor, kitchen, and dining room. The place had clearly been owned by people with some means: there was carpet on the parlor floor and curios on the corner cabinet. A little hallway led to the other rooms.

"Nothing appears to be amiss here," Mr. Leighton said, looking around.

"How can you say that?" Charlotte gasped and clutched at her chest again. Her heart would not slow. "I can barely see anything at all."

"The bodies are upstairs," Mr. Hallorman announced, his feet noiseless as he descended the small staircase in the main hall. Charlotte had not heard him coming, and she looked up, startled. "As I feared. Would you like to see them?"

See them? Charlotte could have laughed until she was sick.

Up there, at the top of the stairs, were the dim outlines of two figures. Staring back at her.

Mr. Leighton's face tightened. "Sir, if you would be a little more considerate of the lady here—"

"This is the frontier, Mr. Leighton," she interrupted, gathering both her courage and her skirt, and started up the stairs. "I have seen the dead before."

There was no escaping them now.

It was a family. An entire family. Two adults, clearly husband and wife, along with four children, none older than age ten. Or at least, what was left of them. Their bodies cast down on the floor of the largest bedroom. Their shades clinging to the shadows.

The latter she ignored. Blocking them out to focus on their more mundane remains.

The bodies were little more than skeletons, as decayed as if they had been left out on the prairie for a year in some undisturbed place. They were still grouped together, all hugging each other tightly. The space stank. Charlotte's eyes stung.

"Killed with a blade," Mr. Hallorman said with a complete lack of emotion, turning one of them over carefully. "You can tell from the score marks on the bones."

Mr. Leighton held a handkerchief up to his nose. "What is that reek?"

"Rapid decay. Same as we saw with the drill back in Leadville." Mr. Hallorman looked to Mr. Leighton. "Do you still believe it's not connected?"

"I don't know what to think right now," Mr. Leighton replied honestly. "How do you account for this?"

"I am not sure," Mr. Hallorman said quietly. "But remember how I told you that even the Otherworld needs its prisons?"

"What does that have to do with anything? Why did you want me to see this?" Charlotte demanded, suddenly angry.

Mr. Hallorman didn't reply. He just turned and left the room.

Mr. Leighton and Charlotte exchanged a glance.

She shook her head.

There was nothing to be done here.

Back outside, Charlotte could once again see the darkness through the windows now. It would always be there, she realized. It would always be in that house, until the structure was no more. She had a sudden powerful desire to set the entire thing on fire.

But she had neither flint nor matches in her own saddlebags, and Charlotte had never been one to give in to her temper. This terrible place was a thing that had to be borne, as so many things in her life were, a small slice of the torment she dealt with.

Perhaps the next people who came here—for surely, somebody would, if only to inquire about their missing friends or neighbors—would be untouched by that which lay within.

Somehow, she didn't believe it.

"You should deal with that, lass," Mr. Hallorman said as they were getting ready to leave, nodding back toward the house. The shades of the dead were still there. Six of them, four small.

How she hated seeing the little ones.

Charlotte shook her head. "I have no power over them."

"I think you'd find you do."

"What are you talkin' about?" Captain Sirok asked, back up on his horse now.

"The dead are still here," Mr. Hallorman replied.

"No, they're not," Charlotte replied. "The catechism is quite clear on the matter. The soul goes to where it is bound, heaven or otherwise, upon the moment of death. We are not left to linger on this fallen earth. Ghosts, as we name them, may be nothing more than an energetic imprint, to borrow a term I have seen used in publications like *Borderlands*."

"A kind of aural body? The leavings of the spirit?" Mr. Leighton asked.

"Shadows they may be, but shadows that can take on lives of their own if left alone," Mr. Hallorman replied. "You know they have to be settled."

"We have to reach my sister," Charlotte said, desperate to be on her way, to have nothing more to do with this cursed place. "We don't have time to give them a proper burial."

"Charlotte, my dear, we shall have an entire cavalcade of dead following us by the time we reach your sister, if Eli Horn continues to drop bodies like this," Mr. Hallorman replied.

"I will not do it," she said, putting as much heat into her words as she could.

"So Christian rites are required to...settle the people who died here?" Mr. Leighton asked, stepping in.

"For these dead, yes."

Captain Sirok shifted in his saddle. "I can send word for the local sheriff to come here when we get to Buena Vista."

"Our trail may not take us through Buena Vista," Mr. Hallorman replied.

"I can do it," Mr. Leighton said suddenly. "I can say a funeral service for them, if Anglican rites are acceptable."

Mr. Hallorman rolled his eyes, then swung lightly back up into his saddle. "I thought you had the stink of the clergy about you, Englishman."

Charlotte saw Mr. Leighton's jaw tighten. He was angry, but he was hiding it well. She doubted anybody not trained on picking up such subtle clues would have noticed. "Would it work?"

"It'd be quicker for Charlotte to have a word with them."

"There's nothing to talk to here," she insisted.

"Have it your way," Mr. Hallorman said with a shrug. "Englishman, say your piece, but do it on the move. We're losing daylight."

The sun was just tipping westward from its noon high, the wind whipping up in chill gusts, when Celeste spotted her chance to escape.

Mr. Abbitt had been called away only a few minutes ago. He and Eli Horn were apart from the rest of the group, distant, discussing something that Celeste took to be of great importance because she could no longer see them, well out of earshot.

And there, rising over the crest of the low southern hills, was smoke.

Celeste smiled at the man who was holding her mount's lead line now. He was one of the older members of the gang; he looked young from a distance, but his hand shook on the line, eyes milky with cataracts.

"Why did we stop?" she asked him sweetly.

He didn't answer.

"Sir, please, help a poor woman understand," she continued. "Why have we stopped? Mr. Abbitt said nothing about—"

"That right," he grunted, and shook his head. "Abbitt didn't say nuthin', did he? So why should I?"

There it was. He was uncertain, perhaps even a bit confused himself, and not happy about it. She could read similar things in the entire gang. The way they were fidgeting, the unease that hung in their conversations.

"Because Mr. Abbitt would not have left me with you if there was not a good reason for it," Celeste pressed on. "He must trust you to some degree, to leave me with you."

"Trust?" The man shifted on his horse. "I trust the boss, not Abbitt."

"And why wouldn't you? Mr. Horn seems like a noble man, under all of..." And Celeste feigned a pause, like she had almost said something she should not have, and smiled ruefully as the outlaw glared at her. "I am sorry, truly. This is the first time I've ever been kidnapped."

"First time we've ever done any kidnappin'."

"So you've been with Mr. Horn long?"

"Seven years," he said, and spat. "Longer than Abbitt."

"And more loyal, too, I'm sure. Mr. Abbitt seems like he's got the devil in him."

The outlaw chuckled. "You ain't never seen the boss when his blood's up."

"Please," Celeste said. "Why did we stop? I'm so cold here, not moving."

The man holding her lead line hesitated but then shook his head. He urged his horse a little closer. "Here," he said, reaching for the bedroll tied to the back of her saddle. "If you wanna use..."

But Celeste didn't listen. He needed both hands to untie her blanket from her saddle. Which meant dropping the line. And the second he did so, she smacked her horse with the reins and slammed her heels into its sides and the animal leapt forward like a cannonball from the breech.

"Hey!" she heard her escort shouting, and other horses were already being turned, but Celeste didn't care. Her horse was off, and all she could do now was hold on.

The hills concealed a fast, steep drop down into a riverbed, but her horse must have been as eager as she was to be free of Eli Horn, because he bounded down it with huge, ground-eating strides. Celeste almost fell off as the animal jumped over a downed tree but managed somehow to stay in the saddle.

There was yelling behind her, screaming, but no gunshots. There was indeed smoke down here, rising from somewhere near the river. There was yelling from that direction, too, now, long gruff voices that carried far on the afternoon wind. Celeste couldn't hear what anybody was saying. But at the first gunshot, she realized that she had forgotten to account for this aspect of things.

"Help!" she screamed as loud as she could. "Help!"

They were running through the riverbed now, sand and water splashing out from her horse's hooves. The gang was all in hot pursuit, whooping and hollering and—it must have been a figment of Celeste's imagination—howling. Her mount was flying. Tears streamed from her eyes and her skin tingled. There were cabins in the distance now, though, multiple cabins, and Celeste urged her horse toward them, slapping him freely with the reins now, anything to reach—

And then he pulled up short, whinnying in fear, rearing up on his hind legs. Celeste was thrown free, landing hard on her side and only barely managing to roll out from under the terrified animal's flashing hooves.

Right onto a pair of weathered old boots.

Celeste looked up then, right into the barrel of a gun, held by a tall but scrawny young man, a scowl on his face.

He cocked back the hammer.

A shot rang out, but not from his weapon.

Instead, Celeste watched as a bullet took the big man in the shoulder, knocking him back. Rough hands grabbed her, yanking her up off the ground, even as the big man roared like an animal and began firing back into the trees.

Celeste struggled against her new captor. A wiry arm had wrapped around her chest, under one armpit with long nails digging painfully into her neck. She slapped at the man dragging her off, angry now. She'd come looking for help and this was the way they treated her? "Stop!" she yelled. "I'm their prisoner, please, I'm a woman, stop!"

"I know you're female," the young man said. "I can smell ya. Shaddup."

What? She twisted herself in his grasp, enough to look up. He was young, she thought, but didn't have time to read anything more from him.

Because just then, Eli Horn appeared, knife in hand. "Drop her, animal," he said coldly.

The young man above her just bared his teeth. His teeth were like daggers in his mouth.

Eli Horn merely drew his revolver with his other hand and fired.

Celeste screamed.

The hand holding her went limp, its owner crumpling to the ground, bleeding horribly from his shoulder. Celeste was pulled down, too, and stared at the boy in horror. He was so young, so terribly young, so—

"Don't run away from me again," Eli Horn growled, and hauled her back to her feet.

Mr. Abbitt appeared from out of the now-smoky trees, two horses pulling themselves along behind his own. Gunshots were still being snapped off all around them; it was impossible to tell where they were coming from or what their intended targets were. "Get on!" Mr. Abbitt yelled.

With no other option available to her, Celeste scrambled up into the saddle. A bullet impacted the tree closest to her head. She screamed. Eli Horn pulled in front of her, between her and the shot, and fired back.

"West!" he yelled. "West!"

And like a thunder cell moving across a valley, the posse all swept west, up the riverbed, into the mountains.

The light was failing fast now, the sun perhaps not below the horizon but absolutely behind the mountains. All was cast in shadow as the gang finally stopped running. They'd come miles up the riverbed, and the horses were all exhausted.

Eli Horn had the lead line, his horse in front of her, any expression on his face invisible. Celeste felt a vague guilt gnaw at her; had anybody died back there because of her? They were outlaws, yes, and that one man had tried to shoot her of course, but it was her actions that had led to conflict.

"Don't blame yourself for this," Eli Horn said suddenly.

Celeste started. His voice was soft but resonant. Perhaps it was some acoustical property of the rocks around them. The riverbed was running upward, into the mountains, and the low earthen hills surrounding it had turned into towering granite outcroppings, channeling the river into an ever-narrowing canyon. At the moment, they were passing between two particularly large cliff faces, guarding the shallow, slight river as surely as castle gates.

"What?" she asked.

"Don't blame yourself. It was that place that Lukas and I were discussing. An old enemy, and not one that would have been receptive to your needs, I'm sure. They were not here when I reconnoitered this route earlier in the year." He chuckled. "You would have liked being with them even less than you like being with me."

She felt like even more of an idiot. Of course, Mr. Horn could be lying. But she had scratches on her neck from the boy, and he had been terribly rough with her, so who knew the truth? "I don't—" she began.

Eli Horn held up a hand. The whole party stopped, the sounds of bridles jingling and saddles creaking. There was a faint rumble from high above. The outlaw pushed back his hat and peered up into the gloom.

"Rockslide!" he yelled suddenly.

There was a terrible sound then, like a thunderstorm brought to earth, like the scream of a hurricane, as hundreds of tons of rock and dirt tore free from their precarious mountainside moorings and poured down toward them. The only thing man or beast could do was follow Eli Horn, and so follow Eli Horn they did. Rocks fell around Celeste, a small one bouncing high to knock her in the shoulder. Screams echoed behind her. Grimly, she clung on to her racing horse, sure that at any moment she would find herself entombed. The noise was enough to knock the sense right out of one's head.

But the roar died to a rumble, then to nothing. A few more rocks rolled down into the thin stream, then stopped.

Dust filled the air, choking and thick. The horses, terrified but exhausted from the earlier chase up the canyon, slowed again to a walk, trudging along. Mr. Abbitt began calling names in some kind of roll call. Eli Horn once again came up alongside Celeste and picked up the trailing lead line.

"We won't have an easy time of it now," he told her.

"What do you mean?"

"Can't you feel it, fáith?" he replied, and laughed. "This mountain hates me."

It wasn't until later that Celeste learned that three men were dead. In the ambush or rockslide, nobody was sure.

Included among the dead was the man who had held her lead line when she had decided to escape.

Chapter Nineteen

Setting out the next morning, Thomas couldn't help but worry about Miss Roseingrave. The path so far had been on established roads or flat ground; today they would be heading into the mountains proper. But beneath her wide-brimmed hat, Miss Roseingrave's expression was set tight and grim.

"Stop fretting over her," Mr. Hallorman told him as they headed out of camp. "She's stronger than she looks."

Thomas shook his head. "I am not worried about her will. I'm worried about the road. I have done but a little mountain riding, but I know that even in Scotland, it can be treacherous."

"We won't have problems with that. They know these lands," Mr. Hallorman said, and patted his mare's neck. The animal whinnied and tossed her head in response. "See?"

Thomas shook his head and didn't say anything more. Arguing with the Irish, even the Otherworld Irish, was an exercise in futility.

The land sloped up gently from their camp, the trail taking them around the edge of a small ridge. Small copses of trees, pines mostly, dotted the rolling landscape, but thin, tall grasses seemed to reign supreme. The mountain peaks were not so far now, and the sun burned overhead in the sky. Thomas could not recall ever feeling its light so keenly.

It was the altitude, he knew. The altitude that made the air thin and his lungs burn with every breath. His body would adjust. But how long that adjustment period would take, and how difficult it would be, he had no idea.

After a while, they left the smooth valley plain, the land growing more rugged. Their trail was dominated now by rocky outcroppings, bursting through the thin foliage like teeth from gums. Here the tilt of the world and the time of year ensured that little sunlight reached the ground. Here lay pockets of unmelted snow.

"It seems an unusual time for it," he commented to Sirok as they plowed through a particularly large section of the stuff, the surface crunching with ice. Mr. Hallorman was in the lead, his horse picking out a trail for the others. "All this snow."

"It'll snow up here any time you please," Sirok replied. He had strapped his saber and gun to the back of his saddle, and both still jiggled with every move of his horse. "And quite a few times you don't."

"Have you been this way before?"

"I've done a few patrols through the mountains. Nasty business. Cavalry favors the plains." He shook his head. "There's enough work out there to keep us all busy forever, I'm afraid."

"What do you mean?"

"My unit, my pack, we get the worst missions. Hardest cases. The most dangerous war bands, the nastiest gangs. Why, before we stopped in at Leadville we was after—"

"Stop your prattling!" Mr. Hallorman called from the front, testy. "It's hard enough to listen to the land without your voice blotting out what she's trying to say."

Thomas had no idea what that meant, but he assumed it was something to do with picking out Eli Horn's trail.

Despite the dire reason for their journey, Thomas could not tamp down his curiosity about their group's non-human members. Traveling with a werewolf and a faery was an opportunity like none he had ever imagined, ever dared hope for. His own personal account would not be enough to sway the Academy to devote more resources to his cause, of course, but perhaps with enough anecdotes and—God willing—a bit of hard evidence, he could at least salvage his reputation.

This kind of knowledge was revelatory. And knowledge and its pursuit, he had always believed, was a noble goal, the purest goal. Nothing of the modern world could exist without knowledge.

And yet...

It was knowledge that came with a cost. A high cost; the grief of one woman and the potential death of another. It was unseemly for his to get lost in his own ambitions, his own theories, while lives were on the line. Why could he not put it aside? Had he only come along to satisfy professional curiosity? Were his intentions noble, righteous? Or was his involvement here based on nothing more than a sudden, foolish desire to help a beautiful woman in need?

All these things turned over in Thomas's head as they followed Eli Horn's gang south, tormenting him.

They didn't break for lunch that day. The outlaws' trail had taken them down into a narrow riverbed sprinkled with scrubby pines and taller cottonwoods. The breadth of the watercourse spoke to seasonal snowmelt floods, but for now, only a small stream flowed between the trees. The horses seemed grateful for it, plodding in and out of the running water, dipping their heads to take big mouthfuls as they walked. Those in the saddles made do with pemmican and their own canteens. The ground was sandy here, though, and the footing unsure. Their progress slowed.

"It seems as if we are headed straight for the mountains," Miss Roseingrave observed, pointing ahead of them to the tall westerly peaks. "Why would they take this route when the way to the south is easier?"

"Trying to avoid attention, perhaps?" Thomas said.

"What I can't understand is why they skipped Buena Vista. Must be aimin' to raid something else," Sirok said, munching on a piece of jerky.

"What reason would a gang of outlaws with a kidnapped woman have to go through a populated area?" Thomas asked.

"Likely to steal something," Captain Sirok replied.

"Like what?" Miss Roseingrave asked.

"Anything, ma'am," he replied. "The Eli Horn gang is the most prolific pack o' horse thieves west of the Mississippi, but they've been known to take anything from jerky to water skins to saddles. And yet somehow, every time we catch one of 'em, their kit seems to be all broken-down and old."

"What about weaponry?" Mr. Hallorman asked. "Does that fail them as well?"

"I reckon so. They steal plenty of that too. Lots o' corrosion on the guns we pull off these boys. Why, a few years back, Horn had the colonel dead to rights and missed the shot cause his damn rifle misfired." The captain laughed. "Not that a lead bullet woulda done much good, but—"

Mr. Hallorman cut him off. "Does this Eli Horn use a gun, then?"

Captain Sirok raised an eyebrow. "Everybody uses a gun out here."

"Does he?" Mr. Hallorman pressed.

"What difference does it make?"

"Rapid aging, decaying equipment, abiotic soil," Mr. Leighton mused, cutting in. "I deduce that this effect is somehow intrinsic to Eli Horn himself, but I have never heard of anything like it, either in the natural world or in...stories." He looked to Mr. Hallorman. "My understanding of Irish folklore is incomplete, it seems."

"That's what happens when your ancestors burn libraries," the faery shot back.

"I assure you, as one who has frequented Trinity College's excellent collection, I do not at all hold with the destruction of—"

"Not meanin' to interrupt y'all's discussion here, but has anyone looked up ahead? I don't much like the looks of that," Captain Sirok said. He nodded at the peaks just to their west. Dark clouds were piling up there, bloated black bellies starting to roll down into the valley. Thomas was amazed; only fifteen minutes ago, the sky had been clear. "Looks like snow."

"Smells like it, too," Mr. Hallorman said, turning his face to the wind. "The whelp is right. We'd best find shelter before that hits."

"Shelter? Where? We're miles from anywhere," Thomas replied.

"What about that?" Miss Roseingrave asked, pointing. Perhaps a quarter mile ahead was a collection of smallish buildings, rough-cut log structures with chimneys all venting smoke.

"I wouldn't recommend it," Captain Sirok replied, wary. "Strangers may not be so friendly out here."

"Whatever it is, it is well within my ability to manage," Mr. Hallorman replied,

"And if it's Eli Horn's gang in the flesh?"

"Then it shall save us a great deal of trouble," Mr. Hallorman said, and looked back at the sky. "That storm is moving fast. Come."

The way to the homestead was trickier than Charlotte expected; the ground was torn up here, full of hidden divots that their horses stumbled on.

But Mr. Hallorman, even more so than the sure-footed Captain Sirok, seemed to know exactly where to go. He flowed across the riverbed, his horse never breaking its stride. Charlotte's own mount, by comparison, seemed reluctant to get any closer to the buildings ahead. A few lengths behind her, Mr. Leighton was likewise struggling to keep up.

The temperature was dropping precipitously now. The light was failing. The storm was upon them. Suddenly desperate, she spurred her animal on.

She missed one of the turns Mr. Hallorman took around a small copse of cottonwoods. The first few flurries of snow whipped around her neck, and when she rounded the corner of a particularly large rock outcropping, instead of Mr. Hallorman, she came face-to-face with a shotgun.

It was held in a pair of big, rough hands, belonging to a big, rough man, dressed all in deerskins. His beard was long, his face thick and broad. What skin was visible looked like old, tanned leather. He squinted at her from under the brim of a battered old hat. There was something about him, something feral and wild, held in check but straining at its bonds, like a wild animal trying to get out of a trap.

That, more than the gun, brought her up cold.

"Now what's a fair little thing like you doing out here?"

"Peace!" she heard Mr. Leighton yell. He wasn't far away, just a few paces to her right, but the growing wind washed out his words. "We mean you no harm!"

"That's what the last one said, too," the man grunted, and took better aim at Charlotte.

"Sir—" she began.

"Don't you breathe, missy, 'less you wanna be breathing out of a second hole in your neck," the man growled. "Tell your man there ta put down his gun."

Out of the corner of her eye, she saw Mr. Leighton. He had his rifle in hand now.

"Drop yours first!" he yelled back.

But before anybody could pull a trigger, the standoff was broken in a most unexpected way.

"Hiram? Is that you?!" It was Captain Sirok, riding up as fast as his horse would allow. The sky to the west was black now. "What the hell are you doin'?"

The man shifted his aim. "Ramage's whelp," he said, his voice a wet, low growl. "I 'member you."

"We mean you and yours no harm!" the cavalry officer insisted.

"What about that one?" he said, and swung his gun over at Mr. Hallorman, who had appeared from nowhere. "I don't like the look o' that one. Like the last."

"Compare me to that thing we're chasing," Mr. Hallorman warned, reaching for his bow, "and it'll be the last thing you do."

"Gentlemen!" Charlotte yelled—for the wind was roaring now—and pointed at the sky. "Might we discuss this inside, where we won't freeze to death?!"

The man, Hiram, faltered for a moment. Then with one last grunt, he slung his gun back around his shoulder. "Well come on then. The missus would never forgive me for leavin' a lady outside on a day like this."

Hiram led them up the valley to the camp they had seen from the trail. It was more extensive than Charlotte would have guessed, with several large dogtrot cabins clustered around a central yard. The signs of inhabitation were everywhere: the remains of cooking fires, bits of broken tools or toys, the faint reek of a garbage pile and latrines some way distant. Inside the yard, a half dozen donkeys were clustered placidly under the overhang of one of the dogtrots, eating their hay. Their party's own horses were on edge, snorting and pawing at the ground, and Charlotte suspected that only Mr. Hallorman's presence was keeping them from bolting.

"Eh, what's this now?" asked a woman, as big and rough as Hiram, looking out from the side of a dogtrot cabin. To Charlotte's surprise, a pair of children were peeking around the woman's patched skirt.

"We've got us some visitors tonight, Hannah," Hiram grunted, and gestured at Captain Sirok. "You'll have to leave your animals out here, but I can't promise they'll be here when the storm is done."

"I'll see to it," Mr. Hallorman replied as he helped Charlotte out of her saddle. He patted her horse's neck once, then started working on its tack.

Hiram looked to Captain Sirok. "Confident, ain't he?"

"Colonel Ramage told 'em the hill-dwellers are arrogant like that."

Charlotte noticed the glare Mr. Hallorman threw in the captain's direction, even if the captain himself seemed to miss it. The faery seemed to have resigned himself to the captain's presence, although what the exact problem was, Charlotte was still not sure. There was something wild lurking inside the captain, that much she could tell. Maybe that was it.

A touch landed on her shoulder, and Charlotte jumped. It was just Hannah, though, a slight smile on her broad face. "Come on then, miss. Let the menfolk work."

Grateful, Charlotte followed her into the relative warmth of the cabin, wind tearing at her hair.

Despite the rough appearance of both the camp and people, the interior of the little cabin was surprisingly comfortable. The logs of the cabin walls were old, cut a few seasons ago, but the chinking was fresh and kept out the wind. The space was well warmed by a small cast-iron stove on which a huge pot had been placed. Gathered bunches of herbs hung from the ceiling in one corner above big barrels of flour and cornmeal, and the beaten earth floor was neatly swept. Furs were everywhere, scattered about.

There were four children here in total, Charlotte saw: the two little ones that had looked out at them, along with a small babe barely big enough to walk, rolling around with its toys near the woman's feet. They had smudged faces, bare feet, clothes that were little more than rags. But unlike many children Charlotte had seen out here on the frontier, these seemed well fed, bright-eyed, and quite alert.

But the fourth child was in a bad way. Maybe fourteen or fifteen, his shirt had been ripped away and some attempts had been made to clean and dress the wounds on his upper chest. He was clearly feverish and moaned as Charlotte looked at him. Unguarded, she caught a glimpse of something she normally tried to ignore. There was a dark pall around him, the world all around him cast in shadow.

Her mother had had the same aura about her, before her death.

Charlotte pulled her eyes away.

"It ain't much we got here, but more bodies'll keep it warmer," Hannah was saying, stirring the huge pot of beans bubbling away on top of the stove. It smelt strongly of cumin and pepper.

"What is this place?" Charlotte asked, trying to warm her hands.

"Our fall camp. In a few weeks, we'll head down south to our winter camp. Like as not, we'll have to kick somebody off it again. Some people don't respect other people's homesteads."

"You have a homestead?" Charlotte asked.

"Three hundred fine acres with a stream runnin' through it. Just for the winter. And for the future," the woman said. "Ain't gonna be forever they'll let us live all peaceful like in the mountains. Whole country's gettin' chopped up. No more trappin' then, and no more free tradin'. We have to secure something for them now." And she nodded at the children, then caught the baby before the little thing could lay a hand on the stove. "Ach, don't you dare! Here, miss, make yourself useful," she said, and with one big hand, scooped up the baby and handed it to Charlotte.

Taking the little body, a rush of imagery flooded Charlotte's mind. The deep shadows of trees, the bare rock plains of the high peaks, raw meat and damp fur, the impression of something huge and dangerous. It was the feel of a predator. But quick as it came it was gone, and all Charlotte saw was a human baby, blinking back up at her with huge brown eyes.

"She likes you," the woman chuckled.

Charlotte looked down at the baby again. Those eyes were beginning to close now. She rubbed the little girl's back. "I guess she does."

The men were in a few moments later. Snow swirled in through the rough-cut door and fell to the floor in wet puddles as they shook out their clothing. Mr. Leighton appeared dazed, his face chapped red from the sudden cold. Even Captain Sirok seemed a bit stunned.

"Nasty one tonight there, Hannah," Hiram said, and gave the woman a kiss on her forehead, "but movin' fast. It'll blow over by midnight."

"Not everyone's back yet," the woman, Hannah, said, as if the storm was a personal and deep insult to her.

"And good thing," Hiram laughed, "or we wouldn't have anything to feed our fine guests here!" He looked over at the bed. "How is he?"

"He's barely woken up," Hannah replied with a sigh. "Nuthin' I can do for him, I'm afraid."

"What happened here?" Captain Sirok asked, brushing the last of the snow from his hat, then laying it aside on the room's table.

"You askin' in an official or unofficial capacity?" the big woman challenged.

He nodded. "I'm askin' for my alpha, ma'am."

Hannah looked at Charlotte and Mr. Leighton, doubt in her eyes. "And those two?"

"They're with me," he replied seriously. "No secrets."

Hiram shook his head. "Big posse came through late last night. Killed two of our clan, hurt my boy, then fled."

"Fled where? Into the mountains?" Sirok asked.

"I reckon so. Didn't get a chance to ask, with the gunfire and all."

"Why attack them?" the officer pressed. "I've never known you to be particularly confrontational, Hiram. At least, not without good reason."

"Their leader was..." Hiram trailed off, like he didn't have the words for it. "An affront to these mountains. We couldn't let him pass."

"What does that mean, an affront to the mountains?" Mr. Leighton asked. Charlotte noticed he had his notebook out.

Hiram, it seemed, noticed as well.

"You talk funny," the huge bear of a man said, turning on the researcher. "Where you from?"

"England, my good man."

"I don't like you writin' what we say."

"He's with me," Sirok said again, getting between them. "Hiram, tell me about this posse."

"Had twelve with them when they came. They left with ten. Least, that's what I smelled." He bared his teeth. "We'd'a killed more, but the boy got hit."

The door banged open, and there Mr. Hallorman was. His clothes were covered in snow, but he didn't seem to notice. "The horses shall stay where they are," he announced, and as he was making for the stove, glanced over at the bed. "That boy of yours is in a bad way, bear."

"You talk funny," Hiram said, accusatorially. "Same as your scholar over here."

"Don't compare me to the Englishman," Mr. Hallorman said, abandoning the stove for a moment, walking over to the bed. He laid the back of his hand against the boy's forehead. The boy moaned and thrashed.

"Is there anything you can do?" Charlotte asked. The baby stirred in her arms, moving to lay a cheek against her shoulder. She began swaying, patting the little girl's back to settle her back down. It was a pleasant feeling. The only babies Charlotte normally encountered, moving in her mother's Spiritualist circles, were dead ones.

"Who is he?" Mr. Hallorman asked. "He doesn't share your blood."

"An orphan," Hannah said, regret in her voice now. "Like all the others. I find them all eventually. You a healer?"

"In my own country, yes, that is one of the gifts my people were granted."

"Don't encourage 'im," Hiram grunted. "You see what he is. Hilldweller. Foreign type. Land don't know him, land won't help him."

"Will he live?" Hannah pressed.

"Infection has set in, riding through the blood," Mr. Hallorman said, and sat back. "Domnu rides with the one who came here. I'm afraid she has your boy now." He laid a hand on the boy's forehead again, eyes closed. The moaning stopped.

"What'd you do?" Hiram asked, suspicious.

"Only thing I could. Gave him one last good dream, instead of the pain," Mr. Hallorman said, and for the first time since meeting him, Charlotte thought she detected a note of regret in the faery's voice. "Then he'll be off to wherever your clan goes when the land calls you home."

Just as Hiram had predicted, the worst of the storm passed quickly. A few hours passed and the wind subsided, leaving behind a thick blanket of white between the trees. It was dark by then, though, with no chance of any further pursuit that day.

Dinner was surprisingly good, beans cooked with chunks of venison and corn bread beside, and if that was a little burnt, Charlotte didn't care. A few more men returned during the meal, bearing wounds and grim expressions. They took their bowls in silence and disappeared off to one of the other cabins. The men in Charlotte's own party were dismissed in time as well,

Mr. Leighton and Captain Sirok to one of the other cabins, Mr. Hallorman heading to the horses' shelter. The last she saw of him before Hannah shut the door was him offering a handful of dry hay to his mare.

This cabin, it seemed, was Hannah's territory, reserved for herself and the children.

"It's better this way. The children are my responsibility, after all. Just mine," Hannah explained as she shut the door again. One last little flurry of glistening snowflakes scurried in behind her. "We ain't naturally social. Prefer solitude, you know. Don't much get along. But there's strength in numbers these days."

"So what are you to each other?" Charlotte asked, still cradling the baby. The little girl had refused to be put down, screaming every time Charlotte attempted it. Charlotte had been obliged to eat dinner one-handed with the baby in her lap, stealing handfuls of beans from her bowl.

"We're clan," Hannah said.

"What clan?"

Hannah didn't answer that. Just smiled and offered to let Charlotte have the only other pallet in the room. She took it, telling herself it was for the sake of the baby.

But later that night, well past midnight and into the early hours before dawn, Charlotte awoke with a start, as if summoned. Anxiety flooded her limbs, urging her to rise. She checked the child beside her—sleeping deeply, sucking on a tiny thumb, with the other two curled up nearby. Hannah was nowhere to be seen, nor was the feverish boy who had been so near death.

Charlotte crept to the door and looked out.

A layer of fresh snow blanketed the entire world in a crisp white blanket. It was cold, that kind of dry chill that bit at the skin and rasped at the nostrils, but was not so unpleasant as to be impossible to bear. The clouds had all blown away, and the world practically glowed under the starlight. Charlotte could see a bonfire beyond the edge of the camp.

Something pulled at her. Some sense she normally ignored. Something she normally would have given anything to not feel.

And yet...

Seized by a sudden, powerful curiosity, Charlotte did something she normally never did.

She pulled on her boots and slipped out into the night.

Drawing closer to the bonfire, she heard the beating of a taut animal skin, the sound of feet drumming in unison on the earth. Dancing. Something was dancing around that fire. Charlotte was drawn on toward it, propelled by something she had not felt in a very long time.

But before she was quite to the clearing, however, a hand caught her wrist and another clamped over her mouth and she was yanked down before she could scream.

It was Captain Sirok. Bare-headed, wearing neither boots nor socks, but he seemed little troubled by the cold. In the light of the half-moon, his eyes almost glowed.

"Shh," he whispered, barely loud enough to hear. "Hannah's friendly enough, but you come upon them like this, they'll kill you without thinking, and that would make Hannah mighty sad, I reckon, when she comes back to herself."

"Like what?" she asked. "What's going on?"

"The boy died," Sirok replied. "They gather to send his spirit on its way."

She looked. She was close enough here to see shadows thrown up by the bonfire. Huge, they were, and dark, not the figures of humans but animals. Bears, it seemed. Massive and eternal. Dancing. A shuffling, heavy dance that should have been graceless but instead flowed as sure and certain as water.

As if they were something that always had been and always would be.

As if they were something that was already vanished, already lost, retreating into the obscurity of the Otherworld, taking just a bit of the mystery of the world with them.

Charlotte felt tears on her cheeks, moved by something she did not understand.

"Come back now with me to the camp, Miss Roseingrave," Captain Sirok said quietly. "This ain't no place for humans."

Charlotte looked back toward the firelight one more time, then nodded. She didn't speak on the way back to the cabin, lost in thought. The children had rolled into her space on the little bed. She grabbed an extra quilt and stretched out on the floor next to them.

Let them have some peace.

Chapter Twenty

That day, Celeste was privately grateful for the men's clothing that had been pushed on her. Riding sidesaddle or being draped over Lukas's pommel through this country would have been utterly unbearable.

The land they found themselves in now was steep and wild. The high peaks of the mountains tumbled down to tight ravines and narrow valleys. Pine forests clung stubbornly to the steep slopes, tall and thick with deep shadows underneath. There was no flat ground anywhere.

As a child growing up in Savannah, Celeste had always imagined mountains as merely large hills, smooth-sided mounds that rose tall from the earth but were largely undifferentiated. Her first train ride through the Appalachians, and a few brief stops in town like Asheville, had not dissuaded her from that notion. It wasn't until she had come west, to the Rockies, that she truly understood.

Mountains rose high, yes, but they were vast agglomerations of earth and rock, worn unevenly by the passage of time, the knees of the mountains all tangled and mixed together. Winding valleys were contained by steep cliffs and ended more often than not in blind canyons.

It was into one of these dead ends that they had now wandered, much to Eli Horn's apparent frustration. Everyone was giving him a huge berth. He had stalked off almost half an hour ago and nobody had dared to follow him.

"The boss might not see it, but I do," Mr. Abbitt told Celeste as they waited, still on horseback. He once again held the lead line attached to her mount. Several feet long, it gave the horse a little leeway, but it didn't seem to need it. The animal seemed beaten, defeated. Tired and old. Everything was tired with the posse, it seemed, a quality that had grown more pronounced since the rockslide.

"See what?"

"The lies, Miss Roseingrave. You stink of it."

She glared back at him levelly. "Your leader had you kidnap me, we were attacked last night, and here we are now, driven into the deep mountains. I do not care for this state of affairs. But if he is searching for something and I may be of assistance, I take that very seriously."

The man's strange gold eyes fixed on her. It was all Celeste could do to return his gaze. But before it became truly uncomfortable, he looked away again, head snapping over to the west. "Well look at that," he drawled. "Got some storm clouds moving in."

Celeste followed his gaze.

The entire sky, at least what could be seen of it here in the mountain canyon, had grown pitch black.

Fear gripped her. "Snow."

"A blizzard, I'd say," Lukas drawled. "The kind of weather that can kill a man out in the open, pretty as you please."

"We need to find shelter."

"No doubt," Lukas said. "But ain't nobody movin' until the boss gets back."

She looked at him. "Are you insane? We shall die!"

"Don't think the boss is too worried about that," Lukas replied, and gave her a flippant smile.

Celeste turned her horse around, facing up the slope in the direction of where Mr. Horn had gotten off to. The wind was beginning to pick up now, bringing with it the promise of deathly cold. "If you won't do something about our lives, I will," she snapped, and spurred her horse forward, only to be caught by the lead line.

He tutted at her but moved his horse forward, keeping pace beside her. "You wanna interrupt him? Your funeral."

Eli Horn was only a little farther up the slope, stopped near where a massive granite face of the mountain's form forced its way out of its earthen wrappings, a rocky mass bigger than the Tabor Opera House. There was no way out here, no shelter to speak of. The trees, while impressively sized, were inadequate to shield them from the storm, and the posse had no time to fell them and build some kind of structure.

"Mr. Horn!" Celeste called. He did not look back at her. Glancing up at the storm, clouds whipping overhead now, she dismounted. Grabbing her bedroll blanket, she draped it around her shoulders as she approached. "Mr. Horn! A word, if you please!"

"You should not be here," he muttered, shoulders stiffening visibly under his dusty trail coat. He waved a hand. "Lukas, you fail me! I said to keep her back."

"She's got a mind of her own, boss."

The outlaw leader chuckled and stood up, brushing off his hands. "It's only the modern man who finds that an inconvenient quality in a woman."

Celeste glanced over his shoulder. Behind him were the remains of what looked like a fox skeleton. "Lukas says a storm is coming!" she said, obliged to raise her voice now.

He looked up. "It does appear that way, doesn't it?"

His nonchalant attitude set her teeth on edge. What was he thinking? This was insane. "I cannot help you find your way home if we all freeze to death out here!"

Eli Horn glanced back at the skeleton, then up at her. "You know," he said, almost cheerfully, as if they were discussing the effects of a light rain on some picnic by the banks of the Trinity River, "the lady is right again. Lukas!"

The number two man nodded from his saddle.

"Round up the men. Bring them up here. Wood, too, if you can manage on the way. We shall have our shelter."

Lukas nodded and spurred his horse.

Eli Horn turned his attention to Celeste. "Would you like to see a little demonstration of the old ways?" he asked.

Celeste had dealt with a great many people over the years who had strong faith. All were always disappointed, from what she could tell, and yet, they never stopped believing. It reminded her of Christian martyrs being put to death in the Colosseum; she had never understood the urge to subordinate one's very life to things that could not be seen nor touched. But it appeared as though tonight, she was to receive a firsthand lesson in such folly.

And yet, if there was the power in this man to get them some kind of shelter, magically...

She pulled the rough wool of her blanket tighter around her. Nodded.

"Then watch," he said, and strode up the slope.

With nothing else to do, she followed him.

Eli Horn did not go far, just up to the base of the cliff. The space here was choked with ferns and lichen and trees growing close to the rock face. He paced for a few moments, studying the stone with an intensity Celeste could not understand nor explain. Was he looking for some cave there, some hidden entrance behind a tree that she had not seen, the presence of which he would no doubt credit to some invisible spirit helper or—

"Stand behind me," he ordered, halting at a shallow impression in the rock. "And don't be afraid, lass."

"Afraid of what?" she managed to ask. The temperature was plummeting, stealing the warmth from her body. Her teeth were starting to chatter.

"This," he said, and touched his hand to the rock face.

For a moment, nothing happened.

But only for a moment.

There came a hiss. A sigh. A creak. As if gas was escaping from somewhere deep inside. Then a rumble started, like the sound of distant thunder. A rumble that grew and grew, becoming a roar. For a terrible moment, Celeste imagined she was to be buried in a fresh rockslide.

But what happened was far stranger.

The front of the cliffside didn't so much explode as it did disintegrate, crumbling like sand on the beach. A great cloud blew out from the rock face. Celeste buried her face in her blanket to keep from being overwhelmed. For a moment, nothing else existed but that strange wall of dust.

Then the winds of the approaching storm blew it away, and she could clearly see what was in front of her.

Where the great slope of granite had once stood, there was now a cave. Broad and wide, it led back into the mountain, back into darkness so complete the weak daylight could not penetrate it. Celeste had a sense of profound sorrow, of loss, and then it was gone, and all she saw was shelter.

Eli Horn was on his knees at the entrance, breathing hard, holding himself off the ground with one arm. There had been ferns, grass, around him. Now, there was only a circle of blasted ground, bare dirt and dead plants.

It reminded Celeste of the garden at Mr. Barton's house.

"Do not run," he panted, and rose with great effort. "Even like this, I would catch you, fáith. Now come. I have not cored out a mountain merely for you to insist on freezing to death."

Still mute from shock, she nodded. Followed.

Unlike an excavation created by dynamite or other modern mining means, this space felt...natural, in some way. The floor was uneven, rising over there and falling here, and the ceiling was likewise sculpted, not blasted. They did not go so far in at first, staying close enough to the entrance to see the light far beyond, to hear Lukas guiding the gang in.

"This way!" he bellowed over the top of the storm. "The boss has found us shelter!"

Celeste looked at Eli Horn. "How does he know there is a cave here?"

The outlaw leader did not meet her eyes. "Lukas has been with me a long time, longer than most. He understands."

"And the others?"

"Mention anything you witnessed," he said, "and we shall have problems, you and I."

"Problems?" she asked, trying to be charming but utterly failing.

"You do not need your tongue to help me open the doorway," he told her bluntly. "Tell anyone of this, and I shall relieve you of it."

That took her aback. "I..." she stammered and then gathered herself. "I do not see why you need me at all, if you can achieve such things as—"

He put a finger to his lips and pointed.

Torches were entering the cave.

With the presence of light, they were able to push further back into the cave, deeper in where the storm's cold air didn't reach them. The space was big enough for all the men and animals as well, and the air was surprisingly comfortable here. Oats for the animals and hot food for the humans soon ensured good spirits.

"Nothing to do but wait out the storm," Mr. Horn told Celeste. He had retreated to a back corner of the cave, a pocket that was partially obscured from the main floor. He had taken Celeste with him; still a little stunned from what she had just witnessed, she had thought it a bad idea to refuse him. He was stoking their own little fire into life. "From what I saw, it will pass quickly."

"How can you tell?"

"The boss is never wrong about the weather." Lukas, standing by the rock at the opening to the smaller room. He had his hat in his hands. He was still giving Celeste that look, the look he'd had on his face outside. It was hunger, she realized, and she pulled her blanket tighter around her shoulders. He had stood up for her that first morning, yes, but who knew what lurked in the heart of such a man? "You'd do well to listen to him."

"Enough, Lukas. The lass has been through enough today." Mr. Horn poked the fire with a fresh piece of wood, dropping it in. Sparks flew. Minerals in the rock around them glittered. "How are the men?"

"Happy."

"Tell them all to get some sleep and eat lightly from the stores. It may be a few days before we emerge from these mountains into civilization again."

Lukas snorted. "Sounds lovely, boss," he said, but nodded and headed off.

"A good lad, that one," Mr. Horn mused. "It's hard to find loyalty like that these days."

"What did you do out there? How did you create this cave?" Celeste asked.

He sighed and leaned back against a rock, one hand resting on a bent knee, the other leg sprawled out in front of him. "I did not," he told her. "One does not create in this world. One asks the land for her blessing, and she gives it when and how it pleases her. Or at least, that is how one properly channels the deep magics, when they will be channeled."

"That sounds...pagan."

"Paganism is your kind's attempt to deal with the forces of nature. But we, we are those forces embodied. We were the powers in this world long before mankind pulled itself from the muck, and we shall be again long after mankind has departed."

"You told me..." Celeste began, and then hesitated. "You told me you were not what you were."

"No, I am not," he said, clearly begrudging the admission. "The Morrigan banished me, cut me off from all that she could, for a crime that was not even my own! Balor, he was the fool who landed us all in this mess.

That is why you see me as human, fáith, instead of my true nature. But not even the Morrigan could sever my connection to the deep magics entirely. She had not the authority to unmake me. Nothing does, except maybe Domnu herself, and I still amuse her, so I live. And yet, with imperfect connection comes imperfect control. I who once commanded the storm?" He held up one of his hands, staring at it, turning his fingers. "My lifespan I retain, and my memories, but little else. All that remains of what I was is most... inconvenient. I am cursed now."

She remembered the coffee cup from that first night. She wondered if the cave had been created in the same way, the destruction of the stone that had once been in this space. "If your curse created this space to shelter us, then perhaps it is not so bad."

The flattery did not seem to soothe him. He clenched a fist. "The power that was once at my command now leaks out of me, dripping like blood from a half-healed wound. Using it is akin to ripping that wound open again. Painful, and dangerous, and not something to do with any frequency. Tonight cost me much. There will be a price to pay. There always is." He sighed. "All that surrounds me, fails me."

"I shall not fail you," she lied.

He smiled back, an expression as vast and terrible as the blizzard raging outside. "I know you won't, fáith. I know you won't." And then he stood. "A pleasure, as always, to spend an evening in the company of a beautiful woman."

Celeste felt her face flush at the compliment—he thought she was beautiful, even like this, dressed in filthy men's clothes and sunburned and her hair a complete mess?—but didn't dare respond. "So where are you going?" she challenged back.

"As far away as I may," he told her. "Prolonged proximity to me right now may have a deleterious effect on your constitution."

"What do you mean?"

"I shall send Lukas back to bind your legs with the irons. I cannot risk you running off, especially not on a night like tonight," he told her, not unkindly. "But do not worry. There will be no repeat of that first morning. You are mine, and none of the lads will go against me on this."

Balor, she found herself thinking as he left her by the dying fire. Balor.

Celeste had heard that name before. In one of Grandmother's old tales. But she couldn't place the story. Couldn't remember the details. Charlotte had always been selfish with those books, never teaching

Celeste the Gaelic, seldom even agreeing to read them aloud to her in English.

But Balor was a name from those stories. The old stories. Before the faery folk and the great kings and the hero Cuchulain. Before the humans.

Who was it? What had they been called?

What manner of creature was Balor?

What was Eli Horn?

CHAPTER TWENTY-ONE

Much to Thomas's surprise, the snow was already melting by the time they gathered for a bite to eat that morning. Hiram and the other men were nowhere to be seen, but Hannah fixed a mountain of flat cakes she called flapjacks that came with wild honey and fresh venison; the deer the meat came from was half-butchered in the yard.

The children, small though they were, tore through the food, consuming quantities far in excess of what Thomas would have thought possible. His own plate was piled too high, he thought, but he accepted it with a smile and went outside to eat with the rest of the group.

"You're certain of this route, wolf?" Mr. Hallorman was saying. He was as composed as he always was, not a speck of dirt on him, not a wrinkle in his clothes, no hint that he had slept with the horses the night before.

Captain Sirok had foregone the flapjacks and was still working on a huge venison steak, cooked very rare. He had a map spread out on the rough boards between them. "We are here, roughly," he said, indicating a spot somewhat south of Buena Vista with his bowie knife, "and the San Juan Mountains are here." The tip of the blade moved south and west.

"That is a huge expanse," Miss Roseingrave said. The baby was once again settled in her lap, eating her food. "How will we find the right place?"

"The San Juans are indeed huge, but rough and hard to navigate. That plays in our favor," Captain Sirok explained. "There are only a few towns, and all the prospectors are obliged to use them as a base."

"So there will be a limit on how far afield this gold mine may be located," the faery mused. His attitude, Thomas thought, had completely changed. Tightly focused, very intent.

"That shall do us no good if Eli Horn has already taken my sister through the portal," Miss Roseingrave said. "We will not have time to conduct a search."

"I already told you, ma'am, pursuit in these conditions is a bad idea. Our best bet is to find where they will emerge and intercept them there."

"That is a gamble we cannot afford."

"You've lost the trail?" Thomas asked, catching on.

The cavalry captain made a face. "I can track in snow, but not after a blizzard like yesterday's. It obliterates the scent."

"Do you need a scent to follow this creature?" Miss Roseingrave asked sharply, looking at Mr. Hallorman, and moved her plate as the baby grabbed for a last bite of flapjack. "We do not detour, we do not guess. We pursue."

"It is a bad choice," Mr. Hallorman replied, but rose to his feet nonetheless. There was a certain grace to his movements, a fluidity, that would have been out of place in a human, Thomas noted. Subtle differences, but differences nonetheless. "But one I will abide by. Finish your food. The sooner we leave, the sooner Charlotte may learn the error of her ways."

Thomas watched the faery stalk off and then looked back to Miss Roseingrave. She was wiping the baby's hands with her handkerchief, a thoughtful expression on her face.

"What power do you have over him?" he asked.

"In truth, I do not know," she told him. "My grandmother always insisted he was real. I assumed that she had met him at some point." Food gone, breakfast done, the baby squirmed out of Miss Roseingrave's lap, giggling as she toddled back toward the cabin where the women and children had slept the night before. "The stories she told me about him made him seem omnipotent, larger than life, affectionate even. Like an angel."

Thomas snorted. "He is not that."

"No," she agreed. "He is not."

Hannah walked with them a little way out of camp, the older children playing barefoot in the already melting snow. The baby clung to the woman's faded calico dress, watching them with big brown eyes.

"You be careful, Isatahkabi," the bear woman said, speaking to Captain Sirok as the party readied itself to leave. "This thing that rides with these men, it's no good."

"I know, Hannah. I've dealt with Eli Horn before."

"The darkness rides with him," Hannah replied. "He ain't human, but he ain't one of us, neither. He's evil. The end of all things. Can't kill somethin' like that."

Thomas glanced over at Mr. Hallorman, who was sitting expressionless on his horse, staring ahead. Trying too hard not to react, he thought.

Captain Sirok smiled and patted his sword. "Never met anything that couldn't be killed, Hannah. 'Sides, we've got ourselves a proper seeress on our side. Don't you worry 'bout us. You take care of those cubs, you hear?"

She placed a big rough hand over her heart, then opened it in some kind of farewell Thomas didn't recognize. "Take care."

Captain Sirok nodded, and that was that.

"Isatahkabi?" Thomas asked as they left the rough little collection of cabins behind.

The cavalry officer ran a hand over his mustache, grimacing a little. "My Comanche name."

"You're Indian?"

"Partially, on my ma's side. Just like Hannah and Hiram, and a lotta people whose families've been out here for a few generations," he said, and grinned. "Whatever you're thinkin', Englishman, ain't nuthin' straightforward out here in the West." Then he spurred his horse. "Come on. Snow'll still be stickin' to the ground further up. We need to move fast while we can."

The bottomlands where the bear clan's fall camp was located quickly closed in, the broad riverbed funneling into a canyon that cut up into the foothills of the Sawatch Range. Shallow at first, the banks quickly rose, turning into low cliffs. The southern rim shaded the interior, and the previous night's snow clung to the ground in big drifts. Still, it did not seem to Thomas to be impassable, and surely the snowstorm would have stopped the brigands as well. He was already thinking of what they would do when they caught up with Eli Horn's posse when their little group was stopped dead.

A landslide choked the canyon. Tall and deep, the rock and earth and tumbled trees looked fresh, unsettled, free of any signs of vegetation growth or the passage of animals. It filled the canyon from bank to bank, fifteen feet at least at its lowest point, well over the tops of the cottonwoods at the other end. At first glance, there did not seem to be a way over it.

Mr. Hallorman laid his reins aside and jumped down from his horse, the beaded fringe of his quiver tinkling quietly.

"Where did this come from?" Thomas asked Captain Sirok, who was scanning the surrounding slopes.

"Hard to tell with the snow, but looks like there," he said, and pointed at a clean strip of hillside, scraped free of its old coverings, a scar in the land-scape. "The angle o' the ground up there don't look all that unstable to me," he said.

"That is because this was not happenstance," Mr. Hallorman said. He was standing at the base of the slide, one foot up on a boulder, glaring up the hill. "This was intentional."

"Intentional by whom?" Thomas asked.

Captain Sirok shook his head. "This don't look like a demolition."

"I made no mention of explosives," Mr. Hallorman said, and went down to a knee, hand on the dirt. "The mountain did this," he said. "It did not want this Eli Horn to pass."

Thomas frowned. "But how could—"

"Silence, all of you," Mr. Hallorman said curtly, cutting him off. "Let me focus. I wish to see if this will move for us."

Thomas looked over at the cavalry officer, who just shrugged. Miss Roseingrave's expression was unmoved. With a sigh, the researcher settled in to wait.

Almost fifteen minutes later, Mr. Hallorman finally rose back to his feet, dusting off his hands, a strange expression on his face.

"Well?" Thomas asked, looking up from his notebook.

"This mountain is quite angry," he told them, "and refuses my requests. Something about not wishing to aid one of my kind after the injury done to it by the other."

"Eli Horn?" Miss Roseingrave asked.

"But you are not entirely similar to him, you said," Thomas said. "Does this mean he is indeed fae as well?"

"With what he is, we are similar enough that the mountain is unwilling to make a distinction between us," Mr. Hallorman said, and paused. "And I am as much a newcomer to these lands as you humans. I am not known here. I am not trusted." This seemed to frustrate the faery greatly. Instead of Mr. Hallorman's usual arrogance, Thomas thought he detected a note of regret in the words. "It will not let me channel the deep magics. This landslide will stay where it is."

"But we must proceed!" Miss Roseingrave protested.

"Captain Sirok, your map, if you will," Mr. Hallorman said, and nodded to Charlotte. "Hours lost this morning, lass. You should have listened to me."

Clearly stung, Miss Roseingrave didn't answer.

In the face of the insurmountable obstacle in their way, the party gathered to discuss their best alternate route. Captain Sirok's map proved invaluable as a reference, but to Thomas, it seemed as if there were no good options. The mountains here all piled up on one another, each taller and more inhospitable than the previous one, unnavigable.

But after a moment or two of study, Mr. Hallorman laid a finger on the map. "Here. The land drains here. They shall have to follow those water courses, especially in terrain like this, and those shall be the most direct route to reach the San Juans. They will come here." He tapped the map. "How large a town is this, wolf?"

Captain Sirok shrugged. "Gunnison? Large enough."

"Supplies? Horses? People to kill?"

"Yes to all of that. It's a major stop on the stagecoach routes."

Mr. Hallorman nodded. "Good for raiding?"

"It would be if you didn't mind dealin' with Sheriff Trumbull. He's a piece of work, no doubt about that."

"Gunnison then," the faery said. "That is where we shall intercept them. We take the easier road, the road they meant to take. Make better time, and arrive before they do."

"I recommend this route," Captain Sirok said, indicating the map.

The massive Sawatch Range stood between their current position and the town, Thomas could see. The distance was not great, in terms of straight miles, but nothing would be straight in these mountains. The route indicated by Captain Sirok went south around the bottom of the range, longer but much flatter.

"There is still a pass there to contend with," Miss Roseingrave mused.

"Monarch Pass ain't so bad," Captain Sirok said.

"You agree with this course of action?" she asked him sharply.

"Of course, ma'am. I have no desire to lead y'all to your deaths in here." And he indicated the mountains again. "'Sides, there's a bit o' official government in Gunnison, and that might help us."

"Your Sheriff Trumbull won't do much against this gang," Mr. Hallorman said.

"Is there nothing else we can do to continue our direct pursuit?" Miss Roseingrave asked Mr. Hallorman, a plea in her words. "I do not like trusting to chance."

The faery shook his head. "This road is closed to us, Charlotte."

Thomas didn't say it, but after the violence of the storm the night before, he was grateful they were not headed deeper into the mountains, where any such blizzards would surely be even more intense, and the bears would be of the more mundane kind.

Still, the look of crushing disappointment on Miss Roseingrave's face was almost more than he could bear.

"South then?" she asked.

"South."

CHAPTER TWENTY-TWO

For Celeste, the next few days were pure misery.

While the snowstorm of the first night was not repeated, the Sawatch Mountains had plenty of other challenges to offer. Steep inclines, thick forest, and precipitous drop-offs were all quite prevalent, as were unpredictable temperatures.

The going was slow. After a day or so, Celeste thought she could discern the outlaw Horn's intentions for their route: he was guiding them alongside the narrow creeks and dry streams of the mountains, letting the water choose the easiest paths between the towering peaks. But it was a strategy fraught with danger; the little canyons sometimes narrowed so severely that everyone was forced to dismount and lead their horses straight through running water, ice cold and providing uncertain footing. In one place, near to sunset on the second day, the water came up to Celeste's waist, and it was only thanks to Mr. Abbitt's intervention that she was not swept downstream.

"I suppose I should thank you," she said later that evening, after camp had been set and fires lit. She was truly grateful for the warmth; she was chilled to the bone, skin tingling, numb from the water. Celeste could feel the current still tugging at her. Shockingly strong, it had been, for how shallow it seemed to be. "Saving me today."

Dropping her chains on the ground beside her, Mr. Abbitt growled a little but would not meet her eye. "No thanks necessary," he said gruffly. "Boss'd kill me if anything happened to you."

Celeste recognized the body language. He was taken with her. But then, that was no surprise. She knew what she was: a pale-faced girl with brilliant red hair and elfin features, a rarity out here on the frontier, and many men seemed to be drawn to her. Under any other circumstances, he might have been the thread she would have pulled on to unravel this mess and effect her escape, but something in her rebelled at his presence.

Lukas Abbitt scared her.

"Still," she said, "I am grateful for it."

Mr. Abbitt stopped, looking her over now. There was definitely hunger in his eyes. Hunger and uncertainty.

"That'll do, Lukas my lad," Eli Horn said, approaching with a metal plate in hand and his long duster jacket cast over his arm. "Fix her leg irons and go."

The gunman obeyed, locking the manacles around her ankles and slipping away again. The other fires were a little way away, down the small hillock where they'd stopped for the night. Down there, the men were talking boisterously, laughing at some raunchy joke and eating so loudly she could almost hear the food falling out of their mouths.

"An uncouth lot," Eli Horn said, sitting down beside her and holding out the food. "But effective."

"At stealing?" Celeste asked, taking the dish from him. Beans and salt pork. It was always beans and salt pork. Too hard, too salty, bitter tonight, as if it was going bad. But it was hot, and right now, she needed that.

Eli Horn settled down next to her. "One only keeps what one can defend."

"Who could defend their homestead against you?" she retorted.

Eli Horn chuckled. "Who indeed?" He set his hat aside, looking up at the stars, just beginning to peek out of the dark, velvety firmament. "It was a better world before your people carved up the land and laid claim to everything. It was better when my people ruled here. So much has been lost since then. So much."

"How old are you?" she asked, intrigued and concerned in equal measure. Before, before the cave, Celeste had been able to dismiss Mr. Horn's strange statements as some figment of a fevered mind, a person lost in their own untrue but deeply held story.

She could not so easily ignore him now.

"We have always been," he said, "and always will be, as long as our stories are told, as long as time endures. We were there at the beginning, and we shall be there at the end."

Celeste shifted. She had been forced to take off her stockings, soaked as they were and drying on a flat rock nearby, and the iron chains were cold against her skin. "At the Rapture?" she asked.

He laughed. "One last grand battle between good and evil? Nothing will be that simple. All is uncertainty, Miss Roseingrave, but what I do know is that all things fail in the end."

"You do not speak like any outlaw I have ever heard of."

"I have not always been an outlaw. Once, dear fáith, I was a king, if you can believe that."

Celeste didn't know what to say to that. It seemed improbable, impossible, and yet, his bearing, just for a moment... "King of what?"

He held out the jacket for her. "I know you were working as a seamstress, and my people always valued a woman's skill with her needle. I was hoping you might mend this for me."

She took the jacket carefully. The fabric was falling to holes in places, so threadbare that the remaining fibers could not hold themselves in their weave. Other sections were almost brittle. It was as if the garment had aged a hundred years in the last few days. "I do not know if I can. The fabric is quite weak," she said. She brushed her thumb across one of the weak spots in the jacket. "How did this happen?"

He rose. "As I said, fáith, the cost for the cave would be, is, significant. We will need to reach a human settlement in the next few days, or risk starvation up here."

Celeste glanced back down at the jacket, wanting to know what he meant by that. "I would need material to patch it with, and, as you say, a needle."

He handed her a small sewing kit, secured in a little case. She opened it to find scissors, needles, and a few spools of thread. Something was gritty on the outside. The tin box was of the newest style, but the paint was already flaking off, and the steel screws holding the hinges in place were rusting.

"I shall do what I can," she told him, looking back up, but he was already gone.

The cost, she wondered. What was the cost?

The answer became clear as they continued to trudge through the mountains.

Eli Horn's curse.

Random, it seemed at first, but undeniable. One morning, she might wake up to a horse whinnying in pain, its shoes rusted in place on its hooves. In the evening, the wood gathered for a fire might fall apart to dust as Eli Horn merely walked by, or the day's ration of hardtack gone so moldy its original surface couldn't be seen. Rockslides became more common. The party was nearly buried twice by avalanches from above, and the packhorse with the cooking pots was lost on the third day, the ground itself giving way mere moments after Eli Horn passed over it. The metal eyelets in Celeste's corset rusted, bleeding red corrosion into the drab cotton of her shirtwaist. Saddles cracked. Clothing fell to rags. Gunpowder failed.

On they pressed, winding their way up through the high mountains, over a series of what Eli Horn insisted were passes. Celeste couldn't tell.

She had spent many a day since Mama's death dreaming about California, about leaving all her sorrow behind her, finding a new life for herself.

But that life had always included clean sheets and comfortable beds and —preferably—a rich husband to dote on her, or at the very least, not mind when she spent his money. It wasn't about hedonism or being spoiled, or whatever Charlotte believed. It was about certainty, about never having to wonder where her next meal was coming from, never getting on a train and leaving her friends behind again, nor being driven out of town by an angry mob of ladies from the local church. Celeste wanted to wake up in the morning, every morning, secure in the knowledge that all was right in the world.

This situation was not that. Not at all.

And yet...

Despite the danger, the forests were peaceful. Despite the cold, the snowcapped peaks were beautiful. Despite their rough ways and hard words, the outlaw gang she rode with was fiercely protective.

Despite his curse, Eli Horn was fascinating.

He brought her supper every night, and while Celeste hated the irons, she always had her own fire. The separation from the others actually gave her and Eli Horn space to talk.

During the day, with the men, she had noticed, he was as rough and unrefined and coarse as they were, and they seemed to love him for it. At night, as they shared a poor meal together, he was different. Noble, and sad, a tragic figure that Lord Byron no doubt would have immortalized in some grand work, if ever the two of them had met. Eli Horn told her stories about Tir na nAill, about the world before. He was an excellent storyteller, and his words wove a beautiful world. Feasts, hunts, battles. Conquests.

"Was she very fair, your Ériu?" Celeste asked him on the fourth night, as he finished an especially sordid tale about a lover he had taken and lost again.

"She was. But as with so many things in my life, she and I were not to be."

"Did you ever see her again?"

"I did," he said, expression almost wistful, eyes focused on something Celeste could not see. "Once. On the battlefield."

"So you fought her?"

"Yes, although it pained me greatly. And when it came to our defeat... she..." He trailed off, scooping up a handful of dirt, thick with little pebbles. The ground here in the mountains was rocky that way, Celeste had noticed, and this night, they'd been able to make camp near a small river. He clenched a fist and opened it again. Fine sand ran out.

The sight of it sent a chill through celeste, but she could not deny that she was enthralled by his story. "Did you love her?"

"I loved many women in my time, fáith. But she is gone, and it is not the way of my people to mourn what has been lost." He looked at her then. "It would be foolish to ignore the beauty around me now."

She stared back at him, wondering where this was headed, trying to fight against the strange rise of emotion she felt at his words. *Find an escape,* she reminded herself, *you're supposed to be finding an escape.* "I am no faery woman from a tale, sir, but a flesh-and-blood human. I am afraid that after such company, I would disappoint."

"No," he said, and pushed himself up to standing, regarding her with dark eyes. "No, you would not."

And leaving Celeste speechless behind him, Eli Horn vanished again into the night.

She watched him go for a moment, then dropped her face into her hands, trying to breathe through the strange heat spreading through her body.

What was wrong with her?

The next morning, after a few hours of riding, they were descending again. Out of the mountains. Toward a small town named Gunnison where, the outlaw leader had assured his men, they would secure fresh horses and supplies. As he had predicted, everything they had was almost spent, rotted away.

It would be Celeste's first, and likely last, chance of escape.

But as her horse obediently followed along behind Lukas's, placidly trotting along on its lead line, a seed of a thought began to grow.

A very dangerous thought.

Was certainty, security, really what she wanted?

CHAPTER TWENTY-THREE

Charlotte's fears about more winter storms proved to be unfounded.

For the next few days, their party made good time across the broad valley plains. They got no more snow, and indeed, by the second morning after the blizzard, temperatures were so high again as to be almost uncomfortable. The horses maintained a good pace, however, and Captain Sirok assured her that they were on course to arrive at Gunnison well ahead of Eli Horn's gang, if Eli Horn's gang reemerged from the Sawatch Range at all.

This was a point he and Mr. Hallorman argued about more than once. Mr. Hallorman was of the opinion that the mountains were actively trying to kill the outlaw fae, roused to unusual wakefulness by his presence.

"I've lived my whole life out west, and I ain't never seen a mountain try to kill a man," Captain Sirok protested.

"I'd wager good cattle you have, wolf, but didn't have the wit to recognize it."

His failure with the landslide seemed to have put Mr. Hallorman in a black mood. Charlotte didn't quite understand it. By rights, no force on earth save time should have moved those rocks, and yet, Mr. Hallorman had taken it as a personal insult.

She had always thought that faeries were tricksters, fey and dangerous in their own way, but commanding little more power than glamours and

simple shape-shifting. For him to be able to move an entire landslide with…
with magic, seemed improbable. But antagonizing him by inquiring about it
would get them nowhere, and besides, Charlotte had had long practice with
ignoring the Otherworld. It seemed a prudent strategy now.

Mr. Leighton did not share that attitude, eagerly jotting notes down
during breaks in their ride, or at night around the campfire.

Still, he was the only other human in their group, and Charlotte was
grateful for his company. Captain Sirok was too jovial, Mr. Hallorman too
grim. Mr. Leighton was the counterbalance to both; she found his company
reassuring.

"At this pace, we'll reach Poncha Springs by midmorning tomorrow,"
Captain Sirok said on the second evening after the snowstorm, as he worked
on a fire. "Then it's through Monarch Pass and down toward Gunnison.
We're makin' good time."

"Familiar with the route then?" Mr. Leighton asked. The captain
shrugged. The researcher pressed. "I wouldn't have thought cavalry would
be so active in the mountains."

"We go where we're ordered," Captain Sirok said, and looked pensive.
"It's the Ute, up here. But not for much longer, I think."

"You've fought the Indians?" Mr. Leighton asked.

"Leighton, we're west of the Mississippi and I'm wearin' a US Army
uniform. Whaddaya think I do?"

"I mean no offense. But you said you were Comanche and—"

"Part," Captain Sirok said testily. "Quarter-Comanche, half-Czech, all
Texan. But let me tell you what, only place in this world I've ever had is
with Colonel Ramage's pack. He tells me to fight the Ute, I fight the
Ute."

"But aren't those your people?"

Sirok narrowed his eyes. "You gone soft in the head, Englishman?"

"Finally somebody else sees it," Mr. Hallorman sighed dramatically.

"The Indians are not a unified single group, as I understand it," Charlotte said, wishing to defuse the growing tension. "The Utes and
Comanches are quite distinct, are they not?"

"And not allies," Sirok said, and looked at Mr. Leighton. "The killin' out
here goes in all directions. Ain't nobody's hands clean."

"But what of the things that are being lost?" Mr. Leighton asked. "Some
of my colleagues have begun to warn of the extinction of language
through—"

"Academic considerations don't matter much when people are dyin',
Leighton."

"I am not talking of academics, but of history, traditions that—"

"It's the way of this world," Mr. Hallorman interjected. "All things flow.
All things change. This land belonged to others, before the Ute. It will
belong to others, after the Americans are gone. All kill to take what they
have. It is the way of things."

For a moment, the others in the group just stared at the faery. Then
Captain Sirok smiled. "And you think I'm the bloodthirsty one."

"I didn't say that I enjoy death, just that it is inevitable," Mr. Hallorman
replied.

"I meant no offense," Mr. Leighton said to Captain Sirok.

"And I ain't sayin' it ain't sad," Captain Sirok replied, voice thoughtful
now. "But ain't no humans, Indians or Anglos or otherwise, my people. I
might look like you but I ain't you."

"Are you indeed a werewolf then? You are not as I imagined such beings
to be," Mr. Leighton admitted.

"That's 'cause I ain't a werewolf. You want that? Should have met my
father b'fore he rightly got put down."

"Who killed him?"

"Colonel Ramage," Captain Sirok said, and would speak no more on
the matter.

The next day was a long one, the road up to Monarch Pass hard-used and
deeply rutted. But it was a proper road at least, and it picked out the easiest
route to the summit. There was nothing to recommend the place, no
sweeping vistas or glorious scenery, and while Charlotte would never have
given voice to it, she did feel a bit of disappointment at that. In Grandmother's stories, the heroes always passed through beautiful lands, through mysterious and magical places.

Her own faery tale, it seemed, was far more mundane.

But she still prayed it might remain so. The world as it was, she believed,
was far preferable to finding themselves in Faeryland, Tir na nAill, or wherever it was this Eli Horn was taking her sister.

If they had to cross that threshold...

Charlotte didn't want to think about it. She had no desire to ever see the true depths of the Otherworld. She dealt with its shallows often enough.

They almost got stuck at the western toll gate, Captain Sirok haggling with the keeper for longer than seemed necessary, protesting the usurious fee.

The gate had been carefully positioned to prevent travelers from merely going around it. They were at the end of an alpine meadow, many acres in size but surrounded by wooded hills. The road passed between two particularly high, rocky outcroppings, dropping sharply to follow a dry streambed down to the flatter lands below. A horse may have picked out a path around it, over the hills, but a wagon would only have been able to pass this way.

Charlotte glanced up the slope. There was a log cabin up there, a few scraggly squash plants bearing huge fruit the last of a small subsistence garden. A cow grazed placidly nearby. Smoke rose from the chimney.

They were almost out of the mountains, but it was late afternoon, and finding another path down likely would have taken hours. And the toll keeper knew these lands better than they. If it came to a shoot-out, or some such foolish thing, they would be at a distinct disadvantage.

This was the only way out. The only way to her sister.

"Do something," she hissed at Mr. Hallorman.

The faery looked at her askance. "Are you sure?" he asked.

"We're losing daylight," she told him.

He laid his reins across his horse's neck. "As you command, milady," he said in his mocking way, and dismounted.

Neither the toll man nor Captain Sirok reacted much as Mr. Hallorman sauntered up. He didn't acknowledge the toll man at all and addressed the cavalry officer alone. "What is the problem? Pay him and let us be on our way."

"He don't want to respect military rates. Which are nothing, let me add," he said, rolling his eyes back to the keeper of the toll gate. "I ain't payin' you to lift this gate. You're gonna do it for free, like you're obliged to."

The toll man folded his arms across his chest. He was dressed in shirt-sleeves and patched old jeans, hat pushed up to look Captain Sirok in the eye. "And I told you, I don't see no military operation, just a group o' people. With a lady, I might add. This ain't no official business. How do I know you didn't kill a man for that uniform you're wearing?"

The captain growled, but Mr. Hallorman stopped him before he could step forward. "It seems the good captain refuses to pay you on principle, which I can appreciate. You are an odious man who keeps a poor road and charges too much for it."

"You're all wastin' my time," the toll man said, and very deliberately laid a hand on his belt, which boasted a revolver in a long holster.

"On the contrary," Mr. Hallorman replied. "I propose a trade."

That took the toll man off guard, and he peered at the faery. "Does this look like a barter economy to you?"

"A trade," Mr. Hallorman continued. "You open the gates and allow us to pass, and the buyout you receive next year from the US government shall make you a very rich man indeed. Refuse, and we shall pass anyway, and the government will all but steal this from you."

The man stared, like he couldn't quite understand what he was hearing, and then scowled. "Get outta here!" he snapped. "Back up the mountain or find your own way down. I ain't got time for this nonsense!"

Charlotte felt something then. A hum, a thrum, like the low notes of an orchestra warming up before the main performance. She could see something that looked almost like a green mist, glowing, little tendrils reaching up from the ground, twisting and turning and winding about it. "Mr. Hallorman," she called out, nervous now.

"A fair trade rejected is an opportunity lost," Mr. Hallorman said with a cruel smile quirking at the corner of his lips.

The toll man made to answer but never got a chance, staring slack-mouthed in horror around him.

Where the road had been only moments before, hard-packed dirt kept clean and empty by the passage of man and beast, there was now grass and weeds and other growing things. It spread fast, a green wildfire sweeping away from them, up the slope. The tendrils of fern unfurled in shaded places. Flowers bloomed on stalks many feet high. The ground broke, rippling under the force of so many little roots. Everywhere, every leaf, every blade of grass, glowed with an inner light.

The effect ended at the gate, Charlotte noticed. A gate whose wood was now erupting with mushrooms. When Mr. Hallorman pushed it open, the wood was already loose and spongy.

Charlotte heard giggling behind her and looked back up the slope. The same infestation of mushrooms was blooming from the log cabin. A trio of children, dirty-faced but smiling, were tumbling out, laughing, dancing in the flowers.

She looked over at Mr. Leighton. He had pulled a notebook and pencil from his coat pocket, furiously writing.

The toll man stood, mouth agape, watching the surrounding prairie reclaim his road and his homestead. "What... How..."

"When the Irish offer you a deal," Mr. Hallorman replied almost sweetly, and swung back up in his saddle, "you'd best take it. Englishman, put your book away! We leave!"

The gate crumbled under the faery's hand, the decayed remains crashing softly to the ground. It startled Mr. Leighton's horse, and he almost fell off, trying as he was to replace his notebook.

Charlotte couldn't look the toll man in the eye as she passed, her own face burning with shame.

"How did you do that?" Mr. Leighton asked, their party headed downward on an easy road once more.

The faery snorted. "He annoyed me."

"That is not an explanation for how—"

"He also annoyed the land here. It was mostly the mountain, if you must know."

"You destroyed their house with that infestation of mushrooms!" Charlotte protested.

"It is not winter yet," the fae said with a shrug. "And the rapidity of that effect will subside. Such things are difficult to maintain."

"There were children there!"

"If you do not want my help, then do not ask for it, Charlotte," he replied, testy. He sounded winded, she noticed, as if he had just exerted a great effort.

She let the subject drop then, keenly aware of her own guilt, and rode on.

They made it down the mountain by sundown, making camp near the start of another set of rolling grasslands. Violet-blue smudging against the western horizon spoke of yet more mountains.

"That'll be the San Juans," Captain Sirok said, indicating the distant peaks.

"They don't look all that different from the rest we've seen," Mr. Leighton commented.

"They ain't. Rugged and nasty, but nothing unusual about them, I'd say."

Mr. Hallorman eyed them as well, but if he had any thoughts, he did not share them. "Where's Gunnison?" he asked.

"Thataway, 'bout twenty, twenty-five miles." And Captain Sirok pointed toward the sinking sun. "With luck, we'll be there tomorrow."

"We ride today until the light gives out," the faery said. "I want us there as soon as possible." And without waiting for an answer or even an acknowledgment from the others, he spurred his horse on, down toward that highland plain.

CHAPTER TWENTY-FOUR

Gunnison came into view just after noon, a collection of buildings scattered across the plains like children's blocks, bright paint peeling and dull wood turning gray under the early afternoon sun.

The terrain that day had been much easier. They had found a good brook to camp next to with plenty of grazing the night before. Well-watered and well-fed, the horses were in good spirits. They had needed little encouragement to move fast, and indeed, Charlotte spent more time trying to keep her gelding from cantering than she did urging him on.

They had not stopped riding all day, not even to eat. Mr. Hallorman had pushed yesterday until the light had completely failed and had woken them all early today, before dawn. What he was worried about, Charlotte couldn't say. His body language was difficult to read most of the time, but today, he was entirely shut down. As if he was trying to hide something from her. But every so often, his gaze would travel northward, toward the peaks of the Sawatch Range.

"The terrain does not seem so unfriendly here," Mr. Leighton observed, about a mile out from Gunnison, according to the markers they passed on the road. "Is it possible that this Eli Horn will circumvent the town entirely?"

"Doubtful," Captain Sirok said. "They'll need supplies. The last year or two, they've been hittin' a target every week. Don't make much sense but..."

"It makes perfect sense," Mr. Leighton replied. "If this entropic effect has something to do with Eli Horn, then a general breakdown of both man and materiel can be expected to—"

"Entropic?" Mr. Hallorman asked sharply.

"Yes, it's a newer concept, but one well founded in thermodynamics," Mr. Leighton continued. "Essentially, the idea is that all things will progress toward static equilibrium. They shall become more disordered and more undifferentiated because disorder is the most statistically likely outcome in—"

"Charlotte, translate this Englishman's babble for me," Mr. Hallorman said, cutting him off. "And tell him that this talk of physics is useless when it comes to my people."

"I confess, I'm not sure what he means either," Charlotte replied honestly.

"Physics is simply an expression of our understanding of the natural world," Mr. Leighton said, pressing on undeterred. "It is my understanding that the fae are embodiments of nature in its many and varied forms. Thus, any discussion of natural science surely must apply to you as well."

Captain Sirok laughed. Mr. Hallorman glowered.

"What is entropy?" Charlotte asked, curious now herself.

Mr. Leighton seemed pleased to explain. "Entropy is the expression of nature's... becoming disordered, for lack of a better term. Things age and die, iron rusts, wood crumbles, all because their entropy increases."

"Would you call this force one of chaos? Of destruction and decay?" Mr. Hallorman asked.

"I suppose one could term it such. Although, from the perspective of thermodynamics, it is more of an equalizing force, as I said, not a—"

"Is this concept widely known?"

"I have attended a few university lectures on the topic, and I have read magazine articles about it, although I would not expect it to be in the average child's lesson book. Why would that matter?"

But whatever Mr. Hallorman was thinking, he didn't share it.

They made Gunnison twenty minutes later.

Like so many other Western towns Charlotte had been through during her travels with Mama, Gunnison was small, compact, industrious. People were out in the wide streets and voices could be heard spilling from multiple saloons.

"Prospectors coming in from the mountains," Captain Sirok explained when Mr. Leighton asked. "This time of year, people are either stocking up for winter before returning to their claims or heading out of the mountains to avoid the snows that are coming. Now, I've been through Gunnison a few times before, and if I recall correctly, the sheriff's office is this way." He guided his horse into the lead, turning down the next street.

"We don't need the sheriff," Mr. Hallorman said. "All you're likely to do is get them all killed."

"How are the four of us going to stop such a murderous posse on our own?" Charlotte asked.

"An excellent question, Charlotte, and as I have told your pet Englishman in the past, one you should have asked yourself before leaving Leadville," Mr. Hallorman said, curt. He was worried about something, she realized. But what?

"Oh, hello," Captain Sirok said, pulling up his horse. "What's this then?"

In front of them was a boy of perhaps fourteen years, mounted on a horse that seemed far too big for him, quite clearly waiting for them. A deputy sheriff's star glinted on his vest. "Are you Captain Sirok?" he asked.

The cavalry officer tipped his head. "Who's askin'?"

"Sheriff Trumbull," the kid replied. "Said he wanted to see a Captain Sirok as soon he gets into town. And you don't look like any of the other cavalry officers we got in town right now, so…"

"Well, you're in luck. Captain Sirok is me," the captain drawled. "Where's the sheriff at?"

"I'll show you the way," the young man said, and hesitated. "Sheriff didn't say nuthin' about anybody else, and seein' as how you have a lady with you—"

"We're coming," Mr. Hallorman said.

"Yes, sir, this way." And the boy gestured for them to follow.

"Sirok," Mr. Hallorman growled as they fell in behind the boy, "what did you do?"

"Colonel Ramage's doing, I reckon, not mine," he said quietly.

"You said you were the official attention this matter would receive."

"The colonel is a very thorough man," Sirok replied. "He sees a threat to the people of this fine state, he's gonna act. It's his job, you know."

"The Army is up here?"

"Army's everywhere," Captain Sirok said, but his good humor seemed strained now.

They were approaching the sheriff's office, a fine brick structure at the corner of the next street, and there wasn't much time to talk about anything else. The boy bade them wait outside, hopping nimbly off his own horse and running inside.

The effect was instantaneous. The door didn't even have a chance to close. Swinging shut, it was thrown open and a pair of men came out.

"Sirok!" roared one of those men, dressed in dusty black with a red waistcoat. He clamped his hat down on his head and scowled at them all. "I wish I could say this was a pleasant surprise."

Captain Sirok's face didn't change, but Charlotte could almost see something stirring in him. That wolf he carried, she figured, and tried not to look at it. It was surprised, and it was angry.

"Wish I could say the same, Sheriff Trumbull," the cavalry officer replied evenly, and he nodded to the other man. "Major Wilson, good to see you, too."

This one was garbed similarly to Captain Sirok, blue uniform with yellow accents, and seemed no more pleased at the sight of Captain Sirok than Sheriff Trumbull was. He just nodded at them, dipping his hat to Charlotte. She nodded back.

The sheriff didn't bother with even those pleasantries. "When Major Wilson arrived in town a few days ago and told me the news, I was a little taken aback. Surely, I said to myself, Colonel Ramage wouldn't be stupid enough to let Captain Sirok handle a pursuit like this all by himself. Not after what happened last time you had a mission up here in these parts."

Now, Sirok's eyes narrowed. "The colonel's never done a stupid thing in his life."

"No doubt the very reason he sent Major Wilson up after you," the sheriff said, and looked at Charlotte like he was just registering her presence. "My apologies, ma'am, for you gettin' stuck with such a barbaric one as this."

Charlotte regarded him coolly. "Captain Sirok's been nothing but a gentleman, I assure you."

"You ain't seen him when his blood's up," Sheriff Trumbull replied.

"Sheriff, that's enough," Major Wilson said calmly. "Nobody's going to have a repeat of the winter of '82 up here. Our good captain was but a young lieutenant then, and I trust that Colonel Ramage, whose reputation is impeccable I might add, has taught him some...self-control since then. Besides"—and he looked directly at the captain—"I outrank him."

"I ain't gonna argue that," Captain Sirok replied, stiff now. "Sir."

The sheriff, seemingly mollified on the subject of the captain, looked now to Mr. Hallorman. "And you, what's your story? I don't like the look of you."

"That is your problem, Sheriff, not mine," Mr. Hallorman replied. "What are you doing interfering in our business?"

"Your business?" the sheriff demanded. "Your business? I've got a mad pack of outlaws who kidnapped a woman loose in my county, and you have the gall to say this is your problem?"

"You do not want to get involved with this, either of you," Mr. Hallorman replied, looking between the sheriff and the senior cavalry officer.

"Like hell I don't," he said, spitting, and then looked at Charlotte. "Beggin' your pardon, ma'am."

She shook her head. "Sheriff, you would do well to listen to Mr. Hallorman here. These men are dangerous."

"So are mine," Major Wilson replied, speaking up again. "Captain, we need to talk."

Captain Sirok hesitated a moment, then dismounted. "I'll only be a moment," he told them, and tossed his horse's reins to Mr. Leighton before following Major Wilson inside. The sheriff slammed the door behind them.

Mr. Leighton folded his arms. "What do you suppose that was all about?" he asked.

"Honestly, I have no idea," Charlotte replied, utterly confused at what had just happened.

The promised moment dragged out for ten, then twenty minutes, before the boy came back out and apologized for the delay but Captain Sirok wanted to see the disposition of the Army detachment that was here and would they be so kind as to wait for an hour or two?

"So we're being dismissed?" Mr. Hallorman asked.

"Beggin' your pardon, sir, they didn't phrase it quite that way, but—"

The faery sniffed. "Any place one might get a half-decent meal around here while we wait?"

They were referred to the Black Horse, a saloon that was—the boy reassured them—not the roughest in town. Charlotte didn't see anything about its unpainted blocky facade to recommend it over the half dozen others on the main street, but it was pleasant enough inside.

They drew a few eyes as they came in, but not many. It appeared to be all locals; hardy people, mountain people, prospectors and ranchers and hired hands. A game of cards was underway at one of the far tables, and a bartender was polishing glasses behind the bar.

"Sit anywhere you like," he called. "I'll be with you shortly, ma'am."

Charlotte nodded her head gratefully and sat down at the nearest table. There were only a few open, and none seemed any better than the others.

"What do you see around us, Charlotte?" Mr. Hallorman asked, placing his hat on the top of his chair. His hair was mussed, strands pulled out of the simple tie at the base of his neck, and there was dust on his hat. His face was as weary and sunburned as Mr. Leighton's. He normally looked untouched by their ride, and Charlotte wondered about this change in his appearance. What was concealed? What was the truth? And why hide it at all?

She smoothed down her skirt unconsciously. "I see honest people relaxing over drinks."

Mr. Hallorman smiled at her. "Is that all you see?"

Charlotte ignored the jab and looked toward the bartender, who was bustling over to them. "Pleasure to have such upstanding folk in the place this afternoon. What can I get you?"

"Whiskey, if you have it," Mr. Hallorman said, and gestured at Charlotte. "And the lady will have a coffee."

"And you, sir?"

Mr. Leighton had pulled out one of his notebooks as soon as they sat down, scribbling notes furiously. "Beer is fine," he said without looking up.

"Anything to eat?"

"Whatever you have in the kitchen," Mr. Hallorman replied, "as long as it's not too burnt or too old."

"I don't hold with servin' spoiled food," the bartender declared, clearly offended, and off he went in a huff.

"There was no reason to insult him," Charlotte said.

"There's no reason to eat terrible food," the faery countered.

"I don't see why we're eating at all," Mr. Leighton said, and pulled out a larger book filled with other notes. Charlotte caught sight of ogham script again. Still working on the translation from the séance then. "Ought we not be preparing for…"

"For what, Englishman?"

"For Eli Horn's gang?"

"Why?" Mr. Hallorman asked and kicked his boots up on the table's empty chair. "It seems the US Army has that problem well in hand for us. Now come, dear Charlotte. Tell me what you see around here."

"I already told you—"

"I don't mean with your eyes."

Charlotte took a deep breath. "I don't care to look that way."

"Won't, or can't?" he replied. "You were not so hesitant when you were a child."

"Things were different before…" … *the fire,* she almost said, but caught herself in time. "The war."

"They usually are. But the thing about wars, Charlotte, is that there's always another one. That's no reason to cut yourself off from a very useful sense."

He stopped then, interrupted by the return of the bartender and the arrival of their drinks.

"I don't need that sense to know what's going on in here," she told him, after the bartender had gone away again, and waved her hand around. "That group of men over there, the three sitting together by the bar, they have recently had a falling-out, likely over money or a lack thereof, and now do not know how to continue their partnership. The woman serving drinks was recently widowed, but I do not think that is the cause of her employment, as she moves like she belongs here." Charlotte folded her hands back upon the table. "I could read anybody here in a similar fashion. I'd have an even better impression if I spoke to them."

"Tricks your mother taught you," he said derisively.

"One need not rely on extrasensory perception to understand the world," Charlotte said, and glanced at the researcher. "Wouldn't you say, Mr. Leighton?"

He shook his head. His hair was slightly too long and fell across his forehead. "It is documented at this point that many mediums do employ such tricks. But even that implies some degree of above-average insight into the human condition, does it not?"

"Ever the believer, aren't you?" Mr. Hallorman asked derisively.

"Sir, I assure you, I am no Spiritualist. This is a matter of...of professional curiosity for me."

"Yes, because one comes halfway across the world to satisfy professional curiosity."

Mr. Leighton said nothing, but Mr. Hallorman had scored a blow. Charlotte saw Mr. Leighton's shoulders tense, his face flush ever so slightly.

What was that about? she wondered.

But just then lunch arrived, beans and beef and day-old bread, and the conversation was dropped.

They were about halfway done with their meal when the saloon doors banged open. All talking in the room ceased. Captain Sirok stood there, scanning the room for them.

Mr. Hallorman held up a hand, and the cavalry officer made his way over. As he did so, a pair of rather rough-looking men from one of the other tables rose. Glaring at him, one very deliberately took aim and spat at Captain Sirok's feet.

If the room had been quiet before, it was silent now.

"Hey! You there!" the bartender said, hurrying over. He was afraid, Charlotte noticed. Probably worried about a gunfight breaking out. "Get out if you can't be civil!"

"I won't share space with the likes o' him," the roughneck growled. "Already too many of the damn cavalry in town as it is."

"All for your protection, sir," Captain Sirok said, nodding a little.

The man scoffed and strode out of the saloon, spurs jingling.

"A brace of traveling cowhands don't speak for the whole town. We're happy to be hostin' the cavalry here right now," the barkeeper said apologetically. "Please don't be insulted, sir."

"It's alright," Captain Sirok said, and eyed Mr. Hallorman's plate. "Got any more of that in the back, my fine man? Rare, if you can manage it?"

"And another beer, if you would," Mr. Leighton added absently, eyes still on his book. He had drained his own mug already.

Everyone in the saloon seemed to relax as Captain Sirok sat down. The chatter and clinking of glasses soon resumed.

More beer and beef was produced, and Captain Sirok tucked in eagerly. "Always nice, gettin' something fresh," he said, and gestured at Charlotte's food. "You best eat while you can, ma'am. No tellin' what tonight's gonna bring."

Charlotte looked down at her plate. She had barely touched her food. "Tonight?"

"There's been a few reports come in from scouts. Looks like the posse is moving this way, and at the rate they're going, won't be in until after dark."

"And the Army presence in town?" Mr. Hallorman asked, testy. "It was supposed to just be you."

"There was a public outcry in Leadville. Lotsa rich people up there, you know. Lotsa influence, deep pockets. Governor has to do something. Colonel Ramage wasn't able to do anything to stop it," the captain said with a shrug. "He talked to his commander out at Fort Carson, convinced him to limit the response to patrols only, at least for now."

"How many men does this patrol have?"

"Fifteen, plus six sheriff's deputies and a whole lotta angry locals who'll jump in, no doubt at the first sign of trouble," Captain Sirok said, and sipped at his beer. "Ambushes are bein' worked on. Sheriff Trumbull's technically supposed to arrest them, but these are horse thieves and murderers. If they get brought in alive, they're gettin' hung anyway."

"Is this Army detachment like you?" Mr. Leighton asked, closing his notebook, tucking his pencil lead carefully back into its holder. "Your, umm, pack?"

"Ain't nobody else in the service like us but us," Sirok declared, but tapped his fork on his plate. "Don't explain why my pack wasn't sent instead. I got a message out to the colonel about that, too."

Mr. Leighton looked intrigued. "A message? Is that some sort of werewolf, umm..."

"Magic? Naw. There's telegraph lines through here," Sirok said, grinning at Mr. Leighton's clear embarrassment. "You and Hallorman're welcome to join in with the volunteers, by the way—"

"How magnanimous of the sheriff," Mr. Hallorman said sarcastically.

"—but we all agree it's best if Miss Roseingrave stays at the sheriff's office. It's the best protected building in town, and the jail's reinforced, too, in case of any shenanigans."

"Didn't you say Eli Horn destroyed a jail in Cheyenne?" Mr. Hallorman asked.

The captain shrugged again. "Are y'all gonna let me enjoy my food or not?"

"The sheriff's office, you say?" Charlotte asked.

The captain nodded, mouth too stuffed to answer.

"Then I shall meet you gentlemen there," she replied, and pushed back from the table. "I think I would like to get some air."

CHAPTER TWENTY-FIVE

The elder Roseingrave sister was a few buildings away from the saloon when Thomas caught up to her. The researcher almost collided with another person on the wooden sidewalk. He pulled back in time but bumped into a hitching post instead.

She smiled at him. "Mr. Leighton?"

He smiled at her ruefully, regaining himself. "With everything going on right now, I should hate to see you wander off alone."

"I suppose," she replied a little hesitantly, but took his arm when it was offered. Together, they began making their way back to the sheriff's office.

Thomas sighed, trying to think of something to say. "Mr. Hallorman is a strange creature, isn't he? I never imagined they could be like this. Flesh and blood and..."

"Petty?" she asked, smiling back now.

He chuckled. "Yes, 'petty' is a good word for it."

A sheriff's deputy, sitting on his horse with a rifle slung across his saddle, tipped his hat to Charlotte as they walked past.

"Thank you," she said. "For being here. With...with me."

"I wouldn't leave you for anything," he said earnestly, and at her questioning look, he added hastily, "I mean, getting to see even this much of the fae up close has been remarkably enlightening."

Miss Roseingrave tensed a little. "Is that all this is to you? Research?"

"I am on a bit of a sabbatical right now, my dear Miss Roseingrave, and—"

She unlinked her arm from his, glaring at him for a moment, expression angry but eyes hurt. "I believe I am expected at the sheriff's office alone," she told him, and stormed off before he could say anything.

Her fists were clenched at her sides. He felt terrible. It had not been his intention to offend her. Of course his interest in this situation was not merely scholastic, but he did not want her to think he was only along because he'd seen a beautiful woman in trouble and...

"You, Englishman, are a fool."

Thomas pulled his eyes away from Miss Roseingrave's retreating figure.

"What do you want?" he asked with a sigh, looking over at Mr. Hallorman.

"You are a fool," the faery said, stepping out of the shadows of an alley that ran between two of Gunnison's many saloons. "Do you suppose there is any threat in this world to the lass that I do not know about? Charlotte is not in need of your protection or your assistance."

Stung and tired of being insulted by this creature, Thomas snapped back. "Except that you have not yet dealt with this Eli Horn, have you?"

"Not yet. But anything can be vanquished."

"You choose your words too carefully," Thomas said sharply. "I notice you did not say 'killed' just now. And even the Tuatha Dé Danann could be slain in battle. So what is this Eli Horn creature? The time for being vague has long passed."

"And what would you do with such knowledge?" Mr. Hallorman sneered. "Write it down in one of your books? Offer it up for debate and testing in the halls of academia? Apply your scientific method to it in some vain attempt to understand?"

"The scientific method is mankind's best chance of gaining mastery over this world and improving its lot. Why, look at the progress that has already been made!"

"At what cost? You build your cities and lose the forests. An Irishman a thousand years ago would have known exactly what he was hunting in this Eli Horn. And more importantly, that Irishman would have known he, as human, was not equal to the task." Mr. Hallorman gave Thomas a nasty look. "Your ancestors would not have interjected themselves in the matters of my kind."

"I gave Mis Roseingrave my word that I would aid her, and I aim to do exactly that," Thomas protested. "I would think that would be something you can respect."

Before Thomas could even breathe, the faery had moved. Grabbed him by the collar and threw him back into the shadows and up against the weathered slats of the saloon, that obsidian blade out and pressed to Thomas's throat. The edge was so close Thomas had to hold his breath for fear of cutting himself.

"Respect you? I, respect you?" the faery growled, and his green eyes flashed in the darkness. "Over a thousand years I've walked your world thanks to an oath that was not even spoken by me, in service of a human bloodline I never wished to be tied to. An oath I have fulfilled a hundred times over. What is your word next to that?"

The faery's grip released, allowing Thomas enough room to speak. He coughed. "I meant the words I spoke to her."

For a moment, he found himself still pinned by those furious green eyes, and then finally, the knife withdrew. "Have a care, Englishman," Mr. Hallorman said, sheathing the black blade. "Antagonize me again and I will not be so gentle, regardless of how she views you."

Thomas blinked. "How she what?"

But somehow, in the space between closing his eyes and opening them again, Mr. Hallorman had vanished. Thomas leaned against the alley wall for a moment, a little stunned by the entire affair. He could still feel the ghost edge of that knife at his throat.

But as strange as their faery companion was, Thomas could not afford to let it distract him. With one last glance over his shoulder and a rub of his throat, he left the alley behind, making for the sheriff's office. He had no desire to leave Miss Roseingrave alone right now.

Oath or not, Thomas did not trust Mr. Hallorman to keep her safe.

The sheriff's office was a hive of activity when Thomas arrived. Sheriff Trumbull nodded at him and directed him to the back of the large open room, where meager accommodation had been made for Miss Roseingrave. A chair had been moved back by the wood-burning stove, next to a huge pile of dried grass in a big barrel. Thomas was confused by the presence of the miniature haystack, and even more puzzled by what Miss Roseingrave was doing with it.

"May I inquire?" he asked.

She didn't look up. She had a handful of straw in her hand, twisting it tightly together. "It seems that Gunnison lacks the budget for coal for this office," she replied, and then held up her work. The straw had been formed into a solid little log. "It burns more slowly like this."

"Surely that does not give off much heat," he said.

"Then we're fortunate today is not so cold," she replied, short, starting on her next twist.

Thomas watched her for a moment, then pulled up a chair on the other side of the barrel. She seemed surprised when he started working on his own handful but answered when he asked about how best to twist it, and it seemed that his earlier words were forgotten.

There was a large coffee pot on the stove, and as the afternoon passed, it was emptied and refilled several times. Miss Roseingrave and Thomas both partook themselves, as did almost everyone who passed through the office.

"You don't have to do that, ma'am," Captain Sirok said a few hours later, filling a tin cup of his own from the coffee pot. His boots were dusty, his normal good humor subdued. "Sheriff Trumbull's own daughters oughta be takin' care of that."

Miss Roseingrave finished the twist and laid it aside in the box next to the stove. Her hands were chapped red, but she seemed not to notice. "Mrs. Trumbull is not here today," she replied. "The sheriff sent her and the children out to her sister's ranch east of here. If there are to be men here guarding me tonight, I would prefer that they are not cold."

Thomas was startled by that; Miss Roseingrave had made no mention of it before. "What a vote of confidence that is," he commented drily. His own hands had started going numb, working on the straw-twists, and in the interest of preserving his trigger finger for the evening, Thomas had switched to cleaning his guns instead. He had them broken apart now, laid out on a small table he had dragged over for this. Nobody else in the room had paid him any heed.

Captain Sirok's face clouded. "Can't blame a man for worryin' 'bout his kin."

"What is the plan right now?" Thomas asked. "I've caught snatches of it but haven't heard the entire thing."

Captain Sirok glanced across the office, over to a far corner where Major

Wilson and Sheriff Trumbull were locked in conversation and had been for the past ten minutes. "The major intends on drawing Horn into an ambush."

"That seems a little dangerous for the people of this town, doesn't it?"

The captain's expression didn't change. His eyes, Thomas noted, were still locked on the sheriff. "Horn don't normally kill indiscriminately, and the main boarding stable's on the far south end of town. He'll be headed there, lookin' for fresh horses. Sheriff's puttin' sharpshooters and the like on rooftops throughout town, and there ain't a man here who won't pick up a gun to defend his own, should it come to that. I don't like it neither, but it's a sound enough strategy for dealing with an outlaw gang."

Miss Roseingrave shook her head. "Eli Horn is no normal outlaw."

"Whaddaya think I've tried to tell 'em?" Captain Sirok replied, bitter now.

"Captain!" Major Wilson called.

"That's my cue," he replied, and looked between them. "Keep her safe, Leighton."

"Of course," he said, and they were alone again.

Miss Roseingrave did not pick up more straw this time, choosing instead to pour herself another cup of coffee and come over to the table. She looked over his gun parts, all spread neatly across the rough oak slab. What she was reading in it all, Thomas had no idea. He hoped it was something good. He still felt like a fool for his comments outside the saloon.

"You seem like you know what you're doing," she commented after a moment's contemplation. "I can't imagine this was a subject in seminary."

He chuckled. "We may not have bears or wolves in the British Isles any longer, but it is still a good idea to carry a weapon while exploring the countryside."

"Oh?"

"And my father was quite fond of bird hunting in his day," Thomas said. He plunged a rag down the barrel of his Winchester with a ramrod. "Something he pursued with relish, apart from his duties as pastor."

"Your father was... Oh."

"Anglican, not Catholic," Thomas replied, a bit stiff. He did not like thinking about this, much less discussing it. "I'm the oldest of six."

"Six?" she said. He nodded. "Perhaps my family would have grown that large, had my father lived."

"What happened?"

"His ship went down with all hands when I was five," she said. "He was first mate on a trading vessel out of Savannah. His ship served as a blockade runner through the entire war, only to sink in peacetime during a storm."

Thomas shook his head, wondering what he could say. He was an observant man—he had no qualms in acknowledging that about himself—but he could not often predict the course of human emotion, nor did he usually know the right words to offer to somebody in distress. "I am sorry to hear that."

She drew in a deep breath, fingers brushing the polished wood butt of the rifle. "And yours?"

"My father is still alive, or at least, he was, last we spoke."

"Before you left?"

"Five years ago," Thomas replied, thinking again about that last argument, and then pushing it from his mind. "Five years."

Miss Roseingrave looked like she wanted to ask more but did not. She folded her hands on the tabletop. "Family," she said with a weak smile.

"Family," he agreed, and started snapping his Winchester back together.

And only just in time, too, it seemed, for it was only a few moments later that the office door banged open and a messenger burst in, breathing hard and hot from the saddle.

"Half a mile. They're half a mile out!"

CHAPTER TWENTY-SIX

Riding into town just before dusk, Celeste pulled her borrowed hat down low over her face. Mr. Abbitt had a tight grip on her horse's lead, their animals close together.

"Careful now, missy," he sneered at her, so close she could smell the reek of his breath, "wouldn't want you getting any ideas, now would we?"

The few people who were out on the streets right now stopped and stared at them. Celeste could see the apprehension on their faces and in their movements, tight and uncertain.

"Why did he bring us here?" she whispered. "They're expecting us."

"Course they are. But there ain't no other choice but to resupply, and the boss, he ain't lettin' you out of his sight."

"Careful there now, Lukas," Mr. Horn called from the front of the group, and tipped his hat to a pair of women passing by. They glared at him and hurried on. He chuckled, easy on his horse. "We're just here to pick up a few things and then we'll be on our way."

As if at some signal, three of the posse broke off, heading down a side street.

"Ain't nothin' to worry 'bout," Mr. Abbitt agreed, giving Celeste one of his terrible smiles.

She sniffed and sat up a little straighter on her horse. Her hand brushed over the saddle horn while she did so; leather, seemingly ancient, flaked away, exposing the metal structure beneath. But that too began rusting, rusting before her very eyes.

The entire expedition was breaking down.

She had been grateful to leave the mountains behind yesterday, their course taking them out of the perilous paths between the high peaks, plunging them down into a small river valley that had grown broader and flatter with the descent today. The men were dressed now in little more than rags, and the food had all spoiled. Nobody had had anything more than water today. The horses were lagging. The men seemed to have aged a decade.

Because of him. Eli Horn. That curse that lay on him. What a terrible burden to bear, Celeste thought, and wondered if she truly did have the power to help him. She would, if she could. Nobody deserved to live with this, and it only made sense that it was likely the driver of all his terrible deeds.

If one could, indeed, call this man terrible.

She knew of his reputation, and certainly his men were rough, but he had been nothing but a gentleman to her. And the reports of his exploits were so dramatic, so ridiculous, that wasn't it more likely that a great deal of them were fabricated, or at least, exaggerated beyond all truth?

Celeste looked around at dusty Gunnison. Here was another chance, a better chance, to slip the leash. And yet...

Another three men peeled off from the main group, leaving their little party with six: Mr. Horn, Mr. Abbitt, Celeste, and three of the gunmen. Their leader had not offered Celeste any details about where they were headed, but she was not surprised to see a large livery building up ahead, on the south edge of town.

Horses.

A man in a straw-strewn apron and white stable clothes met them out front, walking up with his hand up. "That's close enough, thank you!" he called. Lanterns lit the interior of the stable. Horses whinnied and nickered within, boys walking between the stalls with wheelbarrows of fresh hay. "What can I do for you gentlemen?"

Mr. Horn leaned forward. "I've a dozen horses that need stabling tonight. Can you accommodate?"

"A dozen would strain me to the limit. I can put them out to pasture maybe, but not up in the barn," the stableman replied, wiping his hands on his apron. They were calloused and hard, but bore none of the little cuts or ground-in dirt that Celeste might associate with his profession. She looked at Mr. Abbitt. He was relaxed, casual. But it was a feigned ease.

Everyone was on edge, she realized, and she felt her breath coming a little more shallowly now. What was the game here?

"I don't think I like the look of your paddocks," Mr. Horn continued, as if nothing was wrong. "I don't think I like what's camped out there where you think I can't see."

"Come on down from there, and we'll talk about it."

Mr. Horn looked around, nodding at them all. Everyone started dismounting. Celeste felt something hard growing in her gut. If ever there was a time, this was it. Turn her horse, run away, head for...

But Mr. Abbitt was grinning at her, and slowly, she swung down out of her saddle as well.

"That's better," the stableman said. "More civilized, wouldn't you say, Eli Horn?"

Celeste's breath caught. Around her, the men all reached for their guns, but Mr. Horn waved them back, chuckling. "I thought I recognized you there, Captain Wilson."

"It's Major now."

"Major, is it? Coming up in the world, are we?"

"Surrender now, give me the girl over there, and we might just let this thing go to trial," the stableman—officer?—said evenly.

"I don't think I'll do that," Mr. Horn replied, still deadly calm.

"Pity," this Major Wilson said. The boys behind him had disappeared, Celeste noticed. The tension was growing.

"Nobody needs to die here tonight, Major Wilson. I'm just after fresh horses. I'll even pay for them this time." And at that, he raised his voice, calling, Celeste imagined, to whoever truly owned the livery. Major Wilson reached for something concealed under his apron, and in response, Mr. Abbitt's own six-shooter whipped up. Eli Horn sighed. "Lukas, put that away."

"Ain't no thing, sir," Mr. Abbitt replied, and cocked back the hammer. "Been a long time since I got to kill me a military boy."

Mr. Horn held out his hands. "Fresh horses. That's all I want, Wilson, and after this, you'll never see the outlaw Eli Horn again."

"Bullshit, Horn," Major Wilson spat back, and two more men—these in proper cavalry uniforms—stepped out into the gathering gloom. "I know your type. That desire for more death is an addiction with men like you."

"Oh, Major Wilson," said Mr. Horn carefully, his hands straying down now to his guns, "you've never met anything like me."

For a moment, the groups stared each other down

Then a gunshot, three streets away, broke the stalemate.

Inside the jail, with the light failing, Thomas heard the first gunshots echo through the town. But more than that, he saw Miss Roseingrave gasp.

"What?" he asked.

But she didn't answer. From the look on her face, she couldn't. She grabbed for his hand, holding on, eyes closed, even as the gunfire continued, as men began pouring out of the station, shouting and shooting.

The night, it seemed, had just exploded.

Celeste couldn't move, couldn't think, couldn't breathe. All the air had been knocked from her lungs. A weight was crushing her. She was dying. Something screamed. She was...

"Stop fighting!" a familiar voice hissed in her ear.

Eli Horn was on top of her, covering her with his body, her wrists in his hand, and the air around her was growing hot.

That's right. He had grabbed her, borne her to the ground as the shooting started. She had not seen who fired first here, but perhaps it didn't matter. The barn was on fire now, flames licking up the stalls. The screaming was coming from the horses. The ground around her was strewn with dead bodies: Major Wilson and two of his men, along with one of Eli Horn's gang.

He pulled her back up to her feet. Celeste looked around her, mute, unable to process the sight. It had only been a few seconds.

"You with me, fáith?" Mr. Horn demanded. "Are you hurt?"

The horses inside the barn were screaming, terrible sounds, even as both the stable hands and Eli Horn's two remaining gunmen rushed in to open the stalls. There was shouting, human voices. More gunshots. Lots of gunshots, echoing in the town behind them.

"I'm fine," she said, voice shaking.

"Good," he said, and pulled her roughly away.

They were running now, back through the streets. Somebody around the next corner pointed a gun at them; Eli Horn fired back, and a body hit the ground.

"What is happening?" she demanded.

"Ambush," he replied, curt, gun in his free hand. His touch on her wrist was like ice. "They were more prepared than I thought. The Army turning an entire town into a kill box was not a tactic I expected. Not even I would have done that."

"And when have you had a town to lead?"

Mr. Horn turned, dragging Celeste around behind him, gun up. "Major Wilson. And see, I thought you were dead back there."

The man was barely ten paces away, his gun aimed right for them. He was bleeding profusely from one shoulder, and his body was crooked, like something was wrong with his leg. "Surrender, Horn, and let that girl go. You'll stand trial. You have my word on that."

"Trial?" Mr. Horn's face split in a wicked grin as he took aim. "What do you people know about justice?"

"No!" Celeste cried, pushing his arm away before he could pull the trigger. His shot went wide, through the wall of an adjacent building, and the look that Eli Horn gave her chilled her heart. Right before he was hit, dead center, by a round squeezed off by the major.

Something grabbed her around the waist, yanking her back, and Celeste heard an Irish accent whisper in her ear.

"You're coming with me, lass. Now."

The last of Eli Horn that Celeste saw as she was hauled bodily from the alley was the major emptying his revolver point-blank into the outlaw's chest.

The man who had her moved fast, half carrying, half dragging her down the street. She hit at him with her fist, landing several blows, but he just grabbed her wrist and held her tight.

"Stop fighting me, Celeste!"

"You know my name?" she panted, trying to keep up, not wanting to be dragged along. The streets around them were chaos: people running, buildings on fire, men with guns firing into the darkness. Who was who and where the targets were, she couldn't say.

"Not the time, lass," he replied shortly, and pointed.

Up above, silhouetted against the starry sky, a dark shape like some massive beast was leaping on all fours across the rooftops.

Chilled by the sight, Celeste ran faster.

They turned a corner, running across a broad intersection with a few pleasant little trees growing in the middle. They had to duck for cover there, two of Eli Horn's men gunning down three others with bright brass stars pinned to their vests. Celeste screamed, but the stranger clapped a hand over her mouth, holding her still until they had moved on. Then he yanked her along again.

A huge stone building dominated the far side of the street. They were almost there, almost to the sidewalk when the door banged open. A man was standing there, shotgun raised. For one heart-stopping moment, Celeste was sure she was dead.

"Down!" the Irishman yelled and threw her to the ground.

The barrel flashed in the falling night, sending a shot racing overhead, and an animalistic scream rent the air behind them. Celeste looked up just in time to see the creature from the rooftops—for it could only be a creature, not a man, for it to ignore such a mortal blast as that—throw itself toward the door. With unbelievable strength, it hurtled the unfortunate man standing there out into the square, straight into that small group of trees. The man hit one of the boles and did not rise.

Celeste heard a guttural curse growled out by the man who had dragged her here. A dark knife flashed in his hand as he scrambled up and after the thing, but he too was knocked off his feet, borne away.

For a moment, Celeste was all alone in the quiet.

But there were more gunshots, coming closer, more screaming, and she did the only rational thing there was to do: she fled.

CHAPTER TWENTY-SEVEN

Thomas braced his shoulder against the door, desperately trying to secure the bolt in the lock. He didn't know if the wooden planks would hold against whatever it was that was out there, but it was better than nothing.

"What was that?!" somebody yelled at him, rushing over to help with the door. It was one of the last remaining defenders besides Thomas himself, men the sheriff had left here. One had already been shot through a window during the open salvo of the gun battle. Another, a foolhardy deputy who'd been ranting since the shooting started, had just gotten himself killed.

The rest of them had attempted to make barricades with the room's furniture but the posse had come at the sheriff's office hard, and it seemed that not everybody in town was friendly with the local authorities. Instead of a two-way gun battle, it had become a free-for-all out there.

Thomas shook his head, his own body feeling somewhat watery and weak. He tried to fight the sensation down. Now was not the time to lose his nerve. "I don't know," he replied.

And then the latch didn't matter anymore.

For the door simply shattered.

The man beside Thomas died immediately, taking a shot through the head. Thomas rushed for the makeshift barricade of tables and desk, diving over the top as the two other men began firing back. He'd gotten a glimpse of what was coming for them. It couldn't be human. Nothing human moved like that. Nothing human fought like this.

The heavy, solid oak desk they had been sheltering behind was torn away, flung aside and across the room. Another man died.

"Get the girl!" the last man yelled, another sheriff's deputy, firing away.

Thomas didn't hesitate. He was already headed that way himself.

Hopefully, he would find Mr. Hallorman in here, because as much as he disliked the faery, Thomas wasn't sure he had the means to kill this creature himself.

Celeste crawled through the dirt as fast and as low as she could. In the chaos of the gun battle, nobody seemed to notice a slight figure working its way out of the main square, back toward the safety of the shadows. She had no idea what was going on, whom she could trust, whom she could turn to. Her ears were ringing; all other sounds besides the endless gun shots felt very far away.

It was only a few yards to the closest building, but it seemed to take an eternity to reach. Finally, face streaked with mud and tears and snot, Celeste gained the shadows, breathing hard.

"You there! On your feet!"

She turned. It was an older man, a star glinting on his waistcoat. The sheriff. Celeste could have sobbed with happiness.

"I—" she began.

But the man just grabbed her, hauled her up, fury in his movements. His six-shooter was aimed squarely at her chest, and she could see blood and mud caking his face. He had a nasty cut on his forehead. He seemed unsteady.

"You!" he yelled. Or at least, it seemed that he was yelling. The words were dim, far away. "I don't recognize you!"

"Please," she said, "please, Eli Horn—"

"You with him?" the man snarled.

"Yes, I mean no, he—"

The man snarled and yanked her around, driving her back into the side of the building. It was dark in the alley and his vision was compromised, she realized, his hearing momentarily dulled. "You part of his gang?!"

"Please," she said, requiring no effort at all to use her most pathetic, pleading voice, "please don't kill me. I'm... I'm..."

"...with him," the man growled, and put his gun to her forehead.

But before he could pull the trigger, Eli Horn was there. He ripped the man away from her, throwing him across the sidewalk and back into an opposite building. The man grunted and brought up his gun. Eli Horn got between Celeste and the path of the bullets, walking straight into it as the man fired and fired and fired until his gun ran dry.

It availed him not at all.

Mr. Horn produced a bowie knife from out of nowhere and with two quick strokes, ended the unfortunate sheriff's life. The movements were quick, spare, almost too economical to follow. Celeste could only stare as the man's knees buckled but he did not yet fall. He wasn't dead; Eli Horn was holding him up even as his lifeblood gushed away from deep cuts in his chest, into the darkness.

"Nobody touches her but me," Eli Horn growled at the dying man.

What Celeste felt in that moment, she couldn't describe. Didn't dare examine in any detail, lest she find something out about herself she couldn't live with later.

But then, Eli Horn gasped in pain, the shaft of an arrow suddenly quivering in his shoulder.

"Whatever he's told you, lass, it's all lies."

There was the man from before, the strange Irishman, standing with a second arrow nocked to his bow, facing them down with hate in his eyes.

Thomas was met by the barrel of a gun as he flew through the door.

"It's me!" he said quickly, holding his own rifle up, and slammed the door shut. "You're supposed to be in the cells!"

Miss Roseingrave, clearly shaken, stepped back. She'd taken the smallest revolver Mr. Barton had had in his little armory, but even that seemed too heavy for her. She was pale under her freckles and sunburn, and her eyes were unfocused.

"Couldn't," she breathed, and then gasped, grabbing for the wall to steady herself. "They're all dead out there. They're all dead because of me. If I hadn't... If we hadn't..."

And the first blow hit the door.

Thomas gritted his teeth and shouldered his gun. There was no furniture to barricade it with, no furniture for cover. "Not the time," he told her.

She nodded and straightened, clearly putting forth immense effort to gather herself, and then came to stand beside him. There was fear in her eyes, but she held the borrowed gun steady. He wanted to tell her to get behind him, lock herself in a cell, do anything except die next to him, but from the look on her face he knew she wasn't going to listen.

Where in damnation was Mr. Hallorman?

It only took two more hits and the door splintered. A growl and it was torn off its hinges, thrown back into the front room.

Thomas began firing.

The man in front of him just smiled, baring yellowed teeth, curved wickedly. He lunged at Thomas, hand extended, plunging his claws deep into the Englishman's gut. His nails were razor-sharp and Thomas felt a horrible, stabbing pain. He fell back against the wall, staring at the blood pouring from the wound.

But the crazed man was still there. Charlotte was scrambling back, firing wildly. She tumbled into one of the jail cells and pulled the door shut after her. The man roared wordlessly, throwing himself at the bars.

Thomas hauled himself up and raised his rifle, but there was no angle he could find that didn't carry the possibility of hitting Miss Roseingrave, on her back now on the floor. She fired her last shot. Whether intentional or lucky, it caught the man square in the face, the force of it throwing him around, throwing him back.

The crazed man shook himself, turning back again, and without saying a word, raised the same shotgun he had been shot with out on the porch, only moments ago, barrel leveled right at Miss Roseingrave.

Thomas didn't even think. Afterward, he was never sure how he got there in time, got between the bars and the gun before the trigger was pulled, but he did. He leapt in front of the blast and fell into darkness.

Eli Horn dropped the old man with the sheriff's star disdainfully. The arrow still protruded from his shoulder. He made no attempt to break it or pull it out. "Ah. So that explains it. What I was seeing in the entrails."

"Entrails? One of Domnu's finest grubbing around in deer guts for answers?" the Irishman replied coldly. The bow drew back just a little further. "How the mighty have fallen."

"And what do you know of it, hill-dweller?"

"Give me the girl."

"If you could kill me, wouldn't you do it?" Eli Horn taunted. "Or is it something else you're after?"

"Just the girl. She's mine, by right of blood. Give her to me, and we all walk away."

Celeste saw Mr. Horn smile that wicked smile of his. He holstered his gun and spread his hands wide. "Yours, eh?" he said contemptuously. "Then come and get her."

The man with the bow never had a chance to loose his second shot. For Eli Horn clenched his fist and the ground underneath the stranger simply ceased to be.

Charlotte screamed as Mr. Leighton's body hit the floor, bleeding profusely from his shoulder. She barely had time to look down, though, because that monster was still there. It growled at her, blood dripping from its jaw, then threw the gun away and lunged.

She didn't have time to squeeze off a shot of her own.

Instead, everything went sideways.

The entire building shook, timbers groaning, floor shifting. A rumble went up, deep and low, echoing throughout the town. Shots were replaced by screams; the town was being torn apart.

The floor fell, breaking apart, and Charlotte fell with it.

"Mr. Horn? Mr. Horn!"

When Mr. Horn had closed his fist, the entire town had been shaken to its core. The ground beneath it had given out, as if eroded from below, tipping buildings off foundations, rattling others apart. Several, it seemed, were catching fire. Celeste could see it all now from her vantage point in the alley.

Screaming. Everyone was screaming.

Steely fingers closed around Celeste's own. "Get me up, lass," he said, and coughed. There was blood trickling from the corners of his mouth. He tried to push himself up, but his arms wouldn't hold him, and he collapsed again.

"What did you do?" she demanded again, on her knees next to his prone body.

"Tore open the wound again. Now. Get me up," he said, and threw an arm around her shoulders.

With every ounce of her strength, Celeste managed to haul the outlaw to his feet. He leaned on her heavily, still bleeding. The shaft of the arrow was still protruding from his shoulder. They had to step around the sheriff's body. Celeste swallowed and didn't look at him.

Limping out of the alley, she saw what Mr. Horn had done. The tops of the trees at the center of the square were crooked, leaning, and a good yard lower than they had been before.

A sinkhole, shallow but huge, had opened up in the center of town.

"Don't look at it, lass," he gasped.

Shouldering his weight, Celeste averted her eyes and helped him hobble south.

For a moment after the shaking stopped, Charlotte lay on the badly slanted floor, unsure which way was up.

Then she felt something sticky and hot under her fingertips. Mr. Leighton. His body was limp as a rag doll, blood dripping down a loose arm, pooling in his palm, dripping finally down to the floor next to her.

With a cry, she dragged herself up, frantic, not sure what to do. His chest still moved up and down, but his breath sounded wet, labored. He lived, but for how long?

Then she heard a growl.

Above her was a thing that looked like a man but wasn't. Golden eyes glowed in the shadows. A rough hand grabbed her, hauling her up. The stench of death hung all around him, so fresh and terrible that Charlotte could not look it in the face.

"Lovely to see you again, Abbitt."

It was Captain Sirok. The captain was there, Mr. Barton's purloined letter opener in his bare hand. There was a terrible smell like burning flesh, and Charlotte saw smoke leaking out of the captain's clenched fist. He was bleeding from a cut on his face. His smile, teeth stained red, was feral.

"Sirok," the monster growled, the word barely legible. He was still shifting, still changing.

"What a shame it's a full moon tonight. I'd rather you be fully man when I kill you. Ain't no fun, puttin' down a rabid dog," Captain Sirok replied, and threw himself at the other man.

Rabid dogs seemed an apt analogy. The two tore at each other, ripping and snarling, weapons scattering across the floor. Blood splattered the walls of the ruined building. Howls filled the air.

Mr. Leighton was still unmoving on the floor, limbs sprawled out, the cloth Charlotte had pressed to his shoulder stained bright red now. His breath was coming fast and shallow. She couldn't bring herself to look at him. She didn't want to see this man die.

Then she heard a horrendous sound, like the scream of a dying animal. The letter opener was buried in Abbitt's chest, Captain Sirok beside him.

Abbitt rose up on all fours then, and Charlotte was instantly reminded of the creature from Mr. Barton's study. His body was growing, his clothes straining, and everywhere she looked, she saw gray fur. His chest was smoking around the letter opener.

One massive hand, decidedly inhuman now, wrenched the little thing out. "Missed my heart," he growled. His back molars were visible; the skin from cheekbone to chin was torn open.

Captain Sirok looked little better. His eyes, always that strange amber, were glowing gold now. Long fangs shone white against the blood that coated his face, and he spat out a gob of gore, flesh he'd ripped from the other man's cheek with his teeth. He looked like a madman.

With a wordless howl, he launched himself toward them. Charlotte felt her own heart leap into her throat; she couldn't tell if he was coming for Abbitt or for her. She threw herself down.

A bow sang out. An arrow thudded. A wolf howled again.

"By the snow and the ice that bore you, Isatahkabi, stand down!"

Charlotte looked up, sweeping her hair out of her face. Abbitt was nowhere to be seen. Instead, Mr. Hallorman was standing there, bow in one hand and Captain Sirok in the other. He had the cavalry officer, barely recognizable as a man now, by the throat, his feet kicking helplessly off the ground. The captain thrashed and lashed out, his clawed hands ripping through the faery's sleeve, down into the flesh beneath. Charlotte thought, for a wild moment, that she could see light shining through the blood.

Mr. Hallorman tightened his hand. There was an audible crunch, and then Captain Sirok went limp. The faery let the wolf drop then, sliding out of his grip to collapse on the floor like a bag of last year's apples.

For a moment, silence reigned.

"Did you kill him?" Charlotte asked, voice wavering.

Mr. Hallorman slipped his bow back into its quiver. "It'd take much more than that to kill the likes of him, lass," he said, and stepped over the body. He held out his hand to Charlotte. She took it, her own hand shaking, and let him pull her to her feet.

She glanced uncertainly back at Mr. Leighton. "Is he still alive?" she asked, and even to her, it sounded like a plea.

The faery bent down, two fingers to Mr. Leighton's neck. "He has a pulse still, although for how long, I cannot say." And then he lifted the researcher lightly, as if he weighed nothing at all. "Come. We'll see if we can keep him on this side of the veil."

"What about the gunfight?" she asked, uncertain.

"Over," he replied curtly.

"And my sister?"

"One problem at a time, Charlotte. One problem at a time."

CHAPTER TWENTY-EIGHT

Charlotte stood on a plain, barren and empty. There was light, although there was no sun and no moon. There were no trees, no grass, not even moss, growing on the hard-packed ground. It was a land that had given up even the faintest hint of life; a land that had breathed its last long ago.

Silent. Empty. Forsaken.

Then.

A light.

A light. Bobbing along, shining out from a cage of cut glass and beaten silver. A light from a lantern, held up before a pair of dark shapes. A man carrying a rifle across his shoulder. A wolf, padding along beside him.

There were no shadows, but she could not see his face. She tried to call out, but her voice failed. Perhaps sound itself had died in this place.

The solid ground beneath her feet gave way, the dust giving way into nothing. She screamed wordlessly as she was dragged down, scrambling for the edge of the pit, fighting, fighting against—

Charlotte woke up.

Rocking forward, she almost fell out of her chair. It was only by the barest margin that she prevented herself from hitting the floor. She grabbed the arm of it, steadying herself.

A moan from the cot in front of her brought her back to the world.

That was right. Mr. Leighton had been injured, and injured badly, last night. Mr. Hallorman had carried him out of the ruined town, to...

"You alright there, miss?"

It was the camp doctor, kneeling beside Mr. Leighton's cot. "Did I fall asleep here last night?" she asked.

"I offered you my tent," the doctor said, and took the Englishman's wrist between his fingers, pulling out his pocket watch, "but you said you didn't wish to leave him."

Charlotte remembered that. Dimly. "How is he?"

"Not well," the camp doctor replied, and laid the English researcher's arm back down on the cot. "I was able to get the wound cleaned out, but his pulse is slower than I'd like, and not so strong. He lost a lot of blood last night."

"That shot was meant for me," she said.

The doctor gave her a sympathetic look. "He made the gallant choice, ma'am, but it was his choice, if that eases your mind at all. One I'd like to think I'd make for my own wife."

She was still trying to think of a proper response to that when the tent flap flew open.

"Good," Mr. Hallorman said, appearing in the canvas breach. "You're awake. Let's go. We're losing daylight."

"I won't leave him," she insisted.

"Not even to find your sister?"

Charlotte hesitated. Mr. Hallorman smiled at her. In that moment, she hated him. She turned her attention back to the doctor. "Will he die?"

"I'd say it's even odds right now. Mr. Leighton's collarbone was shattered by the shotgun blast. If you can get him back to Colorado Springs or Denver before infection sets in, he might have a chance. If not..."

"Is there nothing you can do?"

"I can give him some laudanum, ease his suffering a little," the doctor told her, but looked away. "Now, ma'am, please don't take this as callousness, but I have other injured men to attend to."

Charlotte waited until he was out of the tent to say anything to her faery guardian.

"Can't you do anything?" she asked, moving over to Mr. Leighton's side.

"I already brought him here to your people's physician." The faery sat down in her chair, kicking his feet up on a nearby footlocker. "Why should I do more?"

"Because this man was performing your job last night," she snapped. Mr. Leighton was terribly pale. "While you were nowhere to be seen!"

Mr. Hallorman pulled his feet down again, leaning forward, a look of profound anger on his face. For a moment, Charlotte thought that perhaps she had pushed him too far. But instead of storming out or biting back, he just smiled and joined her beside Mr. Leighton's cot. He pulled the blanket off, examining him. Charlotte looked away.

Just then, the tent flap flew back again, and there was Captain Sirok, looking as fresh and happy as the first moment she'd encountered him. He had even found a clean shirt somewhere, although the devices on it were wrong. Not a scratch on him. Not the slightest hint of the monster she'd seen last night.

"Ah," the cavalry officer said, coming in, dropping the flap behind him. "So Leighton's still alive."

"Not for long," the faery replied.

"I could bite him," Captain Sirok offered. "But he ain't the wolf type. Not everybody takes to it, you know."

"Yes, the wolf," Charlotte said, not wanting to think about his berserker behavior. "What did happen last night?"

The captain sighed. "Near as we can reckon, Horn had some of his own gang positioned here in town, and once the fightin' started, they joined in. Wasn't no kind of tactic we were expecting from him, and—"

"That's not what I meant," she said, sharper than she meant to.

"Ah, you mean... Ma'am, I'm sorry you had to see me like that."

"What was it?"

"He's got a wolf in his soul, Charlotte, what do you expect? Now you, Sirok, you keep your fangs in your mouth and help me." Mr. Hallorman indicated the other end of the cot, down by Mr. Leighton's feet. "We need to move him."

"Where?" Charlotte asked.

"Where the ground doesn't stink of civilization, lass," Mr. Hallorman said. "Get your boots back on, retrieve his clothes, and accompany us. And grab that kit over there that the doctor left. We might need it."

Charlotte was certain that they would be stopped, carrying a grievously injured man out of an Army encampment on a cot. Instead, not a single person so much as glanced their way. It helped that it was still quite early, the sun barely above the horizon, and not many people were up and about. But not even the doctor, heading into another tent and passing right by them, seemed to register their presence.

"A simple glamour," Mr. Hallorman told her, when Charlotte asked. They were headed down the sandy expanse of the river, well away from the camp and upstream from the still-burning town of Gunnison. "It's tricky, pulling the veil around those who live as solidly in this world as you and our wolf friend here do. Such things shatter easily."

"Fascinating," Captain Sirok mused. He was carrying his half of the cot easily, as if he had not suffered his own injuries last night. "I'd love to see what we could do against the Sioux with it."

"It isn't something I'd use in war," Mr. Hallorman said. "Subterfuge was never our way."

"And whaddaya know about war?"

"Plenty," Mr. Hallorman replied curtly. "Now. Charlotte, hold onto that blanket for me. We'll take him out."

"Into the water? He'll freeze!" Charlotte protested, even as she reached for the blanket.

"Into the water."

The men made their way down the shallow, sandy bank and set the cot down right in the stream. The stream was not especially deep, not even up to the men's knees. But the water was running fast, and Captain Sirok had to hold down the cot lest it drift away. Mr. Leighton groaned as freezing water coursed over him, hands thrashing weakly, but he did not wake up.

At first, it did not seem that Mr. Hallorman was doing anything. He'd positioned himself kneeling beside the cot, facing upstream. He had one hand on Mr. Leighton's bare chest, the long fingers of the other trailing through the current.

Not moving. Not doing anything.

And then Charlotte saw it. A mist, rising up off the water. Little waves rippling. She heard a murmur, like stones over water trying to form words. But even as the sound grew louder, the water coursing across the sand grew less, slowing to a trickle. This strange disparity grew and grew and grew.

Until a four-foot wall of water surged down, streaming, crashing over the three men and sweeping them all from view.

Charlotte scrambled down the bank, frantic. "Mr. Leighton!" she called. "Captain!"

"I notice you don't include me in that," a familiar voice said. And there was Mr. Hallorman, standing next to her. He wasn't even wet, his clothes perfectly clean again, but his head was bowed, his shoulders slumped, as if greatly burdened by something.

She stared at him.

"It's 'cause the lady knows you ain't got to deal with this shit yourself," Captain Sirok called. The captain was hauling himself and Mr. Leighton out of a deeper place in the middle of the creek a few yards downstream, both of them soaking wet, Mr. Leighton shivering violently.

Charlotte remembered the blanket then, hurrying back to retrieve it and pull it around Mr. Leighton's shoulders. His lips were blue, but he nodded at her nonetheless.

The wound had not gone. In fact, it looked worse, the flesh of his shoulder as shredded as if he had taken a shotgun blast from behind and the shot had burst through the skin there. His stomach wound was in a similar condition, the formerly small wound now broken open and raw.

"You're still bleeding," she said, and looked back at Mr. Hallorman. "I thought you said you were going to heal him!"

"His collarbone should be knitted back together now, and the major damage to his internal organs is repaired," Mr. Hallorman replied, words short, voice pained. "I am out of practice with healing humans. Why do you think I told you to bring the physician's bag?"

Still frustrated, Charlotte pulled out the bandages and ointment she had brought from the doctor's tent. But upon touching Mr. Leighton's shoulder, she could feel the bone just beneath the raw skin, whole and smooth, and there was very little blood.

"Why... the water?" Mr. Leighton asked, still gasping from the cold.

"The land here does not want to listen to me. Flowing water is easier to work with than stone. It flows. It forgets. It does not hold grudges. It can sweep away anything it wishes."

Charlotte meant to ask what he meant, then saw the scene upstream. Where green water plants had been growing, even this late in the year, and moss had clung to huge, shadowed boulders, there were only dead things, brown and still.

Mr. Leighton followed her gaze. "You took the life from... from the waters?" He sounded disturbed by the concept.

"I took nothing. I accepted what was offered and accomplished what I could with it. As I told you before, this is not a Tennyson poem. Even the deep magics come with a cost. Like for like. Now cease your complaining, Englishman. You shall live, and more importantly, you shall get back on a horse. We must continue our pursuit."

Charlotte smoothed a last bandage onto Mr. Leighton's raw skin. "You aren't going to once again insist that I remain here?"

"The time for that has passed," Mr. Hallorman said, and something in his manner had changed. To Charlotte's eyes, he was no longer the insouciant creature she had met at Mr. Barton's house. Instead, he had an intensity she had not seen in him before. A warrior of some vanished time, stepped out of an oil painting to regard the modern world with sorrow. "I got a good look at the creature we are dealing with. Whatever we can do to prevent him from reaching that portal, we must do."

"What has changed?" Mr. Leighton panted, even as Captain Sirok helped him stand.

"Eli Horn is a Fomorian."

"I suppose I should thank you. For saving my life, I mean."

Eli Horn didn't look up at Celeste's words.

"I would think you would blame me for getting you shot at in the first place."

"I suppose I should."

They had ridden hard, ridden fast, only stopping when it was too dark for their tired horses to continue on. They had lost the packhorse that had carried her manacles, and so, Eli Horn had sat beside her all night. Celeste wasn't sure he had slept.

She certainly hadn't.

If Celeste had harbored any doubts still about Eli Horn's claims, last night had killed them dead. No human could have done what he had done in Gunnison. Not even the most generous interpretations of witchcraft—something that Celeste had encountered a few times over her mother's career—could have explained it.

He was one of the fair folk, real, in the flesh.

Which meant the rest of it was true, too.

The Otherworld.

The family gift. Mama's gift.

Charlotte's gift.

Charlotte had always known, even as she criticized Mama, even as she'd told Celeste it was all lies. Charlotte could have easily continued Mama's work. Gotten them to San Francisco. Charlotte could have really given Mr. Barton his truth, earned that money, spared Celeste all this pain.

It was this realization that had kept her up all night. This maddening, horrifying realization that Charlotte wasn't just a hypocrite, but a very, very good liar.

Charlotte had lied to Celeste her entire life.

"I am sorry about the events of last night," Eli Horn said now, breaking through her reverie. He was bare-chested, clothes stripped off and laid aside so he could work by touch in the pre-dawn darkness. Celeste was trying very hard not to look directly at him, but she could still see him pulling away the makeshift dressing from his shoulder. "I must apologize to you, fáith. It seems that I have utterly ruined your handkerchief."

Celeste caught sight of the embroidered initials in the corner of it. She personally loathed such handwork; Charlotte had done that, working with Celeste's favorite shade of purple silk thread, telling her—

Damn Charlotte, Celeste thought angrily. "It's no matter," she said, biting her lip. "What's it like?"

"What?"

"The place you are taking me. Faery... I mean, Tir na nAill."

Chuckling, Eli Horn set the handkerchief down. "That is what you wish to talk about here, after last night?"

"I'd wish to talk about anything but last night," she said quietly.

Eli Horn sighed. "My last sight of it was of the ocean. The wild winter seas. The shallow straits in the calmness of twilight, as my boat was set adrift by the Morrigan, bitches that they were."

Celeste made a surprised little noise, and he looked at her, handkerchief still in hand.

"I mean no disrespect to your sex. Among my people, as I told you before, it was not rare to see a woman on the battlefield. The Morrigan were the fiercest of all. It was in their blood. It is in yours, too. I can see it. And yet, you do not let it out." He grunted, looking out across the gray pre-dawn plains. "This time sees all things warped and malformed."

"If you wanted me to fight with you last night, you could have given me a gun," she said. Celeste could not keep the bitterness from her voice. The revelation about her sister had left her exhausted.

He laughed. "It wouldn't do you much good, fáith. You see the effect bullets have had on me." He nodded, as if agreeing with himself. "You thank me for saving you, when I did little to risk myself. I retain little of my old powers, but nothing here now can kill me."

"Then why isn't that arrow wound healing?"

"It was the man who shot it, I believe." He shook out the handkerchief and thin dust flew from it, the blood flaking off, the threads falling to shreds. "The one with the Indian bow. I have not seen his like in...in a very long time."

Celeste remembered that man vaguely. The whole evening was confused in her mind, like paragraphs clipped out of a magazine story and reassembled out of order, without context or explanation. "He was like you?"

"His presence is...concerning," Eli Horn said, and rolled his shoulder. "By Domnu, this stings."

"Let me look at it."

He caught her hand before she could reach for it. His touch burned for a moment, like the feel of cold metal in winter. "You're playing with me," he growled.

Fear thrilled through her. "I am not."

"You've been playing with me this entire time."

"There is a man bleeding in front of me and I fear it's my fault. I only wish to help him," Celeste said, and realized she wasn't lying at all.

He did not let go. "It will heal on its own. Slower, but it will heal."

She shook her head, trying to pull back. "You seem quite miraculous, Mr. Horn, even in your exile."

"I am no miracle. My existence is guaranteed. My kind cannot ever truly be killed without killing nature itself." And he grabbed her hand again, tighter now. "Do not think that just because I am cut off from my power, I cannot see you."

Her heart pounded in her chest. "What do you mean?"

"I see you, fáith," Eli Horn replied, low and soft. "Your hopes, your fears, your dreams. You have been drowning. You do not belong here, in this fallen age. In my age, you would have been as a queen, honored beyond all honor, valued beyond all measure. Your word would have been law, your wisdom above reproach. You would have had your choice of lovers, should you have wanted one, including from my people, should you have found any suitable. You would have been...magnificent." His touch didn't feel so cold now. "Deep down, you know this. And it eats at you, doesn't it?"

Celeste swallowed. "I'm just me, Mr. Eli Horn."

"You are not just anything, Charlotte."

Her sister's name.

Of course.

He wasn't interested in her, the little sister, the one who didn't have the Sight, who didn't have anything.

It cut deeper than Celeste would have liked. She tried to smile, but the words had rattled her more than she cared to admit. His dark eyes were on her, judging, evaluating. Would he kill her, if he knew the truth? Kill her and go back for Charlotte?

Even now, Celeste didn't want her sister to die.

And there was always the possibility, always the chance, that she actually could reach through the veil. She had done automatic writing before during séances, automatic painting, hadn't she? She saw the lights in the shadows sometimes. She had never hated Spiritualism, but had always been curious about its questions, its promises.

Eli Horn may have been using Charlotte's name, but he was looking at her. Celeste. Was it too much to imagine, to hope, that maybe, maybe...

"Would it be like that for me, in your realm?" Celeste asked, voice shaking.

"It would be like that everywhere, if I had my way." And he finally let her go. "It is such a shame, what your time has forced you to be."

Cradling her sore hand, Celeste had no idea what to say to that at all.

Movement. They both heard it, but Eli Horn reacted first, gun whipping up faster than Celeste could blink.

Mr. Abbitt. Standing there, head bowed in that submissive way of his, hat in his hand. There was more gray at his temples than before.

Mr. Horn grunted and slipped his gun back into its holster. "So Arturo's dead then."

"Dead."

For a moment, Celeste saw a look of profound grief pass over the man's face. Then he shook it away. "That's four in the past day."

"Hard price to pay, sir."

"It is indeed. Conceal the body as best you can. Rouse the rest of the lads."

Lukas nodded and retreated again.

The light was growing now, the sun creeping ever closer to the line of distant mountains that marked the eastern horizons. Celeste could see Eli Horn clearly now. He was a tall man and lean, but there was not an ounce of fat on him, keen muscle clear under the alabaster skin of his chest. He looked, she thought, like one of those marble statues of the ancient Hellenic period where the sculptors strove to capture the true perfection of the human form. In the pre-dawn light, she fancied that she could almost see a glow within him. It was a romantic fancy, she told herself, a trick of the mind, and yet, she could not now unsee it.

"What are you really?" she asked.

Eli Horn stood, buttoning his shirt back up, concealing wounds that were already healing. He smiled at her. "As I told you before, I was a king," he said. "And I shall be again, and then our golden age will return, and the world will weep that it forgot about us for so long. Now, see to yourself. We shall be leaving soon."

He turned to go. Confused, she called out, "You're going to leave me alone?"

"Would you like me to watch?"

It was bold, shameless, delivered with the faintest hint of need. Her heart was pounding again, although this time, it had nothing to do with fear. "I meant, aren't you afraid I'm going to escape?"

He smiled back over his shoulder at her, sly and knowing. "No," he replied.

And then he was gone, too.

Dawn was nearly here. A soft breeze whipped up across the high plain, rustling the golden autumn grass. The horses whinnied softly over the crest of the small hill. She could hear the sounds of men moving, packs being reloaded, curses and jeers. And most of all, she could hear Eli Horn's voice, barking out orders.

How was she going to part the mists for him? If she could, should she? Men had died back in Gunnison. Men had been killed back there. Mr. Horn had killed men back there.

And yet...

"A Fomorian? Can somebody tell me what in the blazes a Fomorian is? Leighton?"

Thomas saw Mr. Hallorman glance back at the captain. They had not quite left Gunnison yet, still passing by the last few buildings. Up ahead was open prairie.

Captain Sirok had insisted on having a word with the ranking officer from the cavalry detachment. So their little party had been obliged to take a detour back into town. Back to the Black Horse Saloon, one of the few undamaged structures, serving now as a temporary headquarters for the surviving sheriff's deputies.

The town was in a bad way. The ground in a few places had given way completely, eroding down to the bedrock below. This high in the Rockies, the drop in depth wasn't much, perhaps only a few feet, but that had been enough to cause devastation. Buildings shifted off foundations, cracked apart, even burnt; they had passed at least one structure still on fire, and the whole town smelt of smoke. Tight-faced locals and visitors alike were working on mucking out the mess.

The cavalry detachment was similarly devastated, Captain Sirok had discovered. Many of the patrol's horses had bolted during the fighting and half the men were dead.

Nobody, it seemed, had been properly prepared for Eli Horn last night.

And small wonder, Thomas thought to himself grimly, if they truly were dealing with a Fomorian.

"I am more interested in Mr. Hallorman's answer," Thomas said honestly.

The faery snorted. "Why is that, scholar? Surely you know what they are. The English didn't burn everything."

"As you say, our records are incomplete. I think your perspective would be the more valuable," Thomas replied, but with Captain Sirok staring daggers at him, he sighed and continued. "Have you heard of the Titans, my good man?"

"The what?"

"The Titans. Cronos, Saturn, Uranus…"

"I've heard of the planets. What does that have to do with some gunslinger fae?"

"The Titans were the first generation of gods, in classical Greek mythology," Thomas explained. "They were supplanted, replaced, by the Olympians, Zeus and Ares and Athena and the like."

The captain readjusted his hat. "Are you saying we're up against a god here?"

Miss Roseingrave shifted uncomfortably in her saddle. Thomas spared her a glance, more than a little worried for her. She hadn't spoken since Mr. Hallorman had made his little announcement about Eli Horn's true nature. Thomas suspected that she too understood.

"Here the scholarship fails us. Clearly, the Christian monks who transcribed the old stories cast the Fomorians as demons. Some of my colleagues believe the Fomorians were allegories, mythological stand-ins for the Vikings that used to raid the Irish coasts. Others, including myself, are of the opinion that the Fomorians represent the earliest pantheon of the now-lost ancient Celtic religion of the island, but—"

"Yes, but planets?"

"There was a great war fought between the Titans and the Olympians for control of the earth," Thomas said. "The same happened between the Fomorians and the Tuatha Dé Danann, where—"

"The what?" Captain Sirok asked.

"The ancestors of the hill-dwellers," Mr. Hallorman said.

"Your ancestors?"

"The forebears of all the one the Englishman calls fae, in all their varied forms."

"A heritage that the Fomorians are part of, are they not?" asked Thomas. "Many of the most famous Tuatha Dé Danann are said to be the children of Fomorians, such as Elatha—"

"Who?" Sirok asked.

"One of their kings, I believe. If that is correct."

Mr. Hallorman didn't rise to the bait and didn't answer.

"If Mr. Hallorman had not said the word, I would not have arrived at it myself," Thomas said, continuing. "I would think that Fomorians would be subject to at least some of the same laws as the rest of the faery peoples. The prohibition against iron, for example. And besides, the Fomorians were defeated at the Second Battle of Mag Tuired. At least, that is what the stories say."

"Yes, they were," Mr. Hallorman said grudgingly. "Cast down into the darkness of their own fell nature, locked away until the breaking of the world."

Now there was a nuance Thomas had not heard before. "I thought they were all killed."

"You cannot kill something like that, not truly." And Mr. Hallorman shook his head again. "But it is nonetheless a thing that should not be here walking under the sun."

"Are you sure he is a Fomorian?" Miss Roseingrave asked, finally speaking up.

"The worst of their powers still clings to him, wild and barely controlled," Mr. Hallorman replied. "Only the Fomorians ever commanded those magics, the magics of unmaking, of destruction. Your entropy, Englishman."

She shook her head. "What does such a creature want with my sister?"

"Whatever his intentions, I cannot imagine they will be to anyone's benefit."

Thomas thought there was something evasive in that, but the faery seemed genuinely disturbed by this. "Can you kill him?"

"The Fomorians were long vanquished by the time the mounds were inhabited," Mr. Hallorman said thoughtfully. "It took the full strength of the Tuatha Dé Danann to defeat them, and even then, it came at the cost of several of their greatest heroes and their own eventual defeat by the first humans of the isles. But Eli Horn is clearly weakened in some way, his nature suppressed. As you say, he handles steel guns with ease. We may prevail. But the Englishman's assessment may be correct: like as not, he'll kill us all."

"Ain't too late to turn back," Captain Sirok said gently, and Thomas realized he was talking to Miss Roseingrave.

She roused herself. "Captain, I understand that I cannot ask you to—"

But she didn't get to finish. The captain burst out laughing. "I wouldn't miss this for the world," he told her merrily. "Killing a god. Who could say no to that?"

"He's not a god," Mr. Hallorman said sharply. "None of them were.

Not demons either. Forces of nature, the best and worst of all things, primal and dangerous beyond measure, aye, but fae still, not gods.”

“It’ll still make a great story for the pack,” Captain Sirok said merrily.

Mr. Hallorman just grunted and spurred his horse, leaping forward into a ground-eating canter. The remaining three of them looked at each other, then followed suit.

But even as they raced across the morning plains, the sun moving high, chasing the chill from Thomas’s bones, he had to wonder...

What wasn’t Mr. Hallorman telling them?

CHAPTER TWENTY-NINE

The first horse died on the second afternoon.

It happened suddenly, out of the blue. Nothing dramatic. A grunt, then a scream. A human scream; it had taken its rider down with it.

Today had been hard. All of yesterday had been hard. The plains south of Gunnison were folded and creased like discarded newspaper. Broad flat mesas sloped into a torturous network of valleys and ravines, shallow at first, growing steeper and deeper now, forcing them along a winding and indirect path. It was not country that permitted speed, and yet, Eli Horn pressed them harder and harder.

The ride had been miserable, everyone seemingly picking up on Eli Horn's fell mood. No fires had been lit since leaving Gunnison. They had only managed a meager resupply there and meals were painfully light.

It was not just the humans who were suffering. The dusty ground held only dead grass and few streams. When they had camped the night before, the horses had protested mightily, stamping and pacing, no doubt wanting something to fill their bellies before today's hard push further up into the San Juan foothills.

So perhaps it was no surprise that one had finally died, Celeste thought. And yet—

"Hold," Eli Horn said, reining in his own beast alongside the fallen one.

The great animal had collapsed on its side. The day was cold, but the horse was lathered in sweat. Its chest labored against its girth for air, one hoof feebly pawing at the air, once, twice, then it fell. Boneless. Far from the healthy creature she remembered from only a few days ago, it looked emaciated, ribs showing, flesh sunk from age or privation. It seemed as if the animal had aged a dozen years since setting out that morning.

It was serene, somehow. Serene and terrible.

A hard contrast to the shouting, swearing man trapped beneath it. "Hell and damnation! Get me free of this thing!"

Several of the posse had dismounted by now, going over to help wrestle him out.

The boss leaned forward on his pommel, the brim of his hat shadowing his face, just watching.

Celeste looked over at Mr. Abbitt, whose rough face was inscrutable. He knew something, she thought.

The man was pulled free of the dead animal, but immediately stumbled back, sitting down hard on the ground. His right leg, the one that had been pinned by the horse's fall, was a tangled mess of bone and blood.

"Can't ride like that, can you now?" Eli Horn asked quietly.

Everyone stopped. The man who'd been pinned looked up at him. "Boss, it ain't that bad. Get me up on one of the others and I'll—"

A pistol barked. Celeste screamed and flinched, the sound hitting her like a hammer blow.

The man was silent now, all words driven from him by a bullet round in his forehead.

Feeling somewhat in shock, Celeste looked over at Mr. Abbitt, who was holstering his still-smoking revolver. He, in turn, looked at Mr. Horn. "We're gonna run them all to death at this pace, boss," he said. It was neither approving or disapproving, just a flat statement of fact.

But Eli Horn didn't reply. Didn't acknowledge it at all. Just turned and spurred his horse, heading off again south across the valley.

Mr. Abbitt yanked hard on the lead line. Celeste didn't like what she saw in his eyes when he looked at her, but maybe it was just concern. She realized she was crying.

Two more horses dropped that evening before they finally made camp. The other two riders hadn't suffered the same injuries as the first, but there were no extra saddles to offer them. Eli Horn finally called for a halt, and with one last conversation with Lukas and no word to Celeste, disappeared off into the gathering night.

Perhaps in recognition of the situation, the fae outlaw allowed a few small fires that night, fueled with dead wood from a small copse of pine trees nearby. They were tucked in against the western side of a small hill, and this seemed to be enough for the outlaw gang to feel comfortable. Celeste wondered if it would be sufficient cover for their fire. If it would conceal them from their pursuers, or if they would finally catch up. If she would be set free and the rest of the posse destroyed.

She wondered if that was what she even wanted at this point.

It was a strange thought, but one that had been growing in her since the conversation with Eli Horn the previous morning.

While this road had often been miserable and the conditions abhorrent, there was something about being out here, in the wild places of the country, that she found invigorating. There was beauty here, and much wonder, and something about the land itself seemed to call to her. While Celeste had traveled widely across America over the past fifteen years, she had seldom left its cities, wandered beyond the train tracks that led, so neatly, from place to place now. Despite everything, she wanted to see more of it.

And then there was Eli Horn himself.

Celeste was not sure if he was, as he claimed, some kind of king among the faeries. She did not quite believe his pronouncements about her being some kind of queen. She remembered Grandmother's stories; the fair folk had a way of twisting words, but they could not lie, and when they made deals, they were bound to uphold them. And Faeryland, or whatever it was truly called, was supposed to be a land of great beauty. What if—

Mr. Abbitt sat down next to where he had her chained, offering her his canteen. He had blood on his chest. He had taken some kind of wound back in Gunnison but it didn't seem to be healing. "Haven't had a chance to refill today," he said. "Drink slow."

She took it cautiously, fingers curling around the cold metal and rough canvas. "Why did you kill that man?" she asked.

"Boss was going to leave him there. I reckoned a bullet in the head was better'n dyin' alone out here from thirst or fever." He looked up at the sky. The moon was setting, and it looked huge against the close western peaks of the San Juans. "Or gettin' captured by the Army and dyin' in a fort anyway."

"Then the Army is in pursuit?"

"Don't get your hopes up," he said. "There's a reason we're pressin' so hard, and it ain't the damn cavalry. Boss knows what he's doin'. If he wanted them all dead, they'd be dead."

"Then why not just kill them?" she asked tartly, not really believing a word Mr. Abbitt was saying. Whatever his other faults, she had seen no evidence that Eli Horn was a truly cruel man. His group of outlaws were, of course, but the faery himself was not like that. He was a lord far from home, seeking a return to his former glory, a sad but noble figure. He would not, she was sure, have sanctioned that murder earlier. She wondered why Mr. Abbitt had not been disciplined for it.

There came another pained whinny from beyond the campfire's light.

"What's happening?" she asked.

"Another one's droppin'. Pushed too hard for too long," he said, but it felt evasive. "The boss has a destiny to meet somewhere in these mountains. We can't be late."

Footsteps near the fire made them both look up. It was one of the other outlaws.

"Lukas," he said. "We need to talk."

"Food's going bad already and almost all the horses are dead," the outlaw began. "How the hell did this happen? What the hell has been goin' on?"

Celeste didn't know this one. A few men had joined them on the way out of Gunnison, but she had not yet had time to learn their names or anything else useful about them. They were easy to pick out; they didn't have the same half-starved, gaunt look that the rest of the posse did. From the way this one was standing, the expression on his face and the tension in his shoulders, Charlotte guessed that he was uncomfortable.

Whatever he was used to, running with Eli Horn, something had changed since his group had broken away from the posse. And he didn't like what he had found on his return.

The remainder of the posse—eleven men in all now, including the reinforcements who had joined them during the retreat from Gunnison—were gathered around. They were all standing by the fire, listening. Celeste saw the same tension, the same discomfort, in all of them. She stayed behind Mr. Abbitt, as far from the fire's light as the blasted chain around her ankle would allow. If she guessed correctly, this discussion was going to end in violence.

"What difference does it make? We don't got water for 'em anyway," Lukas said.

"It ain't thirst that killed 'em."

"What're ya gettin' at here, Otis?"

"You know what I'm gettin' at. We can't stay here, Lukas."

"We ain't gonna stay here. The boss—"

"The boss killed Bill today, neat as you please."

Mr. Abbitt looked around, then bared his teeth. "I shot Bill. What you on about?"

"I know you, Lukas. You did it 'cause of him," the one called Otis said. "But we've been together a long time. This ain't like you. This ain't like any of us. We gotta get away while the gettin's good."

Murmurs of agreement swept around the group.

Mr. Abbitt gave them all a nasty look. "What exactly are you fools proposin' here?"

Otis scoffed. "We take the horses that ain't dead, the rest of the supplies, and we head south. Silverton ain't that far, maybe a few days walkin'. We pick up fresh horses there and be done with all this."

Mr. Abbitt's voice got softer. "Sounds like you want to leave the boss out here."

"So what? The man's a monster. You and me, we might be murderers, Lukas, but him? He ain't human."

Celeste watched as Mr. Abbitt's hand slowly fell to his belt. "You best watch what you say."

"Or what? You'll be his good little lapdog and attack?" Then Otis smiled at Celeste. "Whaddaya say, honey? You wanna come with me? I can be sweet when some gal puts me in the mood."

A chorus of laughter went up from the group.

"I'd rather die," she snapped back.

"Pity," Otis said, and something glinted in his hand—a bowie knife.

Mr. Abbitt's hand settled on his pistol butt. "Otis, like you said, we've been with the boss a long time. Don't do this."

"You always were pathetic," Otis snarled.

Before Celeste could blink, guns had left their holsters, barking out in the night, muzzles flashing. Mr. Abbitt's shot went wide, but Otis's hit home, smacking Mr. Abbitt right in the meat of his injured chest. It knocked him back, making him stumble, then trip and fall. There was a sickening thud as he hit the ground.

"Now," Otis said, turning his attention to Celeste, "where were we, little lady?"

Celeste scrambled back, but there was nowhere to go. She picked up a handful of dust and threw it at him, eliciting laughter from the posse. She tugged at the chain, desperately trying to free herself...

... when she ran straight back into a pair of legs.

Eli Horn. Standing there. His own knife in hand. "Did I miss something?" he asked, voice neutral, almost bored.

Otis's prior attitude evaporated instantly, a naughty child called to task by a stern parent. "Just havin' a bit of fun, boss."

"Fun." The boss's deep voice rumbled with the word. "Fun. Are you having fun there, Lukas?"

Mr. Abbitt hunched his shoulders, head lowered. "Grand time, sir."

"And how about you, my fáith?" he asked, looking down at Celeste. "Are you having fun?"

Not trusting herself to speak, Celeste nodded. She wasn't sure what else to do. Everyone here was on a knife's edge.

The boss looked around, shaking his head, then turned to Otis. "Silverton, you say?" he asked, laying a hand on the man's shoulder. "And what would you do there?"

"More 'n this," Otis replied cautiously. "It ain't about abandoning you, boss, but like I said b'fore when you told us 'bout your plan, this ain't the time to gallivant through the mountains, and with the damn US Army on our heels—"

"It's not the entire army. Just one troublesome pup." The boss's voice was understanding, almost kind. He patted Otis's shoulder and then looked around, spreading his arms. "Have I not been good to you? Good raids, good sport? And this is my reward? Betrayal? An attempt to leave me to die here in the mountains?"

There were a few confused murmurs.

"I recruited you for a purpose and this is it." He lifted his hands. "This is our destiny, lads, upon us now. All the suffering, all the struggle, is finally about to be rewarded." He turned, glaring down at Otis. "Would you really give it up now because this coward no longer has the stomach for the fight?"

Otis snarled then, hand diving for his gun.

Eli Horn was faster. His gun sounded out, first and last.

Otis's body hit the ground and did not rise again.

For a moment, silence reigned in camp.

"Drag that out of camp for the buzzards to feed on," Eli Horn finally said, voice cold, and holstered his pistol. "We ride to glory, men. Don't let one coward steer you off course now."

Celeste shrank back as the body was hauled away.

The evening calm descended back onto the camp. Mr. Abbitt left her alone again, pulled away by Eli Horn for some private, distant discussion. The outlaws gathered back around their own fires, talking quietly amongst themselves. There seemed to be an air of resignation about the whole thing, sullen and tired. They were exhausted, she thought, no energy for continuing the fight, no energy for anything. She listened to them talk for a while, and then curled up in her own bedroll, eyes shut tight.

She wished she had Grandmother's old storybook. She wished Charlotte was there to read it to her, voice soft and slow, both of them getting lost in some old tale. Faeries, it seemed, were far more complicated in real life.

"Regrettable. A waste of a good gun hand."

Celeste was startled out of her thoughts but pulled her blanket around her tighter. She didn't know what to say.

"I know you are awake, fáith," Eli Horn continued from somewhere close by. "But you are welcome not to speak. I forget sometimes, in this time and place, modernity has stripped mankind of its familiarity with death."

"I have seen plenty of death," she replied quietly, sitting up then. "Mama made a living off of it."

Eli Horn was sitting on a rock by her own small fire. His expression was pensive. "Perhaps I should have said killing. In my day, many things killed humans. A better time."

"You enjoy this?"

"I did not say that I enjoyed it. Only that it is what the world is. Everything lives and everything dies. Nothing lives without death, fáith. Death is nothing to be afraid of. Your people have cut themselves off from it, wrapped in all your modern comforts, thinking that would save you. But it has not. It will not."

"But—"

"Death sometimes comes at inopportune times," Eli Horn sighed, "and it was not my wish for Otis to die here tonight."

"Why not just let them go?"

"I did not amass this gang of miscreants merely because it amuses me. I need them. It may take all of them to reach my goal." He was quiet for a long while. "Get some sleep while you can, fáith. Tomorrow we start anew."

But Celeste lay awake for a long, long time.

CHAPTER THIRTY

"I 'm sorry," Mr. Leighton finally said on the second night of the pursuit. "About all this. Slowing us down."

Charlotte didn't look up from what she was doing. Captain Sirok had asked her, somewhat abashedly, if she could sew the proper rank and insignia onto his new shirt. He had taken it off an enlisted man. She had already snipped off the chevrons from the arms and was working on reapplying the captain's devices he had salvaged from his ruined shirt. "It's not your fault."

He grimaced slightly, rubbing the shoulder wound through the dressing. Charlotte had changed that a few minutes ago. It was healing rather faster than it should have. At least there was that, she thought. "It has cost us too much time."

"You were wounded for me," Charlotte said. "I can't be angry at you for that."

"Perhaps you should have left me in Gunnison, as Mr. Hallorman said."

And to that, Charlotte was not sure what to say.

It would have been quicker to travel without him, that was certain. Mr. Hallorman's half-completed healing had no doubt saved Mr. Leighton's life, but the jostling on the trail kept reopening the wound on his shoulder. He didn't complain about it, didn't deign to acknowledge it, but Charlotte could see how the wound made it harder for him to grip the reins or even focus on the horse, and at several points today Captain Sirok had been obliged to help guide him.

The pace was brutal, too. That wasn't helping. Mr. Hallorman was pushing them harder than he had before but was forced to stop often to check tracks in the hard, dusty foothills. They were still behind Eli Horn's gang by a good ten miles or more, he said. This seemed especially distressing to him.

And yet, she was grateful for Mr. Leighton's presence. Another human in all this strangeness.

Charlotte had no intention of telling him that, however.

Mama had not raised foolish girls; Charlotte knew a man did not go to these lengths simply for curiosity. He had some kind of interest in her, personal interest. But whether that interest was academic or romantic, she truly could not guess. Charlotte didn't know which prospect scared her more.

She had never much thought about marriage. Marriage meant sharing her life with a man, and what man would understand this curse of hers? Marriage meant children, and children meant daughters, and that meant passing along the Sight. As much as Charlotte longed at times to hold a babe in her arms, it was not something she could allow herself to have.

The things that had happened to her after Grandmother had died, that night when she had very nearly burned, when she had—

No.

She would not perpetuate this.

She would not inflict this on the next generation.

The family's Sight would die with her.

"It is good you are along," she told him instead. "For your knowledge of these things we are up against. Mr. Hallorman volunteers no information at all."

"I am not sure what good my knowledge does you," Mr. Leighton replied. "All of this... it is not what I thought it would be."

"On that, I believe, we agree," she replied. "And yet, here we are."

"Here we are," he said, and threw a handful of dry leaves into the fire. They caught fire and sailed up into the dark night. "Still, I should not be here."

Charlotte watched them until they had flamed out fully and then looked at him. "Where should you be, Mr. Leighton?"

"That depends on who you ask. Mr. Holzworth would no doubt say the

Academy's research library. My more enthusiastic friends? They would say I should be nowhere else, but preferably packing around a camera rig and a case of sample bottles like some Arctic explorer." He paused for a moment. "My father would say that I belonged at his old parish, watching over his old flock."

"What did happen with your seminary studies?"

"The bishop didn't take kindly, it turns out, to one of his pupils pursuing a personal interest in ancient folklore, faeries and ghosts and all the rest. Smacked of witchcraft, I was told, and was a straight road to damnation." Mr. Leighton's voice took on a bitter note. "I do not see archaeologists subjected to such criticism. Why our own history is so objectionable but the study of ancient pagan Egypt is celebrated, I have never understood."

"So you left?"

"Quite," Mr. Leighton said. There was a story in that one little word. A long story, most likely quite painful. But Charlotte had no desire to drag it out of him. Not because she was not curious—she was, intensely—but because she did not wish to force him to say it. Ferreting out secrets may have been the family business, but it was not hers. She saw no gain in stripping his pride from him, frayed as it was right now after the ambush in Gunnison. "I wished to parse the truth of things, of all things."

"Is not our faith the greatest of truths?" Charlotte asked gently.

"Perhaps, but that does not mean there is nothing else worth pursuing. There are many disciplines within science. Botany and zoology concern themselves with the natural world, with setting out to discover and describe all the species of the earth. I see no reason why we should not attempt to discover the supernatural species of this world as well." He stared into the fire. "This portal in the mountains, the Land of Faery... do you think we will see it?"

Charlotte thought of her earlier question, the nature of his interest in her. Academic, she decided. She had been distracted long enough. She refocused on Captain Sirok's blouse. "I certainly hope not. It is not a place that we belong, no matter how curious we may be," she told him firmly, perhaps just a little angrily.

The Englishman didn't answer for a few moments, still writing, and then he closed his book, drawing his pencil lead back into its little brass housing. "Why do you avoid this so? I know many people who would give anything to see what you see."

Memories scratched at the back of her mind, things as sharp and wicked as the first time she had encountered their contents. Old memories, bad memories, of bad things. She breathed out, pushing them down.

"They wouldn't be so keen for it if they had it," Charlotte replied.

"Tell me."

"So you can write it down and report it to your organization?" she said, a little harsher than she intended. "I don't think so."

He had the good grace to look embarrassed. "These notes are for my own edification, not the Academy. The Academy feels it must maintain a narrow focus, a scientific focus, if it is to ever convince anyone to take psychical endeavors seriously as a science. Monster hunting, I'm afraid, does not fit the bill." He hesitated. "I had to take...a prolonged leave of absence to come here. Mr. Holzworth, if you must know, flat out refused to allow it."

She frowned. What? "But you said..."

"I do work for the Academy. Did, perhaps. We did get Mr. Barton's correspondence, and I did champion it to our steering committee. They denied his request for assistance in his investigation. But the photographs we received had ogham script in them. I thought it significant enough to be worth pursuing. I contacted Mr. Barton separately. He agreed to pay my way, in exchange for also serving as collector and courier for some books and objects he wanted for his Spiritualist library, of course, and I..."

"You lied?"

Mr. Leighton's expression was pained. "Mr. Barton knew our arrangement. He was the one who created the ambiguity about this being an official... Miss Roseingrave? Miss Roseingrave!"

She had stood, unable to bear this a moment longer. "Good night, Mr. Leighton," she said, and headed off into the night.

The moon, just waning now from full, was high over the trees. Beyond the campfire's light, the darkness was far from complete. She could see almost as well as if it was daylight. So Charlotte found herself wandering down the hill, toward the soft whinnying of their sleeping horses.

Overhead, the stars wheeled in brilliant indifference.

Charlotte suddenly felt as if she was the last woman alive, all alone in the wilderness.

For so long, she would have said this was all she wanted. Solitude. Silence. Nothing bothering her. No people to deal with. And yet, the sense of loneliness that suffused her now was unbearable.

She was angry at Mr. Leighton for lying. She was angry at herself for trusting him. But most of all, the conversation had stirred old memories, and those, she wished to leave behind.

Those memories...

She remembered the funeral. Grandmother's funeral.

Papa had been gone years at that point. Mama had relied on their savings, then the charity of friends, to carry them after that. At the point when Grandmother passed, Mama had been eking out a living conducting séances for the well-heeled women of Savannah. It had not been a hard sell; the Civil War had stirred up a deep and intense interest in speaking with the dead, and séances were very much in vogue. There was not a weekend that passed where Mama was not at the lecture hall or in the drawing room, talking to spirits.

It paid, but not very well. An old friend of the family—Mrs. O'Malley, wife of the man who had owned Papa's shipping line—had graciously granted them room and board. For a fee. The rest of Mama's money went into maintaining her facade of being an upper-middle-class housewife, and later, into caring for Grandmother in her last days.

So when Grandmother had passed, there was no money to spare for the funeral. The service had been little more than the priest standing in the cemetery over a pinewood box. Charlotte had cried her way through all of it. Celeste, barely four, hadn't really understood what was going on, and had spent the brief service playing amongst the headstones. They'd gone home to a poor meal in the small room they shared in the servants' quarters at old Mrs. O'Malley's fine mansion, and it was with tears in her eyes that Charlotte had drifted off to sleep.

She had woken long after midnight, with Mama and little Celeste sleeping in bed next to her. She had heard music, drums and pipes, wild and sweet, exactly the sort of thing from Grandmother's stories. She had heard Grandmother's voice.

Charlotte had snuck out of bed then, barefooted and wearing nothing but her old, patched nightgown, following the sound. Always it seemed out of reach, playing down the bend in the hall or in the next room.

Finally, after what seemed like a lifetime, she had stumbled into what seemed like a grand clearing in the deep woods, every aspect of it cast in the most exquisite detail, more real than the most real thing she had ever seen. Grass was thick beneath her feet. Wild music filled the air, laughter and singing mingling with it, inseparable. A bonfire roared. Figures danced.

And all stopped as she entered.

A woman stepped forward.

Her grandmother, Charlotte had thought. It looked so much like her. Not as she had been before her death, old and wasted from consumption, but young and healthy, not so much older than Charlotte herself.

Or so it had seemed.

They had embraced, the hug the warmest thing Charlotte had ever felt. Talked, although about what, Charlotte couldn't recall. Only that it was time for Charlotte to learn the full depths of her talents, and that the thing wearing her grandmother's face was there to guide her, teach her, bring her into her power.

"All you have to do is walk forward," it said, holding out a hand. "Walk forward and be with me forever."

Charlotte, six years old and grieving, hadn't cared about power. What she wanted, more than anything, was another hug and another story and to hear Grandmother tell her that everything was alright.

She had taken the hand.

Stepped forward.

Into the bonfire.

Into the main fireplace of the O'Malleys' breakfast room, the flames there stoked high against the winter morning's chill.

It was the night she'd learned what kind of terror the Otherworld truly held. How false its promises were.

How wrong all of Grandmother's stories had been.

How alone she was.

"Where do you think you're off to?"

Mr. Hallorman. Leaning back against a tree, legs kicked out in front of him and hat cast aside on the ground.

"It's none of your business what I do with myself," she told him, and instantly regretted how bratty it sounded.

He smiled at her and got to his feet. "Best not go too far, lass. I don't fancy having to watch you and them."

A thought came to her, sudden and hard, that memory Mr. Leighton had stirred up. A thought, and a question. She bit it back before it could escape, but the faery seemed to catch it anyway, cocking his head.

"Ah," he said. "I see."

"I would appreciate it if you didn't do that."

"What, read your thoughts? I can't. But I did hear your conversation with that damned Englishman, and I see the look on your face." He cast his face up at the moon. "You blame me for it."

"I blame you for nothing," she said, rather taken aback. "I did not believe you were even real before this business with my sister."

"You do blame me," he said. "You wonder why I didn't save you that night."

She stared at him, saying nothing.

"I am not omnipotent, Charlotte, not some avenging angel sent by your desert god. I have my limitations. There are places not even I may go. Things I cannot fight."

"This Fomorian. Are you his match?"

"We shall find out," Mr. Hallorman said, and settled back down. "Tomorrow, I believe. The land protests his every footstep. We are getting close."

"Good," Charlotte replied, and made to go.

"Hate me, if you must. But don't hate your mother," he called after her, before she could get too far.

That stopped her cold. "Excuse me?"

"You hate your mother. You resent her choices. You resent her bringing you into this life, for dragging you closer to all the things that hurt you. You think she took the easy way out. She didn't. She had daughters to feed."

"And social status to maintain," Charlotte said coldly, turning back to him. "The wife of a ship's first mate, a future captain's wife, would not lower herself to scrubbing floors or working in a factory. She wished to remain in her socialite circles. She—"

"She would have worked in rags the rest of her life, but she wanted you girls to have the life your father had tried so hard to secure for you," he told her. "She and I talked about it often."

"You talked to her?" Charlotte asked, taken aback.

He shrugged. "We had a deal, she and I. She rarely used her true gifts, and I helped her when she needed it. But she always skirted the deep places. Unwilling to claim her power. After what happened to you, she didn't feel it was worth the risk."

Charlotte swallowed, wavering. By god, she wanted to believe him, but wasn't that a reason to doubt? "You spin a fine story but have no evidence for it. That seems convenient."

"You humans possess a degree of separation from our world, it is true, and there is some protection in that. But when you look into the darkness, the darkness looks back. Your grandmother did what she could to shield you. Your mother was desperate, not thinking about the consequences at first, until..." Mr. Hallorman trailed off. "She listened to me. And I protected you as best I could. But Charlotte, the time has come for you to protect yourself. You can't do that if you hate what you are."

"Goodnight, Mr. Hallorman," Charlotte told him, unwilling to speak any more to him.

He inclined his head in a silent farewell, turning his attention back up to the night sky.

Leaving Charlotte only with her memories.

CHAPTER THIRTY-ONE

They had not been on the trail long that morning when Captain Sirok smelled something.

"Blood. And rot."

Another half hour of riding brought them to the source of the reek. A dead horse with a dead man pinned beneath it. A sight that would have been terrible enough on its own, but made worse by the state of the bodies. Charlotte could not stand looking at them, and turned away, handkerchief to her nose. It didn't help much.

"Looks to be about a week dead," Captain Sirok said on the ground next to the bodies, inspecting them close. "But not touched by any scavengers. Strange."

"Not so strange," Mr. Hallorman replied. "This is one of Eli Horn's lads, isn't it?"

"Looks to be. Whatcha thinkin'?"

"How did they die?" Charlotte asked. She could see no ghost, no shade. The horse would not have left anything but a passing shadow, but the man... There was not even an echo of his passing on the land. Normally she could see something, whether she wanted to or not. This emptiness disturbed her.

"This man? Bullet to the brain," the cavalry officer said, mustache twitching a little as he sniffed the air. "From the look of it and the smell of the horse, though, I'd say it died of old age."

"Entropy," Charlotte said, turning to Mr. Leighton. "Didn't you speak to us a few days ago of that force you called entropy? Where things inevitably fall apart?"

The researcher looked startled. "That's an oversimplification. If you look at it more holistically it..." he began, then caught himself. "Yes, I suppose we did talk of it."

"Does it include aging?"

"Yes, but so quickly... I don't know. The wearing away of things is a slow process."

"Clearly, Eli Horn's weaponized it in some way. Or perhaps death is the inevitable result," Charlotte replied, and thought of the void, the darkness, the nothingness she had seen around Eli Horn. "If all things progress toward one steady, unordered state, then surely all things would become faceless? The rivers would wear away all mountains until no mountains were left. The fires would burn all until nothing was left but ashes. How could anything live in such a world?"

Mr. Leighton looked at her for a moment, blinking behind his spectacles. Then, as if noticing for the first time that they were dirty, he took them off, polishing them on a bit of his shirt. "It would go beyond that, perhaps," he said. "Some theories I have read state that matter itself may fall apart in the end, although there is as yet no instrumentation that allows us to verify that atomic theory itself is correct."

Charlotte thought of the darkness she had seen around the drill, in that farmhouse. She shivered. "What a horrible vision for the future."

He nodded. "I agree. But it may be inferred from the concept."

"The gods help me. Atomic theory," Mr. Hallorman muttered.

"I don't know about any of this philosophical talk," Captain Sirok said, wiping his hands off on the butt of his uniform pants as he rose again. "But every second we linger, they get further away. We should go."

On they rode, following the trail of Eli Horn's gang. It was not hard to follow now. There was a strip of dead grass to follow, clear as a road, left, Charlotte presumed, by Eli Horn's passing.

They came upon a campsite about an hour later, where a dozen horses lay scattered about, dead on the grass. All were emaciated, spent. This seemed to enrage Mr. Hallorman. Cold anger burned in him so brightly that in Charlotte's vision, he positively glowed with it.

Mr. Leighton was examining a few of the bodies, writing furiously in his little notebook. "If I had to guess," he said, "this is due to age, just like the horse back there."

"You ever seen this before, Captain?" Mr. Hallorman asked, pointedly ignoring the Englishman.

Captain Sirok looked equally disgusted by the scene. "No, but he does usually leave old horses behind when he steals new 'uns. Explains why he does it, I reckon. If his mere presence kills 'em all like this."

"This is quite pronounced," Mr. Leighton said, sitting back over his heels. "And did they not steal a few horses in Gunnison? For a horse to age to the point of death in less than thirty-six hours, the number of new horses he would need and how often would be—"

"Shut up," Mr. Hallorman said tightly, coming back from around the edge of the hill. "No more talk of statistics and science."

"But if we extrapolate—"

"I do not care for your extrapolations, Englishman. Even a Fomorian would not be so stupid as to do this. Something is wrong with him. Dangerously wrong."

"Such as...?" Mr. Leighton asked.

Mr. Hallorman pointed to the east, up the slopes, covered now with pine trees instead of juniper scrub. Charlotte could see smoke rising in the distance. "The horses came from that direction. It is there we will go."

"But my sister!" Charlotte protested. "Captain Sirok, did you not say the trail heads this way?" And she pointed due south.

"We are no more than a few hours behind them now," Mr. Hallorman insisted. "If the portal is here in these mountains, it will not be accessible until twilight. We have the time."

"But—"

"It ain't far," Captain Sirok told her. "Maybe a mile."

Charlotte wanted to scream. No matter how close she got to Celeste, her sister was ever just out of her grasp. "Fine," she said.

Mr. Hallorman had already turned his horse up the slope.

Over the next half hour, as they worked their way through thickening forest, moving ever upward, the smell became stronger until it stung the eyes. The smoke gathered under the branching arms of the pines, greasy and dark in the fine morning. The trees grew increasingly unhealthy, needles brown, limbs bare and falling.

Finally, emerging from a grove of aspens as dead as anything, they saw the source of the miasma.

Mr. Hallorman was the first to speak. "I feared it so."

Charlotte looked around in horror. The place wasn't large, just a low, long main house with a whole series of scattered outbuildings. Kitchen, ironworks, bunkhouse, barn. A ranch, no different from dozens, hundreds, that dotted the country from here to the Mississippi.

Except this one looked as if it had been abandoned for hundreds of years.

And everywhere Charlotte looked, there were bodies.

Decaying, rotting bodies. Dozens of them. Animals mostly, but a few humans here and there, ruined flesh peeled back from stark white ribs. The stream was choked with dead things: cattle, a trio of dogs. The trees on its bank had lost both limbs and bark, broken forms still reaching for the sky. Up the slopes, scattered across the dead grass, more cattle lay dead or dying. The lowing of the few still alive was piteous.

"Trees dead, bodies decomposed. Even the rock is crumbling," Captain Sirok said, kicking at a boulder near one the blacksmith's shop, disgust on his face. "Is this Eli Horn?"

"Yes," Mr. Hallorman said. "Either his power is growing, or he is losing the ability to contain it. Or..."

"Or what?" Mr. Leighton asked.

"Enough of that!" a female voice yelled, and around the edge of one of the buildings, there she was, a woman in a bloodstained calico dress, half-torn from her body. Her hair was loose, her lightweight corset clearly showing through the tears in her bodice, a nasty wound creasing her face from temple to chin. Dirt coated her arms. But she had a shotgun in hand, aimed right for them. "Come back for more, have you?"

Charlotte frowned. Beyond the injuries to her dignity and her person, there was something about the woman. Something wild. Something not entirely human. Charlotte's breath caught in her throat. "Mr. Hallorman," she gasped.

"I know, I see her," he said, and swung his horse around, addressing the woman directly. "We're not here to hurt you. Although I scarcely think we could do worse than what has already been done."

The woman tightened her grip on her weapon. "What's your business?"

Mr. Hallorman held out a hand then, just for a moment, and Charlotte almost saw a light there. The woman must have seen it, too, because she faltered. But then, just as quickly, the gun came back up.

"Stay where you are!" she ordered.

The faery ignored her. He pointed at one of the cows, lying on its side on the ground. "I can hear this one. She's in pain."

For a moment, the end of the barrel tipped down. "I haven't had time to put them all down yet."

"Let me help," he said.

The woman stared at him a moment more, then looked around at the rest of the small group, as if seeing them for the first time. Her gun moved, right over to Captain Sirok.

"We're huntin' the ones who did this," Captain Sirok told her, seemingly unperturbed. "I ain't here for your cattle."

She stared at him for a moment more, eyes narrowing, but finally lowered the gun. "You, faery, you do what you can."

Mr. Hallorman dismounted and went over to the cow. One hand flat to the earth, the other on the cow's neck. Charlotte was no expert on cattle, but the poor thing looked starved. Needle-thin, eyes sunken, nostrils flaring red and dry. It pawed at the earth.

"Shh," Mr. Hallorman said, murmuring something else in a language that was neither English nor Gaelic. Charlotte had no idea what he was saying, but it was warm and rich, deep and sonorous. It soothed the cow; its lowing stopped, and its breathing began to even out. The air grew sweet and still. The day seemed to darken around them, but perhaps only by comparison; a brilliant light shone out of the trees.

For a moment, it felt as if all the forest were watching them.

Mr. Hallorman exhaled slowly, sitting back over his heels, and patted the cow's neck, its flesh restored now to health. He was sweating, paler than usual, visibly tired. Unlike at Gunnison, however, there was no sign of dead things around him. Whatever he had traded for the cow's healing, it hadn't come from the land.

The woman had tears in her eyes as the cow got back to its feet, mooing softly. "Even I couldn't do that," she muttered, coming over to rub the animal's face.

Mr. Hallorman shook his head, looking around at the other cattle. "A feat I do not have the strength to repeat."

The woman sighed. "What's the bargain, faery? And make it reasonable. You offered no terms."

"I shall accept a story," Mr. Hallorman said, gentle now. "What can you tell me about the one who did this?"

The woman nodded. "Come on. Let's get out of this killing field," she said, and laying a hand against the lone cow's neck, began walking west up the flow of the creek. The animal followed her.

It was then that Charlotte noticed.

The woman had a tail to match the cow's, poking out from under the edge of her ruined skirt.

"A Fomorian, you say?" the woman with the cow's tail said as they reached a place where she had clearly made camp. There was grass in the clearing beyond, and the cow trundled out to tuck in. "We know them by other names."

"You know the same powers under different aspects," he corrected. "These are not the same as—"

"Don't speak of it," she said sharply, and sighed again. "This land was supposed to be empty, new. Untouched, I thought."

"Where one human passes, the Otherworld presses close," he said. "You should know this."

"Still. Fomorians. Never thought I'd see the day. Next thing you'll be telling me we have a troll problem here." The woman rubbed a hand over her face, smearing more dirt there. "The gods help us if trolls find these mountains."

"What happened here?" Mr. Hallorman asked.

"A stranger came through last night," she said. "Late, well after sundown. Said he needed horses. He had the darkness in him, but they wouldn't listen to me. My husband and I ranch round these parts." She looked at her sole surviving cow, sadness in her eyes. "Or did. The human men refused to give the stranger what he wanted, told him to leave. That's when...that's when the dying started. I tried to tell my husband, but..."

"He stayed to fight."

"What was there to fight?" the woman asked bitterly. "Death and dark-

270

ness, that's what bled from that thing. Death and darkness." She looked at them all. "What's your interest in this creature?"

"He took my sister," Charlotte said.

"Then I pity you," the woman replied, "because in him is the end of all things."

"We believe this creature is searching for something," Mr. Leighton said. "Some kind of...liminal place."

"Lima-what?" she asked.

"The Fomorian is trying to pierce the veil," Mr. Hallorman said, rolling his eyes. "Cross back into the deep places."

"Ah, well, the Otherworld isn't any of my concern," the woman replied. "The forest here, that's what matters to me. Not the realm of gods and nightmares."

"We're all denizens of it, in one way or another," Mr Hallorman replied.

"Excuse me," Mr. Leighton asked the woman, "but are you saying you aren't human?"

She looked at him askance and then pointed at Charlotte. "Ask her there," she said. "She can see me."

Charlotte was startled by that. "I don't... Mr. Leighton!"

He had pulled a large, overstuffed book from his saddlebags. "I'm not taking notes," he said defensively, brandishing the thing. "But ma'am, I do have a sketch here, if I can find it. One that was done by Miss Roseingrave's sister. Do you think you might take a look and—"

"Roseingrave?" And the woman snapped her fingers. "As in, Madame Aine Roseingrave?"

"She was my mother," Charlotte said, confused. "You know her?"

"I loved her articles in *Borderlands*. Insightful for a human." The cow-tailed woman tapped a finger to her lips. "So she had the true Sight after all, then. Interesting."

"I don't find it so," Charlotte replied.

"None of us escape our true natures. We always come back to what we are," the woman said. Her voice was sad. "Maybe it's better this way. My husband won't have to live with the pain of losing me to the forest again."

"My dear lady," Mr. Hallorman pressed, "we must find this portal before nightfall."

At that, her expression shifted. "You said you have a sketch of the place?"

Mr. Leighton produced it, pulling it from between the sheets and handing it over. The woman took it carefully, examining it.

"You think this is here in these mountains somewhere?" she asked.

"There can't be that many waterfalls like this around," Captain Sirok said.

She gave him a dirty look but nodded. "There aren't. I know this one. Could show you myself, if I didn't have her to think about." And she nodded at the cow.

"It's just a cow, ma'am," Captain Sirok said.

"I wouldn't expect a wolf to understand," the strange woman shot back.

"Peace," Mr. Hallorman said. "Can you provide directions, at least?"

The woman nodded and started talking.

Within the hour, they were off again.

The directions the woman had provided seemed nonsensical to Charlotte. Nothing about major landmarks or anything corresponding to Captain Sirok's map. Instead, it was *turn west at the sighing tree* or *once past the canyon of the shouting wind, continue past the grieving rocks*. But it must have made sense to their faery companion, because he nodded and thanked her for the exceptionally clear path.

The only thing Charlotte understood was the distance. Five miles. They were less than five miles from their destination, and it was barely noon.

Perhaps they had not yet lost Celeste after all.

Mr. Hallorman had left a full saddlebag of their supplies with the woman, jerky and hardtack and water, warning her against any further contact with the ruined town.

She had taken the supplies and the advice with a stone-faced expression but waved to them as they departed. Her plan, she told them, was to make her way down to Silverton or Durango, find a stable for her cow and work for herself over the winter.

"What was she?" Charlotte asked as they headed off toward the mountains.

"Huldra," Mr. Hallorman told her.

"What is that?"

"A forest spirit," Mr. Leighton supplied. "From Norway, if I'm not mistaken. They are said to lure men to their doom in the forest."

"Humans have always feared the wild places of the world. But from one such as her, you have little to fear," Mr. Hallorman said.

"Why wasn't she affected by the Fomorian?" Mr. Leighton pressed.

"She likely was. But the forests are old, long-lived, in a constant state of death and renewal." He was silent for a moment, and his next words were spoken grudgingly. "Death is a part of life. Even the Fomorians used to know this, before they made their choices."

"And that would be enough to keep her safe?" Mr. Leighton asked.

"If we want to find Celeste before twilight falls, we need to pick up our pace," he said curtly, and spurred his horse.

They passed beyond the ruined mining camp, back into the forest.

CHAPTER THIRTY-TWO

As nonsensical as the huldra's directions had been, they seemed to be sound. Mr. Hallorman set as fast a pace as the terrain would allow, glancing here and there at rocky outcroppings or cliff faces or certain trees, gauging their position and moving on without hesitation.

Their way eventually took them into a steep-sided gorge, where a narrow creek ran between sheer granite cliffs. Their horses splashed on through the water more often than not, the land on either side of the small watercourse so narrow that in places it was too choked with vegetation or fallen rocks to be passable, or it vanished entirely.

To Charlotte, there was an air of watchfulness here. She began to imagine that the mountains themselves were observing them, evaluating them, and if they were found wanting, a cliff might shear free or a boulder come tumbling down from above and they would be no more.

When she said this to Mr. Hallorman, he just chuckled. "They might at that. They know what lies ahead of us, and they know what we are."

"Do they know about the portal?"

"How could they not?" He paused for a moment, considering an old, gnarled oak tree planted in the middle of the stream. "It is not so easy, moving through the veil. Its thinning is rare. Its crossing can be painful."

"For the land or for us?"

Mr. Hallorman snorted. "Are you asking if we can cross the veil now, Charlotte?"

"No," she said, a chill running through her at the very thought of it. "No. But this Fomorian wishes to, clearly. If he takes my sister through—"

"If he does take the paths into the mist, it will have to be you who leads."

"What do you mean?"

He gave her a look. Behind them, Captain Sirok and Mr. Leighton were finally catching up. "My oath binds me to you, and in turn, your world."

"Are you saying you haven't been there since becoming bound to us?"

"Yes," he said. "I can't part the mists."

That stunned her. She had never considered where the family protector might reside when not directly involved in their lives, but something like that would not have occurred to her. "Can Eli Horn?"

"I don't know," Mr. Hallorman said, and pointed to the left, up the steeper slope. "We proceed this way."

Mr. Leighton pulled his horse up alongside Charlotte's as Mr. Hallorman rode off again. "What was that all about?" he asked.

Charlotte stared up after the faery. "There's something he's not telling us."

"Assuredly," Mr. Leighton said.

There was no help for it, though. She patted her horse's neck and urged the gelding forward.

Celeste was close now. She could feel it.

Everything else would just have to wait.

The way was steep, winding up to a small, open meadow clinging almost sideways to the mountainside. Above that was a game trail, barely visible, a tight squeeze between huge boulders. The party was forced to dismount here and continue on foot. Mr. Hallorman had a word with the horses while Captain Sirok retrieved a bandolier and Mr. Leighton shouldered his saddlebag, the one with the oilskin-wrapped books.

"Surely you won't need that?" Charlotte asked him. Her entire being was on fire with nervous energy.

"There was ogham script on your sister's drawing," he said, cleaning his spectacles. "I want to capture that, if it's here."

"Leave the bags," Mr. Hallorman told them, coming over. He had left the horses fully tacked up, but removed their bits so they could better eat. "This is not some archaeological expedition."

"I will not," Mr. Leighton replied, and replaced his spectacles on his face. "I will not be reliant on you if we encounter something that requires translation."

The faery gave him a strange look, then the edges of his mouth quirked up in a faint smile. "Well then, Englishman, let us go. Would you like to lead the way? It is not far, maybe a hundred yards or less."

"You take the lead," Charlotte ordered, her nerves making her irritated. "If any of us should be shot at, it should be you."

Mr. Hallorman chuckled and, loosening his knife in its sheath, strode up the narrow, half-hidden game trail. "As the lady commands," he said with a laugh, and disappeared into the trees.

Charlotte felt her heart sink, but then Captain Sirok snorted and moved ahead. "I can smell him, don't worry," he said. "We ain't lost yet."

And so, the three of them struggled up the last leg of their journey.

Had they come here on their own, Charlotte thought, they never would have found the place.

Twenty minutes after leaving the horses behind, the party emerged from a maze of boulders and scraggly pine into an aspen grove. The trees still clung tenaciously to the faded summer, and so Charlotte's impression of the place was a world of white bark and rustling golden leaves.

It reminded her of her dream.

Mr. Hallorman pointed, but Charlotte didn't need the guidance. She could feel what waited for them. His way through the mists. The portal to Tir na nAill, the Otherworld. Charlotte could feel her heart hammering in her chest in a way that had nothing to do with the thin air or the exertion of climbing up the narrow canyon.

Emerging again from the aspen grove, they found themselves at the dead end of the canyon. Sheer granite walls rose up all around. A waterfall, thin and spidery, fell from above. Only a trickle of water reached the ground. There was a small pool, mostly dry, and the stream that straggled away from the place was small indeed, disappearing somewhere in the grass. All was cast in shadow here, which did not seem right; the day was failing fast, but the sun was still above the mountains, above the trees.

Sirok looked up, clearly gauging the position of the canyon walls around them. "Unnatural," he muttered. "This should still be awash in sunlight."

Mr. Hallorman moved past them, toward the waterfall. "Yes, it should be."

But if Charlotte had felt uneasy in the trees, this strange little meadow was worse. Her mind suddenly filled with things she didn't want to know: angry words, the tension of a standoff, gunshots, blood, death. People had died here, at least a dozen.

Anxiety rushed through her. Her heart pounded. Her palms went weak. She felt as if she would pass out.

"What is it?" Mr. Leighton asked, coming over.

"Something is wrong here," she replied, grabbing for him, trying to steady herself. The warmth of his arm lessened her inner turmoil. "Very wrong."

"What do you see, Charlotte?" Mr. Hallorman called back, up ahead.

The question made her queasy. "I don't want to look."

"Anything you can—"

"The lady said no," Mr. Leighton snapped.

"It's alright," Charlotte said, forcing herself to stand on her own feet. She felt better, but still shaky. "I think...there was an ambush. People died here."

Captain Sirok held up a lumpy object he'd just scrounged from the thin grass. It was badly corroded, rusted almost entirely away, but enough was left of the bottom to identify it. A cast-iron Dutch oven. "There was a camp, I'd say."

"Mr. Barton's expedition?" Mr. Leighton asked.

Sirok set the pot aside and went over to the pool, bending down. "I'd say so."

Mr. Leighton followed. "Is that..."

"Yup," Sirok said, and tossed him something that looked like a peanut. Mr. Leighton caught it, and even in the strange gloom, Charlotte could see the glint off it. "Gold."

"This is where the portal is?" Charlotte asked and shivered.

"Yes," the faery replied, still looking around. "But where?"

"Is that something?" Mr. Leighton asked, pointing.

The waterfall's bowl was a little way out from the base of the cliffs. Behind it, tucked into the blunt end of the canyon, was a cave mouth.

And Charlotte realized, with terrifying clarity, that there was no rock. It was all an illusion. The finest of illusions. They were not in a cave, but in a pocket of open air within a drifting mist. She could hear the cry of seabirds, smell the scent of the sea, sweet and sharp and—

She closed her eyes, scrubbing her hands across her face, trying to block it out. "No," she muttered. "No, no, no, no."

"That is not natural," Sirok commented.

"Indeed not. Our friends here must have been digging already," Mr. Hallorman said, and set his course for it. "Captain, keep watch out here."

"I ain't your guard dog," Sirok replied, but unslung his rifle nonetheless, taking up position at the edge of the trees.

Mr. Leighton looked at Charlotte. She straightened as best she could, smoothing down her skirt, and followed Mr. Hallorman.

For all the buildup, all the effort, all the suffering they had endured to reach this place, the portal itself was rather disappointing.

Thomas didn't know what he'd expected. Something grand perhaps, like the megalithic structures of the British Isles. Something fanciful, like a giant tree with darkness under its roots, broad enough for a human to easily pass through. But like all else Thomas had seen of the Otherworld on this journey, the truth was more mundane and yet more strange than he could have guessed.

The ill-fated mine was shallow, barely twenty feet deep, with a sandy floor and smooth walls. The afternoon sun didn't penetrate far into the gloom, and Thomas found himself wishing they had brought a lantern with them.

"This looks to be somewhat natural after all," Mr. Hallorman commented as they entered. Miss Roseingrave shivered. What she saw, she didn't say.

"Except for this," Thomas replied, catching sight of something in the shadows. In the back of the cave, there was writing. Scratches set around a tall curving line.

Miss Roseingrave reached for it, but Mr. Hallorman pulled her away again. "Best you not touch that," he said.

"What is it?" she asked.

"An incantation," he replied, stony-faced. "Or close enough to it."

"So is that the portal?" she asked.

"You're thinking about this too literally," he replied, lips pursed. "This entire hollow is the portal. But that is a statement of intention."

"Might I examine it?" Thomas said.

Mr. Hallorman glared at him, his disapproval palpable. "This is no research expedition."

"This is ogham script, found in a cave in North America," Thomas replied, laying a careful finger against one of the lines. "This is extremely significant."

"Very well. But be quick," Mr. Hallorman sighed. "The veil is thin here and twilight approaches. That posse will be here soon."

Gauging his options, Thomas swiftly tore a handful of pages from his notebook, retrieved one of his pencils, and got to work.

He worked as quickly as he could, confused by what he was seeing. While a full translation would require some time and focus, he recognized at least some of the writing without having to consult his notes. Ogham recorded names and family relationships almost exclusively, and yet here in the stone was the old Irish word for *crow*. Perhaps it was part of a name, or perhaps this was an entirely new usage of the characters, one unknown to science.

Mr. Hallorman watched him for a moment, then stepped in. He looked at the writing, eyes roaming around the doorway, taking it in. "By the stars below," he muttered.

"What?"

"We leave," he said, and there was fear in his voice. True fear, for the first time in the entire journey. Thomas wondered at hearing it. "Now."

"But my sister!" Miss Roseingrave protested.

Outside, a wolf began howling.

And Thomas didn't need to see the expression on Mr. Hallorman's face to know that it was too late.

"This is it. Here we are. At the start of all things to come."

Celeste didn't dare look Eli Horn in the face. She wasn't sure what he would see in her eyes. She didn't know what she felt herself. Excitement? Naturally. It wasn't every day that a girl got the chance to see Faeryland. Fear? Of course.

Could she actually open this portal? The question had dogged her all day. It had been a hard ride through the mountains today, hard and quiet, everyone in the posse seeming to retreat back into themselves as they passed through the winding, steep canyons of the San Juans. The attempted mutiny had been thoroughly shattered; nobody had dared gainsay a thing Eli Horn had told them today.

Right now, the rest of the posse was hanging back, even as Mr. Horn led Celeste through a fine autumnal aspen grove. Mr. Horn had given them the order with a kind of breathless urgency, telling them to guard this canyon's end with every last fiber of their strength. "If you do not, all is lost."

What he had told them to make them follow him on this hard, desperate road, Celeste did not know. There was love there, yes, but fear as well. A powerful combination, Celeste thought to herself, and wondered which was holding her to him as well.

You can do this, she told herself.

Spiritualism held that psychic talent ran through even the most hardened human heart, and Celeste was determined to make this work. She would not be the Roseingrave sister who denied the Otherworld.

"I will do what I can for you," Celeste told him now. "I have never opened a portal before."

"It is a simple matter," he told her softly, pausing between two white-barked trees. "I shall walk you through it, should you falter. But I do not think you will. This is—"

"Boss."

Anger passed over Eli Horn's face, swift as a thunder cell moving across a valley, and he turned. "I told you to stay back."

"Boss," Mr. Abbitt pressed again. He was the only one of the posse that Mr. Horn had brought with them. All the rest had been told to hang back, beyond the aspen grove. "I smell something."

"I know," Mr. Horn replied, and resumed walking. "We aren't alone here."

And a wolf started howling.

Emerging a few moments later from the deep shadows of the trees, Celeste's palms were clammy, her body positively vibrating with anticipation.

But then her heart fell to her feet, because stepping out of the gathering darkness into the last rays of day were a pair of men. One of them was the man who had threatened them before back in Gunnison. The other, Celeste realized with a start, was Mr. Leighton, the researcher from the Academy who had come to see her and her sister.

Both of them had weapons pointed straight toward them.

"Release the girl…" the man with the bow ordered. Celeste had the feeling of being observed by something far older, far more vicious, than anything she had ever known. It was like witnessing the enmity of a mountain. "… and maybe I'll let you live."

Eli Horn just laughed and stepped forward, hands wide. "So here we are again. You don't have the power to kill me, hill-dweller."

"Should we test it?" the strange archer replied.

And before she knew what was happening, Celeste was grabbed by the hair and jerked back, a knife at her throat. She screamed, caught between the blade and Eli Horn's body.

"What are you doing?!" she yelped.

"Play along. These faeries are all cowards," he murmured in her ear, and then he straightened, smiling at the man in front of them. "How much do you value her life?"

The arrow did not waver. "You won't kill her."

"Are you so sure of that?"

Celeste saw a muscle in the other man's jaw twitch. His arrow dipped for a moment, almost imperceptible. "I cannot let you take the road through the mists."

He jerked her back, cruel and hard, and Celeste whimpered, perhaps a little more than she otherwise would have. "Then it seems we are at an impasse," Eli Horn chuckled.

And perhaps they would have resolved their argument, perhaps Eli Horn would have talked the archer down, except that just then a third figure came out of the cave.

"Sister!"

Charlotte. It was Charlotte. Running for her. She got no more than a few paces, however, before the strange Irishman grabbed her, dropping his weapon in favor of catching her by the waist.

Celeste stared at her in shock and only barely kept herself from blurting out Charlotte's name.

Eli Horn, on the other hand, began roaring with laughter and walked forward across the grass as easily as if he were strolling through a park or across some dance floor. "Two of them," he chuckled. "Aine did have two daughters, didn't she? How wonderful of you to bring the other to me, hill-dweller. One and a spare. How—"

Then his forehead exploded in a burst of blood and bone, knocking him down to the ground. Celeste stared, too shocked to even scream. Mr. Leighton was standing there, rifle smoking, a startled expression on his face as if he too couldn't believe what he had just done.

Then the Irishman was at her side. "Best come with us now, lass, before he—"

"Before I what?" Mr. Horn growled, and Celeste saw him stand, the wound already knitting shut. "That's not enough to kill me."

"Time to go," the strange Irishman said, grabbing Celeste by the elbow, but no sooner had they taken two steps back toward the aspen grove than the posse started shooting.

That, Celeste did scream at.

Running now, the Irishman snatched Charlotte from where she was standing, too shocked to move, and yanked Celeste around, pushing them into what seemed like a shallow cave, keeping his body between them and the grove. Celeste saw blood on his sleeve. The Irishman had taken a round right through the arm. He seemed not even to notice, focused instead on shoving the two women into the furthest corner he could manage before positioning himself at the entrance. His bow sang out once, and a scream echoed from the aspens.

Mr. Leighton dived in after them, firing as well. The noise was horrific, and Celeste clutched at her ears. She was still screaming, she realized, but she couldn't seem to stop herself.

Then—

"Stop firing, you damned fools!" Eli Horn's voice rose, finally, over the din. "Stop!"

Mr. Leighton squeezed off one more shot, but the Irishman grabbed his arm. "Save your ammunition," he said grimly.

The evening fell silent, still. Nothing stirred.

"Are you hurt?" Charlotte whispered to Celeste.

"What are you even doing here?" her sister hissed back.

"I was at Gunnison! We came to rescue you."

"Rescue me from what?"

Charlotte stared at her, like this was yet another stupid question from her dumb little sister. "From that... that thing out there! Eli Horn!"

"Why?"

"Why? Why? What do you mean, why?"

"He just needs my help. He's just trying to get home," Celeste explained. How to make Charlotte understand? "How can I refuse that?"

"Ahh. So here we all are."

It was Eli Horn, his voice soft, soothing, after the tumult of the gunfight. He stood there in the cave entrance, framed by the last rays of the dying sun, Mr. Abbitt at his side. Mr. Horn was no longer holding his guns, but Mr. Abbitt had his own six-shooter trained right at Charlotte.

The Irishman lunged for him then, knife out. Eli Horn didn't budge, his gaze fixed on Celeste. Mr. Abbitt, on the other hand, fired right through the man's trouser leg, above his knee. The Irishman groaned, falling to the sandy floor of the cave.

"Stay out of the business of your betters," Eli Horn growled, kicking the Irishman as he walked past, closing the small distance to where Celeste and Charlotte were huddled. Charlotte gasped, grabbing at Celeste as he knelt down in front of them, hand out. "Now, my little fáith, are you ready?"

"Don't do this," Charlotte begged, eyes closed, breathing heavy. "Sister, please..."

And for a moment, Celeste wavered. Hesitated. Torn.

But then she saw moisture collecting in her older sister's lashes and was filled by a sudden, blinding rage.

"Tears?" she snapped. "You didn't even cry at Mama's funeral, but you'll do it now?"

"Please," Charlotte panted, "you have to see it. How can you not see it? You can't go in there with him."

"Why not? So I can go back to working twelve-hour days at the opera workshop for pennies? So you can continue to lie to me about everything?"

Charlotte was crying properly now, silent tears running down her face that she didn't seem to even notice. Her body was shaking. She was as close to a breakdown as Celeste had ever seen her.

And it was infuriating.

This wasn't Charlotte. Charlotte wasn't this weak, this emotional, this raw. Ever. About anything. It had to be an act. Just an attempt at manipulating her, getting Celeste back under her thumb, her suffocating control.

"That's not... This isn't..."

"You knew!" Celeste yelled, years of frustration finally boiling over. "You knew about all of this! You knew about our family, you knew about Mama, you knew about...about them! And you never said a word to me!"

"I was trying to protect you!"

"From what?!"

"From them!" Charlotte yelled back, pulling herself up, dashing the tears from her face. "Do you have any idea what he is?"

Celeste looked back at Eli Horn. For a moment, they locked eyes, and if Celeste had had any doubt before, it was washed away now.

"Yes," she said, and took his hand.

"Come now, Charlotte my dear. Let's go home," he said with a gentle smile, pulling her back up to her feet.

"No!" Charlotte cried. "Sister, you have to understand, he's—"

But whatever words she was trying to get out were lost in the mists, mists that sprung up all around them.

There was only silence.

Silence, and then, the sound of the sea.

Chapter Thirty-Three

Charlotte collapsed to the rocky floor of the cave, arms empty, bereft.

Celeste was gone. Celeste and Eli Horn and that strange brutal man they had had with them, swallowed up by mist. Tendrils of it still played around her hand on the cave floor.

Celeste was gone.

Vanished.

Into Tir na nAill. Into the Otherworld.

"Miss Roseingrave," she heard, and looked up to see Mr. Leighton squatting on the floor next to her. He had a hand out. "May I help you up?"

It was so painfully polite, so kind, she felt like striking him. But fresh tears came instead, and she collapsed down, head in her hands.

"What do we do?" she heard the researcher asking their faery companion. "What do we do now?"

Mr. Hallorman was leaning against the back of the cave, the tip of his knife hidden beneath the ripped fabric of his trousers, digging around. A shot like that would have cost a mortal man his leg, if not his life. The faery just looked resigned, as if this was an annoyance and nothing more. "It's the lady's call."

"What do you mean?"

"You let her go," he said, and then grunted. A small object popped up out of the wound and landed in the dirt beside him. The bullet. "Or we follow."

Cold fear gripped Charlotte. "Into Tir na nAill?"

"Where else, lass?"

Captain Sirok came running into the cave, panting hard. "We've got trouble," he panted.

And that was when the shooting resumed.

"I got one of them with my knife," the captain explained in between shots, "but there's at least eight out there still. Eli Horn musta left them with some kinda order to kill us or they're crazed or they're doin' it out of some kind of instinct, I don't know. What difference does it make, Leighton?"

The small party was huddled back in the further recesses of the cave, sheltering as best they could. Mr. Hallorman had shoved Charlotte back into the space where she had been before, blocking her view of the exit with his own body. His quiver, she noticed with a kind of wild clarity, never seemed to run empty. Why was that? What power refilled it, and how, and from where, and—

"If we knew what their problem was, maybe we could get them to stop?"

"Stop? This ain't some damn debate in some fancy college hall somewhere!"

"Can't you do what you did in Gunnison?" Charlotte asked, desperate to be heard over the gunfire. The sun had set by now, though, and the world outside of their little cave was dark, too dark to pick out targets under the shadow of the trees. The men were firing blind. "Go berserk?"

"Not a chance in hell," Captain Sirok snapped back. "Do you have any idea how dangerous it is, lettin' the wolf out? I'm not sure even Hallorman there could stop me if it had the mind to go after y'all."

Charlotte exchanged a quick glance with Mr. Leighton, who just shook his head. "Mr. Hallorman!" he called.

But the faery, eyeing a shot into the darkness, didn't answer.

"Is there no way out?" Mr. Leighton pressed, looking back and forth between the two others.

Captain Sirok shook his head, expression flat, loading another round. He fired, reloaded, fired, reloaded, before answering. "Not unless you fancy a climb up a thousand-foot rock face in the dark. This is a shooting gallery. We're pinned down, pretty as you please."

"There has to be something we can do!"

"There is," Mr. Hallorman said, turning to face Charlotte.

"What?" she asked. A bullet impacted the cave wall just above her then, showering her with shrapnel. The hot lead bounced, striking the floor only a few inches away from her hand. She couldn't stifle her cry. And when she looked up, Mr. Hallorman was right there.

"Charlotte," Mr. Hallorman told her. "Charlotte, you have to open the way! It's the only retreat we have!"

"What?" she asked, struggling to catch up with what was going on right now.

"Part the mists!"

"I can't," she said, brutally ashamed of herself but unable to stop the words. "I can't."

He was on her in a flash, hand grabbing her collar. "You are going to die here, lass, and if you die, I die, and then there is no hope of recovering your sister. She will die alone with not even the crows to pick over her bones. Is that what you want?"

Charlotte blinked, shaking her head. Mr. Leighton and Captain Sirok were still firing, shouting. There was shouting outside now, too. "No."

"Then part the damn mists!"

Never had Charlotte willingly looked at anything in the Otherworld. When the shades of the dead gathered by her bed, she ignored them. When she caught the sound of wild music or lights that were not there, she walked the other way. She had prayed all her life for it to stop, although it never had. But now she found herself on her knees, trying desperately to do what he said.

The mists were there, like a foggy morning by the sea. She could feel it. She *knew* it. And yet—

"I can't," she panted. "I can't."

Mr. Hallorman knelt down beside her. Put his hand over hers. His voice was softer now. "You can do this."

She couldn't look at him. Tears were rolling down her cheeks, hot with shame.

Mr. Leighton ran back, throwing himself down. He was bleeding from a cut above his left eye; he seemed not to notice. "Miss Roseingrave?" he asked, panting.

She shook her head, squeezing her eyes shut, trying to stop the blasted tears.

"Can't you do it?" Mr. Leighton demanded. "She's too terrified to move, my good man!"

Mr. Hallorman looked up, face in the direction of the cave entrance. "Aspens."

"What?" Charlotte asked, dazed, pulling her head up.

"Aspens," he said again, mouth set in a thin line, and stood. "Stay here," he ordered.

Then the faery adjusted his waistcoat, placed his bow back into its quiver, and strode out of the cave.

The men outside were as confused as they were, it seemed; for a moment, the gunfire faltered. But when it resumed, it did so with ear-shattering ferocity.

Mr. Hallorman waked straight out into the hail of bullets. Several found their mark in him, blowing holes through whatever he had that passed for flesh, almost knocking him down, but he didn't stop. Something was growing around him, something Charlotte could feel as well as see, a green light flickering and licking around him like tongues of flame. Like at the toll gate, she thought, but much more powerful now.

It whispered. Whispered of the deep forest and thick moss, of sunlight on the mountainside and rain sweeping down the rocks. It was the feel of growing things, living things, and she realized that where he stepped, wild-flowers were waking from autumnal slumber. Growing, reaching, blooming, dying again.

He raised his hand as he approached the tree line. Several outlaws concealed within kept firing, but others had stopped, perhaps confused by this change in tactics.

"I pity you," Mr. Hallorman said, and his voice had taken on a strange timbre. "All this time following that thing. Now, see the deep magics as they were meant to be."

And with that, he knelt down and plunged both hands into the loam at the edge of the trees.

For a moment, nothing happened.

Then.

Around him, the white-skinned trees that had been losing their leaves for the winter suddenly burst into life. Green erupted anew from their branches, first pale, then dark, shivering.

Around him, out of the soil, there burst saplings. Small at first, then growing rapidly. The taller trees shook as if caught in a gale. They grew, too, taller and taller, thicker and broader. Somebody screamed, and Charlotte saw a man on the edge of the grove, being dragged back inside by a sapling that seemed to have curled around his leg, growing thicker with every passing second.

A tree crashed down, bark peeling, limbs bare. Dead, Charlotte realized. Two more saplings pushed up around the hole its roots had left in the soil. Faster and faster it went now, the trees coming almost too quickly to comprehend.

For the next few minutes, she was treated to the sight of an entire forest living out its full cycle of life and death. Growing, dying, growing again. The trees grew so thick that the outlaws could no longer be seen; only their agonized screams could be heard, echoing far up the sheer cliffs of the canyon's end.

Finally, it ended. The madness faded. One last tree pushed its way free of the tangle of dead, burst into life, then faded away again, red-gold leaves blown away on the last of the breeze. The waning moon finally lifted over the dark peaks of the San Juan. The young night was silent.

Eli Horn's gang was no more.

Mr. Hallorman made his way back toward them. He could barely stand, his skin gone pale, almost translucent. The veins in his face and neck glowed with that same green energy as before, but it too faded. Something remained, though, something Charlotte couldn't quite place.

He wheezed hard and only just stopped himself from falling over by grabbing the rock of the cave entrance. Blood flecked the back of his hand. "A grove that might have stood for a thousand years gave its life for you tonight, Miss Roseingrave."

"I don't understand," she admitted.

He coughed again. "I know you don't," he told her, and it sounded like an accusation.

Making their way out of the mountains was a miserable task.

While the sun had fallen completely during the gunfight, the moon was already rising in a cloudless sky, nearly full, giving off enough light to see by. Even with that, though, the path back to the horses took them through the now-dead grove. The trees had come up, so thick and dense that, in the few places where it was even visible, the ground was cracked and tortured. They had to scramble over fallen boles and through half-rotten branches, piled up in big drifts like seaweed thrown up on the beach after a storm.

"What happened to the men in here?" Mr. Leighton asked at one point, helping Charlotte over a particularly rough patch.

"Crushed," Captain Sirok said with a sniff. "Between the trees, or impaled by them'd be my guess." Charlotte looked at him in horror, and he shrugged. "There's a fair bit o' blood in the air."

Charlotte choked back her guilt and kept moving. They may have been thieves and murderers, but they were dead because of her. Because of her fear.

Opening the way into Tir na nAill would have saved them all, and she had been too weak, too afraid, to do it. The mists had been right there. She could have seen the way through. She could have.

Mr. Hallorman's normal sure-footedness had deserted him after his little demonstration with the forest. They were forced to help him through the grove, but once they had started down the narrow path to the lower meadow, he had recovered himself somewhat.

"Are there any settlements nearby?" the faery asked Captain Sirok as they reached their horses. The animals were all sweating despite the evening chill, wild-eyed and snorting. But the mare that Mr. Hallorman had been riding came over, nickering softly. The faery stroked the animal's face absently.

"I can't be sure of exactly where we are, but there are a few towns in the area, and lots of mining claims," Captain Sirok said. "If we're lucky, we might be able to reach Silverton or Capital City without too much trouble."

"We should not linger in the mountains, not after what I did here." Mr. Hallorman nodded, as if bowed by a great weight. "I am spent. Do you think you can take the lead for tonight?"

Surprise flitted over the cavalry officer's face, but he nodded nonetheless. Then he went over to his own horse—who was holding up somewhat better than the others—and pulled his overcoat from where it was rolled up on the saddle.

"You couldn't'a done anything more for her," he told Charlotte gently.

She pulled the jacket tightly around her, grateful for the warmth. She couldn't even respond. She just felt numb.

Her sister was gone.

What was she going to do with herself now?

BOOK THREE
STEEL

CHAPTER THIRTY-FOUR

It was a somber group that reached civilization the next morning.

Miss Roseingrave hadn't spoken to anybody since the night before. She stayed silent in her saddle, wrapped in Captain Sirok's greatcoat and refusing to look any of them in the eye.

Thomas wasn't sure what had happened back there at the canyon. He was still struggling to make sense of it. Faeryland. Even after all these days on the road with Mr. Hallorman, after the demonstrations of...of magic, for lack of a better word, he had not quite accepted the reality of it. And yet, last night he had seen the mists swallow Eli Horn and Miss Celeste Roseingrave.

There was truth to the old stories.

But even now, even with everything that had happened, he could not suppress the satisfaction, the glee, that part of him took in these revelations. Faeries were real. Faeryland—Mag Mell, Tir na nAill, the Otherworld—was real. His personal theories, pursued at enormous personal cost, were correct.

He would have vindication when he returned to England.

Thomas had thought their party was in some remote corner of this vast wilderness, days or perhaps weeks from any other human life. But they had passed a significant mining operation only a few hours after leaving the portal canyon, and from there, found themselves on a wagon road. Despite the late hour they were able to make their way safely down from the heights, and by the time the sky had turned its dusty daytime blue, they found themselves once again in a town.

"Ouray," Captain Sirok observed as they passed onto a broad, well-maintained avenue. Of all their party, he seemed the least impacted by what had happened last night. "Lots of mines in the San Juans here. Some silver, some gold, and sometimes they uncover other things, too, I'm told."

"Gemstones?" Thomas asked, curious.

"Semiprecious," Sirok said. "Or quartz, which has industrial uses, I've heard."

"Quite," Thomas replied, and only barely caught himself from launching into a diatribe about some of the advancements that had been made in scientific instrumentation of late. Now wasn't the time. "So what manner of place is Ouray?"

"Nice as anything you'll find around here," Sirok told him. "And wealthy, like I said. I've heard they've even got an opera house up here now."

"An opera house?"

"It ain't London, but if entertainment's your goal, I'm sure it does its job."

A proper little city, this Ouray, with straight streets and solid structures. Brick storefronts lined wooden boardwalks, facing each other across dusty, well-trodden streets. If anything, it reminded him of Leadville. Some of the buildings were quite grand, the wealth of the mountains no doubt tumbling down to be spent on elaborate stonework or fine carpentry.

It was a new town, a young town, and the Englishman in Thomas marveled at that aspect of it. While there were areas of Britain which had certainly been freshly constructed, this country had a vigor to it that no place in Europe could hope to match. Ouray had a sense of weightlessness, of strangeness, as if it had been placed here through no less mysterious means than Mr. Hallorman's own faery-magic.

He heard a soft sigh beside him and immediately felt ashamed. It was Miss Roseingrave, swaying dangerously in her saddle. The reins were loose in her hand. She looked more pale than usual.

"Is there any lodging available here, do you think?" he asked Captain Sirok.

"There are a few hotels. Only one I would recommend with present company," the captain said, nodding at Miss Roseingrave. "It's almost always full but I can make inquiries."

"I shall do it," Mr. Hallorman said wearily. He, too, had been silent for most of the ride. "Your uniform will scare people, and the Englishman will be utterly useless, of course."

Thomas was too tired to object to the insult.

And on they went through the quiet morning streets.

Captain Sirok's recommended hotel, the McKenney, stood on the corner of two busy streets, its intricate two-story facade boasting a fine shaded porch looking south and west, the broad windows on the upper story no doubt offering excellent views of the mountains.

The innkeeper's wife who came out to greet them must have been charmed out of the kitchens by Mr. Hallorman, her apron covered in flour and old stains. She looked them all over with an appraising eye.

"Your father tells me you ran into some trouble in the mountains," she said, speaking directly to Miss Roseingrave. "We're hard-pressed on space right now, and I can't spare you more than one suite, and it'll take me some time to get it ready. But you're welcome to stay with us. If you'd like to accompany me, Missus…"

"Miss," Miss Roseingrave supplied.

"Miss then. Come have a bite and a sup in the kitchen, nice and private, while the men tend to your horses." She looked at Captain Sirok. "Stable's around back thataway. Should be hay and whatnot available."

"Might there be any way to wash up?" Miss Roseingrave asked, dismounting and following the caretaker up onto the porch.

"I can draw you a bath, once we get you settled, but for now, I can have one of my girls get you a basin."

"That would be lovely."

And the two women disappeared into the hotel.

"Reckon we've been dismissed," Captain Sirok said, stifling a yawn. "C'mon."

Thomas cast a glance back up at the porch. He was worried for Miss Roseingrave. She seemed to be blaming herself for this, but he couldn't fathom why.

Long strands of red pulled free as Charlotte attacked her hair with her brush.

The suite was more than she would have hoped for after so miserable a journey; a set of two small bedrooms opened into a central sitting area, with a bathroom down the hall that Charlotte had just come from. The innkeeper's wife had lent her a dressing gown and towel and gave her the key to the bathroom, "So you won't be disturbed, dear. It's mostly menfolk I have in right now."

Clean and dry now, the grime of the road scrubbed away with homemade lye soap, Charlotte felt almost ashamed of herself. Sitting here in comfort while her sister...her sister...

The brush hit a bad snarl.

She huffed and set it down. As she started to work the knot free with her fingers, she stared at herself in the guest room's small mirror. She didn't like what she saw. A sunburned, freckled face stared back at her, blue eyes tired. Her hair frizzed out around her like an auburn mist. She looked like a mess.

Celeste had been right there. So close. Within reach.

All Charlotte had needed to do was reach out. Reach through, open the doorway.

She hadn't. She couldn't.

And now her sister was going to pay the price.

Her hair really was a disaster. One snarl came free while another almost instantly appeared. She hissed in frustration and picked her brush back up.

All this time. All these miles. All the struggle and the effort and the blood and the terror and she had failed. Failed her sister. Failed everyone.

"It's not really you, lass."

Charlotte yelped in shock and dropped her brush. There, behind her, sitting in the room's small chair, was Mr. Hallorman. She clutched at the neck of her borrowed dressing gown, feeling horribly exposed.

"What are you doing in here?" she demanded.

He tapped his temple. "Your thoughts are loud right now, Charlotte."

She clutched the edge of the vanity table, feeling a little unsteady. "And what gives you the right to simply barge into my room?"

He didn't answer for a moment. And then, when he did, it was nothing that Charlotte might have expected. "I wanted to apologize."

"What?"

He crossed his legs. Picked at the fabric of the chair arm. Did not meet her eye. "Your gift is something you have never been comfortable with. Asking you to part the mists was quite unfair of me."

She could feel her heart slowing back to its normal rhythm. "If I had, could we have rescued my sister?"

Mr. Hallorman stared back at her, level and emotionless, and Charlotte was on the verge of ordering him to answer her when there came a knock on the door.

"Miss Roseingrave? Are you alright?"

"Your damn Englishman is back."

"Leave him alone, would you?" Charlotte snapped and went to the door. She opened it just a crack. Mr. Leighton, in shirtsleeves and suspenders, concern on his half-shaven face. He flushed a little when he saw the state she was in.

"Forgive me," he said, "but I was just... and I thought I heard a cry and voices and—"

"I'm quite alright," she said.

"I am sorry if I..."

"It's alright, Mr. Leighton."

He hesitated, dabbing at his face with a towel that was cast over his shoulder. "I did want to say, if we are alone, that what happened with your sister was not your fault. If she chose to—"

"Glamour and lies, Mr. Leighton," Charlotte said softly. "That's the power of the fae. Who knows what Eli Horn said to her?"

"It's not your fault," he told her again, and shook his head. "Will you join us for lunch? Mrs. McKenney says it will be ready for us in half an hour in the main room."

Charlotte was ashamed, and she was exhausted, and not much in the mood for company. But Mr. Leighton seemed so earnest about it, Charlotte found herself nodding. "Of course."

"Miss Roseingrave," he said with a nod.

She shut the door again and turned back to her unwelcome guest. He had picked up her grandmother's chatelaine, turning it over in his hands.

"What are you doing?" she demanded, storming over.

"Do you know what this is?" he asked.

"It's my sewing equipment and the last thing I have left of my grandmother," she said. "Give it back."

"This is more than a mere accessory," he said, holding it out. "Just as you are more than a mere seamstress."

Charlotte grabbed at it. "There is no shame in being a seamstress."

"I never said there was," he said, and laid a hand over hers. "Now listen to me. Your sister is lost. She has made her choice, and such things have a great deal of power. Charlotte, you have a long life in front of you. Don't waste it on worrying over things that cannot be changed."

"I promised our mother that I would take care of her," she said.

"I know. I remember that conversation."

"What parts of my life haven't you spied on?"

But there was no answer. He had already gone.

She looked around the room for a moment, wondering how he was able to pull off such a trick. "Infuriating creature," she muttered to herself, and went back to venting her frustrations on her hair.

The day passed more slowly than Thomas would have liked.

Lunch had been served in the main dining room, a simple affair of corn bread and some local dish that Mrs. McKenney had called chili. It boasted a high quantity of pepper, and Captain Sirok had found Thomas's reaction to that first bite to be highly entertaining. The room was full of other people, though, and their party didn't talk about anything of any importance.

After that, Thomas had wanted to work on translating his rubbings from the night before but was too exhausted to manage it. Fearing he might fall asleep on top of his precious sheets, he folded them neatly back into the notebook and fell into bed instead.

The next thing he knew, Captain Sirok was rousing him for dinner.

A small table had been set up in the sitting room this time, with four chairs and a heap of food. Venison and root vegetables, fresh bread and an excellent German-style lager. There was plenty to go around, but of all of them, only Captain Sirok seemed to have an appetite.

"Pass the bread, would you?" he asked Thomas, indicating a basket in the center of the table. Thomas handed it over, watching as the cavalry officer grabbed out another two slices and began slathering them with butter.

"How can you eat at a time like this?" Thomas asked.

Captain Sirok wiped beer foam from the edge of his mustache. He'd oiled it and shaped it and to Thomas in that moment, it resembled nothing so much as Mr. Hallorman's strange stone knife. "There's nothing we can do about Miss Celeste Roseingrave tonight, and it's a poor soldier who lets food go to waste."

"How did you get Mrs. McKenney to be so generous with us?" Thomas asked Mr. Hallorman.

The faery picked at his venison. "I gave her a rather large pouch of silver dollars and told her I was terribly worried for my poor daughter's health."

"Your daughter?" Thomas asked.

"Silver dollars?" Captain Sirok asked, raising an eyebrow. "I thought there was a stink to you."

"Where did you get it?" Miss Roseingrave asked, more pointedly.

"Mr. Barton offered us any assistance we needed, and I needed a few bags of his silver," Mr. Hallorman said. "He has plenty more of it to go around. I'd hardly call it theft."

"But the bit about a daughter..." Thomas pressed.

"I employed a simple glamour, making me look older and more sympathetic. It's even less remarkable than the silver. Only humans would be amazed by something so basic." The faery was, Thomas thought, quite a bit more testy than he normally was.

"Isn't there something we can do for my sister?" the elder Miss Roseingrave asked. Her own food was virtually untouched. She had been fiddling with her fork for most of the meal. "Mr. Hallorman?"

"I do not think it worth the risk," he said.

"Do not evade me, sir," Miss Roseingrave said, suddenly angry. "Is there still a way to save my sister? I order you to answer me!"

Mr. Hallorman sipped his beer. "Walking into Tir na nAill is a dangerous proposition under the best of circumstances. Time runs different there. We could enter, find that no time at all had passed for Celeste, rescue her, and then emerge again to find a thousand years had passed, and then you would all be quite dead of old age."

"Even me?" Captain Sirok asked.

"Your... nature would not protect you there," Mr Hallorman said, and delicately cut off a morsel of meat. He held it on his fork, staring at it as if it were some sort of mystery to be solved. "It would likely be a hindrance."

"What did this Fomorian want with Miss Roseingrave?" Thomas asked.

"What do any of my people want from humans? A bit of sport, a bit of fun. Perhaps he intends to eat her when he has bored of bedding her. Fomorians were notorious for—"

But he didn't get the chance to finish his sentence. The elder Miss Roseingrave pushed her chair back from the table then, making a terrible noise across the floorboards. Glaring at him, she took her plate and fork and stormed into her own room, slamming the door behind her.

Mr. Hallorman looked after her, and then with a shrug, went back to his venison. "How am I supposed to know what a Fomorian does with his prey?"

"So is this a common thing, then?" Captain Sirok asked. "Fae draggin' human women into the Otherworld?"

"So it says in the folklore," Thomas told him, taking a sip of beer himself. Mr. Hallorman's lack of decorum appalled him, but he could not fault the assessment. "Humans are often charmed by fae creatures and taken down to their doom."

The captain nodded. "With the lady gone, perhaps I can speak a little more freely." He poured himself a glass of whiskey from a decanter on the sitting room's sideboard and paced to the window. "I've seen plenty o' bad things out there in the West. Things like rape. You familiar with that concept, faery?"

"What's your point?" Mr. Hallorman asked, suddenly very tense.

"My point is, faery, that if all Eli Horn wanted was a tumble, he didn't need to drag a gal halfway across the state. Hell, he didn't need to kidnap any gal to begin with. Spare change'll get you that in any town in the West, if you catch my meaning."

"I do."

"That mine was a hell of a long way from Leadville. That drill was sent back as provocation, and to a wealthy Spiritualist to boot. Might have been bait, I'm thinkin'. After all, didn't it attract the attention of his organization?" And here the captain waved at Thomas. "Didn't it get Mrs. Roseingrave's attention, the attention of an actual medium?"

"Am I supposed to delve into the minds of humans now?"

"No," Captain Sirok said, his good nature falling away and a deadly seriousness in its place. "I want you to explain to me why some devil from Ireland went to all this trouble to find a medium, kidnap her, and pull her down into the Otherworld, if all he wanted was a good fuck. There's something else going on here, and I think you know what it is."

Thomas blinked, a little taken aback by the captain's manner and his words. Mr. Hallorman didn't seem to know what to do with them, either, and seemed to settle for draining his beer and pushing away from the table.

"I must bid you gentlemen a good night," he said curtly. He grabbed his hat from its peg on the wall. He paused with his hand on the knob. "Don't presume to get in the middle of fae business. Such things usually end poorly."

And with that, he was gone.

Thomas folded his arms, rubbing one hand over his mouth.

"Your thoughts?"

He started a bit. Captain Sirok was looking at him, eyes gleaming gold.

"What do you mean?"

"I mean, what do you think about all this?"

Thomas huffed out a breath, trying to sort out the available information in his mind. "Something is not quite right here. He knows more than he's saying. But then, there is probably much he knows and doesn't say that has nothing to do with our current predicament." The captain looked irritated now, and Thomas held up a hand. "But in regard to our current predicament, I wonder if the Fomorian needed somebody to open the portal for him. Mr. Hallorman himself cannot enter there. So, it stands to reason that it is possible to banish a fae from Faeryland."

"But why Miss Celeste Roseingrave? What was special about her?" Captain Sirok asked.

"I don't know."

"Guess."

"Perhaps the way can only be opened by one with the Sight. A seer, if you will."

"But then he would have needed to take the elder sister, not the younger," Captain Sirok pointed out. "And wouldn't he have noticed the one he took lacked the Sight? I can smell the power on Miss Roseingrave. Why would he come all this way with the wrong woman?"

"Perhaps my sister convinced him she was me."

The bedroom door was open and Miss Roseingrave stood there, smiling sadly. "I did not intend to eavesdrop, but you were rather loud, Captain Sirok."

He bowed his head a little. "My apologies for the foul language, ma'am."

She brushed it off. "Where did Mr. Hallorman go?"

Both men shrugged. She rubbed a hand over her face and sank back into her chair from dinner. "My sister was...skilled in my mother's more mundane arts. The ability to anticipate what others wanted. Present herself in any manner she chose."

"She's a con woman?" Captain Sirok asked with a slight smile.

"She's a good woman," Miss Roseingrave retorted.

He held up his hands. "I wasn't criticizin' her."

"If she didn't really know she was dealing with some kind of, of…Other-world creature, a fae, and thought he was merely some human who wanted her for her perceived abilities, she might have played those abilities up." She was quiet for a moment. "And I heard him use my name, addressing her."

"That still doesn't answer the question as to why he didn't know she wasn't you," the captain said.

"We all saw him handling guns. He didn't seem to be in control of what magic he had. All the rot and decay we've seen, terribly conspicuous, isn't it?" Thomas replied. "Perhaps his banishment saw his command of his powers stripped away."

"Conjecture."

"You asked for conjecture, Captain."

The cavalry officer eyed him. "Any way to prove any of it?"

Thomas shook his head. "Our most immediate and best clue are the rubbings I took. Mr. Hallorman seemed alarmed at what he read in the writing. That is where I shall focus my efforts."

Captain Sirok set his drink aside. "I think I'll take a walk down to the sheriff's station, see if there's anything official I might find out."

"Your sister may not be lost forever," Thomas told Miss Roseingrave gently, as the captain took his leave. "We need not give up our pursuit. It may be that we labor all through the winter to find an answer and make our way to her in the spring only to find that mere minutes have passed in Faeryland."

Miss Roseingrave nodded but got up and poured herself a glass of whiskey as well. "A great many things may happen in a few minutes," she said, and shut herself into her room again.

Thomas watched her go, sitting at the dinner table all alone for a few moments. Then he cleared a space by his plate and went to get his notebooks.

Mr. Hallorman had paid Mrs. McKenney for an evening's worth of lamp oil.

Best put it to use.

CHAPTER THIRTY-FIVE

It seemed to Celeste that they were walking forever, a journey far longer and somehow, more exhilarating than the one already undertaken. And yet, it seemed no time at all before the mists parted again, revealing a rolling, rocky landscape and the sound of the sea beyond.

It was twilight, or dawn. There seemed to be no discernible source of light; the sky was overcast. No sun, no stars. No wind.

They had emerged at the edge of a stone circle. But unlike the etchings she had seen of places like Stonehenge in England, all tumbledown and broken by time, this one was pristine. All stones even and upright, capped with vast lintels and carved with strange, swirling designs. The circle sat at the top of a hill, and down the slopes lay more stone structures, menhirs standing like the rails in a fence, encompassing little hills, covered in grass.

And unlike the pictures she'd seen of Stonehenge, there was a hill in the center of this circle, a great earthen mound ringed with rock and closed with the largest boulder Celeste had ever seen.

At least, that was how it seemed at first.

For as soon as Eli Horn approached, the scene changed. The great standing stones remained, but their appearance shifted. No longer neolithic, but something altogether stranger. Headstones, as if she and Eli Horn had emerged inside a cemetery.

Perhaps they had.

That hill was no longer so plain.

Instead, there now stood a mausoleum in the latest style. The grass was gone. Only dirt and rock stretched out around them now.

She didn't understand. This wasn't what Faeryland looked like in Grandmother's stories.

"Too far. I've come too far from home."

Eli Horn. Beside her, driven down to one knee. He was leaning hard on one of the tombstones, holding himself up with what seemed like an enormous effort. Celeste hurried over to him, laying a hand on his arm.

"What's wrong?"

He smiled at her. There was blood on his teeth, on his face. It was streaming from every orifice, glittering with some inner light. "If homecomings were easy, I could have accomplished it without you, fáith. I am... I am not supposed to be here."

"What can I do?"

He ignored her. "Lukas," he coughed instead, and held out his free arm. "Help me."

Celeste started; instead of the man she had known these past days, up bounded something monstrous, a terrible amalgamation of wolf and human, drool dripping from its jaws as it considered her.

The great wolfman half carried, half dragged Eli Horn over to the mausoleum. The thing boasted great iron doors, wrought in the shape of leering demons and locked with chains, with a padlock larger than her head. The scale of it made no sense at all. Eli Horn staggered to the doors and collapsed again, one hand gripping the chains that bound the great doors shut.

She had no idea how long they stood there, silent, still, while Eli Horn bled out onto the naked earth.

Then.

The gates shifted. A wisp of wind escaped, whispering through her hair. In the terrible stillness, it felt like a hurricane.

Eli Horn stood again, pulled up as surely as a marionette on its strings, jerked upright by a force more powerful than he. His body convulsed, head snapping back. Every muscle in his neck stood out, corded and taut, as if he was being pulled apart from the inside. He screamed then, a long and terrible sound that froze Celeste's heart.

It echoed long among the tombstones, his head bowed, body shaking.

Before he rose. And looked at her.

"A sister," he rumbled. "An older sister."

Something in the words made her quail inside, and she turned hesitantly to meet his eyes, only to drop her gaze again; she could not look him in the face. He had not changed in appearance, except he had, in some way that would have been impossible to describe. That thing which had seemed to be missing in him was finally here, and it was terrible to behold.

He strode toward her, unbuckling his gun belt as he did so. The weapons in their leather holsters fell away behind him. There was still blood on his clothes. A darkness poured from him, lashing out against her mind, and she collapsed.

"I see now," he said, and knelt down beside her, lifting her chin, examining her face, like a man buying a horse at an auction. "You lied to me... Celeste, younger daughter of Aine."

She couldn't answer. She didn't trust any of the words that would come from her mouth.

He took a handful of her hair, cruel and hard, and she whimpered. He forced her head back, still looking her over. A horse at auction? No. It was the action of a man examining a pig for the slaughter.

"You can't hide from me here," he said, almost conversationally. A cold finger traced her cheekbone. "I am returned to myself, and I see everything again."

She was petrified, unable to move even while everything in her screamed at her to run.

"There is something in you," he continued. "Enough to bring us here. But you're not a fáith, are you? Not a fáith at all."

"Please..." she stammered. "I didn't know, I didn't know, I didn't—"

"Shh," he said, and laid that finger on her lips. "You didn't. How could you? Even your sister, with the true Sight, would not have been able to see me fully. Not as I was." He took a deep breath, clenched a fist. "That banishment has been broken. All things fail in the end. Even the power of the Tuatha Dé Danann. They always thought themselves better than us, you know. In their arrogance, they forgot how beholden they were to my people."

Tuatha Dé Danann. She had heard that word before. Where? Grandmother's stories? She couldn't remember. Her fear was clawing at her, screaming, a trapped animal seeking any escape it could find. If she could have moved, she would have run until her heart gave out.

And yet, a not-insignificant corner of her soul was screaming why, why, why at her. Eli Horn had promised, he had said...

"I thought..."

He chuckled. "You thought I would kill you and go back for your sister instead if I found out you couldn't help me," he said, smiling indulgently. "And of course I would have. But don't cry, lass," he said, and raised her chin with his burning cold touch. "You'll get to see the dead here soon enough. All the secrets of creation will be laid bare for you, and maybe you will even thank me for it in the end. I was rather looking forward to that, but my favor shall have to wait for your sister. Lukas!"

The wolfman was back, hunched, hungry.

"I know you desire this one. She's yours," Eli Horn continued. Celeste stared at him. He didn't give her any heed. "Do anything you wish. Make it bloody. Make it painful. Be noisy. Her sister will hear, and she will come."

"No, no, not Charlotte, please," Celeste said. "She's done nothing, she knows nothing about—"

"I care nothing for what she's done or what she knows. All that matters is what she is," Eli snarled. "The gift passes to the eldest daughter of the bloodline, no other, lest it dilute itself and become useless. Do you suppose she'll come again for you, after you betrayed her? She will. She had that look about her. Anything for her beloved little sister, no matter the circumstances, no matter how undeserving the bitch is." He threw Celeste down. "And then, Celeste daughter of Aine, I will make you watch while I tear her soul from her body."

Celeste collapsed, crying freely now.

She was still crying when Mr. Abbitt grabbed her in one monstrous claw and began to pull her away.

Charlotte couldn't sleep.

The bed was soft, the night air cool, the hotel surprisingly quiet.

Charlotte couldn't sleep.

Every time she closed her eyes, she saw blood. Hot, red human blood. Splashed all around in what looked to be a graveyard, the tombstones swollen to the size of houses, hanging in the air like a mist. And screaming, there was screaming. No words, just an endless chorus of pain, sung out in a woman's voice.

Her sister's voice.

Her sister...

Charlotte paced, tears clouding her eyes, hands over her ears, trying to blot out the noise. But there was no help for it. It came and came and came, filling her mind in a manner that had nothing to do with her more natural sense. Who said the Sight was a gift? It was a curse, it was an agony, it was...

Please, she heard her sister sob, pleading now, in between the screams, *please...*

Charlotte sat down at the room's small table, dropping her head into a hand, the other going to the crucifix around her neck, mentally reciting a prayer.

But somehow, even in her desperation, she doubted it would be enough. The mercy of the Lord may have been boundless, but sometimes, as with so many things out here on the frontier, one had to take matters into one's own hands.

She had been afraid of the portal, yes. Afraid of what lay on the other side. Afraid of what it all might mean. But what was the fear of such things compared to allowing her sister to be tortured to death?

Charlotte took a deep breath. Sat for one more moment, crucifix in hand.

Then she threw on her clothes.

Corset, stockings, boots. Two of the buttons were missing and she had not had time to replace them. It didn't matter. With trembling fingers, she wrestled the remaining buttons into place and went to work on her dress.

Five minutes later, she was making her way through the silent hotel to the ground floor to the back courtyard, out to the small stables there.

Her horse nickered at her softly as she roused it from sleep; Charlotte felt a brief moment of guilt for this. The animal was no doubt as tired as she was, and likely terrified from the night before.

"I am sorry about this," she told the horse as she stepped into the stall, holding the bridle. "It's not too far at least, and the moon's just past full. You'll be alright."

The horse regarded her with its huge eyes and tossed back its head, pulling away. Charlotte sighed and moved in closer.

"Going somewhere?"

She startled.

"Here," Mr. Hallorman said, and took the bridle from her. "He does remember what happened back there. You'd be hard-pressed convincing him to go back, if it was just you alone." The faery rubbed a long-fingered hand up the horse's broad face, ruffling the shank of hair that fell forward between its ears. "He might throw you if you take him out alone."

She frowned. "Were they that scared?"

"Weren't you? You didn't do your job. Why should you expect them to do theirs?"

Charlotte didn't answer that. "What are you doing here?"

He chuckled again, although there was less amusement in it now. "What are you?" he challenged back. "I thought you wanted nothing to do with us and Tir na nAill and all the rest of it."

"I don't. But my sister is there."

"She might be beyond saving, you know."

"Nobody is beyond saving. That I truly believe."

The faery snorted. "The reasoning of your desert god won't hold much sway there."

"He is everywhere, because all of existence is His creation. How could He not be there as well?"

"And you think he would help you? Even though you betray him by this course of action?"

Charlotte felt a rush of guilt, then something hardened in her gut. "My faith warns against worshipping anything other than God or trusting the designs of the devil. I did not ask for the Sight. I do not seek to profit from it. I could gouge my eyes out but still I would see what I see. I do not think that is witchcraft. And if it is, then may He forgive me, but I cannot leave my sister to die in that place."

Mr. Hallorman looked at her for a moment more, then smiled. Not his normal mocking smile, but something gentler, fonder. Proud, in some strange way. It was a smile she had not seen him wear before, and she did not know what it meant. "I know you think me a curse, lass, and all too often, I've had the same thought myself. Neither of us chose this, but neither of us can reject it. If you're fool enough to walk into a Fomorian's hold, then you won't walk in alone."

An unexpected lump formed in Charlotte's throat, and it took her two tries to get any words out. "Why?"

"Why am I bound to your family?" he asked and smiled. "That's a story too long to tell now. Now, let's get you saddled up. It'll be a hard ride back to that canyon and we'd best part the mists in the daylight."

There were many questions Charlotte wanted to ask him. So many things she wanted to press him on. But for the moment, she didn't give voice to any of them. Instead, she pulled her saddle off its post and lugged it over to him.

"Thank you," she said as he took it from her.

"Don't thank me yet," he said, and laid it easily on the horse's back. She looked behind him and saw that his mare was already saddled and ready to go. Charlotte realized that she had been expected. "Like as not, we'll both die there. But never let it be said a fae broke his oath."

"What does this Fomorian want with my sister?"

"Whatever it is, it will not be to the benefit of anything but their own wickedness."

"Then all the more reason to get her back."

"Indeed."

Ten minutes later they were back in the saddle, heading south out of town.

Mr. Hallorman was quiet for most of the ride. Charlotte was used to his silence by this point, after so much time spent on the trail with him. But where it had previously felt like he simply didn't want to be bothered with human conversation, this was different. She could almost feel a strange sort of energy, radiating out of him like heat from a campfire.

Magic, she thought at one point, and dismissed it. Even after everything that had happened on their journey so far, she still could not quite accept the concept as real. Glimpsing the echoes of the dead, seeing things move in the shadows, having strange dreams and intense emotions that weren't her own had been part of her life, all her life. But magic was something entirely different, something that was still in the realm of children's stories or pagan mythology.

But Mr. Hallorman was real in a way she couldn't deny or dismiss.

Magic he may have had, but it was radically different from anything she'd ever expected.

The road took them most of the way, eventually turning west where they had to turn east, and they spent long, cold hours picking their way back up toward the canyon's end. The sky was lightening by the time they made a broad shelf, enough to give Charlotte a view of the land below.

Trudging through in the dark, it had been impossible to see the details of the landscape. Now it was laid clear, this tightly bunched collection of cliffs and hills, canyons dug deep into the sheer, steep sides of the San Juan mountains. A maze it seemed from this position, and this position especially was quite exposed to the slopes above. She was grateful for the huldra's alternate route. If they had encountered Eli Horn's gang here, they would have been easily overpowered and killed.

"We'll need to leave the horses here," Mr. Hallorman said, squinting up at the sky. "And we'll need to climb quickly. Dawn is coming."

If the climb up from the hidden meadow had been hard, this was worse. The canyon was choked with huge boulders that they had to scramble over. But then they were through and facing the aspen grove once more.

Dead now, the grove resembled nothing so much as a giant's bonfire, waiting for the spark that would set it aflame. But getting closer, Charlotte realized that it was not just a pile of dead wood. The advancement of time that had overtaken the place seemed to have continued in some way. The dead wood was already alive with mushrooms and lichens, and many trunks had already collapsed under that relentless consumption. It reminded her of the toll gate, but on a far larger scale.

Of the men who had died here, there was no sign. It was far easier to cross than it had been the night before, and all too soon, they were back at the cave. All was as they had left it the night before. The bullets, the blood. The place where her sister had vanished into the mists.

Mists that Charlotte herself needed to access.

Mr. Hallorman sat down on the cave floor, brushing aside a few stray bits of lead. They had deformed from their impact on the rock. He closed his eyes and leaned back against the raw rock.

Charlotte held a hand out, feeling very silly. "What is this supposed to look like?" she asked. "What am I to do?"

"I don't know. I'm not a human, I don't know how our doorways appear to you."

"What do you see?"

"Right now? Nothing. But I know what lies beyond. The dark gray sea, lapping softly at the rocky beaches. The grassy hills that stretch out under the quiet sky, endless and eternal."

Charlotte huffed. "That sounds like the stories my grandmother used to read me."

"The stories you often reread yourself," he replied without accusation or humor. "Why do you think my liege gave your ancestor that book?"

Her storybook was that old? Charlotte marveled at the idea. "What do you mean?"

"You may be tempted to think, dear Charlotte, that I am mightier than you, possessed of greater power, based on what happened last night. But humans possess a power of their own, and I do not speak of your Sight. The stories you tell..." And then he trailed off. "Stories are the medium through which our worlds meet. Your people's stories. You hold all the power here. You know what Tir na nAill is. You've seen it a hundred times in that book. Now find it here."

Charlotte tried, she did. She closed her eyes, reaching for the memory of those places she had read about so many times. The land beyond time, without light or shadow, without wind or rain or time itself. But every time she tried to conjure the images from Grandmother's old book, her mind strayed back to her sister. Her sister, four years old and tucked into bed next to her, listening wide-eyed as Grandmother read them the story of Bran's voyage into the Otherworld. Her sister, twelve and up well past their bedtime, copying one of the knotwork animals in the book into her own sketch pad again. Her sister, twenty-one and demanding to know why Charlotte was reading about—

"I do not know if I can do this," Charlotte admitted.

"Check the time, Charlotte."

She glanced down. There was a light coming from her pocket, the pocket where she'd placed her chatelaine for this journey. Pulling it out now, she saw where the light was coming from: under the cover of the small watch she wore there. Popping open the cover now, the light faded, but even in the gloom of the cave, she could see the second hand ticking.

Tick. Tick. Tick.

Slower and slower.

Until it stopped altogether.

Charlotte meant to ask what was going on, but then she noticed mist around her feet. Heard the sound of surf.

Fear ran through her.

They were here.

CHAPTER THIRTY-SIX

"Gone? What do you mean, gone?"

"I checked the horses this morning. Two are missing. The two they was ridin'." Captain Sirok sipped his coffee. "And clearly neither one has emerged to join us. Now siddown."

To Thomas, this didn't seem like a conversation to be having in the hotel's main dining room. But it was early still and they were the only people in the bright, sunny space, the only other sound in the place that of the fire crackling merrily in the rough stone hearth. Thomas had woken to find the suite completely empty. He had dressed and come down here only to get this news from a seemingly indifferent cavalry captain, eating his breakfast at a truly leisurely pace.

"And you're here, eating breakfast?" Thomas demanded, shifting his notebook under his elbow. He was most of the way done with the translation and was loath to lose any chance of finishing it.

"What else should I be doing?" Captain Sirok asked and waved a hand at the spread in front of him. The food looked good, bacon and fresh eggs and hot rustic bread, along with some sort of preserved fish and a few sundry other items. "I don't fancy the idea of settin' out on pursuit with an empty stomach."

"But Miss Roseingrave—"

"Is out there with that faery fella. He ain't gonna let nothin' happen to her," the captain said, and eyed him. It was like being watched by some feral, hungry thing. "And ain't neither of us doin' anything just yet, so you might as well eat."

Miserable, Thomas sank down into a chair.

As if by magic, Mrs. McKenney appeared with a fresh rack of toast and a pot of tea on a silver tray. Thomas frowned as fine porcelain was set down on the table beside him; he hadn't seen tea since leaving St. Louis. "I like to keep a well-stocked larder here," she explained as she poured him a cup. "Never know what kind of people might come through, and some folks be wantin' their tea. Is Earl Grey alright?"

"Quite." The brew smelled heavenly, especially after so many days of the nerve-rattling swill that Captain Sirok referred to as coffee. Thomas sniffed appreciatively. "Might you have any milk?"

"I do. Would you care for any eggs with your toast?"

Thomas wanted to tell her that they would be off again, quick as could be, but the expression on Captain Sirok's face was unmistakable. The shifter was going to finish his breakfast, come hell or high water. "Eggs would be lovely, if you have them. Over medium?"

She nodded and was off again.

The toast was accompanied by more butter and a small pot of some kind of berry jam. Thomas didn't recognize the taste, but it was quite good.

"Mighty nice for a minin' town," Captain Sirok said thoughtfully, coffee in hand. "I don't normally enjoy things this fancy when I'm with the unit. I'll hafta have Colonel Ramage offer my services to you more often."

"Captain, I appreciate your observations about our accommodations, but I doubt I shall hunt any more monsters after this," Thomas said. Captain Sirok snorted. Thomas pressed on. "Might we talk about how we are going to reach Miss Roseingrave?"

"Why would we?" Captain Sirok asked and finally set his coffee aside. He leaned forward, elbows on the knees of his uniform breeches, suddenly serious again. "You and I both know where she's goin'."

"The portal. The Otherworld. Exactly."

"Do you think you can just...write your way in there, scholar? And what would we do there, even if we got there? What kills these things?"

"I don't know," Thomas replied honestly, "but in the tales, they die rather frequently."

"Maybe they can only be killed by each other. We've both seen the damage Mr. Hallorman's taken from regular ol' human weapons and it don't seem to stop him," the captain pointed out. "Maybe it ain't our place to worry. Miss Roseingrave's goin' ta Otherworld with Hallorman at least, and he seems to know all 'bout this business."

"I don't trust him."

"That's 'cause he's been ridin' your ass the entire trip."

"It's not about the insults," Thomas insisted, leaning over his toast. "Something is wrong here. He was lying to us about what he knew about this situation. Miss Roseingrave is most likely headed into some grave danger."

Captain Sirok huffed, rolling his eyes, silent for a moment. "I have to send a report back to Fort Carson, let my colonel know what we've seen. I'll be headin' down to the telegraph office after I finish this magnificent breakfast. Don't get anything like this down at the fort." He picked up a piece of smoked trout and chewed thoughtfully. "Gettin' an answer back'll take a few hours, of course. You've got until I get the colonel's answer to figure something out."

"I don't catch your meaning."

"I mean, I want to see Eli Horn dead and the Roseingrave sisters safe and sound as much as you do," Sirok replied. "But my commander might have a different opinion on it. He may order me to disengage pursuit. So I reckon you better find us a way to get us through that portal before I get any such telegraph."

"You would disobey your commanding officer?"

Sirok grinned then. "I can't disobey an order I haven't received."

It was, Thomas thought, the most American thing he had yet heard anyone say. "Alright. Alright. I'll figure it out."

"Excellent," Sirok said, and his grin widened as the door opened again. "Mrs. McKenney, what would we do without you?"

She was back with Thomas's milk and eggs and a fresh pot of coffee for the cavalry officer. She smiled at them, setting the plates down, but Thomas barely noticed. He was working on his translation again.

Captain Sirok, despite his nonchalant attitude, finished his breakfast quickly and was off before Thomas had even gotten a chance to finish his tea. The silence was welcome, and Thomas used the newfound solitude to make more progress on the translation.

It was a strange collection of words, the oddest he had ever seen or heard of with ogham script, and Thomas was so engrossed in the work he barely noticed time passing. It was only when Mrs. McKenney brought him a fresh pot of tea and inquired when his traveling companions might be joining him that he remembered.

Right.

Guilt roiling in his gut—how could he have forgotten?—he made his excuses and set the translation aside. What he had deciphered made no sense, and there was still that tantalizing clue, the only standard form of ogham in the entire thing.

Father of B.

It would have to wait. There was nothing in the folklore—at least, nothing Thomas was aware of—that would answer his specific questions now. The name of the specific Fomorian they were pursuing would likely not be the deciding factor in how to enter the Land of Faery.

Instead, he had to consider other things.

Like Miss Roseingrave herself. She was a direct sort of woman, and not at all comfortable with the things that she saw nor the things they had encountered. Practical, she was, and cautious. She would not have returned to the portal unless she was certain that she could open it. But she had not been able to the night before last.

So what had changed?

And as Thomas finished his breakfast, he was left with only one course of action.

A search of Miss Roseingrave's room.

Thomas knocked before he entered, hoping against hope that this was all just conjecture. That Miss Roseingrave was indeed here, merely oversleeping or grieving in private.

But there was no answer. The room was empty. Empty and silent.

Like the other room in the suite, this was finely appointed, although clearly decorated for a woman's taste: lighter colors, a more delicate look to the bedframe and furniture. A large mirror stood watch over the place from the vanity. Thomas wondered if the hotel received many female visitors. Was the room intended for women traveling with their husbands, or ladies entertaining men with less honorable intentions? Was—

He tamped the curiosity down.

Time to focus.

There was very little to see beyond the furniture, though. Charlotte had had nothing more with her on this journey than her clothes and boots and chatelaine, all of which were absent. The only indication that she had been here at all was her hairbrush, set aside on the vanity top. Feeling suddenly guilty for snooping, Thomas turned to go.

And that was when he saw it.

There, glinting in the morning light, half-hidden under a knitted towel by the washbasin, were the gilded edges of a book.

With a frown, Thomas went over. He hadn't noticed either the towel or book when he had entered. That didn't necessarily mean anything, of course.

But going over, looking in...

Thomas felt the hair raise on the back of his neck.

It was indeed a book. One that belonged to Miss Roseingrave. The book she had accused him of snatching from her apartment at the workshop. The storybook. He thought she had left it behind in Leadville. How had it come to be here?

Taking a deep breath, Thomas forced himself to be logical. Miss Roseingrave could have brought it with her, the same way he had brought his own books. Perhaps Mrs. Coulton had tucked it into her bag at the last minute. Charlotte could have left it here, unwilling to take it with her into Faeryland.

But he couldn't shake the feeling that something else was going on here.

A feeling that was confirmed when he flipped open the cover.

The book fell open to a random page. A page with a fine illustration on it in an antiquated style. A young man, speaking to a monster with a head swollen to vast proportions, one vast eye blinking there, and even without translating the Gaelic fully, Thomas could read the names.

Bres. Talking to Balor.

He had found something indeed.

"Messages are sent," Captain Sirok announced, tossing his hat down on the sitting room's table. "I reckon it'll be a few hours before I get a response. Uncle Sam hasn't seen fit to install a telegraph office into our garrison yet, so somebody'll have to go fetch him, if he is on post at all."

"Uh-huh," Thomas said, distracted. He had a notebook next to the storybook he'd found in Miss Roseingrave's room, writing out his translation slowly and carefully.

"You figure anything out?"

"The more I read, the less sense it makes," he admitted, and set his pencil down. His hand was starting to cramp. It had been a while since he'd been able to just sit and write, and it seemed like with all his time in the saddle, his fingers had forgotten a little of their usual skill. "This tome contains references to an event I've heard of before, normally referenced in the Irish mythological cycle, which is criminally understudied, if you ask me. Comparable to early Greek mythology in scope and scale, but lacking in the same wider cultural impact on—"

"Leighton," Sirok said warningly.

"Of course. Well, the Second Battle of Mag Tuired—"

"Battle? Now that sounds more interesting."

"It was a war between the Tuatha Dé Danann and the Fomorians. Mythical," Thomas said, and tapped his pencil on the paper. "Or at least, so I thought. The battle was instigated by a half-Fomorian king named Bres, along with his ally, the monstrous Balor of the Evil Eye."

Sirok really did look more interested now. "What were they fightin' over?"

"Control of Ireland, I have always assumed." And Thomas frowned. "Although it could be that they were fighting for control of Faeryland, Tir na nAill, itself. It's a little unclear where the boundaries are in Irish mythology. But despite the loss of their own king and many of their greatest heroes, the Tuatha Dé Danann were victorious and drove the Fomorians from what we now know as Ireland. As I have observed before, the parallels between this and the war of the Titans against the Olympians are unmistakable. Considering that similar stories crop up all over the world, one might imagine that—"

"Leighton."

"Yes?"

"I don't think no Greek god is botherin' us now. But you've mentioned these Tuatha folk a few times. Who are they?"

"Oh, of course. The Tuatha Dé Danann were…nature gods, I suppose you'd say. Warriors and healers and the forebears of the fae. Mortal enemies of the Fomorians, too, although they had many dealings together and even intermarried." Thomas tapped the cover of the book thoughtfully. "The stories from *The Book of Invasions* don't go into much detail about what happened after Mag Tuired. This claims that the Fomorians were sealed away in a barrow, isolated in a realm of their own nightmares. Only four Fomorians, out of the countless force that went up against the Tuatha Dé Danann, were permitted to live. Banished, stripped of power and driven from the land that provided it, but alive."

"Eli Horn?"

"Logic seems to dictate that he is one of those four, yes."

"So…" Sirok rolled his eyes and sat back in his chair, putting his booted feet up on the seat of another. "The others. Why lock 'em up if they were dead?"

"I'm not sure the Fomorians were. Or, at least, I'm not sure they could be killed in any way that we understand it." Thomas paged idly back through the book, pausing at a lurid illustration of the monstrous Balor on the battlefield. "If they are linked to the primordial force of entropy, of decay, then there really is no stopping them. Death might only make them stronger, if one applies a little modern logic."

The captain did not look convinced. "Uh-huh…"

"And then, there is the writing from the cave, the ogham script." And Thomas shuffled out his pile of rubbings. "Every example I've ever seen of this type of writing contains only names and relationships. The father of, the son of, the master of. But this contains only one such name. Father of B. Which could be Bres or Balor or half a dozen others I know or one I don't. Doesn't matter. The bulk of this seems to be some kind of incantation, for lack of a better word."

"Incantation?"

"Magic," Thomas said. "This is a rough translation at best, but it reads, 'Father of…' the name I cannot translate, 'in exile no more, claims the tombs and conquers the…seals, or locks,' I think. 'The blood of a bean fáith,' a female seer you understand, 'opens the way into the formless lands, where all waits as death, and death will spill forth as her blood pours out.'"

Captain Sirok raised an eyebrow. "These little scratches say all that?"

"As I said, it's a rough translation, with a few liberties on my part. See, this word here means 'crow,' but it can also indicate—"

Sirok held up a hand. "Eli Horn, some banished evil fae thing, needs Miss Roseingrave in order to reach the place where all his dead kin were sealed in?"

"It stands to reason."

"And what happens when these things get out?"

"I have no idea."

The captain paused. "Would this ogham script be something our friend Hallorman could read?"

Thomas pulled his spectacles off, rubbing them clean as he considered that. "It is the oldest script in Ireland and was said to be taught to humans by Ogma of the Tuatha Dé Danann. As a descendent of that race..."

"Hallorman woulda read it. He'd know what Eli Horn is up to. And he's leading Miss Roseingrave right back into it," Captain Sirok finished, grim.

For a moment, the two men just sat there, struck by the revelation.

"We have to get to her," Thomas said.

"I agree," Sirok said grimly, "but how are we gonna do that? How do we open the portal? It's one question we don't got answered yet."

Frustrated, Thomas cast down his pencil, rubbing his temples. But when he tilted his head, his eyes fell on the dishes from last night's supper, stacked up neatly but not yet removed. Beer glasses.

The beer.

"There might be somebody in town that can help," he said, already moving, grabbing for his jacket and hat and heading for the door.

CHAPTER THIRTY-SEVEN

"So where are we going?"

"There," Thomas said, and pointed down toward the end of the street, toward a large brick building with a finely painted sign. BLACK MOUNTAIN GOLDSMITHS.

He had asked Mrs. McKenney about the beer, and she had confirmed what he suspected. "One of the families up here brews it as a side business," she'd told him. "Doesn't come cheap, but we can't run the finest hotel in the region if we let our competitors have the finest beer, now can we?" And she'd given him the address for their main shop.

"What makes you think there'll be help here?"

"There was a Mr. Dvalinsson in Leadville who was involved in the events leading up to the séance, and owned a place with the Black Mountain name. In speaking to him later, I had the distinct impression he had some kind of magical or occult knowledge. Now"—and he gestured at the store's facade—"here that name is again. It is a slim lead, but a lead nonetheless."

Sirok cocked his head, sniffing a little. "It certainly has the stink of something otherworldly."

"The fae?"

"I don't know," he said, and strode forward. "Let's find out, shall we?"

Inside, the place seemed to be nothing more than a normal jeweler's shop, albeit one with cases of decidedly ethnic pieces, dusty silver and turquoise and other, odder stones. Those pieces were scattered through cases containing interesting minerals, some of which were labeled. Thomas was admiring a rather interesting hunk of tanzanite next to a set of oblong beads when a door opened and a bell chimed.

"Who's there now?" a female voice called. "How can I help you, my fine..." And she trailed off.

The voice belonged to a short woman, small and swarthy, barely five feet tall. She was broad through the shoulders and waist, with thick wrists and calloused fingers. Her dark green wool dress was plain and simple; Thomas got the impression that she would have hit a dressmaker who suggested she wear a bustle. She crossed her arms, looking back and forth between them, glowering.

"Good day," Thomas said, leaping in. "My name is Thomas Leighton, and this is my associate, Captain Sirok, a—"

"A cavalry officer," she interjected, and huffed, tilting her head. She had an accent that might once have been German or Norwegian. Thomas couldn't properly tell. "Among other things. You aren't my usual customers."

"This is your establishment?" Thomas asked, a little surprised.

The swarthy woman looked askance over at Sirok. "What can I do to get the pair of you out of my shop?"

"We have a portal to open," the captain drawled. "Up in the mountains. Where, I believe, a family member of yours died. Now that I stand here, I recognize the smell of his blood."

She looked between them for a moment, eyes landing once again on Captain Sirok with one rough finger of hers pointed at Thomas. "He's a human and you're talking like this?"

"Beggin' your permission, ma'am, but he's seen much worse in the last few weeks than you."

Thomas braced himself for some kind of rejection, a denouncement, a decree to vacate the premises immediately. Instead, the woman's stony facade seemed to crack a little. She rubbed a hand across her eyes. "Did you find any bones up there?"

"Not a single one, ma'am. But then, we wouldn't, would we? For one o' your kind."

For a moment more, she said nothing. Then she sighed and waved them back. "You'd best come with me," she grumbled. "I have an appointment in half an hour with a dealer out of San Francisco for a few of my more choice Navajo pieces. Wouldn't do to have him walk in on this conversation."

Thomas glanced back at the case. "You deal in Indian jewelry? Is that what this is?"

"You sure about this one?" the woman demanded of Captain Sirok.

He just shrugged. "You'll have to forgive him. He's foreign."

"Aren't we all?" she grumbled. "Well, don't just stand there like bats in shit. Come with me."

The strange little woman led them back into a workspace that could have been a cave, for how little natural light there was. The stonework was immaculate here, the furnishings minimal. A double-headed axe of exquisite craftsmanship was mounted over the back door, the room's only other exit.

It was lit with gas lanterns, all cheerfully burning away in glass covers. The place was immaculate, despite its obvious hard use. A potbelly stove sat in the far corner with a few chairs arranged near it and a black iron kettle on the top. It was to this that the diminutive woman led them, past a pair of similarly proportioned men sat working at their stations.

"I understand the wolf here," the woman said without preamble, opening the cast-iron stove with one bare hand, leveling a finger at Thomas, "but you, you I don't know."

"Mrs. Dvalinsson, I—"

"Ha! Humans with all your bowing and scraping and specificity. I'm no Mrs. Dvalinsson. Dvalinsdoter would be more accurate, but America don't recognize the old names. Call me Inga."

"Is that your name?" Thomas asked.

"As good a name as any," she told him, an ugly smile on her face. "So wolf, why are you hauling this one around?"

"He's with the Academy for Psychical Inquiry," Captain Sirok said.

She paused, log in hand. "And you came from Leadville? You associated with Lane Barton in any way?"

"He commissioned me to assist him in verifying the results of a séance," Thomas confirmed.

"Séances. Ha! Humans are idiots, doing things like that. Talking to the dead? The dead have nothing to say. Nothing worth listening to anyway." The fire fed now, she slammed the cast-iron door shut. Her hand wasn't even red. "But I heard about Barton's séance. What happened?"

Thomas gave her a brief rundown of the situation, pausing only here and there to answer questions and allow Captain Sirok to offer his perspective. The chase through the mountains, the battle at Gunnison, the ruined town, and the final showdown at the cave he laid out as quickly as he could.

Inga took it all in, her shrewd face betraying not a single thought, although her eyes did seem to gleam when he described the cave, and she questioned Sirok extensively on the details. Both of them had to describe the canyon to her multiple times before she was satisfied.

"So you need to make your way into the Otherworld and rescue your woman?" she asked when they had finally finished.

"In short, yes," Thomas replied. "Can you help us with that?"

"Won't be easy," Inga replied. "That seeress friend of yours may have one foot in the Otherworld, Englishman, but only one, and you lack even that. Your souls keep you tethered here."

"Soul?" Mr. Leighton asked. "You don't have a soul?"

"We're made of different stuff, our kind and yours," Inga replied.

Fascinating. The whole thing was fascinating. "I have heard this about the fae in some folklore, but—"

He was interrupted as the woman burst out laughing. "Fae? Ha! An Englishman's word for an Englishman's myths. Not ours."

"What should I call you then?"

"We are all of the Otherworld. But not all the same kind."

"There are difference species of, err, Otherworlders?" Mr. Leighton asked.

"As many as there are human cultures in this world, and a great many beyond those. Some forgotten, and some not found yet." She waved it off. "The old word for us might have been 'dwergaz.' I'm not sure what it is now."

It took Thomas a moment to process that. But then, he recognized the word. "A dwarf. You're a dwarf? The kind that the sagas tell of? The craftsmen and engineers of the gods?"

"The gods? Once we served them, in our way, but no more. They're so far away now it may be impossible to ever reach them again. Humans have forgotten them, forgotten the stories that allowed for connection with them, or changed the stories so greatly that the truth and the tale no longer align. Like using the wrong key for a lock. And thus, we drift even further from each other." She interlocked her fingers, then pulled them slowly apart. "Cut off from what we were, we can only be what you perceive us to be. Pure spirit no more, we're locked into these shapes, become more like you with every passing year."

"What does that all mean?" Thomas asked, utterly intrigued now. Captain Sirok cleared his throat, and Thomas remembered himself. "I mean, what bearing does that have on getting through this portal?"

"Absolutely none," she said, voice calm but the words punctuated by a loud crack. Thomas looked; the back of the nearest chair, where her hands were resting, had just snapped in half. She barely seemed to notice. "I thank you for bringing me the news about my son, but I won't take you there. Better a few humans lost than the entire state."

"What do you mean?"

"If we're lucky, that Fomorian of yours will keep his revenge to his own lands and not bother my mountains any. I won't provoke him by barging in on whatever nonsense he no doubt has planned," she said, and stood. "Now, will you see yourselves out, or should I send one of the boys to escort you off my premises?"

"It's been a long time," Mr. Hallorman said beside Charlotte, and his voice was different. She looked over at him. They were standing on a rocky shore. He was looking out to sea. It felt like the most natural thing in all the world, and yet, everything was wrong.

There was no sunlight here, no discernible source for the weak daylight around them. The ocean did not move, the surface still as a millpond. And Mr. Hallorman...

Gone was the man who had hiked up the canyon with her, dusty from the trail. Standing next to her on the eternal, unchanging shore was a luminous being, tall and proud, untouched by age or infirmity, illuminated from within by a light that, Charlotte realized now, was older than humanity itself.

She looked down at her own hands. No glow. Nothing special about her at all. She was nothing but a human adrift in a place she didn't belong.

"It is not what I thought," she admitted, looking around.

He took a deep breath. "Ahh, I have missed the sea."

If he had been odd before, he was stranger still now. He was still wearing the same clothes, the same modern suit and trousers and cravat, which did not seem to fit the old stories at all. And yet, around his neck there was a golden torque, thin but undeniable, the ends of which were twisted into fearsome faces, glittering as if under a strong sun.

He caught her looking at it and tapped it with two fingers. "My bond," he said simply.

Charlotte shook her head, not knowing what to say. Her family had never kept slaves, not even before the war, but she was familiar with the old accoutrements. The chains, the neck irons. She found it uncomfortable to know that the family guardian wore such a thing.

"How are we supposed to find my sister in all of this?"

"This is the realm of my people, Charlotte, and nothing may hide from me here. Now. Let me see your thimble."

"My thimble?"

"Even here there is a certain flow to events, and right now, the tide is ebbing," he snapped, suddenly impatient. "Do you wish to see your sister again or not? Thimble now, if you please."

Frowning, Charlotte opened the small cage hanging from one of her chatelaine chains and handed over the thimble. It was a simple thing, sized for her right ring finger, plain beaten brass. "What are you going to do with it?"

But he was already moving down the gray, rocky beach, into the quiet lapping waves. "Our world and yours are not so different," he told her, and set the thimble down. "What one perceives is what there is, and the underlying truth pokes through where it may."

Charlotte started; instead of a small sewing accessory, a large coracle now lay on the beach, wide enough for both of them to sit comfortably in. It was far broader than the thimble had been, proportionately, but the outside still had the beaten dimples that the thimble had possessed.

"Of course," he said with a self-satisfied smile, "it doesn't work with everything. You should be grateful nobody would purchase your chatelaine."

"What do you mean?" she asked.

He looked down the beach for a moment, and then strode off, water around his ankles, after something carried in one of the waves. "Did you imagine my service was the only token of my old lord's favor?" he called back and grabbed at the thing. He began walking back, dragging a piece of driftwood almost his own height. "There was great affection between him and your ancestor."

She looked down at the innocuous little object. "Are you saying this is magic?"

He laughed, reaching her again. He hefted the driftwood, staring down its gray length. "What is magic, Charlotte?" he asked, almost leisurely, and hit the wood with the flat of a hand. To her dismay, it shattered apart, and yet, when the splinters all fell, he had in his hand a oar of gray wood, finely shaped as if by great labor.

Standing there on that strangest of shores, Charlotte felt entirely out of her depth. "I don't know. I never thought any of this was real."

He smiled at her, stepping into the boat and holding out a hand. "Now that's a lie if ever I've heard one."

She hesitated then, unsure of herself, unsure of any of this. But Celeste was somewhere out there in that ocean, and Charlotte had come this far already. She took Mr. Hallorman's hand and, lifting her skirt, stepped aboard.

"Well, Leighton, any other ideas?" Captain Sirok asked, his long strides eating up the ground.

Thomas looked back down the street at the goldsmith's shop. Unable to convince Mrs. Dvalinsdoter any further, they had taken their leave of the strange little woman. He felt utterly lost. There were no other leads. No way in.

"I'm not sure," he admitted as they walked. "But I still have Miss Roseingrave's book. Perhaps an answer may still be found in its pages, some way to enter the Land of Faery safely without—"

"Risking the temporal displacement effect?"

Both men stopped, for in front of them was one of the younger dwergaz from Mrs. Dvalinsdoter's workshop. He was short and swarthy and had a full beard already, but he looked young, barely into his adulthood.

"Temporal displacement effect?" Captain Sirok asked, bemused.

"Too scientific a term maybe, but that's how the human here thinks about things," the young dwergaz man said, and tipped his hat. "Andrew Dvalinsson, you can call me."

"That's a very American name," Thomas commented.

"Why shouldn't it be? I am American, every bit as much as your wolf friend here is."

Captain Sirok inclined his own head. "Don't mind him, he's foreign."

"I can tell. It's the accent," Andrew replied. "Mama might want to avoid any further entanglements with the Otherworld, but if my brother's bones are there, I'd like the chance to lay him to rest."

"You leave bodies?" Captain Sirok asked, sounding surprised.

Andrew shook his head. "Every year, Mama says, we become more like you."

"Don't seem worth it."

"There's gold to be had here."

Thomas broke back in, interrupting the odd argument. "So, young Master Andrew, can you help us with this temporal effect?"

"Certainly," he said with confidence.

"You have a horse and kit you can take?" Captain Sirok asked. "We're travelin' light ourselves. Don't have anything to spare."

The young dwergaz shrugged. "I'll stop by Dunlop Livery and get one of our mules. I can get us anything else we need, too. And we'll need proper kerosene for the lamp, none of that rendered whale fat. That won't guide us right."

"The lamp?" Thomas asked.

"The lamp," Andrew said, like this was something both of them should have known already. "How else do you think we're gonna mitigate the temporal displacement effect? Gotta take your own light in."

Captain Sirok tugged at Thomas's elbow. "Give us a moment to confer, kid," he said, and yanked Thomas around, voice dropping. "Whaddaya thinkin'?"

"I think we should accept. He is of the Otherworld, is he not?"

"He is like me. Grounded here. He may not be able to help us."

"It's the best lead we have."

"Ain't you worried about tricks?"

"No."

"You're far too trusting, Leighton. I don't know what London's like, but this is the frontier, and people ain't always what they seem to be."

"London is a viper's pit of crime," Thomas retorted, irritated now. "And the dwarves of legend are not tricksters or deceivers or liars. They honor their pacts and take pride in their work. I say his offer is genuine. Unless you're questioning my expertise."

Sirok looked at him for a moment more, golden eyes piercing, and then he laughed uproariously, slapping Thomas on the back. "This is why I like you, Leighton. Expertise. Right," he chortled, and turned back to the boy. "When can you leave?"

"How far is it?"

"Eight miles, perhaps."

"Eight miles?" The boy's face contorted. "My brother died eight miles from here? By the gods, he's been so close all this time."

"It's not an easy ride," Sirok continued, "but we did it in the dark last night. If we leave by noon, we might make it by twilight."

"Then we'll leave by eleven," Andrew replied firmly. "I just need to, uhh, get the right lamp outta Mama's safe."

"Wait," Thomas began, but Captain Sirok cut in.

"We'll see you at eleven, kid," he said. "We're at the McKenney Hotel. You know it?"

"Of course. They buy our beer."

Two and a half hours later, with a padded bag dangling from the pommel of Andrew Dvalinsson's saddle and a can of kerosene in Captain Sirok's bags, the three of them set off south, back into the mountains, toward whatever madness awaited them.

Chapter Thirty-Eight

"Something's wrong here."

It was the first time Mr. Hallorman had spoken in...how long? Charlotte couldn't tell. The length of the journey had left no impression on her.

The arms on her pocket watch had moved, forward and back, swinging forward by hours only to drag out the seconds on the few occasions she had looked. Mist had swirled across the water, and dark shapes loomed here and there in the distance. Islands, she had thought, and she had asked when the first one had appeared, but Mr. Hallorman had just shaken his head and rowed on. How many had they passed? Ten, fifty, a hundred? Attempting to understand the lay of time and place here was like trying to plot the cartography of a dream.

Up ahead now were more dim shapes, but unlike all the others—had there been others?—these dark smudges resolved, coming into focus.

Land. Just as Mr. Hallorman had said.

"What do you mean, wrong?" she asked. "It looks like an island."

"An island with cliffs." The faery's voice sounded cagey. The torque around his neck looked strange against the standing collar of his shirt. "Those should not be there."

The thimble-turned-coracle moved without urgency under his guidance, turning into the cliffs. It was strange, Charlotte thought. The daughter of a seafarer, and a child of the Atlantic coast, she would have expected terrible wave action so close to this kind of shoreline. Instead, the water remained as still as a millpond, as quiet as a highland lake at midday.

"It's too shallow here," Mr. Hallorman told her when she asked about this, and to emphasize his point, pushed the oar down. It went barely a foot more under the water, then stopped. "Something has happened to the sea."

"Like what?"

"I don't know."

As they neared the cliffs, Charlotte could make out details there. To her surprise, she saw the shapes of seashells clinging to the rocks, desiccated coral, the look of land that had once been underwater. The bodies of sea creatures lay beside their path now. A great whale was visible far down the shoreline, beached but still moving, tail beating the shallow surf. In front of them, seal carcasses littered the sand. The closer they got to shore, the more decayed those carcasses became, until Mr. Hallorman was picking their path only through bones.

The coracle finally ground to a halt, the water too shallow to carry them anymore. Mr. Hallorman jumped out into the shin-deep water and began dragging the little boat toward the cliffs. Charlotte made to get out herself, but he just shook his head. She wondered about it and then looked down.

Where the water touched him, his trousers and boots were being eaten away. The effect seemed to extend deeper. Wounds appeared on his legs. Trickles of bright red blood ran out into the water.

She swallowed and stayed where she was.

Finally, Mr. Hallorman drew the coracle up into a cleft in the cliffs. It was a fit so tight, Charlotte could have reached out with both hands and touched the sheer walls of weather-eaten rock on either side. The little coracle barely fit. Here, the quiet waters deposited them on a narrow strip of rocky ground, a small scattering of gravel over dirt that almost immediately gave way to wet stone, boulders having tumbled into the narrow gap within the cliffs.

Hundreds of feet up, silhouettes of tree limbs half blocked the gray, sunless sky. There was no noise of animals, of breeze, of the distant passage of trains, of the sea they had just left. Even Mr. Hallorman's movements seemed muffled. The silence was complete, and suffocating.

"You should be safe now," he told her, holding out a hand. She glanced down at his feet. His boots and trousers seemed to be intact, and yet, when she looked back, she could see bloody footprints in the sand. Gathering her courage, she took his hand and stepped out of the coracle.

As soon as she did so, the shape of it collapsed, flowing like water until it was nothing more than a thimble again. Mr. Hallorman picked it up and passed it back to her, a ghost of a smile on his lips. "Always trust a seamstress to have the right tool for the job at hand."

"What is this?" Charlotte asked, feeling very much out of her depth. He tucked the thimble back into its little hanging case. "I can't remember anything like this from Grandmother's stories."

"This is something new," he replied. "Something's happening here. Something's changing."

"But I thought you said stories are what connect us to the...the Otherworld. If I understand it in a certain way, then surely—"

"Stories are more than what is written in books, and they are more than an individual experience. But your grandmother taught you what she could of the old ways, and that, dear Charlotte, may protect you here more than anything else. Trust her wisdom. Unless, of course, you wish to turn back." His eyes were a burning green.

Charlotte ignored the chord of fear those simple words struck in her but turned her face to the thin sliver of light above.

It was, Charlotte thought, a scene that would not have been out of place in the mountains they had just left. If anything, that made her sense of dislocation even worse. Instead of being in some magical realm where all was different, it felt like a strange shadow of the world she knew. So similar, and yet, utterly different.

"I had thought nothing would be alive here," Charlotte said, indicating the trees.

"It will not be, closer in."

"Closer in to what?"

"The barrowland," he said.

Her confidence in this course of action, weak as it was, was flagging. It was one thing to contemplate crossing the veil into Faeryland to in pursuit of some ancient monster, but it was another thing entirely to actually do it. She would have run from this screaming, had it not been for—

"My sister is here?"

"Yes." He hesitated. "And she is in agony."

Charlotte closed her eyes. Because of her failure. A mistake she would not repeat a second time. "Then we go to the barrowland," she told him.

"Step where I step. We must proceed with caution."

Entropy, Charlotte found herself thinking as they gained the upper plateau. What had Mr. Leighton said about entropy? That it was not so much about destruction as it was disorder, a state in which all things became equal and no differences could be found. Equilibrium reached, with no potential for anything to build upon itself or become anything new.

Such a strange concept.

And yet, it was what she saw on this strange island.

Mostly.

The cliffs gave way to a rolling landscape, as if the mountains themselves wore down as they walked. The dead forest faded along with the peaks, dwindling to scrub brush, and then, to nothing more than thin grass and lichen clinging to the rocks.

Charlotte, having grown up on her grandmother's secondhand tales of the wild green beauty of Ireland, had expected something of that here. Instead, it looked like the bare lands around the peaks they had already passed in Colorado, and she said so to Mr. Hallorman.

But he just shook his head, and on they pressed.

Eventually, even the grass gave out and they were nearly on what looked like a great dirt plain, as flat as could be.

It was a strange land. Nothing seemed to change. The ground was an undifferentiated gray grit that ground underfoot. There was no wind, no sound, nothing to distinguish one place from another. They could have been standing still, if not for the movement of their feet.

Charlotte remembered the first time she had seen the Great Plains. The curvature of the earth had been clear to her then, nothing but sun and grass and the endless expanse. But this was different. The perspective was wrong. Instead of being at the top of a vast curve, she felt as though she was in the center dip, inside a giant bowl she could not leave. A bowl where she might be trapped forever.

And yet, even with that, Charlotte could see shapes, hazy in the distance. Getting larger. Ever on the horizon, but growing.

"I did not want this," Mr. Hallorman said suddenly, glancing over at her.

All she could see were his brilliant green eyes. He had pulled a handkerchief up over his nose and mouth. Dust clung to the cloth, little dots in front of what must have been his nostrils. Charlotte found it odd; the air was dry and unpleasant, tasting of nothing, but she felt no dust on her face. He seemed to be struggling far more than she with the passage.

"Excuse me?"

"If given my choice, I would not have chosen to be bound to you," he continued, all expression lost behind the handkerchief. "But I have spent long centuries walking beside the women of your clan, and I have found them...less boring than most humans. Allowing your line to die out would be, I estimate, a loss to your race."

"Am I to say thank you for that?" she asked, in no mood for his games.

Mr. Hallorman pulled the cloth up a little higher and started walking again. "You should," he told her. "If I liked you any less, even with the oath between us, I would have refused to come here at all. And even with this, the cost of victory, if victory can be achieved at all, will be excruciatingly unpleasant."

"What a comforting thought," she replied sarcastically, her own fear nipping at her humor.

"Understand this, lass," he told her. "Oaths can be spoken. Oaths can be broken. But some things run deeper even than that."

She wanted to ask him what he meant, but with her next step, everything changed.

They had closed the distance between themselves and the barrows with surprising speed. One moment, they had been far distant. The next, they were among them. But it wasn't any barrow that Charlotte was familiar with.

"It looks like a tombstone," she said as they stopped in front of the first.

And it did. Fifteen feet high, at least, and shaped like any monument in any modern cemetery—Charlotte thought about her mother's own resting place, the sad little plaque that marked the grave, the most they had been able to afford, alone in a sea of finely engraved monuments. But this tombstone was not like those; this one sat in the ground slightly crooked, and the surface was carved not with kind words about the deceased, but huge, uneven slashes set on lines.

"Ogham," Mr. Hallorman said in a low voice, taking a step back to look up at it. "It gives the name of a dead Fomorian, killed at the second battle of Mag Tuired."

"Mag Tuired?" Charlotte asked, thinking again of Grandmother's book. "That actually happened?"

"Of course it did," he said, and pulled his bow from its quiver. Nocking an arrow, he jerked his head around the stone, indicating that she should follow. "Not the first of the wars between the Tuatha Dé Danann and the Fomorians, but the last and most decisive one."

"What happened? Really?"

"Really?" Mr. Hallorman shook his head. "One of the most formidable of the Fomorian kings, Elatha, used his son to provoke the Tuatha Dé Danann. He wished to avoid any responsibility for the outcome, as well as utilize the battle as a convenient way to rid himself of anyone who might challenge his leadership. His goal was to create chaos, then step in to reclaim control. He wanted the Tuatha Dé Danann under his thumb once again. Instead, he ended the Fomorian dominion forever."

Charlotte looked around at the tombstones. It was easy to imagine them as headstones for dead monsters, and she shivered.

"What happened after that?"

"Your grandmother's book has most of the details. There was a conclave. The Tuatha Dé Danann offered a few of the survivors terms. Some, like Bres, were permitted to remain in Ireland at first. They repaid that kindness with horror, and finally, they were hunted down and banished by the Morrigan."

"But the rest of them?"

"Executed," he said, and spread an arm around. "And buried here."

"You talk like you were there," Charlotte said. The headstones were scattered without rhyme or reason, it seemed. No pattern in their positioning, no change in the flatness of the plain. The only thing she could discern was that they seemed to be getting taller and more elaborate, the script on them smaller and denser.

Mr. Hallorman scoffed. "Any of the fair folk could tell you of Mag Tuired. Children are taught those sagas from a young age, melancholy and violent though they are. But we never sing them for humans."

"Perhaps that is because such sagas are lies, and you're afraid of getting called out for it. You should know, Miss Roseingrave, that the Tuatha Dé Danann always did have a terrible relationship with the truth," a voice said.

Its owner stepped out from behind a headstone.

And everything changed.

Thomas didn't know what to expect as he shouldered his pack. Loath to leave his books behind, he had brought them all with him. It seemed foolish; either he succeeded in this rescue attempt and returned unharmed to Ouray to reclaim his precious tomes, or he died there and then. What did it matter to him what happened to his physical possessions? But Thomas could not bear the thought of his notes being thrown out nor Miss Roseingrave's splendid storybook ending up in the hotel's small lending library. Even sitting forever unread in a dusty cave was preferable. Perhaps one day they would be found by other explorers or scientists, pondered and admired and—

"Leighton! A little help here!" Captain Sirok called.

He shook it off and went to help pull tack.

As before, the party was forced to dismount before reaching the end of the canyon; even on the main approach, there was no way to bring horses all the way up. There were already two horses grazing here, Mr. Hallorman's mare and Miss Roseingrave's gelding. The mare came over to sniff at their horses, eyeing the dwergaz boy's mule with naked suspicion.

Captain Sirok had brought a small quantity of molasses-soaked oat clusters with him and was talking quietly to Mr. Hallorman's mare as she took them nervously from his hand.

"She don't like me," he told Thomas as he pulled the bridle off his own gelding, "but I think we've got an understanding."

"Oh?"

"She'll try to keep them here. It's good grazing and water's over yonder but it ain't enough for all five of them for more than a day or so. They might not stay through tomorrow night." He looked to Andrew. "We'll need to be quick."

"Time's got no meaning in there," Andrew replied, peering up at the sky. He had twin rock axes hooked through metal loops on his belt on either hip, and the motion made them sway. "Sun'll be down over the mountains soon. We need to go. Show me where this portal is."

"Up."

"Then up we go."

As stocky as Andrew was, he was surprisingly spry with the climb, moving up the tumbled, tortured rockfall with ease. Thomas, on the other hand, was puffing hard by the time they'd climbed to the upper plateau.

As they neared the place where the aspen grove had stood, Thomas expected to see the same pile of dead wood they had clambered over the night before. Instead, there was grass, deep alpine grass, flowers blooming in it even at this late hour of autumn. It stretched out as far as the aspens had once grown, and at the edge, deer grazed.

Andrew, however, stared in horror. "What happened here?" he asked.

"What do you mean?" Thomas asked.

"What do you mean, what do I mean?" he asked, putting one hand to the ground. "By the gods, the deep magic was worked here. Anybody could feel it."

Thomas looked over at Sirok, who just shook his head. "Our companion, the one we told you about, forced the aspens here to cycle through their entire lifespan in a few minutes."

Disbelief showed on the young dwergaz man's face, but whatever else he was thinking, he didn't give it voice. Instead, he nodded toward the waterfall. "That's it then? The portal?"

"Indeed so," Sirok replied.

Despite his stated eagerness to see the place where his brother died, Andrew lingered a little while beside the waterfall pool, sifting a few small nuggets of gold from the water. He stood admiring them until Sirok barked at him. Pocketing the gold, he shook his head.

"No wonder he liked this place," he said. "He'd told us he'd found something up here but wouldn't say where. Shame we can't mine it."

"Why not?" Thomas asked.

"Even we don't mess with portals if we don't need to," Andrew said. "There are things in the Otherworld that would chill your heart, if only you could see them. The stories are gone, burned or melted down, the people who knew them all dead, and the ways are shut. Unless you find a place like this, where the walls between the worlds wear thin. And then there's no telling what you might stumble into in the dark."

The cave was exactly how Thomas had left it. The carvings still stood out on the rock faces. Bullets still lay strewn about the ground. And yet, something had changed.

Andrew gave no heed to any of it. Instead, he crouched down, running his fingers through the dirt. But for that simple movement, he would have looked like a statue, so still and gray he was. Thomas was beginning to wonder if the dwergaz was looking for more gold when Andrew finally spoke again.

"You are fortunate. Fortunate you came to a dwarf and not another fae-thing for this."

"What do you mean?"

"I smell their sea. Without me, you'd be forced to take those routes yourself, and no human navigates their way through that. You only reach their lands if you're lost. Least, that's what the stories say."

Thomas didn't rise to the bait. "But you have another way?"

Andrew hit his chest with a big, broad hand. "Rock and stone, human. Right through the foundations of the world. But not without light. Come on."

Andrew stomped outside the cave again, unwrapping the lantern that he had brought from Ouray. Thomas, curious, followed, not really paying attention to how Captain Sirok had sat down to start removing his boots.

The lantern looked relatively normal, except for a few key details. It was smaller than a regular lantern, made out of what looked to be pure silver. Instead of glass, however, cut panes of some mineral sat in the frame.

"Pure quartz," Andrew explained, and brandished a small, strange magnifying glass, this cut from some type of blue stone and inlaid with more of the clear quartz. "The wick must be lit directly from the sun's dying rays. That's how we take time in with us."

"But the sun ain't time!" Captain Sirok called from the cave.

But Thomas's mind was already at work on the problem, and he snapped his fingers. "I think I understand Master Andrew's logic. If we look at the work of such luminaries as Foucault, and more recently, Albert Michelson, then it indeed appears that light waves travel at a certain speed, which may be used to measured time."

Andrew sighed, looking at him. The boy reminded Thomas strongly of Mr. Hallorman. "I am speaking more fundamentally than that."

"I assure you, young Master Andrew, there is nothing more fundamental than the discipline of physics."

"If my Mama was here, she'd tell you that it's all about symbolism. Humans have always looked to the sun to inform them of time's passage. The march of days, the turning of the seasons, even England's mastery of oceanic navigation. All revealed through the movement of the sun."

"Technically, the sun doesn't move. Our planet—"

"I'm not talking about astronomy. I don't care what time actually is, if it's anything at all. The only thing that matters is how humans experience it. The passage of the sun is how you measure time. So we take it with us."

The day was failing fast now, but thanks to the saddle in the western range, there was still light falling in the small glen. Andrew positioned the lantern on a small boulder, squinting at the sun, making minute adjustments.

"So you ask the sun to ignite the wick or…"

Thomas trailed off, the dwergaz boy staring at him for a moment. Then Andrew burst into laughter.

"You've spent too much time with the fae. Asking the sun. Ha! Nobody asks the sun anything. It doesn't care about what happens to us. It's too old and too far away to care about even our lives." And he thumped his chest again. "Our people do not ask for permission to use the deep magic, like the faeries do. It is part of us already. Why should we plead for what is rightfully ours?"

"Then how—"

"Make the right tool and it'll never fail you." Andrew opened the small door on the lantern and positioned the magnifying glass in front of it, his hand perfectly steady. "Now be quiet."

Thomas was familiar with the concept of focusing sunlight through a glass to start a fire, but especially so late in the day, he didn't see what such a flawed tool could accomplish. And indeed, for a few minutes, nothing happened.

He was about to protest, to ask Andrew what he thought he was doing, when the last rays of daylight washed over the canyon's end, gold and warm. Thomas thought he heard something, like the whisper of water across stone, wind in some barren, rocky place. Power surged. His soul swelled.

There was a flame on the wick.

Andrew slipped the magnifying glass back into his pocket, giving Thomas a triumphant smile. He couldn't help but smile back.

They headed back inside. Thomas was surprised to see that Sirok had laid aside his saber and rifle and was stripped down to his long underwear already.

The cavalry officer smiled at his confusion. "I know, damned inconvenient, isn't it?"

"You're going to walk into Faeryland naked?"

"It's either that or ruin my clothes, and I don't fancy doin' the hike back to Ouray in my skivvies."

"Wolves," Andrew grumbled, rolling his eyes.

They were obliged to wait until Sirok had stripped to the skin. Only then did Andrew put his hand to the wall and whisper something Thomas did not understand.

A chill gust of wind washed through the cave. The light outside grew darker while the lantern's flickering light grew brighter.

Andrew pressed his ear to the rock for a moment, then sighed and stepped back. "It's done."

"I say," Thomas began, "nothing seems…"

Then he stopped.

Then he saw Sirok.

Where the man had stood beside him, there was now a wolf.

A huge, lean, black-furred wolf with brilliant gold eyes.

"Can you talk?" Thomas asked.

The wolf looked at him, silent.

"Can you, er, understand us?" Thomas asked.

The Sirok-wolf pawed at the ground and tossed its head.

"That's something, at least," Andrew said.

The wolf growled.

"Where do we go?" Thomas asked, forcing himself to stay objective. "The world around us looks much the same as the place we just left."

"As I said, human"—and Andrew pointed—"we proceed through the foundation of the world."

Where the blank wall of the cave had once been, there was now a passage.

Thomas felt a chill go through him. "How extraordinary."

The wolf that was Sirok merely snapped its jaws, then trotted ahead.

"What is it?" Andrew said, a note of impatience in his voice.

Thomas looked back over his shoulder. "Perhaps we should go back so I may retrieve Sirok's saber for—"

"Ha!" Andrew's laugh was harsh in the space. Here, he seemed less like a boy and more like some force of nature, young, yes, but still eternal, like a rock freshly fallen from the mountainside. "Go back and we'll have to relight this, and there's no guarantee the light will still be there. If you're to save your woman and I to find my brother, we go forward now."

The rock axes that Andrew had brought with him had changed in their sheaths by his side, turning from simple tools into something lethal.

Thomas checked his own guns. Both revolver and rifle seemed

unchanged, except for there being a slight gleam to the steel barrels that he had not noticed before. There was nothing in any of his research, any of the stories he had heard or translated, to let him know how this worked. But Miss Roseingrave was in there, and if this was the only way to reach her—

"Lead on, my good man," Thomas replied.

Andrew nodded and produced a second lantern, seemingly from nowhere. He lit it from the other lantern and held it high. "Don't fall behind," he warned, but there was a note of fear in his voice as well. "Older things than my people live in the darkness here."

Heart in his throat, and nothing but a revolver by his side and a Winchester rifle over his shoulder, Thomas Leighton walked into Faeryland.

CHAPTER THIRTY-NINE

Charlotte stopped cold.

There was Eli Horn. The outlaw. The man they had been chasing. Utterly transformed.

Charlotte remembered the way he had looked in the cave. No different than a human man, gray-haired and dark-eyed and wearied unto the point of death, clad in an old long coat and worn hat.

Now, he was different. Now he stood tall, taller than she would have guessed, no weariness in his posture or expression. His hair fell around his shoulders and his dark eyes blazed. The trail wear was gone, replaced by an ensemble that would not have been out of place in a performance of Wagner at the Tabor Opera House, garish and outlandish. And yet, it was no affectation, no pantomime or costume. There was a sense of utter and deadly purpose around him.

"So," she heard Mr. Hallorman say, "it is you."

"You presume to know me?"

Mr. Hallorman said nothing.

"Of course you don't. The lesser child of a failing people, you see a Fomorian but have no idea what we are." Eli Horn laughed. "Your ancestors were so proud of the slaughter they inflicted on our kind that fateful day. Like cattle. Just look at this killing field."

Mr. Hallorman placed himself between Charlotte and the outlaw, knife in hand. "What are you doing back here?"

"I could ask you the same question," the Fomorian replied, smiling. "You don't belong here anymore, that much I can tell. You have the stink of the human world about you. But ahh, you found a loophole, did you not? This human child, you're bound to her. If she walks here, so too must you."

"And what was yours?"

"Humans themselves." And Eli Horn spread his arms. "Look at this place. Look at what they have reduced it to. They try so hard these days, don't they, to render everything down to principles and theories, to strip away any deeper meaning? No longer does the storm have its own voice! No longer is destruction a terrible thing to behold, but inevitable, an exhausting matter of probabilities, everything failing, even light dying in the end. Entropic theory! Have you heard of it? We win in the end. That is what they believe now." He chuckled. "Under these new ideas, cracks appear in the old ways. The old wards. Of course, it will all drift away from them soon enough, lost forever, but for now, paths appear where no paths were before."

"And you slipped through one, like a rat through refuse, with the help of a human girl," Mr. Hallorman replied, condescension dripping from his words. "Give her to me. You have no claim on her."

Eli Horn smiled, and it was terrible to behold. "Yes, the false fáith. I found her quite charming. The perfect innocent, so guilty and yet so unblemished. What a shame."

"What did you do to my sister?" Charlotte demanded, stepping forward, anger overcoming her fear now. Mr. Hallorman thrust out an arm, holding her back.

The Fomorian burst out laughing, clapping his hands. "I can see your gifts, eldest daughter of Aine," he told her lightly, and smiled at Mr. Hallorman. "How kind of you to bring her to me, saving me the trouble of"—and he sighed happily—"another messy raid."

Throughout this conversation, Charlotte had seen the faery almost buzzing with some kind of furious, barely checked energy, but at those words, he finally moved.

Almost too fast for her to see, fluid and smooth, drawing his bow and an arrow and firing off a shot within the span of a heartbeat. A human opponent would have been killed in an instant. But not Eli Horn. He turned, catching the arrow as it grazed his neck and snapping the shaft in half. Then he came on, ploughing into Mr. Hallorman like a freight train.

The faery collided hard with the ground.

Blood, black and viscous, red and bright, dripped on the hardpan.

Eli Horn clenched his hand around the captured bow. It cracked and rotted, dust falling away through his fingers.

"A sloppy attempt," he snarled. "The human world has made you weak."

Mr. Hallorman smiled, looking up from where he was on hands and knees, and lunged up, knife in hand now. That earned him a kick to his ribs, so hard that it sent him flying back and up, into one of the monstrous tombstones. Mr. Hallorman hit it hard, and did not rise this time.

Charlotte tried to run to him then, but was grabbed from behind by huge, steely-strong hands. She heard a growl, smelt rotten meat, and looked back into a huge pair of jaws.

It was the wolfman again, the one from Gunnison, but warped and shifted almost beyond recognition. Fear rolled through her, and anger. She knew—just knew—that this was the thing that had tortured her sister. She tried to jerk away and then yelped; the pressure of his grip on her forearm was so great, she felt her bones shift.

"Don't hurt her, Lukas," Eli Horn said, sounding like an exasperated man talking to his pet dog, and went over to the tombstone where Mr. Hallorman lay. The Fomorian knelt down by the prone faery, grabbing a handful of his hair and forcing his face up, neck twisted terribly. Eli Horn had a knife in hand himself now, Charlotte saw, bronze and broad-bladed. "Get up, vermin," he growled. "Or have I killed you already?"

Mr. Hallorman turned his head slightly, eyes glittering, the metal of his torque glinting. Charlotte's mouth was dry. He was going to die here, and all because of her. But if such thoughts had seized him, too, he gave no sign; his gaze didn't waver.

But Eli Horn didn't move in for a killing blow. Instead, his blade traced the edge of the torque. "And now it is clear to me," he said. "Why you brought her here. Why you follow this pathetic human girl."

The faery's eyes pulled up, looking at the Fomorian. "Just strike, if you will."

"What was the oath that made this?" Eli Horn demanded. Mr. Hallorman was silent. One clawed hand clamped down around Charlotte's throat. "Speak!"

Mr. Hallorman glanced back at Charlotte one time and then fixed his eyes on the Fomorian in front of him. "To protect her and her blood. Until the stars go out."

"Was it your oath?"

The faery hesitated. The fingers around Charlotte's throat tightened. She struggled helplessly, her body fighting as the air was crushed from it.

"No. My lord's. He made a gift of my service."

"The oath of a dead man, then." Eli Horn smiled then, a terrible expression. "What would you give me to remove this from you?"

Mr. Hallorman did not speak.

"I offer you mercy and you ignore me," the Fomorian said with mock suffering. "Fine, I shall—"

"It binds me to her," Mr. Hallorman said. "While she lives, you cannot kill me."

"But you'll die all the same."

"While I live, you cannot kill her," Mr. Hallorman tapped the torque. "You came here to open these barrows, did you not? To force open the gates that locked your miserable kind away in the world of the dead. Only a seer's blood will move those doors, one who walks in both worlds. But you can't have it, Fomorian. I assure you, even with your pet werewolf over there, I can make things very, very annoying for you before she bleeds her last."

"What do you want?"

"If you give me my life back, you'd be free to take hers."

Charlotte felt the bottom fall out of her world. Eli Horn seemed to notice, and chuckled. "One thing you should know about the ones your people call the fae is that they honor the letter, not the spirit, of their agreements," he told her, almost conversationally. "Glamour and lies. That's all they offer your kind. And Lukas, what are you doing? Get your hand off her throat before you choke her to death."

The pressure around her neck vanished, the hand releasing. Charlotte tumbled to the ground.

"I trusted you," Charlotte coughed, unable to believe what was happening here. "My grandmother trusted you!"

Mr. Hallorman did not meet her eye. "This oath between us was never my choice, Charlotte."

"Lukas, bring her," Eli Horn ordered, already laying a hand on Mr. Hallorman's shoulders and leading him away. "I want her to see this."

Thomas would have been hard-pressed to describe the journey through the darkness.

It seemed as though they passed through caves, but they were not like any caves he had ever heard of. Here, there were no stalactites and the smooth organic curves of water's slow, long craftsmanship, nor was there the working of man, brutal and obvious, with trusses to hold up the ceiling and rails for some mining cart to follow. It was more akin to being in a badger den, Thomas found himself thinking, the lair of something indifferent to design or sense, burrowing ever deeper from instinct alone.

But when he asked Andrew about this, the boy just shuddered.

"You would not like to meet the ones that made this place."

"I would," Thomas said. "Or at least, I would like to know the stories that were told of them once."

A growl beside him. Sirok, padding along in that wolf form, looking up at him. Even like this, Thomas could see the cavalry officer's disapproval in his eyes.

"Some things are best left forgotten," Andrew said, and led on.

Eventually, the utter blackness of the strange tunnels gave way to a gray glow, like the light of a cloudy day. Andrew stopped and sniffed the air. "Bah, close," he snarled, and stepped forward more cautiously.

The tunnel bent, then turned sharply upward. Thomas had to clamber up the rocks, rifle slung back across his shoulder. What would a gun do in Faeryland? Would it even work? Would the laws of physics hold out here, igniting gunpowder, propelling bullets? He had no idea. The stories didn't say. Even the heroes of legend who dared enter the Celtic Otherworld were often met with ruin, and Thomas was no warrior.

Andrew went up before them, as graceful and easy as a mountain goat. He disappeared over the lip of the incline by the time Thomas was only a few yards up. When he pulled himself up to the top, huffing from the effort, the dwergaz boy was nowhere to be seen. But unlike many other places in the tunnels, there was only one clear exit here: a narrow doorway of rock, beyond which was daylight.

A grunt. Panting. The Sirok-wolf was beside him, having just bounded up the rocks himself. Those gold eyes pinned Thomas for a moment, then the beast clacked its jaws and strode through the doorway. Thomas followed.

The world that waited for them aboveground made no more sense than the world below. They emerged into the occluded daylight in a place that was much the same as the one they had left. A mirror image of it, Thomas realized, as if they had gone into the cave and come right back out again. But there was little alive here, nothing but straggling weeds where the alpine meadow had been.

Out there, crouched where once there had been long grass but was now only dead weeds, was Andrew. He had his hand on a small bundle of what looked like rags at first, but coming closer, Thomas could see it was a body.

"Mama and my uncle argued when Lane Barton proposed the partnership between our clans," Andrew said quietly, regarding his brother's body. "Mama said that nothing good will come of partnering with a human. But my brothers and I were raised around humans, been with 'em all our lives. We didn't think anything of it, and Ove here especially was eager to make something for himself. He agreed to lead the expedition, show Mr. Barton's son the ropes out here in the mountains. Told Mama he could smell the gold." The dwergaz rubbed a hand over his beard. "Ove. He must have fled here, after they were ambushed out there. Dying alone in the realm of our ancestors." Andrew shook his head sadly but rose, unclipping the lantern from his belt, holding it out. "You'll need this to make your way home. Don't let the light go out. No power here will relight it, and you'll lose the trail anyway."

"Trail?" Thomas asked, but as soon as the little silver lantern was fully in his hand, he could see what Andrew meant. Behind them, glowing like mist backlit by the morning sun, was a ribbon of light. "Ah, I see it."

"Follow that back, and you'll emerge when and where you left."

The tales made no mention of such devices, Thomas thought, but then, he had taken a sidestep into other folkloric traditions here. It was a fascinating concept, and if he survived this, he would have to look into it more. But for the moment, he nodded to the boy. "Thank you. What about you?"

Andrew was gathering up his brother's body now, and didn't look at them. "Don't wander. Make for your woman and nothing else," he said, and raised the spare lantern.

"How will we find her?" Thomas asked.

But Andrew opened the glass. Blew out the lamp.

And then there was nobody else with them.

Cursing himself for not working out this most important of details prior to leaving the human world, Thomas looked at Sirok. "I don't suppose you can smell them, can you?" he asked. It felt strange to be talking to a wolf, and Thomas had to fight to remind himself that this was the same man he'd been riding with all this time. The wolf was the captain's true nature, it seemed, made manifest here in this strange place. Sirok just yawned, as unconcerned as any true animal would be. "Surely there's something you can do to at least signal yes or no."

The wolf huffed and got off his haunches, trotting forward.

With nothing else to do, Thomas followed.

Back in the San Juans, in the real world—the human world, Thomas admonished himself—the canyon tumbled down, steep and precipitous, but also green and alive. Here, the rock was bare and the ground dead, and even the geography seemed to give up, because where there should have been steep slopes and close peaks of other mountains, the canyon soon gave way to a flat, featureless plain.

It was an uncanny sight. The similarities of the place made the differences all the more stark, but it wasn't that that caused the hair on Thomas's arms to stand up. Down across that plain was a sense of unspeakable menace. He hesitated then, torn between his intentions and the reality facing him. Had he ever really believed that this place existed? Could he, a human with nothing more than a magic lantern and a pair of guns, really stand up to the power that lay in this place?

How was he going to prevail?

Some creatures, in the old stories, could be deterred with garlic or salt or holy water. Hurt by cold iron. Killed by silver. Thomas knew many of these stories, although he recognized now that his studies on European folklore were woefully insufficient.

He was a fool, coming here. The Fomorians had been like gods in their own time. But he would not simply abandon the woman with whom he had already come so far. And if his suppositions were true, if this was some kind of plot by Eli Horn to unleash a gang of Fomorians from prison or death or wherever they were, the results of not intervening might well be disastrous.

But this was an age of knowledge, of discovery, not superstition.

They would prevail.

Somehow.

The Sirok-wolf sat down next to him, panting like a nervous dog. Thomas wondered what he was thinking. Would he be taking this all in stride, as he had with so much so far? Or was Tir na nAill as much of a shock for him as well?

There was no way to know. If they made it out again, Thomas could ask him then. For the moment, he had to stay focused on the problem at hand. Somewhere out on that plain were the Roseingrave sisters.

Shouldering his rifle, Thomas started down the slope. Sirok followed. And out they passed into the barren wastes.

Chapter Forty

Charlotte was half carried, half dragged through the barrowland, past tombstones ever larger and more elaborate, until at last she was thrown down again, nearly dashing her head on the stones.

Stone.

Instead of that hard-packed dirt under her fingers, there was stone. Cut and dressed stone, a gray, gloomy granite that seemed quite out of place here. It was cold, so cold it burned, and she recoiled from it.

Behind her, she heard a sharp intake of breath. A chuckle.

"Yes, yes, so you have the wit to recognize it, at least," Eli Horn said.

In front of her was a mausoleum. It was of the same gray granite, formed into a structure eerily similar to anything one might find out in the human world. Mr. Leighton had shown Charlotte a few of his drawings of ancient British monuments. Skye. The Hebrides. Newgrange. She had expected that, not this strange parody of a modern crypt. It could have been any monument in any cemetery.

Except that it was not.

It was pitted and worn, aged a thousand years, and the huge wrought iron gates were chained and locked with a massive padlock.

The outlaw brushed that lock with his fingers now. "A fine piece of craftsmanship," he said coolly. "Wouldn't you agree, faery?"

Mr. Hallorman shrugged. "As the lid for the box of maggots your kin have no doubt become, I suppose it isn't bad."

Eli Horn whirled around, and his long duster swirled behind him like smoke. "Mock me, and I just might risk killing you." The Fomorian laid both hands on the door now, tapping with the tips of his fingers. "This is the way. This is the door that must be opened. After the Tuatha Dé Danann achieved their craven, cowardly victory over my people, they raised a great barrow over the slain and threw the still-living in after them, thinking that would be enough to kill them, too."

"It should have been."

"Mind your tongue, hill-dweller," the outlaw Horn snapped. "You have no idea what it was like! Banished, first from my rightful place in Tir na nAill, and then from Ireland entirely. I despaired, cut off from the land, from my true nature, but I endured. Do you know what drove me, hill-dweller?"

Mr. Hallorman shrugged. "Does it matter?"

"Of course!" Horn snapped, pacing now. "All things change, all things... decay. Humans used to see the world so differently." He chuckled. "The storm that kills you or the disease that wears you away is no longer evil, but merely a mystery to be solved. Destruction has no moral value but has been recast as a phenomenon that is inevitable, undeniable. Entropy, I think they call it. A force that cannot be destroyed. That shall always win in the end. Look what this shift in understanding has done to this place!" He chuckled. "And yet, something in these wretched creatures still understands. enough for a few paths to still be open between our world and theirs. Like you, woman. What do you believe in?"

Charlotte's mouth was dry. She couldn't answer.

But Mr. Hallorman had his arms crossed, considering those words. "You were all executed. But if humans believe that the forces you represent are eternal..."

"Then the difference between our lives and our deaths is gone. And beyond this door is no barrow of broken bodies, but an endless night filled with ceaseless rage," the outlaw Horn said, and tapped on the gate. "Bring her, Lukas."

Charlotte looked to Mr. Hallorman in disbelief, unsure of what was happening here, pleading silently with him to stop it.

He did not.

Charlotte was grabbed then, brought up to the doors. The wolfman holding her was fantastically strong and she yelped in pain. Eli Horn took out a knife, small and of strange design, and sliced it across her palm.

"Just a bit, for now," he said, almost gently. "Just enough to drag your guardian into the place where the stars themselves have died."

And with that, Eli Horn pressed her bleeding hand to the gates.

What Charlotte saw next, she didn't understand.

The world was gone. The tombstones, the mausoleum, the leaden, lightless sky. Around her now was nothing.

There was no ground under her feet. Nothing to hold her down. No light, no sound, no scent. Her clothing and hair drifted around her. She floated in a formless void, a void that even now, she could feel pulling at her, tugging at her sanity, at her body, some great malice threatening to unmake her very—

And then, as suddenly as it had started, it was over, and Charlotte was crumbling to the ground, cradling her cut hand. It had scabbed over. How long had she been in that place? How long had she been standing here? She was exhausted.

Eli Horn knelt down beside her, hand on her back. "You still believe in evil, don't you? You've seen it. You might not believe in anything else, but you believe in that."

She shuddered, but didn't have the strength to throw him off. "What is that place?"

"The end of all things," he said seriously, no hint of his earlier gloating on his face. "The emptiness your people are beginning to believe in, my little fáith."

Charlotte heard a groan. Mr. Hallorman, she realized. He was collapsed against the mausoleum wall a few paces away from her, sprawled on the ground like a marionette with its strings cut. Eli Horn left her and walked over to him.

"Are you still alive?" the outlaw asked, prodding Mr. Hallorman with the tip of a boot. "Until the stars go out, yes?" Mr. Hallorman groaned. The golden torque around his neck had tarnished, dulled to black. Eli Horn grabbed it now, hauling the faery up. His feet dangled. Eli Horn narrowed his eyes. "Answer me!"

"You...did not tell me...what...what that would require," Mr. Hallorman said, his words thick and ungainly. His teeth were streaked with red. He had bitten through his tongue, Charlotte realized with horror. The flesh was still knitting back together.

Eli Horn laughed and then crushed the torque with one hand. It crumbled into dust, falling away again, and Mr. Hallorman fell once more, unable to stand. Charlotte stared at him mutely, rage warring with sympathy in her heart; he was suffering, that much was clear from his expression. For a moment, their eyes locked, and it seemed like he was trying to tell her something.

But then he smiled, scrubbing both hands across his face. "Ahh. That's been a long time coming."

Eli Horn laughed. "Indeed. Lukas, remove her, please." And he held out a hand to Mr. Hallorman. "Come, come, don't sit there looking as if someone has just slaughtered all your cattle. This is a time for rejoicing. A homecoming for both of us. Freedom from the restrictions laid on us for so long, imprisoned in the human world. Won't you take a drink with me?"

Charlotte watched in despair as her once guardian allowed himself to be pulled to his feet. "I think I shall," he said, and the words were like a hammer blow to her heart.

Celeste wasn't sure how long she lay there.

Her body was a mass of agony. Her blood was on fire.

Mr. Abbitt, or whatever that wolf-thing was, had not been gentle with her. He had clamped his jaws into her shoulder and dragged her off, across the rocky ground of this strange place. His bite was excruciating, grinding down into sinew and bone.

She wasn't sure how far he'd taken her before he let go. He'd licked the wound. That she remembered clearly. Celeste had thrashed out at him, kicking and screaming, half in rage, half in pain, but the wolf-thing had ignored it all.

Considered her for a moment with those gold eyes.

Before latching its huge jaws around her neck.

Celeste had been convinced she was going to die. The pain in her shoulder was nothing compared to that. Teeth punctured skin, arteries, blood pouring out. Her breath came wrong; her throat had been torn open. She remembered desperately trying to hold it shut, but her hands wouldn't work right. Her heart beat wrong. Everything ceased to exist but the pain.

Black dreams overtook her. Unwelcome dreams, memories that weren't hers, of padding through dark forests under moonless lights, the world bright and bare before her, the smell of some scared thing huddled in the underbrush, terrified.

Terrified of *her*.

Celeste had not expected to wake up. But eventually more mundane sensations reasserted themselves. Dirt under her fingers. Rock against her head. The taste of blood in her mouth.

And a voice she had never thought she would hear again.

"Celeste! Celeste, oh my lord... Celeste! Please wake up!"

Celeste was so weary, so tired. She just wanted to sleep. Even in those black dreams, there was some form of rest. Waking would be agony enough, she knew. Waking with her sister there would be even worse. Celeste wouldn't have put it past Charlotte to come all the way here just to tell her *I told you so*. And yet...

"Celeste, please, can you hear me?"

With great effort, Celeste forced her eyelids open. They felt wrong, as if her own eyes had been torn out, replaced with something that didn't fit. But they worked, at least, and the scene they revealed almost stopped her heart all over again.

It was indeed Charlotte there with her. Charlotte, on her knees beside her, daubing Celeste's head with a strip of fabric torn from a petticoat. The cloth was soaked red already. There were a few similar strips cast off on the ground, already crumbling to dust, Celeste noticed dumbly.

"Oh, thank god," she heard her sister breathe. "You are alive."

"Maybe not for long," Celeste tried to say. Surely the damage to her throat meant she only had moments left and likely no voice left. But the words came out, pure and true. If anything, that just scared her more.

"Don't talk like that," Charlotte snapped, wiping Celeste's face. "Tell me, what happened to you? All this blood and not a scratch on you."

Not a scratch? Automatically, Celeste's hand went her throat. She froze when she felt what was there. Nothing. Unbroken, unblemished skin. The realization rocked her back, causing her to pull away from her sister's touch.

Charlotte stopped, sitting back again. For a moment, Celeste thought that meant her sister was leaving and grabbed for her. Her hand caught Charlotte's wrist, lightning fast, faster than she had meant to move or even thought she could, and she didn't miss the way her sister's eyes widened.

There was a scent in the air. Fear. Charlotte was afraid.

Celeste let go, forcing her hand to open, and looked away. "Don't go," she said.

"Where could I go? We are both prisoners of Eli Horn now, I fear."

There was an accusation in her sister's words, and hesitation as well, as if she didn't want to hurt Celeste's feelings by bringing up the man she had thought...the man she had hoped... Celeste shook her head. "Bastard," Celeste muttered.

"Celeste!"

"What? He's a monster," she said, and finally dared to look her sister in the face. As she did so, all the emotion of the past few days finally caught up with her. A great wave of shame came over her, and she burst into tears.

Charlotte caught Celeste as she pitched forward, hugging her tight. Celeste clung on, desperate as she had been at four when Papa hadn't come home, at six when Grandmother died, as she had been a few months ago, when Mama had left them, too. Charlotte's hands twisted in the back of Celeste's ruined shirt, holding on, as it all spilled out.

Finally, the storm passed, and Celeste felt empty, but better, and when Charlotte put a hand on Celeste's shoulder, Celeste laid her own hand over it.

"What happened?" Charlotte asked.

"Mr. Abbitt, he..." Celeste began, but just shook her head. "I don't know."

"Is he the wolfman with the Fomorian?"

"Fomorian?"

"Eli Horn. But I don't think his real name is Eli Horn," Charlotte said. "Is it, sister?"

Celeste felt the bitterness in her sister's words. A fresh wave of shame passed through her. Eli Horn's stories had been beautiful. Lies, but beautiful lies. Was that why she hadn't seen the ugly truth underneath? Or had she just wanted to believe it? "I'm not looking for a fight about this."

"Really?" Charlotte asked wearily. "All we do is fight these days."

Celeste closed her eyes then. "What is going on here, Charlotte? Eli Horn, or whoever he is, said he needed my help to open some kind of door, but when we got here, he...he got angry. Started saying I was false. He said he needed you."

"He needs a woman with the Sight, it seems," Charlotte said stiffly. "He used a word with me. Umm..."

"Fáith," Celeste replied, her momentary calm already subsiding, eaten away by fresh anger. "So you actually do have the Sight, then?"

"Celeste—"

"Can you see the dead?" Celeste asked. "Truly?"

It was a long time before Charlotte answered. "Yes," she finally said. "Or at least, I see what's left behind. The shades of people with their heads blown open or their faces mottled red from disease or so much water in their bloated lungs that they can't speak. And...other things, too."

"Things like Eli Horn?"

"Things like him."

"Are there a lot of them, everywhere?"

Charlotte just shook her head, turning her eyes to the sky above. "I don't know. I've never wanted to see them. I never wanted to know about them. I never wanted you to know about them." Charlotte replied, and all the fight seemed to be gone from her now. She slumped back against a headstone. "But perhaps if I had told you, none of this would have happened. Perhaps if I had, you wouldn't hate me now."

Celeste bit her lip. "I have never hated you."

"Maybe you should. Look at what I've brought down on us."

For a little while, the sisters sat in silence. Then Celeste snapped her fingers. "If Grandmother's stories are all real, or some of them are at least, what about the family guardian? Isn't there some sort of faery who's bound to us?"

"I came here with him," Charlotte said, the words grudging. "He betrayed me."

"How is that possible? Grandmother always said—"

"We can't look to him. It's on us to figure out a way out of here now," Charlotte said grimly. "But how does one escape from the Otherworld?"

Celeste didn't have an answer for that, and before she could stop herself, the most ridiculous thing came out of her mouth. "I wish Mama was here," she said, and leaned into Charlotte's shoulder.

But Charlotte, for once, didn't snap at her for mentioning their mother. Instead, she laid an arm around Celeste's shoulders. "Me too."

CHAPTER FORTY-ONE

The Fomorian who the humans called Eli Horn couldn't quite identify when his plans had gone awry.

He had had much time since his exile to ponder this question, and he had never been able to determine the answer. There was no single moment, no one action, to which he could trace the ruin of his people and their kingdom. He had made mistakes, of course—trusting Bres and Balor to handle the Tuatha Dé Danann on their own had been a poor plan, in retrospect—but it was not his fault.

Everyone around him had failed him. Everyone around him always failed him. Weak. Pathetic.

Just like this creature he'd found, this hill-dweller. Weak and pathetic, so eager to betray that which had been entrusted to him by his liege lord, long ago.

But then, all things failed.

Only the darkness endured forever.

That was the way of Domnu.

"What did you think of it?" the Fomorian asked conversationally, genuinely curious, as he led the way away from the mausoleum. The human fáith had been dragged off already. Less spirited than her sister, which was a disappointment. But then, humans so often were disappointing. He would be glad to be rid of his dependence on them. "Our true domain?"

The hill-dweller, walking next to him through the thicket of tombstones, shook his head. "Is that the future that awaits all things?"

"It awaits us," the Fomorian said seriously. "Your kind? You will die when the sun finally eats this world. We, on the other hand, shall endure forever."

"Good," the hill-dweller said. "I would not like to endure any amount of time in that darkness."

"Perhaps we understand each other a little better now," the Fomorian replied.

"Perhaps," the other replied, obviously cautious, and eyed him. Sizing him up. The evaluation of a lesser creature. What did it matter? The Fomorian paid him no heed, glancing back at the mausoleum instead.

What had he told the false fáith, the younger sister? That eventually, the human world would drift too far in its understanding of the old ways for any there to take the path through the mists back here. That time was coming. That time was coming soon.

Humans were such fools.

Just because they were losing the knowledge to reach Tir na nAill, didn't mean Tir na nAill couldn't reach back. All their vaunted modern wisdom did was leave them vulnerable to the ancient things lurking on the edges of their dreams.

"Elatha."

The statement brought the Fomorian out of his reverie. "What did you say?"

"Four escaped the slaughter," the faery said casually. "Nemain's name I saw on a tombstone, so I assume she succumbed to her rage and died out in the human world somewhere. Balor was slain by the Morrigan after the banishment and cast back here. It is possible you are Bres, but you don't seem like an idiot. Which makes you the last of the banished. The father of Bres, like it says in your incantation. Elatha mac Delbaith."

The Fomorian held back his snarl. His name, his rightful name. He had worn so many others in the years between Mag Tuired and now, he had almost forgotten his true name. To hear it from the lips of some hill-dweller, this faery, one of the debased and degraded descendants of his archenemies, seemed the greatest of insults.

This creature was barely worth Elatha's time, and something he would have killed out of hand under any other circumstance, the way one might swat away a mosquito.

But all things had their uses.

"Lord," he said.

"Excuse me?"

"I would have you refer to me properly, as is my right as the once and future king of all of Tir na nAill."

"Lord, then. As you will it. Lord." The faery smiled as he spoke the words, mocking and sarcastic.

Elatha pictured himself killing this one. Perhaps he would, after the barrows were opened and the fáith dispatched. Or maybe he would make her watch. A shame she had to die so quickly. He had such torments he could visit on both her and her sister. They deserved nothing else.

Maybe he'd kill the sister first, the one who had lied to him.

Yes, Elatha decided. Yes, that would be fitting. Slow, this could be now. Slow, now that he was back in this place with no time.

He led the faery on.

Back in the glory days, when the humans were inconsequential and the Tuatha Dé Danann had accepted the primacy of the Fomorians, they had built many fine things together. Towers, castles, grand fortifications.

But the same forces that had made it possible for him to step back into Tir na nAill had changed it, and his own palace was no exception.

Instead of the old halls woven from living willow and oak, or the glittering heights of caves carved out by water and wind, Elatha's abode here was marked by tombstones that stood closely together like the upright walls of some ruined hunting lodge.

By his will, and his alone, the space was furnished and set as if for a great feast. Huge, hewn ash tables were here, the finest of silver knives and gold goblets laid out. Of course, it was not new, not fresh in the way that the Tuatha Dé Danann had always insisted on. The tables were half-eaten with rot, the coverings of the chairs threadbare and musty, the goblets tarnished, the knives bent. The space was not huge, but it was endless, with enough room for all of his clan to gather and enjoy themselves, once they had satisfied themselves elsewhere.

The faery whose name was not actually Hallorman looked past him, at the fine tapestries and laden tables between the barrow stones. "Who else are we expecting?"

"My entire clan. The fáith's death will open the way for them, and then they shall glut themselves as they will. I think they will be quite pleased with the human world in these days." Elatha smiled, thinking about it. "Not even we had invented something quite as devilish as TNT."

"Is that your plan?" the faery asked.

"My plan? What plan?" Elatha said, and bade the faery sit down. A flagon of mead appeared next to them, along with filled goblets. "My brothers and sisters shall indulge themselves as they will. What need is there for plans?"

"Probably wise, considering how poorly your plans went before Mag Tuired." The hill-dweller—insolent creature—sniffed as he picked up his drink. In his hand, the metal of the goblet seemed a little less tarnished. "At least this appears to be in good condition, milord."

"Good condition?" Elatha spread an arm around. "That was ever the problem with your forebears. They spoke of accepting change, and yet, they wanted nothing to ever decay. But a thing is decaying from the moment it comes into being, and denying the beauty in that is to deny yourself the true pleasures of life."

The hill-dweller shrugged and sipped his mead. "That was all before my time."

"Don't worry. I will show you. We will all show you how it is truly meant to be."

"Then you aim to conquer the human world?"

"Conquer?" Elatha scoffed. "One does not conquer that which was wrongfully taken from him. My banishment is ended. I have reclaimed my power. And soon enough, I shall reclaim what is mine. My kingdom. Nothing more, nothing less."

"What, Ireland?"

"I rather like this country. Unsettled and violent," Elatha replied. "Quite enjoyable when the damn cavalry isn't insistent on ruining the fun."

"And how do you plan on making this conquest? This is the only gateway I've seen in this entire state," the hill-dweller said, "and it is far from any major human settlements."

Elatha picked idly at a roast seabird that he had commanded for himself. Food tasted better here. No longer of ash, falling apart even as he ate. This was tender and succulent, the tough flesh made soft by rot. He found the sustenance wonderful; it had been exhausting, freeing the faery, more so than he would have thought. A foolish thing to do, perhaps, but a temporary weariness to neutralize the only thing here that might have threatened him was well worth the effort. And he had time enough to rest. He had all the time the world. "Anything I've sunk my influence into has worn the veil between the worlds thin. It is from there that we will emerge."

"Like that drill, rotting the very earth in Leadville?"

Elatha smiled, thinking of it, sucking meat and feathers free of the bone. "Yes, exactly. Won't they enjoy the revelation?"

The faery smiled right along with him. "So why do you wait here? Open the barrow."

"Are you truly that eager to see the end of the world?"

"I am eager to see her die."

"Would you like to watch while I kill her?"

"Nothing would bring me greater pleasure."

"Then watch it with me you shall," Elatha said, and tore off the bird's beak, crunching down on it thoughtfully.

Oh, yes. He would remind the humans of the old ways. He would show it to them at the tip of his sword, the edge of his knife. He would show them the truth they seemed so desperate to believe.

Everything they loved, everything they thought eternal, was an error. A temporary misalignment of the universe. The true nature of all things was the darkness, the equilibrium of nothingness.

The purpose of life was to end.

What fun it would be.

CHAPTER FORTY-TWO

Charlotte wasn't sure how long she and Celeste sat there together in silence. It was disquieting in a way; they had been quarreling so much the last few months that to have Celeste looking to her for comfort seemed strange. But then, Charlotte told herself, look where they were.

She found herself fingering the little pocket watch that hung from her chatelaine. Flipping open the cover now, Charlotte could see the hands ticking away unevenly, no rhyme or reason to their movements. While she was watching, the hour hand moved backwards.

With a sigh, she was thinking of putting it away again when she remembered that comment from Mr. Hallorman. A seamstress having the right tool for the job, or something like that. Seized by a sudden thought, Charlotte drew the chatelaine out fully.

She took stock of her chatelaine. All her little accessories were still there. The pocket watch. The needle case. Her thimble cage. The little purse, now empty, only ever big enough for a few coins anyway. A brass key taken from their old house after Papa died at sea and Mama had been forced to sell it, a key that now opened nothing. The empty chain, the chain that Charlotte had always left empty because Grandmother had left it empty.

And her scissors.

Her little sterling silver scissors, only big enough for snipping threads in whatever project she happened to be working on.

But they had an edge to them. And silver was supposed to be anathema to all evil things, wasn't it? Iron hadn't worked on Eli Horn, but perhaps silver would.

Maybe that would be enough. It would have to be enough.

A growl and a moan brought her attention up.

It was that beast again, the one that had brought her here, the one that had torn her sister apart.

He was monstrous, but she realized with a start that she could see the man in the core of him, the human man who had been bitten against his will, taken and twisted into a thing that hunted the innocent in the light of the full moon. He had been driven from his home, his family all forsaking him. Haunted by his own nature but unable to escape it, he had fled. Elatha had found him in the darkness, made promises, given him a chance at dignity and purpose again.

She could see it, but she could do nothing about it. Perhaps he had been innocent once, but he had beaten that same infection deep into her sister. Charlotte could find no sympathy in her heart for him now.

"Charlotte," Celeste whispered, fear in her voice.

Charlotte swallowed her own terror down. "I won't die on my knees," she said, and stood up, looking at the creature in front of her. "Leave my sister alone," she said, and slipped the scissors up inside her sleeve, "and I'll come."

A horrible smile split the twisted wolf's head of the creature. He grabbed them both and pulled them away.

Thomas and Captain Sirok soon entered a dusty graveyard of bizarre scale, one that seemed to be decaying back into the hardpan on which it sat. The place bore no resemblance to any ruin that Thomas knew from his own country, a question that tugged at his mind. But they had a mission here, and whatever the place appeared to be, rescuing the Roseingrave sisters and thwarting this creature's plans was the more important objective.

On the weather-eaten stone, however, was carved more script. More ogham lines. Thomas didn't have time to stop but he found he could read the names, the words coming now with strange familiarity. He recognized some. Figures from *The Book of Invasions*, Fomorians all.

Cethlinn, She of the Poison.

Ochtriallach, Son of Indech King of All.

Nemain, the War-Wife.

And on and on.

Looking down, Thomas realized the light from the lantern had dimmed, as if it too was in fear of discovery. When he looked back at their path, the ribbon of light was barely visible.

And then, noise. Voices. The Sirok-wolf pricked up its ears, growling, the hair standing up along its spine.

"Shh," Thomas admonished, but the wolf was already moving. Cursing under his breath, Thomas followed.

They came to a place where the headstones were larger and denser, clustered around the base of a hill. Low though it was, it was the only such feature Thomas had seen since leaving the portal's canyon, and it seemed as high as the moon. In front of it, leading back into it, was as fine a mausoleum as could be found in London's best cemeteries, and quite a bit larger. They took refuge behind a large headstone a little way away, peeking around the edge at the source of the voices.

There, Thomas saw. There were the sisters. Some huge, ungainly thing had them both. The elder Miss Roseingrave was already on the ground, and as Thomas watched, it threw down the other. The younger Miss Roseingrave hit the ground hard. Reaching a hand out to her sister, the elder Miss Roseingrave glared at Eli Horn. "You have me. At least let her go!"

"No," he said. "For her lies? She gets to watch you die."

Celeste screamed then and lashed out, but the wolfman caught her and flung her back down, one clawlike foot on her back.

"Hallorman," Thomas muttered, taking in the scene. "Where is he? Why isn't he stopping this?"

The Sirok-wolf growled again, the sound low. It was bloody inconvenient that the captain couldn't talk in this form, Thomas thought to himself. But the wolf's gaze was trained on something, and with a start, Thomas saw it, too.

Mr. Hallorman was indeed there, leaning back against one of the gravestones with a smile on his face, arms crossed, nonchalant.

"Some guardian you are," the elder Miss Roseingrave said, and even from his vantage point, Thomas could see that she was furious.

Mr. Hallorman regarded her coldly. "Two millennia of following your family like a kicked dog is enough, I daresay."

"Did you not see what nightmares wait in there?" she demanded, casting a hand back toward the mausoleum.

He shook his head. "Charlotte, my dear Charlotte, I did say we shouldn't have come."

"And yet, you did. I am thankful for it. You have no idea how long I have waited for this," Eli Horn said, circling the elder Miss Roseingrave. "But the great goddess Dea Domnu rewards patience, now doesn't she?" Miss Roseingrave very deliberately turned her head away. He grabbed her by the hair, forcing her head back cruelly. "Doesn't she?"

Suddenly incensed, Thomas almost stepped out from behind the headstone, only to have huge teeth clamp down around his ankle. It wasn't a hard bite—enough to warn, but not to break the skin—but he still glared back at the Sirok-wolf. Despite the cavalry officer's much-changed appearance, there was still something human in his eyes. Something clear enough to read.

Wait.

"I don't know what you're talking about," Miss Roseingrave was saying.

"Your kind has forgotten the old ways," he growled, and knelt down in front of her. "Don't worry. You'll learn soon enough. You'll remember. You all will. Now stand up, eldest daughter of Aine."

She shook his hand off. "I won't help you."

"Fortunately," he said, and pulled a knife from his belt, "your consent is not required."

Thomas aimed his rifle. Captain Sirok tensed. Miss Celeste Roseingrave, sprawled out flat on the ground next to her sister with the creature's foot on her back, glared upwards. Everything was still for a moment.

And then Thomas saw it. Something long and silver in Charlotte's hand. With an angry cry, she drove it toward the Fomorian...

... only to have her wrist caught by Mr. Hallorman. Miss Roseingrave cried out in agony, and the thing fell from her hand. Scissors, Thomas could see. They had almost looked like a hunting knife in her hand, but there, on the ground, they looked tiny. He glanced back at Sirok. The wolf shook its head. Gritting his teeth, Thomas readied his rifle.

"Charlotte, my darling, where were you hiding those?" the faery asked, retrieving the things from the ground. Thomas could have asked the same question; the scissors were ten inches long now, and wickedly sharp-looking. Miss Roseingrave didn't answer, except to spit in his face. He wiped it away, then handed the sewing implement to Eli Horn. "Looks like she had a surprise, even from me, lord."

The Fomorian took the things contemptuously. "Silver," he said, and shook his head. In his grip, the bright metal began to tarnish. "You'd need more than this to hurt me."

Then Mr. Hallorman smiled. "I have an amusing idea, milord," he said cheerfully, and leaned in, whispering something in Eli Horn's ear. Thomas couldn't hear it from his position, but he saw Miss Roseingrave's face fall. She started backing away as best she could, Eli Horn following. Her back hit the mausoleum.

What would work? What would stop this thing? Thomas wracked his brain, looking for the answer. What scrap of knowledge, what piece of trivia, had he collected over the years that would help him now? There was something, there had to be something...

Eli Horn brandished the scissors. "Celebrate, daughter of Aine, child of the old ways," he said, and grabbed her wrist. She cried out as he wrenched her arm out, twisting it. "Your death will bring back that which should have always been. Your blood opens our way back into your world. And to be killed by your own weapon, betrayed by your own bodyguard. What wonderful irony, don't you think?"

Silver. Iron. Lead. Thomas didn't know what would hurt this thing, what would kill it, but he realized then that it didn't matter. He was getting lost in the details. Fomorians could bleed. Fomorians could die. The stories all said so. The evidence was all around him. Thomas only had one weapon at his disposal. It would either be enough, or it wouldn't, but he couldn't live with himself if he didn't try.

"Enough," Thomas muttered, and pulled the trigger.

The moment her own scissors buried themselves in her arm, Charlotte was certain she was going to die. It was pain unlike anything she'd ever felt before, the silver blade tearing through sleeve and skin alike, and yet...

There was a gunshot. A howl of frustration from Eli Horn, and his hand left the scissors.

"You dare challenge me in my domain?!" the Fomorian roared. "Lukas!"

Dazed, Charlotte looked up, just in time to see Thomas Leighton fire off a second shot. In time to see the wolfman leave her sister, bounding up over her toward the headstone where the Englishman had concealed himself. In time to see something dark and massive bowl into the wolfman, howling as it did so.

Eli Horn's lip curled in disgust as his hand clutched at a bleeding wound in his shoulder. "Lead bullets?" he sneered. "It'll take more than that to kill me!"

There were more shots. More howling, loud and close enough to curdle the blood. But Charlotte didn't have time to think about any of it. She felt her sister's hand on her arm, saw the fear in Celeste's eyes, but couldn't do anything.

She was bleeding, red welling up around the tips of the scissors, and as the first drop hit the ground there came the sound of shearing metal.

The gates on the mausoleum were opening.

But barely had she time to take this in when a hand grabbed her by the throat, lifting her clean off her feet. Eli Horn, a half dozen holes punched through his chest and arms, and inside of him was darkness. A bloated, hungry, gaping darkness, patient and wicked, the end of all things.

"I had thought to let you bleed out slowly," he hissed, and pulled out the scissors. Blood poured from the wound. Charlotte screamed in pain. He flicked open the scissors, revealing a razor-sharp blade. "But I think I'll just end you instead. Don't worry, little fáith, it'll be quicker than the death I deal your world."

Celeste was screaming at her now. Mr. Leighton was running. Charlotte couldn't move, couldn't breathe. All she could do was stare in horror, transfixed by what she saw echoed in Eli Horn's eyes.

But the killing strike never fell.

Instead, the strength in that hand failed, fingers releasing her, and she dropped to the ground.

Mr. Hallorman had just buried one blade of the scissors in Eli Horn's neck, all the way up to the handle, pinning him to the gate of the crypt through the meat of his throat. Something inside him rattled and screamed.

"Go," the faery said in a low voice, pulling her roughly to her feet, the other half of the scissors held out between them and the struggling Fomorian, grown huge now, large as a sword. "Back to the portal. Back to your realm. Nothing I do may heal you here."

Mr. Leighton and Celeste were both there now, Mr. Leighton helping to hold her up, Celeste desperately wrapping Charlotte's arm with the remains of her own shirt. Charlotte realized how very cold she was starting to feel.

"Get her there before she bleeds out," Mr. Hallorman said, and Charlotte realized he was talking to Mr. Leighton, "or everything's lost."

"You son of a bitch," Mr. Leighton growled. "You've killed her."

"It was the only way."

"Why?" she asked, dazed.

The faery smiled grimly at her. "Glamour and lies, Charlotte."

"What?"

Behind him, Eli Horn was struggling with the blade buried in his throat, even as darkness continued to pour from the gates, like water leaking from a pierced bottle.

"Run!" Mr. Hallorman snapped and turned around to face the gate.

Celeste grabbed at Charlotte's hand, pulling hard. Her sister's touch brought Charlotte back to herself, and with nothing more than a nod, she turned and fled.

As darkness poured from the crypt, the small group of humans fled through the graveyard.

Thomas had dropped his rifle as the wolfman rushed them. The damned thing had rusted to nothing almost as soon as it had hit the ground. All he had left was his Colt revolver and a pocketful of ammunition.

Ammunition that—for the moment anyway—seemed to be working.

"Mr.... Leighton!" Miss Roseingrave gasped, and her younger sister screamed.

Behind them, leaping over one of the tombstones, was a shape, all shadows and claws, chortling as it fell on them. Without even thinking, Thomas brought up his gun and fired. The shape fell back, blown apart like smoke in the wind. On they ran.

"What was that?" the younger Miss Roseingrave asked. She was wearing nothing but a bloodstained corset cover and a pair of men's pants, and her hair had fallen down around her shoulders. She seemed in little better shape than her older sister, but at least she wasn't wounded.

"A Fomorian, I think!" Thomas said. The light twisted through a set of smaller tombstones, turning sharply. Behind them, the strange, gray half-light of the Faeryland sky was being consumed by black. "They must be escaping."

"Fomorian?" she demanded. "Escaping?"

Thomas was about to answer her, but a bloodcurdling howl from his left stopped him in his tracks. And a good thing, too, because no sooner had they stopped than a dark shape barreled in front of them.

"Lukas," he heard the younger Miss Roseingrave breathe.

Thomas found himself staring up into a pair of pitiless red eyes. The wolfman stood seven feet tall if he was an inch, and when he opened his mouth to roar at them, his breath smelled like a slaughterhouse. The fur of his clawlike hands was matted in blood, and he was bleeding from a dozen serious-looking wounds.

But before Thomas could so much as bring up his gun, another shape careened back out of the forest of gravestones on all fours, knocking the wolfman to the ground. A brief, bloody struggle ensued, blood and fur flying everywhere. He watched in mute horror as Captain Sirok leapt on top of his enemy and sank his massive jaws into the back of the wolfman's head, right where skull met spine.

The body went limp, and Sirok stood over him, howling.

The younger Miss Roseingrave whined and turned her face into Thomas's shoulder. He wasn't sure if the elder sister even noticed; her head was bowed, her eyes closed.

But the Sirok-wolf looked at Thomas and bounded over them, leaping at something else coming in behind them.

Thomas needed no more encouragement. He gathered the two women and ran, finally clearing the tombstones and heading out into the barren waste. Thomas, for one wild moment, recalled the dead patch in Mr. Barton's garden. Would the Fomorians make all the world like this if they left this place? Would everything, everywhere, die?

But then Miss Charlotte Roseingrave's hand pulled at his shirt, her strength failing her, the woman stumbling so badly that she almost pulled him down with her. Thomas caught her with both arms, keeping her from falling.

"I can't," she panted, eyes half-closed. "I'm sorry, I can't."

"Charlotte, get up!" the younger Miss Roseingrave snapped, glancing back toward the darkness, spreading like a storm across the strange lightless sky. "Get up!"

She was too pale, had lost too much blood. Thomas thrust his Colt at the younger sister and gathered the elder up into his arms.

They had to get her out of here.

CHAPTER FORTY-THREE

Lane Barton was dreaming.

At least, it felt like a dream, everything cast in extreme clarity, like he was watching the entire world through the lens of a jeweler's glass. The sound of leaves brushing against the window of the drawing room, the tink of fine cut crystal on wood as he set his drink down on a table so polished it reflected the firelight, the feel of his cambric nightgown, soft as the fleeting clouds in the moonless night beyond.

He was talking to somebody. Somebody he hadn't seen in a while. Mikael Dvalinsson, his old business partner, the one who had cut ties with him over the San Juan mining expedition, the one who had disapproved of the entire scheme with Madame Aine, the one who—

Why was he here?

A dream, Barton told himself. This was all just a dream.

"Godsdamn it, would you focus?" the man growled, pacing about on Barton's fine Persian rug with muddy boots. "Do you not see what's going on here?"

They were talking about something. But what? "I don't like your tone, Dvalinsson."

"And I don't like your taste in liquor, but we all have our problems tonight, don't we, Barton?" the short, stocky man snapped, draining his drink despite the protestations. He went to the sideboard to pour himself another. "I've heard about what you brought here. Why did you keep the damned thing?"

And now Barton remembered. They'd had this conversation months ago when the rock drill had shown back up, tied to the saddle of that mule, the one that had dropped dead in his garden. They'd fought then, Barton and Dvalinsson had, and after that night, his former business partner had never set foot in his house again.

But it had to be a dream. Dvalinsson was different now. His presence seemed to fill the entire room, that feeling of excitement and dread one had when deep underground, the claustrophobia, the sense of time and space ceasing to exist. Everything about him was terrifyingly inhuman.

"I'm not having this conversation again about the drill," Barton sneered, still looking out the window. Had it been a moonless night, all those months ago? "A few days from now, you tell me about the iron ring. And look, it's working, isn't it?"

Dvalinsson stared at him. "Has your head gone soft, Barton? It's the end of the month of October, a time your people used to fear, if I recall, and you've got a godsdamn piece of hell in your garden. Have you even seen what's going on out there tonight?"

A wave of unease washed over Barton. This certainly was not the conversation they'd had before. "What are you talking about?"

"You've damned the entire town. It's a weak point in the fabric of reality. Don't you get it? Like lava pushing its way to the surface. It's opened up a path for them, and now that they're out, they're all gonna leak through," Dvalinsson said, and looked out the window, shaking his head. "Although maybe it don't matter where it starts. There won't be any hiding anywhere when they break through proper."

Barton looked out.

The drink fell from his hand, crystal shattering on the imported parquet floor.

There was a monster standing in his garden.

Elatha was not pleased.

This was not how all his plans were supposed to go.

He struggled against the scissors buried in his neck. They burned, oh, by the darkness, how they burned. The faery had struck true. The tip was buried deep in the stone of the barrow gateway and would not come free. Silver. They were only plated. Silver-plated steel. And now, fully in possession of himself once again, Elatha's old powers came with the old weaknesses.

Nor would his kin come to his aid. Ingrates, fools. The smaller ones grasped and clawed at him in their haste to get out of the gate. In their eagerness, they threw themselves at the hill-dweller standing before them. A pale echo of their ancient enemy. The first chance to kill after being locked away in the final darkness where even light itself had been murdered.

The faery was wielding his makeshift sword like a madman, laughing as he cut down one after another, grappling and punching, kicking and slicing. The edges of his blade glittered with fell silver light, even as his hands smoked from the contact with the underlying metal.

Elatha couldn't talk, couldn't call, couldn't warn or give orders or tell the damn fools to pull back, to go after the main target. The scissors had severed his windpipe. But he would heal from this all too quickly, once he got the accursed metal out of his neck.

But the fáith's wound was only as good as the weapon that made it. Only here were the scissors something long and brutal enough to do what they were doing to him. Back in the human world, her body would recognize the wound for what it was. A scratch, a trifle. Nothing fatal.

"After her!" he tried to scream. "After the human girl!"

He hissed and raged, but none heeded him. He fought to free the scissors from his neck. In his anger, his touch burnt through the silver plating, down into the metal underneath. It burned him. He kept pulling.

The humans were fleeing, he realized.

Fleeing.

And then the mausoleum shook. The entire graveyard shook. The shadows of his lesser kin scattered, no doubt feeling all the weak spots in the veil, the places where Elatha's past influence had been forced deep into the human world, the places where they might pass. He almost had them out, the blade almost free...

And then there was the blade's mate, inches from his face.

"Having fun with your new world yet?" the hill-dweller asked.

Trying to answer, spit out a curse, only blood poured out of Elatha's neck. His hands were slippery from it.

"I know, I'm a faithless bastard," the hill-dweller laughed, bisecting one of Elatha's lesser kin and sending it hurtling back into the endless night beyond the doors. "But what did you expect?" A new Fomorian leaped at the faery like an owl at a rat, and the faery's blade tore it apart. "Some things run deeper than words." And, kicking another scurrying sliver of darkness away, the faery pulled back his sword for what was unmistakably a decapitation strike. "Things, great King Elatha, that you never cared about."

But before the miserable little wretch could land his blow, Elatha yanked the scissors free.

Only just in time, because the great metal doors were flung wide, hitting Elatha with enough force to knock him into the closest tombstone. Throat still bleeding freely, he got to his knees.

And then started laughing when he saw who it was.

Not too bright. But then, who would be, with an eye that large pressing in on their brain?

"What is that?" Barton demanded, backing away from the window. Outside, in the garden, the iron ring was gone. The drill was gone. The garden itself was gone.

Instead, Barton beheld a scene unlike anything he'd ever imagined.

There was a graveyard there, crooked stones set into barren earth. A graveyard through which corrupted figures streamed, cackling and hooting, dragging the darkness with them, and at their head was a giant, lumpen and misshapen, its head bulging on one side as if some tumor had grown there unchecked. But it held its head easily, as if there was no extra weight at all, hands curled around the hilt of what looked to be some kind of sword. Facing town, the streetlights from Leadville shone through it, as if it was not fully there.

Barton had the distinct impression that it was sniffing the air.

The smaller creatures raced forward, out into the unsuspecting night.

"Fucking Irish."

Barton turned, Dvalinsson's rude manner enough to pull him from the horrible sight. "Excuse me?"

"This is the problem with your Spiritualism nonsense," Dvalinsson continued, as if he hadn't heard Barton at all. "You think only of what you can gain from it. You believe that if you understand it, you can control it, like fire or water or stone. You think you can look into the Otherworld and it won't look back at you. You forget what your ancestors knew. That there are monsters in the darkness."

The door to the study banged open. "Sir, there's something wrong with the—oh my god!"

"Yes, yes, Mrs. Coulton," Dvalinsson said, rolling his eyes and grabbing the whiskey bottle. "There it is. Thank your employer for this little slice of the spirit world."

Mr. Barton looked at his housekeeper. She was frozen to the spot, shaking, mouth open.

"None of this is happening," Mr. Barton said defiantly. "None of this is real."

"Suit yourself," Mr. Dvalinsson said, and inclined his head a little. "I consider our partnership ended tonight. If we're lucky, that thing won't find its way to Denver or anywhere else, when it's done killing its way through this place."

"Killing?" Barton asked, startled now. This felt so real, all of it. It was hard to remember that it was a dream, that he wasn't awake, that hell itself wasn't streaming out of his garden like gold through a sluice.

"Yes, I would think so. It reeks of the ending of things, and the Irish always did love a good fight." Dvalinsson held out his elbow to Mrs. Coulton. "Can I offer you an escort out?"

She reached out, hands moving blindly, eyes fixed on the horror outside the window. "I... I..."

"It's alright, ma'am." And he patted the rock axe at his side. "You're safe with me."

Barton was held transfixed by the sight outside. More real than real. Too real to be anything in the waking world. Monsters didn't exist. "You've got it wrong, Mikael," he breathed. "Spiritualism isn't about superstition or ignorance, it's..."

But he trailed off. His old friend was gone, along with his housekeeper, as if they were never there.

Outside, in the garden, more dark shapes were emerging. Running forth, cackling, howling, hooting, as the crouching giant laughed and swung a hand toward his stable. The roof on the building collapsed at once.

Suddenly seized by a blinding rage—because dream or not, this was unacceptable—Mr. Barton grabbed his shotgun from its mount beside the door and stalked toward his back porch. The doors seemed to fly open before him, banging open as they hit the fine woodwork on either side of the inside wall. He didn't care. He just started firing.

One, two, three of the dark shapes he hit, their substance blowing apart like dust in the wind. But before he could get off a fourth shot, the monster finally turned.

The last thing Mr. Barton ever saw was the swollen tumor on the side of its head spilling open, pulled open by what looked to be dirty bronze meathooks fixed on chains, revealing a twisted parody of a human eye.

Its gaze fell on Mr. Barton.

As he stared back at it, Mr. Barton finally found the truth he had always sought, the answers to the questions he had first started asking on the blood-soaked battlegrounds of the Civil War.

But he didn't have the chance to enjoy the revelation.

For fifty tons of stone and brick and wood and metal collapsed on top of him, and he died to the sound of that creature laughing at him.

CHAPTER FORTY-FOUR

The flight back to the portal was one of the strangest of Thomas's life.

Unlike the journey here, where every moment bled into the next, indistinguishable, until all sense of time and place was gone, Thomas was horribly aware of every second of their run. Every breath, every footfall, every aching muscle. Every drop of Miss Roseingrave's blood hitting the ground.

Every scream and hoot and cackle and wail coming from the direction of the graveyard.

They had the light to guide them, which certainly helped as they fled across the empty plain. It was more than just a trail to follow. Thomas had clipped the lantern onto his borrowed ammo belt, and it seemed to him that the light was spooling back up into the cut crystal, like fishing line returning to the reel. And he did feel like a fish on a line; he could feel the light tugging at him, calling to him. He couldn't have deviated from it if he'd wanted to.

The elder Miss Roseingrave was in a bad way. Cradled in his arms, she was getting weaker by the second. Her sister had attempted to bind the deep gash in her left forearm, but Thomas had gotten a look at it. He had seen bone; it was a fatal wound, and he wondered why she wasn't dead already. But she wasn't. She was holding on, muttering words that he couldn't quite make out.

"Mama," he thought he heard at one point. "Mama."

Smaller things pursued them. The younger Miss Roseingrave fired off more than a few shots, although how much good that did, Thomas didn't know. The Sirok-wolf kept up a steady orbit around them, running ahead to chase the light one moment, falling behind to rip apart one of their pursuers the next.

Soon—sooner than he had dared hope, but not soon enough—they were back into the low hills, climbing steeply into the mountains. It seemed to take only moments to reach the final boulder scramble up into the canyon's end where the portal lay. Whereas it had only been a minor inconvenience before, it now seemed the worst obstacle in the world.

"We need to climb, Miss Roseingrave," Thomas said, shaking the woman in his arms, but she didn't answer.

"Can you wake her?" the younger sister asked as Thomas laid her down, desperately searching out the easiest path up.

"I don't know," he said. "I'm not sure I should, even if I could."

A grunt and Captain Sirok was back, his wolf form bleeding freely from its hindquarters and shoulders. One ear had been almost torn off. In an all-too-human gesture, he motioned with his muzzle toward the plains below.

It looked like a storm cloud was moving across a valley floor. A writhing, laughing, screaming mass of darkness, headed their way. For a moment, Thomas was struck by a mad thought: the old tales never gave him a sense of how magnificent, how horrific, these things could be.

But then the elder Roseingrave sister moaned, and Thomas pulled himself from his reverie.

He looked to Captain Sirok. "Can you carry her?" he asked.

The wolf tossed his head, body language unsure, uneasy.

The gun was held out to Thomas. "I'll help," the younger sister said.

Holstering the pistol again, Thomas looked out on the plain. The storm was moving fast. What good was his gun against that?

It took all three of them to rouse the elder Miss Roseingrave and get her onto Captain Sirok's back. She seemed to be present enough to understand what was going on; the wound did not seem as bad now as it was when they had first started, and the bleeding had slowed greatly. Thomas did not understand the cause of that effect, but he was grateful; he didn't think she had much more blood to spare. But Miss Roseingrave had little strength left in her hands, and her younger sister had to scramble up next to her, pushing and pulling to keep her level.

"I'm sorry," she panted as they climbed, grabbing for Thomas. "I couldn't make them grow. I thought I could make them grow. Like he did."

"Save your strength," Thomas replied.

The storm was almost upon them now.

But there was also a light above them like the last rays of sunset. The coming of night, yes, but a reminder of the warmth of the day and the change of the seasons and an ordered world that made sense. Thomas felt something in his chest swell to see it, and it seemed to give them all a second wind, but even Captain Sirok was flagging by the time they reached the top.

And not a moment too soon, too. Because as they limped back to the cave, the storm broke around them. Darkness swirled around them.

And out of it strode Eli Horn, his neck torn open to the bone and a knife in his hand.

Thomas recognized the glint of obsidian.

Charlotte had thought herself dead.

She had felt little of the journey back here. Just impressions. Mr. Leighton's concern. Her sister's fear. The strange lupine thoughts of Captain Sirok. The endless emptiness they sought to cross. And the darkness beyond it all. That darkness...

It had felt like that dream from her childhood all over again. The woods, the bonfire, the hearth. Because out of that storm came a voice. A man's voice. Eli Horn's.

Fall and be at peace, Charlotte. Let go and let me take you far from all concern and pain and sorrow.

The promise of the Otherworld. The same promise it had made her, all those years ago.

A lie.

She was so tired of lies.

There was a light ahead, a light that both pulled and repulsed. It was the light of her own world, the world she had grown up in and known all her life, and yet, there was some part of her, some part of her that had always been and always would be, that longed to walk in this place. Know its ways, drink of its power, claim—

And then Charlotte stumbled, falling to her knees again. She felt hands on her trying to pull her up, but she couldn't rise. She heard screaming but couldn't make out the words. All she could see was the man in front of her, holding out a hand.

"Be at peace," Eli Horn told her, a kind of gentleness in his terrible voice. "What difference does it make, when and how you meet your death? All things end. All things are meaningless."

But the light behind her swelled, wrapping Charlotte in its embrace, and for a moment, one terrible moment, she was back in Mrs. O'Malley's dining room.

Charlotte blinked, but the vision didn't fade. Eli Horn was gone. The dead mountains were gone. In their place was a smooth marble floor and finely carved oak panels and the sunlight of a cold December morning streaming through plate glass. She looked at her hands, a child's hands, streaked with ash, the skin blistering.

A wet cloth swiped across her face, a cloth held by—

"Mama?" Charlotte asked, throat as dry as a desert.

Her mother—as young as she had been once—swept a wet cloth across Charlotte's face. Tears were welling up in the corners of Mama's eyes, but she was trying to smile.

"Mama?"

Charlotte didn't remember this. She didn't remember much from those days after the spirits had tried to kill her. She couldn't rightly say if this was a memory or a vision or a visitation or something cooked up by her dying mind to comfort her in her last moments.

"What is this?" Charlotte begged. "Mama, what is this?"

Her mother set the cloth down then and tugged her shawl a little tighter around Charlotte's shoulders. "You don't have to listen to them. You don't have to give in to their lies. No matter how they might seem to us, they are not omnipotent. Oh, my daughter, you wouldn't have this gift if you didn't have the strength to bear it, that I truly believe," her mother told her, and took Charlotte's unburned hand in her own. She placed something there in Charlotte's palm, closing Charlotte's fingers around it. "But when your own strength fails—"

But whatever Mama meant to say—had said?—Charlotte didn't hear. The vision fell apart.

Charlotte was on her knees in the dead dust, her sister and Mr. Leighton both there trying to pull her to her feet. Captain Sirok was in front of her, fur bristled, growling.

And there was Eli Horn, stalking toward them out of the storm's black howl. Holding a stolen blade, a black blade, Mr. Hallorman's obsidian knife grown to the proportions of a great sword.

Obsidian.

Volcanic glass.

Glass, because he could no longer touch—

Charlotte opened her hand.

It was her needle case, cradled in her palm. The needle case still hooked to its chain, the rest of the chatelaine dangling free.

"Pathetic creatures," she heard above her, the words delivered from a mangled, barely functional throat, and she looked up, horror rippling through her, at the sight of Eli Horn holding Mr. Hallorman's knife. "What he saw in you, I'll never know."

And down he swung.

But the blade didn't land.

Instead, there was a terrific sound, like a glass bottle hitting a wall, and sparkling shards of obsidian rained down around them.

There was Mr. Leighton, holding up her chatelaine like a shield above them. It had grown to the size of a wagon wheel, the knotwork filigree wider now than her wrist.

"Fools!" Eli Horn roared, hacking away. The blade cracked more with each blow, but the enraged Fomorian didn't seem to notice. "I am the end of all things! I am inevitable! Did I promise quick deaths? Slow they shall be, and agonizing. You'll watch as I rip your world apart."

Mr. Leighton was driven down to a knee by the furious assault, but still the chatelaine shield held. A chip of the volcanic glass caught him across the face, cutting his cheek. Splinters rained down on them all.

"Death!" Eli Horn was roaring now, all sense having seemingly fled from him. "Death!"

Celeste grabbed Charlotte's arm, murmuring words that Charlotte couldn't hear. If her sister was praying, it was for the first time in years, she thought wryly, and yanked the case open. Something fell into her palm, catching in the sticky blood that seemed to be everywhere right now. A needle.

"God help us," she muttered, and thrust up.

Mama had believed in buying quality things, when possible. "They'll last longer," she always said, "and they'll serve you well for all that time." So these were good needles, the best, rolled and tempered steel with wicked sharp ends. They were the kind of needles that swam through the toughest silks and dove through the thickest wools with ease, the kind of needles that made sewing a joy and the finished product that much more beautiful.

That quality seemed to hold firm, because Charlotte felt no resistance at all as she shoved the thing up through Eli Horn's heart, only stopping when her closed fist hit the barrier of the chatelaine shield.

The Fomorian stumbled back, looking at the yard-long spike now protruding from his chest. His eyes rolled down to meet hers, just before he crashed to his knees. "What are you?" he burbled, that dark, horrible blood of his burbling up through his clammy lips.

But then there was a light, and a whisper of wind, and the dark shapes scrambling to reach them were no more.

CHAPTER FORTY-FIVE

Passing through Denver's Union Station once again, Thomas couldn't help but stop at the board holding the public notices. Eli Horn's wanted poster still hung there, offering its five-hundred-dollar reward for his capture. The psychical researcher looked at it for a moment, and then with a smile, pulled it gently from its nails and rolled it up in his hands.

It wasn't needed here anymore. And perhaps, in his care, it could serve as an interesting data point for future investigations.

He donned his hat as he headed out to the main passenger platform. It was a new hat, this one, fresh and clean, suited for the city, whereas his old one had been quite thoroughly ruined by his recent adventures. Outside, he could see dark clouds piling up over the western mountains, a sure sign in these parts of snow.

It reminded him of Eli Horn. He shuddered a little to see it.

But now wasn't the time to worry about such things. The train was already in the station, and according to the clocks hanging from the wrought iron beams out here, was due to depart in less than ten minutes. He was late. He just hoped he hadn't missed—

But they were were, up near the first-class cars. With a sigh of relief, Thomas headed there now. As he approached, he was able to pick familiar voices out of the crowd.

"Are you certain you want to leave?"

"It's not so much a wanting as it is a...a necessity, I think."

"Quite necessary, if we're to salvage anything from all this."

And then there they were. A tall, lanky man who was not a man at all, wrapped in the uniform of the US Army Cavalry, mustache freshly waxed. A slender woman in purple-trimmed black with flaming red hair, barely contained in its coiffure. And, of course...

Gold eyes turned on Thomas. "Leighton, what happened? You missed lunch."

"You almost missed the train entirely," the younger Miss Roseingrave added.

But before Thomas could stammer an apology, that third figure nodded at him, bonnet dipping. "I would imagine Mr. Leighton here was distracted by something," the elder Miss Roseingrave said with a smile. "A book, perhaps?"

Thomas found himself smiling back, all his earlier nervousness somehow melting away at the sight of her. As if nothing at all could be wrong, as long as she was alive.

Every time he saw her now, he had this feeling. It was strange, but not necessarily unwelcome. Thomas wondered if it could be some sort of residual emotion, some holdover from the battle against Eli Horn in that strange Fomorian barrowland.

He distinctly remembered grabbing a shield he saw beside them on the ground—which he had been shocked to learn later was merely her chatelaine—and he remembered Horn hacking at it, screaming at them. Then the mists had come, and the flame in his lantern guttered low. For a moment, Thomas had feared that they were all lost, but then the mists broke and starlight washed over them and they were back in the real world once again.

He had found himself sprawled out on his back in the grass. The sound of birds calling softly in the night was the most beautiful thing Thomas had ever heard, he thought. He heard flapping and looked out to see a crow land on the ground near the entrance of the cave. The dark-feathered thing looked at him for a moment, head cocking this way and that, then it flapped away again, cawing.

It was the world. The human world. He lay on the ground for a moment, just soaking it in, breathing in the free air.

Then a sob brought him back to reality.

"Charlotte! Charlotte!"

Thomas had hurried back to the younger Miss Roseingrave. She had been on her knees by her sister's prone body, frantic. She looked up at Thomas with teary eyes.

Then, a cough. Movement. And then the elder Miss Roseingrave had been pushing herself up, pulling off the makeshift bandage. There was nothing on her arm but a shallow scratch and a tiny puncture wound, visible through the torn sleeve of her dress. "I'm alright," she'd said, voice still weak. "I'll live."

She sounded stronger now, here on the train platform, the damage to her mourning dress cleverly mended and her face no longer streaked with sweat and blood, a parasol in one gloved hand and her chatelaine clipped back onto her belt. The little device was its proper size and configuration again, although she had been forced to replace her scissors with a new pair. There was a new charm too, a little silver lantern. Andrew Dvalinsson's timepiece had shrunk to miniature proportions once they had returned to the real world. Thomas had almost lost it in the grass of the meadow.

"It is good to see you out and about," Thomas told her now.

"Well, *Carmen* is scheduled to open next week, and Mr. Dunn does need his costumes done," the elder Miss Roseingrave replied. "A scandalous story, I'm told, so I'm sure it will play well out here." Her words were resigned but there was a smile tugging at the corners of her mouth.

"I've seen it," Thomas said. "Once, in London, last year. It is a bit scandalous."

"Sounds fun," Captain Sirok said. "Pity we won't be there for it."

"Yes, terribly sad," the younger Miss Roseingrave replied, and she, too, was smiling. "All that basting and sewing and buttonholes and trim application I shan't be able to help you with, dear sister."

The elder Miss Roseingrave rolled her eyes.

But Thomas still remembered the look on Miss Celeste Roseingrave's face when she had heard her sister speak, back on the mountainside. With a noise that was somewhere between a laugh and a sob, the younger sister had thrown her arms around the elder, holding on tight. "What happened back there? What was all of that?"

"We're alive," Captain Sirok had said, coming out of the cave, snapping his suspenders onto his trousers. Just like before, Thomas had made note of the wolf shifter's complete lack of shame in being in a state of undress in front of the women. At least he'd had his undershirt on. "And there ain't a pack of Fomorians trying to eat us alive right now, so I'd say that's as good as it's gonna get."

The younger Miss Roseingrave looked up at him. "Who are you?"

The cavalry officer pulled his outer shirt back up, nodding a bit. "You may have noticed the big ol' wolf runnin' with you, Miss Celeste."

"That was you?"

"We've got some things we need to talk about, you and me."

The younger Miss Roseingrave, Thomas had noted, had blushed a little at that.

"I don't know about all that shit," Captain Sirok said now, and picked up the younger sister's suitcase, "but we've got plenty of our own work to do."

"Will it work?" the elder Miss Roseingrave asked. "Can you keep my sister from turning into... into..."

"Lukas?" he replied and shook his head. "Ain't no promises I can make. It ain't up to me. But"—and here to he looked at the younger Miss Roseingrave—"you've got a fighting spirit, and that counts for a lot."

"I still wish I could accompany you," Thomas said. "Understanding how the nature of the werewolf has evolved here in America, being able to witness how that is accomplished would be quite the feat of—"

"I ain't no werewolf," the captain interrupted, cutting him off, nodding to the younger Miss Roseingrave. "And you won't be neither, if we have anything to do with it."

She nodded and gave her sister one more hug. The elder Miss Roseingrave embraced her tightly, and there were tears in her eyes when she let go again. "Come home."

But the younger sister smiled. "Like him," she said, and nodded at Captain Sirok, "or not at all. I won't live my life as a monster."

The train whistle called out a warning. A conductor came walking up the platform, ringing a handbell. "Time to go," Captain Sirok told her.

The younger Miss Roseingrave took his arm and, head held high, stepped onto the train.

The elder Miss Roseingrave stayed on the platform, watching as the train pulled out of the station, bound for Colorado Springs and Captain Sirok's pack, and whatever it was that came next for her sister. Thomas waited there patiently until the last train car was away, and then held out his elbow. After a moment's hesitation, Miss Roseingrave slipped her arm into his.

"Do you suppose your sister will find what she's looking for?" Thomas asked her as they strolled away, back out into Denver's streets. The early

November day was crisp, chill. The air was dry, and the temperature did not feel as low as it was—50 degrees per the mercury thermometer at Mr. Barton's house. To the west, over the rim of the Front Range, snow threatened. There were a few people out and about, but for the most part, everyone seemed to be hurrying home ahead of the coming storm.

"A way to be the sort of wolf that Captain Sirok is? I hope so. He said it's possible."

"Did he tell you how?"

"All he would say is that the decision belongs to the land," Miss Roseingrave said, and sighed. "Sounds like something *he* would have said."

He. Thomas shook his head.

Mr. Hallorman.

Miss Roseingrave had asked about the faery when they'd all reemerged from the portal. The last Thomas had personally seen of the faery was of him standing in front of the mausoleum, laughing uproariously as he swung his scissor-sword up through one of the abominations pouring forth from the open gates.

"Do you suppose he survived?" Miss Roseingrave asked.

"I don't know," Thomas replied honestly. "After what he did, though, I'm not sure I would care to see him again."

"I have thought a lot about this over the past few weeks," Miss Roseingrave replied, "and I believe he did it for me. Whatever the Fomorian did to him in order to break the oath, it hurt him deeply. I do not think he would have done that under anything but extreme duress."

"He got you stabbed!"

"With my own scissors, creating a wound that could be mended. Would I have escaped death had Eli Horn opened my arm with his own knife?"

"How could he have possibly known you would attempt to stab Eli Horn yourself?" Thomas pointed out.

Miss Roseingrave just sighed and laid her other hand on Thomas's arm. "He knew me better than I know myself, I think."

They walked on.

After reemerging from the Land of Faery, the Otherworld, Tir na nAill, whatever Thomas was to call the place, none of them had been willing to camp that night in the mountains. They had once again descended down in the dark, back to Ouray. The horses had been quite scared of the younger Miss Roseingrave, and only Mr. Hallorman's brave mare would carry her. They had stayed at the same hotel as before, but this time, when Thomas had asked for a lager, he had only gotten a blank stare.

It seemed that there was no Dvalinsson family in town. Even the building had been missing when Thomas had gone looking for it.

A glamour, most likely, but one that not even the elder Miss Roseingrave had been able to see through.

A mystery for another time.

Captain Sirok would not be parted from his own mount, but the younger Miss Roseingrave's new supernatural infection, as Thomas had taken to thinking of it, made the horses terribly nervous. It had been impossible for her to ride all the way back to Leadville, much less Denver. Mr. Leighton had accompanied the sisters by stagecoach and train, while Captain Sirok had vowed to meet them back in Denver in due time—before the next full moon.

He had kept his word, at least. Thomas had been glad for it. The captain seemed to think he could save Miss Celeste Roseingrave from becoming a wolf-thing like the one they'd fought in the barrowland. What that entailed, he had no idea. Another mystery.

Thomas was quite certain his life would be full of such things now.

"What will you do with yourself, Mr. Leighton?" Miss Roseingrave asked as they turned the corner of 14th Street. "Back to England, I suppose?"

"I had always intended to do a survey of local folklore here in America," he said, "as well as meet with a few of the lesser-known mediums, see what kind of information I could gather."

"That seems a reasonable task."

"Indeed. But there is no real reason for me to return home just yet," he said. Miss Roseingrave stopped walking, looking at him with a curious expression on her face. Thomas hurried to explain. "I suspect I will no longer be welcome at the Academy for Psychical Inquiry, considering that I inserted myself into an investigation and came here without authorization. Mr. Holzworth does not take kindly to betrayal."

"How can you call it betrayal?" she asked. "After...after all you did?"

"Unfortunately, I brought no proof with me from Faeryland that might save my career," Thomas said wryly. "But there is that matter of Mr. Barton's institute to consider."

And there was that, wasn't there?

The story was already a scandal across the state. Mr. Barton's grand new mansion in Leadville had completely collapsed. A police investigation was still underway but already the story was that he had blown it up himself in a fit of rage. Or some such nonsense.

Thomas's notes had survived, though, delivered in a big bundle to his hotel in Denver with a note on them: *Courtesy of Mr. D.* When Thomas had gone by Mr. Barton's Denver residence to inquire, he had found Mrs. Coulton not polishing the brass or dusting the woodwork but reading a book in the library. They had talked for quite a long time that day, and she had eventually mentioned that, per Mr. Barton's will, an advisory board had been convened from prominent local Spiritualists to choose a director for the Barton Memorial Rocky Mountain Psychical Institute.

With little reason to return to England, and one very good reason to stay here in Denver, Thomas had submitted his application.

"Ah. Then you're considering the offer?"

"I have already accepted," Thomas told her. "I had my second interview this morning with the steering committee. That is why I was late today."

She didn't break her stride. "Congratulations."

"It should be a good position. The committee has asked for quarterly reports on my activities in building up the institute. Representative Childs especially seemed interested in a quality lecture program. But other than that, it is largely self-directed. It comes with a stipend, too, of course, and room and board at the old Barton mansion."

"Convenient, if you are to turn the place into a library."

"Exactly my thoughts. You should see the state of his collections. Terrible. Something I will have to correct straightaway. But while I expect mostly to be collecting and consolidating oral traditions or emerging folktales, if I do happen to come across something that requires a bit more insight, I would love to be able to call on you for assistance."

"Assistance. As in, psychical assistance?"

"Precisely so."

Miss Roseingrave did not answer right away. But neither did she push away. Thomas kept pace, kept silent.

"All my life, I've been terrified of the things that I see," she finally said, soft and gentle, finally slowing to a halt. "This existence is a lonely one. To see into that other world is to be part of it, a place where humans are not supposed to go. To be totally alone in the darkness. Few people acknowledge it, and those who do are lost in the popular notions of Spiritualism, which do not include all the unpleasant realities."

He laid his free hand over hers. "The truth is all I am concerned with."

"But I see now that I am not alone, and I cannot forever regard what I see with nothing but fear in my heart. Indeed, facing it may do some good for others. And if uncovering the truth helps people like my sister..." She trailed off. "... then I am willing to help you."

"Thank you, Miss Roseingrave."

"At my discretion, of course."

"Of course."

Her mouth quirked upward then. "And for a fee. Such commissions will no doubt take me away from Mr. Dunn's sewing rooms, something he will not much care for."

Thomas smiled. "I am sure the committee would not hesitate at bringing such a figure as a Roseingrave on as a paid consultant from time to time."

"I think," Miss Roseingrave replied gently, a serious expression on her face now, "they will soon come to value the asset they have in you."

It was a generous compliment, and one Thomas was not sure what to do with. He looked toward the mountains, to the storm gathering there and the winter that was coming. "What do you think we shall discover?"

"More than either of us can imagine," she replied, and leaned into him.

Afterword

Historical fiction is an interesting exercise.

I do historical costuming as a hobby and one thing you learn pretty quick is that you can never be one hundred percent authentic. Whalebone isn't available anymore for stiffening corsets, after all, and we have nice hair products like shampoo now, instead of beef tallow and cornstarch.

So what do you do? What parts of the modern world do you include in your work? What elements simply must be authentic? Do you put that meat grease in your hair? Or do you use hairspray?

These questions get even more complex with writing. Do you stick with a period style? Do you make the characters reflections of their time or ours? Do you make it a fun, historical-themed adventure that plays fast and loose with the facts, or do you spend days researching the most minute of details? There's no wrong answer, but you have determine your direction and stick to it.

For me, I wanted to tell you a good story. Give you a vision of the American West balanced between what it was and what it might have been if the creatures and being from our legends were real.

For me, setting a fantasy story there is as natural as breathing.

I grew up in Tucson, Arizona, hiking and camping with my family out in the desert. I went to the Air Force Academy and later served at Space Command in Colorado Springs, where the Rocky Mountains became my escape. And I can tell you unequivocally that there is a magic in the land there, a power that sleeps in the rocks, in the air, in the great silence you feel when you're out in the wilderness.

I really wanted to explore that in one of my favorite time periods, the late Victorian era. What if our legends were real, and what would that look like in this time period? What if they came west with us? How would this new age, new ideas, new environments, impact them? And what would it be like if our world collided with theirs?

I hope you had as much fun reading this as I did writing it. And if you did like it, please consider leaving a review! Reviews help other readers find new books, and gives more people a chance to enjoy the story for themselves.

If you'd like to read more of my work and find more speculative worlds to get lost in, head on over to my website and sign up for my newsletter to stay up to date on all release news and book progress.

There will definitely be more *Scholar and Seer* in the future. I've barely scratched the surface of this world and I cannot wait to share more of it with you!

Kindest Regards,
    Eryn

About the Author

After a childhood spent in the desert Southwest, E.M. Rensing's first posting to Tokyo, Japan with the US Air Force was quite the change. At least Japan had plenty of its own mountains and ancient ruins to explore.

E.M. Rensing enjoyed a thirteen year career as a Cyber Operations Officer, traveling all over the world, working everywhere from Space Command Headquarters to the Texas Air National Guard. Now, she writes what she loves; hidden worlds, brave characters, and fantastical adventures you'll love to get lost in.

When not writing, she enjoys historical costuming, raising the next generation of little readers, and planning her next big adventure. E.M. Rensing lives in South Texas with her husband and daughters.